BRIAN O'SULLIVAN

THE PUPPETEER

A NOVEL

BIG B PUBLISHING

B

ACKNOWLEDGEMENTS:

To my editor, Sarah, who doesn't use social media, preferring to live a quiet life reading and editing. The novel wouldn't be the same without you. Thanks!

To Elisabeth Brizzi, who designed the fantastic cover that has so many people talking. She captured exactly what I was looking for. Contact her if you need some exemplary work done.

To all my friends and family who have read the novel since its infancy. There's too many to list here, but you know who you are. Thank you!

There's a certain New York Times bestselling author who gave me some detailed notes that improved the novel immensely.

To my vast Twitter following, who have helped promote this novel and get it out to the masses. Keep fighting the good fight!

This novel is dedicated to my loving parents. It's been a tough year, but my father is still around to see the launch of this book, and I'm grateful for that.

THE PUPPETEER
Copyright © **2017 Brian O'Sullivan**
All rights reserved.
ISBN: 978-0-9992956-0-1
Published by **Big B Publishing**
San Francisco, CA

Cover Photography from **Elisabeth Brizzi**
lizbrizzi.com

THE PUPPETEER

PROLOGUE

The congresswoman looked at the man facing her. In her profession, she had met all types of scumbags, reprobates, and degenerates, but this guy may have been the worst of all.

"Boy, am I glad you aren't in the White House," she said.

"Oh, you are so naive. I can put up an article on my website and drop the president's approval rating 10 points in a day. I could release a story about a cabinet member that would get everyone so up in arms they would have to resign within days. I can make a war sound necessary and inevitable. I can make an enemy sound sympathetic or a long-time ally sound conniving. I have dirt on some of the biggest people in Washington. And if I don't, I'll make shit up! No one cares what the truth is anymore. They only care about what will advance their cause."

"Not everyone is as cynical as you," the congresswoman said.

The man ignored her statement, staring intently at her instead. After a few seconds, he finally responded.

"I know you deal with all those politicians and statesmen all the time, including the President, but you know what?"

"What?"

"I'm the one pulling all the strings. I'm the fucking Puppeteer!"

PART 1:
THE GREATEST NOVEL EVER

1

"This is the greatest novel ever!" Uncle Owen said, but as I read the opening sentence, even the sixteen-year-old me knew that wasn't the case. "But if I'm going to let you keep it, you have to make me a couple of promises first."

"I'm listening," I said.

"First, I want a promise that you won't read this novel until you've turned 18. Second, you have to assure me you'll at least read until Chapter 5."

Judging by the considerable thickness of the novel, I didn't think waiting till 18 would be any problem at all.

"I'll read it, Uncle Owen." I half-heartedly said.

I peeked a look at the second sentence. This was as much a great book as Owen was my real uncle, which was to say, not at all.

Owen Harding was a friend of my father's since childhood and every six months, or so he would sleep on my parents' couch for a few weeks. A freeloader was what my Mom had commonly referred to him as.

When we were children, my father thought it would be cute if we started calling him Uncle Owen and it stuck, much to my mother's chagrin. Despite her obvious objections, my younger sister Fiona and I both grew fond of Uncle Owen. He was fun. He'd take us to ball games, go fishing with us, and drive us to get ice cream. One time he even showed me a Playboy magazine. My ten-year-old self stared at the women in awe, before my Mom walked in and Uncle Owen hastily hid the magazine. He was the guy who would do all the fun stuff with you, and never had to do any of the disciplining. Of course, we liked him.

I'd periodically ask my parents as a young child where Uncle Owen was, and they would not so subtly say 'Owen is inside again.' I knew that meant he had landed back in jail. This happened a lot during our childhood, and we'd go months, and sometimes years without seeing him.

One time, when I was just a little kid, I asked him about all of his tattoos, and he showed me several that he received in jail. I remember asking him if he was allowed to leave the jail and go to a tattoo parlor in order to get it done. Uncle Owen smiled at me and patted me on the head.

"You're alright, Sport."

That's what he always referred to me as. Sport. Never called me by my given name, Francis Edward Waters, or even by my adopted nickname, Frankie. I had come to like being called Sport. I knew that Uncle Owen didn't fit in the suburbs where we lived, but I didn't care. I would notice the disapproving looks of my Mom's friends as she introduced the heavily tattooed man who was sleeping on the couch. Their looks didn't matter to me one bit. I liked Uncle Owen.

My appreciation for Uncle Owen had been tested earlier that year, however. My father, Eddie Waters, had died in a game of pickup basketball six months previously. His friends would ask him what he was doing playing basketball in his mid-40s, fearing he might tear an ACL or sprain an ankle. Turned out, it wasn't his joints or bones that couldn't handle it. It was his heart.

The death of my father impacted my life in every way imaginable. I was absolutely crushed. I had loved him more than life itself, and I knew our family would never be the same. All of my sports teams were coached by him. He would help me with homework or answer my questions about high school girls. He was a hands-on father in the best way possible. In my mind, he was perfect and then one day he wasn't there. It was cruel.

It also affected me in different ways than if he had died in a car accident or some random occurrence. I started wondering if I had a limited time on earth. Doctors said he had an enlarged heart and while my tests came back normal, it's always there in the back of your mind, no matter what the doctors say. Not only did I have to deal with the loss of my father, but I was now questioning my own mortality. As a teenager, no less.

Uncle Owen was the closest I had left to a father figure, and I really could have used him during that time. Not to take me fishing or to ball games, but to tell me that somehow, despite the death of my father, that it was all going to be all right. Or at the very least, to let me know that the world wasn't swallowing me whole.

But as he was prone to be, Uncle Owen was in jail when my father died.

Finally, four months after my father had passed away, Owen was released from jail. He came down and stayed with us. My mother had never taken a liking to Uncle Owen, but she sensed I was becoming a lost soul and could do well by having a man around the house. Even if it was one who slept on the couch.

It didn't last long. Uncle Owen was coughing from the moment he arrived in Oakland, and after several days of it persisting, my mother suggested going to the doctor. After seeing several specialists over the coming days, he got his prognosis. It wasn't good.

Uncle Owen was dying of lung cancer. He was only 45, but 30 years of smoking had caught up to him prematurely. I'd see people much older than Uncle Owen going to town on a Marlboro Light, and they were doing just fine. I remember thinking that life could be so unfair.

But then I realized that what happened to Uncle Owen was unlucky, but not unfair. At least he knew the risks he had undertaken by smoking for 30 years. All my father had done was agree to go out and play a game of basketball with some friends. That was truly unfair.

Although he had spent years of his life in a prison cell, on the day he handed me the novel, Uncle Owen was inside the one room that was worse. He was inside a hospital room. The Intensive Care Unit to be precise. It was the second time in six months that I had been in the ICU. My father was alive for a few hours after the initial heart attack before his heart gave out for the final time. Here I was, a young man, with my whole life to look forward to, and I was back in the ICU. "Sweet" would not be the adjective I would use to characterize my 16th year.

Even though I was in the hospital room of Uncle Owen, my father's death kept entering my thoughts. It wasn't fair to Owen, and I knew it.

He grabbed my wrist, noticing my attention was waning.

"Remember to at least read to Chapter 5, and to wait till you are 18."

Even in his weakened condition, his grip was very tight, and it hurt my wrist. I pulled away.

"I said that I promise."

"And you promise to look after your little sister too?"

"Of course, Uncle Owen."

"Good job, Sport. You are going to have to grow up fast. Your father is gone, and I'm going to be gone too, so you are going to have to be the man of the house. It's not going to be easy, but I know you can do it. I was a punk kid and started getting into trouble around your age. You can't afford to do that. You need to be there for your mother and sister. Do you understand?"

"Of course," I said.

"You can go back and grab them now."

"Okay," I said.

I looked forward to getting the hell out of the hospital room. I truly had looked up to Uncle Owen, and I hated seeing him with all the tubes coming out of God knows where. He had been the cool, vibrant "Uncle" who rode motorcycles and dated hot women. He wasn't the type of man who died in a hospital. And at 45, no less.

I went outside the hospital room and motioned to my mother and my younger sister, Fiona. If they saw the book underneath my arm, they didn't mention it. We walked back in, and we spent the next half hour talking to Uncle Owen. As we began to leave, I saw tears in my mother's eyes which I took as a sign that Owen wasn't going to live much longer. We headed towards the door, but I went back for a final goodbye. As I hugged him, Uncle Owen grabbed me close and reiterated to read to Chapter 5, and left me with a warning to be safe. I had no idea what he was referring to.

We drove home from the UC San Francisco Medical Center to our childhood home in the Oakland Hills. As we crossed the Bay Bridge that connected the two cities, I looked out at the beautiful lights, hills, bridges, and bodies of water that permeated the San Francisco Bay Area. They weren't doing it for me on this night, however. The death of my father and the impending death of Uncle Owen had temporarily blinded me to the beauty of the area that I called home.

Our tan, two-story ranch style home was equally beautiful and decadent, but it had pained me to look at it ever since my father had died. First and foremost, because I knew that it was now just a house. It would never be the home that it was while my father was alive. It's like it had lost its soul. Second, I knew that we weren't going to last long in it. Without my father's paycheck coming in, the writing was on the wall. We were going to have to move.

Not much was said on the ride, and when we did arrive home, I walked up the stairs to my room and stared at the book Uncle Owen had given me. It was a paperback at least three inches thick. As a sixteen-year-old, reading a book that long was just below eating brussels sprouts or sitting in a hospital on the list of things I wanted to do. Plus, he had said I should wait till I was 18, so I decided to honor his request. At least, that's how I rationalized not reading it.

I looked up at the bookcase in my room. My mother was a bit of a bookworm, and she tried to keep all of the books that either Fiona or I had read stocked in our respective rooms. I looked up and scanned all the books that adorned the bookshelf. Not bad for a sixteen-year-old uninterested in reading. I took one last look at the novel I had been gifted and slotted it in between *Green Eggs and Ham* and *Jonathan Livingston Seagull*.

A half hour later, Fiona and I made our ways downstairs. We had a mostly somber dinner as my mother told stories of having to deal with the always incorrigible Owen throughout her marriage to our father.

"How about one from their childhood? One that will make us laugh?" Fiona pleaded. We needed something light, a reason to laugh.

"Did you ever hear the one about the crickets?"

"No," Fiona and I said in unison.

"This is a great one. Of course, this was all second hand since I didn't meet Owen until your father and I started dating. But your Dad would tell this story every few years."

I saw a tear in my mother's eye. I couldn't imagine how tough our father's death must have been on her. They had been married 18 years, were raising two beautiful children and had built a successful life for themselves. And now it was all gone. As I saw the tear start to slide down her cheek, I hoped we could enjoy this story. Our little family of three needed it.

"They were seniors in high school, and Owen had been fired from the local movie theater he was working at. According to your father, Owen was already trouble at this point, and I have no doubt he was fired for a legitimate reason. He vowed revenge, however."

Fiona and I looked on in expectation. It was nice to hear stories about our father and Uncle Owen together. Especially now.

"So Owen was trying to figure out a way to get back at the movie theater. He had considered throwing paint on the front entrance and other silly things."

"Sounds like Dad sure knew a lot about this," Fiona said.

"He told me he was there to weed through Owen's bad ideas," my mother replied. "Seemed to be a common theme with them. Anyway, Owen finally came up with his master plan."

"Well, what was it?" Fiona showed the exuberance that only a young girl could.

"There was a local fishing store that sold live crickets as fishing bait. Owen had come up with the idea of buying up all of the crickets he could and unleashing them in the crowded movie theaters."

Fiona and I smiled at the thought of it.

"So Owen went to the store and bought up all the available crickets they had. Your father said Owen didn't have much money to his name and spent nearly all of it on his plan. He was that hell-bent on getting back at the movie theater. He collected all the crickets he had bought and put them in two big cereal boxes. Apparently, they were packed to the brim, and there were hundreds, or possibly thousands of the little guys. The tiny movie theater only had two screens, and he had a cereal box for each theater. He waited till eight p.m. that night when he knew both screens would have a new movie starting. A few minutes after the lights went down and the movies commenced, Owen walked down one of the theaters, subtly dropping the crickets out of the cereal box. Your father did the same in the other theater."

"Dad!" I found myself smiling for one of the first time in months. Our father had always been the strait-laced one compared to Uncle Owen, and the visual of him dropping crickets in a crowded movie theater made me really happy for some reason.

"So, what happened?" Fiona asked. She was fully immersed in the story.

"They met up in the lobby and waited. Your father said it didn't take long. They started hearing the low buzz that crickets make within seconds. Then they started hearing people yelling and heading towards the lobby. Whenever your Dad told this story, this is the point where he'd start tearing up he'd be laughing so hard."

Fiona and I looked at each other, laughing heartily.

"People started running out of the two theaters, shaking their hands through their hair, yelling that they were being attacked. Crickets were jumping from the hair of old ladies who entered the lobby. A few crickets made their way to the candy section and started hopping around. Several made their way to the popcorn machine. As the lobby was being overrun, you could still hear the hum of crickets coming from the theaters. Everyone was running from the theater into the lobby and then running outside, hoping to get the crickets off of them. It was mass hysteria, and your father said he and Owen sat there and enjoyed every second of it."

Fiona and I were laughing, enjoying the visual of crickets jumping around a crowded movie theater as people fled. I imagined old ladies with even older hairdos having crickets leaping out of their beehives or whatever hairdos people had back then. I looked at Fiona and could tell she was imagining something similar.

My mother looked at us and joined in the laughter. Our guards were down, and we couldn't stop laughing. It truly was one of the best moments we all had together since the death of our father.

After our laughter subsided, I asked, "Did they get caught?"

"Well unfortunately for Owen, he hadn't been very stealth, and several of his former employees saw him laughing at the commotion going on around him. It wasn't long before the police came looking for him. But he never told them that your father was part of it. Your father would always close the story by saying that's why he loved Owen. He took the blame for both of them."

It was the perfect story at the perfect time. It should have been a terribly sad occasion, but we had managed to find a way to laugh, something that hadn't been easy to come by.

"Everything is going to be all right," our mother said and brought us in for a group hug.

Dinner ended, and Fiona and I went to our respective rooms. Our mother tucked us in and told us to say our nightly prayers. I was way too old to get tucked in, but I knew it was a tough night, so I didn't protest. I prayed that Uncle Owen would be cured of this awful thing called cancer, knowing it was likely too late. To distract me from the thoughts of Owen's impending death I started imagining the crickets jumping all over a crowded theater. I fell asleep with a smile on my face.

Uncle Owen died three days later, but it would be five years until I started reading Chapter 5 of "The Greatest Novel Ever," and my life would change forever.

2

"Frankie, time for dinner," my mother yelled from the kitchen.

By the time I was 21 years old in 2017, I had lost my childhood commitment to nightly praying, but I hadn't lost the nickname Frankie. I was fine with that. Frank sounded like an old man's name, and Francis sounded feminine to me. My mother told me that Francis was Frank Sinatra's real name, so I asked, if it was such a great name why hadn't he stuck with it. She had no comeback to that, and people continued calling me Frankie through my teenage years and into college.

It was December 10th, and while most of my friends were arriving home over the next few days for their winter break from college, it was merely another day at home for me. I was now a junior at San Francisco State University.

Of course, that hadn't been the plan. I got into two Ivy League schools, Dartmouth and Brown, as well as UCLA, but it wasn't meant to be. After the death of my father when I was 16, it was just a matter of time before money became an issue. He had a little bit of life insurance, but by the time I had graduated from high school, that well had run dry. My mother worked hard as an administrative assistant, but raising two kids and paying a huge mortgage just wasn't possible.

The Waters' family, or more specifically, our mother, had to sell our beautiful house in the Oakland Hills, and we moved to a cheaper part of town. The days of living on a Cul-de-sac in a ranch style home high up in the hills were gone. We now lived in a tiny, three-bedroom house, where the backyard consisted of a 10-foot lawn and a chain linked fence. Our old backyard with a swimming pool and recliners was a distant memory.

My mother had pleaded with me to attend UCLA, telling me she would send all the money she could and that I could work for the rest. I had strongly considered it, but in the end, decided to stay home and enroll at San Francisco State. Truth be told, I could have made it work, but I couldn't leave my mother and sister alone. After the death of my father, I had told myself I would be the man of the house, and a man wouldn't leave his mother and baby sister to fend for themselves.

Of course, things were beginning to change. My sister was now a freshman in college at Cal-Berkeley, and I was an old man of 21. I had been toying with the idea of transferring schools and/or moving out of my mother's house. I had to be honest with myself, it was becoming tougher telling girls I lived at home with my mother. I had dated a few girls since college began, but when it came to getting down to business, it was almost always at their place. Not only did I live with my sister and mother, but the three rooms were right next to each other, and let's just say the house wasn't properly insulated. I had made that mistake a few times.

I also had a very unselfish reason for wanting to move out. With Fiona and I at home, my mother would conveniently say that she had no time to date. That's not what I wanted. Sure, there was a time where I was happy that my mother was not dating following my father's death. I admired it, and I took it as a badge of honor that their love was truly everlasting.

That opinion lasted for about a year, but it had long since passed. It had now been over five years since my father had been taken from us. Long enough for anyone to grieve. She had been on dates of course, and she would occasionally bring a man home, but once that man saw the tiny three bedroom place was inhabited by her two children, we wouldn't see him again. My mother was a beautiful woman who was still only in her mid-40s. She had kept her figure, and everyone always said how great she looked. It wasn't lip service, she truly did. I knew she could easily find a new man if Fiona and I would just get out of her way. And my Mom deserved that.

Sally Anderson had met Eddie Waters 25 years ago at an outdoor play in San Francisco at the beautiful Golden Gate Park. They were both on blind dates, but not with each other. They happened to be sitting within 10 feet of one another watching some Shakespearian play. My father could tell she didn't like the guy she was with, and because my father wasn't hitting it off with his own date, he subtly slid his business card in my mother's hand when he had the chance. It had been a bit presumptuous, but they had exchanged some friendly smiles with each other, commiserating about their woeful blind dates.

Two days later, having nearly forgotten about the woman in the park, my father answered a call at the Pacific Gas & Electric office he was working at. He was an engineer and had been there less than a year. Sure enough, it was Sally, the woman he had slid his business card to. They started dating immediately, were married two years later, and 18 months after that, I was born.

Sally Anderson had become Sally Waters, and she couldn't have been happier. Two and a half years after I was born, Fiona was brought into this world, and they bought the house in the Oakland Hills shortly thereafter. Eddie Waters was successful and made enough for Sally to be a stay at home Mom while he paid the mortgage on the million dollar house. They had a great life together and loved their two children with all their hearts.

And then one day, a man in seemingly great health fell to the ground while playing basketball with some friends. He would never regain consciousness, and Sally Waters' life had changed forever. She persevered through the pain of losing her husband and put all of her love into raising both Fiona and I. She did a great job. There was a time after my father's death where I was a bit of a lost soul, getting in moderate trouble and running with the wrong crowd. My mother put an end to that immediately, and I had been a responsible, respectable, loving son ever since.

And that's why I knew I needed to move out. Sally Waters, i.e. Mom, needed to have her own life again. She had done everything she could for Fiona and I, and we were adults now. It was time for our mother to be able to enjoy being an adult as well.

So I vowed that over the next few months I would start looking at apartments. Possibly schools to transfer to as well. My grades would be no problem. I was putting up straight A's and many a teacher asked why I was still at San Francisco State. They did have a great computer science program, and that's one of the reasons I stayed.

As you can see, it wasn't all bad. The three of us had grown very tight over the years. I guess there are two ways a family can go after the premature death of a loved one, and instead of fighting and saying "Why us?", we became closer, and we all truly loved each other.

Wherever my father was, I'm sure he was smiling when he looked down at us. We had a hole in our lives that would never be filled, but we were a happy family nonetheless.

I had grown up a lot since the year of my father and Uncle Owen's death. Both figuratively and literally. At 16, I was a bit of a small fry and was generally looking up at people my own age. That changed in my last few years of high school as I grew to 6'1". I continued my growth spurt early on in college and now stood 6'3". At 21, I had grown into my body, and now people were looking up at me. My light brown hair was very short on the sides, but I let the top go a little wild. Girls seemed to consider me handsome.

An athlete but also a bit of a computer nerd, I had been between social classes in high school. I gained some confidence since I had started college and some of my friends thought I had gotten a little cocky, but that wasn't the case. I was still a grounded individual and treated others with respect. My parents had done a great job in that area when we were little kids, and my mother had now taken the baton with the death of my father. She wouldn't allow either of the Waters' children to be seen as impolite.

"Frankie, time for dinner," my mother repeated.

I walked downstairs and was greeted by the two women in my life, Fiona having beaten me to the table. My mother had made chicken piccata over some noodles with a side of brussels sprouts. Like the nightly prayer, I had outgrown my distaste of brussels sprouts and actually enjoyed the little buggers these days.

"Your computer was a little loud last night, Frankie," my mother said.

I took a bite of the chicken, making sure to get some of the wine-lemon-butter sauce and the capers that came with it. I knew that when I did move out, I'd truly miss the home cooked meals.

"Wow, this is delicious," I said, and then answered her. "I'll turn it down. Sorry about that."

"What were you watching? I heard a lot of swearing?" she asked.

"I heard it too. Bad, bad boy," Fiona said.

She made the tsk tsk motion with her thumb and index fingers. I only needed my index finger to make the Shhh motion to her.

"Chapter 5 of this Netflix series I've been watching."

"Do you mean Episode 5?"

"Same thing, but this show calls them Chapters instead of Episodes. Thus, Chapter 5."

My mother looked like she had seen a ghost. It was an altogether weird reaction.

"What?" I asked.

"Oh, it's nothing. Just something about the phrase Chapter 5," she said.

Something entered the back of my consciousness, but I couldn't place it just yet.

"It's obviously something, Mom," I said.

"Do you remember when Uncle Owen died? I took you and Fiona to the hospital a few days before he passed."

"Of course I remember. I was 16 years old, Mom," I said, and then I realized why I should have remembered the phrase 'Chapter 5.' My stomach quickly started forming a few knots.

"Well, the hospital called me a few days later saying he could go at any time. I sent you and Fiona to Cindy Johnson's house, and I raced to the hospital. There's no secret that I didn't always see eye to eye with Owen, but he was Eddie's best friend, and since he had no family, I thought I should be there if he passed on. By the time I got there he was so drugged up, he didn't even recognize me. His breathing was labored, and I could tell he wasn't going to last long."

My mother looked at both of us before continuing.

"Between his labored breaths, he kept saying 'Chapter 5.' He must have said it 10 times. Maybe more. Finally, he started to go into convulsions, and the nurses escorted me from the room. He died a few minutes later. From time to time, I still think back to him repeating 'Chapter 5' in between those strained breaths."

The hair on my arm stood up, rivaling the knots in my stomach for most un-welcomed bodily reaction. I had only been 16 years old at the time, and five years had passed, but now I remembered it like it was yesterday. Uncle Owen grabbing my arm and making me promise I would at least read to Chapter 5 in the novel he had given me.

"Why didn't you ever tell me?" My question came out loud and accusatory. I regretted it immediately.

"About him saying Chapter 5? It didn't seem important Frankie. He was on loads of drugs and probably didn't know where he was or what he was saying," my mother said. "And you and Fiona were still very young. I didn't want to tell you about seeing Owen's final breaths."

My mother never called him Uncle Owen. It was her form of civil disobedience since she had always considered him, at the very least, a nuisance. If truth be told, she would more likely have described him as a felon, occasionally living under the same roof as her two young children. She wouldn't have been wrong.

But she invited him to stay when our father died. And she was there for him when he died. My father would have been proud of that.

Things would have turned out differently if I had just told my mother right then about Chapter 5 and what Uncle Owen had told me five years previously, but I decided not to. After all, he had given the book to me, and it was about time that I read it. I thought back to our conversation and remembered he had wanted me to read it when I was 18. Sorry Uncle Owen, but I was going to be three years late.

I excused myself after finishing every morsel on my plate, and walked up the stairs, hoping a book I had set on my bookshelf years earlier was still there. It was time to find out why a man would spend his final breaths mentioning a chapter in a novel...

3

The year was 1968. In a city named Broken Arrow, located in the northeastern part of Oklahoma, Richard Bowles put a dollar bill in the jukebox and put on as many Johnny Cash songs as it would allow. A dollar was actually worth something back then, but if it meant hearing all of his favorite Cash songs while enjoying some bourbon and a beer, well that was money well spent to Bowles.

The bar, unironically named Happy's, was one of the biggest dive bars in rural Oklahoma, and that was saying something. The sawdust on the ground barely masked the blood, dirt, and whiskey stains that had accumulated below it over the years. If you dared bring a woman, you were likely to hear catcalls that would make a sailor blush.

Bowles and his two friends sat at the bar, talking about the work they were doing at the local pork farm, and of Hollywood starlets they'd love to screw. They talked about football as well, and as the only native Oklahoman of the three, Bowles was outnumbered when it came to the famous Texas/Oklahoma football rivalry.

When they weren't talking football or women, Bowles sang along quite loudly to Johnny Cash.

The bartender was a tall, fat man in his mid-50s with red and white suspenders that barely kept his pants up, but did nothing to hide his enormous gut. He endured Bowles screaming the lyrics of the first Johnny Cash song and then the second, but by the time Bowles started yelling the lyrics to *Ring of Fire,* the bartender had enough and walked over to Bowles.

"How many Johnny Cash songs you play in a row?"

"I reckon it's none of your business."

"I work here, so I *reckon* it is," the bartender said, accentuating reckon in the same manner that Bowles had.

The bartender was a good six and a half feet tall and towered over Richard Bowles. The difference was underscored by the fact that the bartender was standing above Bowles, who remained seated in his chair. Bowles made up for his lack of stature with a pit bull's persona, and this big fat blob in front of him didn't scare Richard Bowles one bit.

"I put my hard earned money in the jukebox, so I'm just going to sit here and enjoy the greatest singer on earth," Bowles said as he ashed his cigarette in the direction of the bartender.

As Richard Bowles joined Johnny Cash in singing "*I went down, down, down,*" the bartender headed back towards the jukebox. Richard Bowles got up off his bar stool and started following directly behind the man. The bartender arrived at the jukebox and grabbed a cord that led to a little button that would skip from one song to the next.

He smiled at Bowles, pressed the button and "Ring of Fire" came to a scratching halt, sounding like someone had ripped the needle off a turntable. Another Johnny Cash song came on, and once again the bartender pressed the button. He did this five more times until you began to hear Mick Jagger singing the lyrics *"She would never say where she came from."*

The man stared at Bowles. "The Rolling Stones. Ruby Tuesday. Now we're talking."

Richard Bowles laughed as the bartender approached, but it was hardly a congenial laugh. It was a knowing laugh of what was to come. The bartender approached Bowles, and the next few seconds were so violent that those who witnessed it would never forget what they saw.

As the red and white suspenders slowly waddled past him, Bowles broke his Bud bottle on the pool table next to him and rammed the broken shard up the nostril of the passing bartender. It happened so quickly the bartender had no time to put up a defense.

A split second later, Bowles grabbed the man's head and slammed it into the pool table, sending him immediately to the ground, bleeding profusely from both his forehead and his mangled nose. Not done yet, Bowles grabbed the closest pool cue and hit the defenseless bartender in the face as he lay on the ground. After the fourth hit, his friends finally grabbed Bowles, pulling him away just in time to save the bartender's life.

Two days later, the police caught up to Richard Bowles and arrested him. When pressed for a motive, all he could muster was 'No one turns off Johnny Cash.' Richard Bowles got 30 months in jail for the brutal assault, and almost everyone involved agreed he got off easy.

To say Richard Bowles was a huge Johnny Cash fan would be one of the biggest understatements of all time. He had every record Cash ever released, and he was pretty sure he knew every lyric of every song he had ever recorded. This was the 1960's and 1970's, and the Internet was a long way off, so Bowles would read the liner notes as he listened to the albums, memorizing all the song lyrics.

His trailer in rural Oklahoma had three full-sized posters of Cash adorning the walls. He would have had more, but Richard Bowles was not a rich man, and his trailer was one of the smallest on the lot. Not that you would find anyone making fun of his trailer as Bowles was feared by about everyone he came in contact with. He was mean, he was a drunk, and he had a vicious right hook that he had perfected in numerous bar fights in and around the rural outskirts of Oklahoma City.

He had resorted to using a pool cue and a broken beer bottle in Broken Arrow, but there had been upwards of 10 fights that Bowles' ended merely with his right hook. It was usually enough. The fat slob of a bartender got more than knocked out because he had the audacity to turn off Johnny Cash.

The year was now 1975, and Richard Bowles was on his third wife, and they were about to have their first child together. Bowles didn't have any children from his first two wives, but when the marriages lasted a combined seven months, it's no surprise why.

Bowles had always joked that he probably had a few kids littered throughout Oklahoma and possibly Texas, but this time it was real. He loved the former Mabel Midgely, now Mabel Bowles, a simple, yet loving, fellow Oklahoman. At 35 years old, Richard was thinking it might be time to reign in his aggressive behavior a little bit. After all, he was about to be a father.

Sitting in his trailer one day with "The Man in Black" quietly playing in the background, Mabel turned to Bowles, her large stomach in plain view. She was only four months pregnant, but Mabel had a rotund figure at all times.

"So what do you think we should name it?" Mabel asked, her thick Oklahoma drawl on full display.

"Sue." Richard Bowles was brief and to the point.

"Sue is a very pretty name. What if it's a boy?"

"Sue," Bowles repeated himself. "And what do you mean if? I already told you it's going to be a son."

Mabel looked at Richard. "OK, I get it. Your favorite song ever is *A Boy Named Sue*, right? Are you freaking crazy, Richard! We can't name our son Sue. He'll get an ass whoopin' every day at school."

"That's the point."

"Huh?"

"Oh Mabel, why don't you try listening to the lyrics once in a while. The man named his son Sue so he will become tough."

"Sue is out of the question."

"How about Kim?"

"Even worse."

Mabel was generally a pretty weak-willed woman, and she acquiesced to Richard Bowles on a daily basis. She remained steadfast on this issue, however. Richard was impressed. He knew in the end that he would get his way, but he respected Mabel for holding out as long as she could. While it may not be Sue or Kim, he was going to give his son a feminine name. Men were turning into pansies these days, and if his son had to take a few ass kickings due to his name, then so be it. Toughen the little fucker up.

After several months of going over prospective names, most of which Mabel deemed too feminine, they finally agreed on one. Richard Bowles wasn't right about many things in his life, but his inclination that he was going to have a son proved correct, and on November 1st, 1975, Darby Cash Bowles was born.

The first few months of Darby Cash Bowles life were some of the best of Richard Bowles's life. He would look at the huge, brown eyes of his son, and knew that for better or worse, he had contributed something to this world. He started drinking less and staying at home more.

It wouldn't last, unfortunately. After a few months of behaving himself, Richard Bowles fell back into old habits and was hitting up the local bars three or four times a week, leaving Mabel by herself to look after young Darby.

In the song "A Boy named Sue," after years apart, the father and son make up after almost killing each other first. The tale of Richard and Darby Bowles wouldn't last nearly that long, as Richard Bowles was dead before Darby's first birthday. His intention of mellowing never came to fruition, and his final bar fight ended with him on the ground, eyes wide open, a knife protruding from his chest.

Darby Cash Bowles would be growing up in a tough area of rural Oklahoma without a father and with a feminine name to boot. If he was going to survive, he was probably going to turn into a mean son of a bitch, and that's exactly what ended out happening.

4

As a child, I always thought church lasted longer than anything else in the world. That was until I started reading the first chapter of Uncle Owen's 'Greatest Novel Ever.' It was just as interminable and without the promise of donuts at the end. The first chapter was 30 pages and took me 45 minutes to read. What's the matter with a brief, to the point, opening chapter?

It was the story of Arthur Billingsley, a 19th century widowed farmer, who lusted for his best friend's wife. Pardon my French, but it was boring as fuck! Uncle Owen had been a cool guy; he had tattoos and cute girlfriends. What was he doing reading this garbage and much less labeling it the greatest ever? Damn him.

And then I felt a tinge of regret, as I remembered Uncle Owen kept saying Chapter 5 on his deathbed, and I realized I owed him to at least read up to that point. But if it didn't pick up by then, it was going to become *The Greatest Novel Ever That I Accidentally Tossed In The Garbage.*

As I started on Chapter 2 of the Most Boring Novel Ever, I heard my Mom talking to some woman in the kitchen. I wasn't really paying attention, at least not consciously, until I heard the woman say, "Yeah, Evie is back for Christmas break also." I closed the novel and started heading towards the kitchen.

Evie Somerset had been the most beautiful girl at Bishop O'Dowd High School in Oakland. Well, let me clarify that. I thought Evie was the most beautiful girl at our high school. Most people dismissed her as the dorky brunette with glasses who was always reading, but I knew better. Evie was like that girl in movies who gets a makeover, and everyone suddenly realizes how beautiful she really is. But while her makeover came gradually, I knew it from the day I met her.

She moved to Oakland from Lawrence, Kansas the summer before our senior year. Her father was a professor of English and had taken a job at UC Berkeley. As nice as the University of Kansas was, a job at a school as prestigious as Cal was something he couldn't pass up. He moved his wife and Evie, their only child, to Northern California.

They moved into the house directly across the Cul-de-sac from my home. This would prove to be the final year that we could afford the house in the Oakland Hills, and even as we enjoyed it, I realized that we weren't going to be there forever. I remember being grateful that at the very least, we had held on long enough to have Evie move in next door.

Evie had been given her father's love of English and was a voracious reader, spending hours a day wrapped up in her books. Partly because of this, she was quite shy and had trouble making friends in that first summer. In fact,

I was probably the only true friend she had those first few months. I didn't know if it was due to proximity or whether we had a blossoming romance on our hands, but I was just happy to have a pretty girl coming over to my house a few times a week.

I'd ask her about Kansas, and she'd wonder what to expect at our high school. We got along great. On one beautiful, late August day when it was a good 80 degrees out, I suggested she bring over something to go swimming in. I had moved slow with her, not wanting to alienate my new next door neighbor, but I was starting to have feelings for her. I figured getting her in a bikini was a good place to start.

She accepted, but when I got to the door and saw her usual baggy clothes, I was let down. That wouldn't last. We got to the pool, and she slowly took off her long, loose-fitting sweatshirt to reveal her curvy body underneath. I knew at that very moment that I didn't want to just be friends with this girl.

Two weeks later after another swimming session, we sat in the two poolside recliners and were talking how school was only one week away. I was still a shy 17-year-old and hadn't gained the confidence I would in later years, so I had yet to make a move. Getting her in a bikini and staring at the curves of her breasts and hips were as close as I had gotten to first base. I knew it was pathetic, and I vowed to try and kiss her if the time was right.

I felt like she was giving off positive vibes on that day, so I was on my toes waiting for the right moment. I looked over at her, taking off my bright yellow sunglasses that I was positive made me look *soooo* cool. She smiled back at me, and I was pretty sure a wink followed, but it was tough to tell with the glare of the late summer sun.

I took it as a sign to kiss her, so after an excruciating few seconds of self-doubt, I leaned over from my recliner towards hers and kissed her on the lips. I looked at her for a reaction, but it seemed like she was looking right through me.

She had winked and smiled at me, right? As I repositioned my hands on her recliner, my hand fell through the little ruffles, and I lost my balance. My hands fell off her recliner, and my legs were pushed up into the air by my own recliner. I ended up in the position of doing a hand stand, and I knew what was going to happen next. I came down with a splash, landing in the pool.

As I made it to the surface of the water and swam to the edge, I looked out and saw why Evie had been looking right through me.

"Evie honey, I think it is time to go," Mrs. Somerset said.

It's the most embarrassed I had ever been. I raised myself out of the water and saw my mother and Mrs. Somerset looking at me. I looked at Evie, to see what kind of reaction she had on her face. I had to know if she had wanted me to kiss her. She had winked at me after all. At least, I thought so. But when I looked at her, all I could see were equal parts empathy and sadness. Evie walked towards her Mom, and I knew I had lost any chance with her.

The last week of summer ended without Evie coming back, and our senior year of high school started soon thereafter. I'd run into Evie occasionally at school, but it wasn't the same. She was meeting new people and never seemed to have much time when we talked. I soon found out why.

About a month into the school year, Evie had started dating Stuart Conley, debate class president, chess club president, French club president, and president of seemingly every other freaking club our school had. Only he didn't look the part. Stuart Conley was probably 6' 5" and certainly not the stereotype of a guy involved in debate, chess, or French.

Evie and I remained friendly through our senior year, but it was more of a neighborly friendship. Something born out of necessity more than anything else. Don't get me wrong, she was still very polite and warm towards me, but she had a boyfriend and we just kind of went our separate ways.

She went back east to college, getting accepted into Brown. She had always been very smart, and no one was surprised when she ended out enrolling in an Ivy League school. Of course, I had been accepted into Brown as well, but my family's lack of money had contributed to me staying home and enrolling in San Francisco State.

I saw her randomly over Christmas our freshman year, but I hadn't seen her in almost two years now. I assumed Evie's parents still lived in the Oakland Hills, so I was curious why her mother was down in this part of town.

And last I had heard, Evie was still dating Stuart Conley, so I wasn't quite sure why I was sprinting the 30 feet to the kitchen.

I realized my exuberance was probably a bit much as I slid past the kitchen, my socks unable to stop on a dime. I tried to play it cool as I doubled back and enter the kitchen. It appeared to be too late as my mother and Mrs. Somerset looked at me with curiosity as I arrived at the bottom.

"Hi, Mrs. Somerset," I said.

"Oh, hello Frankie. That was quite the entrance."

I was embarrassed, so I smiled and then lied.

"Just a little hungry."

I started looking around the fridge, pretending that's why I had entered the kitchen like a bat out of hell. My mother knew I had eaten 30 minutes earlier, but I figured I could count on her to keep my little secret.

"I was just telling your Mom that Evie is home for the holidays."

"You don't say," I said. I had never uttered that phrase in my life. Why did girls make me act so weird?

"Why don't you come by and say hello today or tomorrow?"

It was time to be honest. "That's really nice Mrs. Somerset, but I haven't seen Evie in a few years."

"Well, she asked me yesterday if you were still in town, so maybe she'd like to catch up. I remember that first summer when you guys would hang out all the time."

My mind raced back to the incident in the lounge chair and falling into the pool. I should have been embarrassed at the recollection, but I was too busy soaking in the good news that Evie had asked about me.

"We were just kids back then, but I'd love to come by and say hi."

"You two are still kids," Mrs. Somerset said, and judging by my entrance, it was hard to disagree with her.

"You still live on our old street?" I asked.

"We do," she responded.

I realized it was time to get out of there while I was still ahead, so I grabbed a banana I had no intentions of eating and excused myself, telling Mrs. Somerset I'd stop in soon. My Mom shot me a look saying she knew exactly what I was doing.

I walked upstairs, but couldn't go back to reading that boring novel. How could I concentrate when I knew Evie Somerset wanted to see me?

5

Darby Cash Bowles ran roughshod over his mother from a very young age. Mabel Bowles was passive by nature, and with her husband dead by Darby's first birthday, she struggled to say no to the hyperactive, precocious child. Darby developed a potty mouth early in life, incorporating the words the older boys used, and Mabel didn't do anything to help stop it. "Boys will be boys" was oft repeated by Mabel.

Most people who met Darby thought he had a good heart for a young child, but he fell under the spell of the wrong neighborhood kids. With no father there to discipline him, Darby didn't realize the fault of his ways and continued hanging out with kids who would be the downfall of him. At some point, you are who you are, and although Darby Bowles had potential, he was turning into a troublesome youth.

He started missing school and was often seen smoking cigarettes at the local seedy hangouts. And this was when he was 12. By the time he was 14, he was drinking beers with kids three and four years older than him. At 16, he was collecting debts for a school bookie. Darby Cash Bowles was headed down the wrong path, and no one could stop it.

One incident stood out above the rest.

Darby had just turned 17, and he was returning from one of his many school suspensions. The latest one had come because Ms. Genova, a graying Geometry spinster in her 50's, had the gall to tell Jeff Odmark, the school principal, that Darby had told her to "Fuck off" when she asked him to make a presentation in class.

"Fuck that. I'm not letting some Old Maid tell me what to do," was the exact words that Darby had said, and he tried to tell Principal Odmark that he hadn't directly told Ms. Genova to fuck off. Darby pled his case to the principal to no avail and was suspended a week for his actions.

Darby spent the whole week stewing at home. Mabel tried to settle him down, telling him this was his chance to take a look at himself and to start becoming a better person. Darby would nod when his mother said this, but all the while he was thinking about a way to get back at Ms. Genova. No wonder that old bitch couldn't find someone to marry her, Darby thought to himself.

The week went by quickly with Darby looking forward to his revenge. He had the period off before Ms. Genova's class so he'd have time to implement his plan. It was a Tuesday when Darby's suspension ended, and he went to his first few classes without incident.

The third period was the one that Darby had off. He loitered around his locker, waiting until everyone went into their classrooms for their own third-period classes. He then made his way to Room 218, knowing the room was free before Ms. Genova taught Geometry for fourth period.

Looking around to make sure no one was watching, Darby opened the door to Room 218 and entered the barren classroom. He immediately went to work on loosening the screws in Ms. Genova's chair. She always put her chair in front of her desk, sitting in full view of all of her students. Darby knew this was going to make things even better. Falling behind a huge desk wouldn't get the laughs that falling directly in front of all her students would.

Darby worried that when Ms. Genova moved the chair from behind the desk to the front, that possibly the screws would fall out then. He hadn't taken them all the way out, however, and he assumed it would take the pressure of someone sitting on the chair to have it collapse under its own weight.

As if that wasn't enough, Darby went to the blackboard and wrote in big letters: **SYNONYMS OF AN OLD, UNMARRIED WOMAN: OLD MAID. SPINSTER. MAIDEN. MS. GENOVA.**

Looking up at the writing and back down at the chair a final time, Darby went to leave the room. He walked out and saw Tiffany Yates, a petite junior, grabbing something from her nearby locker. Fuck, Darby thought. He tried to cover his face and started walking away from her. Going back into the room and retightening the screws wasn't even a consideration. Darby just hoped Tiffany Yates wasn't a tattletale.

Thirty minutes later, Darby returned to Room 218. He didn't want to be the first one in class, less they suspect him later, but he did want to make sure he was there before Ms. Genova. Of course, he wanted to see her fall off the chair, but he also wanted to see her face when she saw the chalkboard.

Darby took his seat in the back left of the classroom and waited for Ms. Genova to make her way in. Two minutes later, she did just that. She looked towards the students first.

"Everyone take their seats," the always perfunctory Ms. Genova said.

She went towards her desk, and that's when she saw the writing on the chalkboard. She quickly shielded it with her body, grabbing an eraser to wipe the chalkboard clean. There were small pockets of laughter in the classroom, but many students hadn't seen it, so the reaction was rather pedestrian.

After erasing the chalkboard, Ms. Genova's eyes bore down on Darby. For a good 10 seconds, she just sat and stared at him, her eyes staring into his. It was at that moment that Darby knew this was his last day at Western Heights high school. There was no way he was going to get away with what was to come.

As she always did, Ms. Genova grabbed the chair from behind the desk and started moving it to the front of the class. While she was carrying the chair, Darby started to hope that the screws would fall out right then. Darby was a bad kid, but he wasn't a monster. He realized that he had gone overboard with this prank.

Ms. Genova finished bringing the chair up and set it down between her desk and the row of students. Darby had a bad feeling. As Ms. Genova started to put her butt on the chair, Darby yelled out, "Don't sit down!"

It was too late.

Ms. Genova's didn't have time to heed Darby's warning, and her butt hit the chair a split-second after he spoke. The chair collapsed almost immediately, but instead of falling straight down, Ms. Genova's momentum had her falling back in the direction of the desk. Her butt hit the ground behind the chair, but this sent her head snapping back. Her head hit the thick, front part of the desk with a huge thud, and most of the students started screaming.

Darby saw Ms. Genova's head hit, and then her whole body went prone to the ground. Darby's immediate thought was that he had killed her, but knew that was unlikely. He was the first one at her side, encapsulating the good and bad of Darby Bowles in one fell swoop.

Within seconds, Ms. Genova came to, and Darby felt relief that she was alive. He wasn't a killer. But he knew he had done a terrible thing.

The shrieks from the classroom had led a passing student to go get Principal Odmark. He walked in, and a few students started telling him that Darby had warned Ms. Genova before she sat down. It was a condemnation, not a commendation.

Darby looked up at Principal Odmark, fully aware that he was a goner.

"I assume I should go," Darby said.

"No, you should stay," Jeff Odmark said.

Darby was thinking he might have to fill out some paperwork for Mr. Odmark, confessing to what he had done. Of course, the real report he was going to have to fill out was a police report. Several Oklahoma City officers arrived minutes later, and Darby Cash Bowles was led out in handcuffs. Darby had been right, he would never set foot in Western Heights high school again.

Darby's actions finally caught up to his mother, and Mabel Bowles passed away from a massive heart attack at 50, only two weeks after Darby had been expelled from school. He was serving time in juvenile hall and had to be released for the day in order to go to his mother's funeral. He cried and cried, knowing Mabel had tried her best with him. He loved his mother, but he had been a horrible son, and he knew he had helped contribute to her premature death.

Being only 17 years old and having no legal guardian or close relatives, Darby Bowles entered a foster home once he was released from Juvenile Hall. The end couldn't come fast enough for Billy and Sue Baker, who had put up dozens of wayward teenagers in their life. Years later, they would both recall that Darby Bowles was one of the worst.

At 18, Darby was now an adult, and responsible for his own actions, but that didn't knock any sense into him. He was still a conflicted teenager. Some people saw him as a misguided soul, but not irreparable, more like the boy who warned the teacher than the boy who orchestrated the terrible prank. Others saw him as a bad seed beyond help. The truth was he was somewhere in the middle.

Regardless of others opinion's, when you are 18, the court of law sees you as an adult. And when Darby knocked out a guy who looked at his girlfriend a second too long, he served a year and a half in jail for assault. Darby had been dating her for all of four days.

When he got out this time, he was 20 years old, and by some miracle, he managed to stay out of jail for 14 months.

He had inherited his father's affinity for bar fights, however, and a vicious right hand that put a bar patron into a brief coma landed him back in jail for a three-year stint. He had been sent to Lawton Correctional Facility in southwestern Oklahoma. It's where he would spend his 22nd, 23rd, and 24th birthdays.

It was during this stretch that Darby Bowles started to change slightly. He softened just a bit, realizing all his anger had gotten him nowhere. He was by no means a saint, but he knew he wasn't as bad as the convicts he was surrounded by in the Lawton Correctional Facility. His father had been a barroom brawler, but that didn't mean that Darby had to be.

He could handle jail, he knew that, but if he was going to land there again, it would be for a good reason. He decided he was done with bar fights and stupid shit like that. If he was going to land back in jail, it would be while trying to make some money.

6

Oakland, CA is a city that everyone has heard of, but it still lives in the shadows of its richer, more highly thought of neighbor, San Francisco. They are only separated by eight miles, the length of the Bay Bridge, which led renowned sports columnist Jim Murray to say "Oakland is this kind of town: You have to pay 50 cents to go from Oakland to San Francisco, but coming to Oakland from San Francisco is free." Yeah, he wrote it a long time ago, and the bridge toll is now $5, but the sentiment is still pervasive.

Anyone who has been to places like Lake Merritt or Jack London Square can tell you the numerous attributes of Oakland, but it often rings on deaf ears who consider it the ugly, younger brother of San Francisco. People often have the impression that it is filled with rowdy Raider fans and that's a tough stereotype to overcome.

In the Oakland Hills where I grew up, the streets were lined with huge trees, and it was generally a sleepy, quiet area. It didn't have the city feel that most parts of Oakland had, and was considered by the suburbs of Oakland.

That all changed when we moved down to 26th street and left behind our house in the suburbs. I had since come to the conclusion that if you moved from an address with a name to one with a number, you were probably downgrading. Taking it further, drive, court, and lane were almost always preferable to Street, Avenue, or Boulevard. In our case, 26th Street was a huge step-down from Gravatt Drive.

There were worse parts of 26th than the area we lived on, but our neighborhood would never be confused with the suburbs.

It was the day after Mrs. Somerset's surprise visit, and I had decided to take her up on her offer to go and see Evie. It was only four miles from our tiny little house on 26th Street to the Cul-de-Sac on Gravatt Drive, but it felt like a different world. I parked in front of Evie's parents' house and walked over to our old house, spending a good two minutes looking at it. They had repainted it, from the tan that we had to a light green color. It wasn't an improvement.

I said a silent prayer for my father and walked back towards the Somerset's. Unlike our old house, their house hadn't change a bit. It was a white style ranch home, upper middle class in all its glory.

Mrs. Somerset answered the door and led me back towards Evie's room. I was starting to question her motives. I hadn't spent any quality time with Evie in over three years, and now her mother was walking me back towards Evie's room to likely be alone with her daughter. What was going on here?

"Evie honey, Frankie is here."

Evie opened the door, and even though I was standing before the gorgeous girl I remembered, it was obvious that something had changed. There was a sadness to her that I had never seen, and it was more than just the 'having a bad day' type of sadness. Her mascara had smeared, and her eyes had the hint of someone who had been crying recently. There was a blue tint to her skin around her eye, and it looked like she might be recovering from a black eye as well.

Despite this, she greeted me with a big smile, and this lit up her whole face, revealing the beauty I remembered. She was still a brunette, but it was a lighter shade than I had remembered. Her hairstyle was shorter as well. I had always imagined her as a sexy librarian, and that image came back to me now. Of course, this librarian had been crying, and I shouldn't have been thinking of her looks.

"Hi, Frankie."

"Great to see you, Evie."

I brought her in for a hug. I wasn't sure if I just imagined it, but she seemed to resist it at first, but then held on a little longer than I expected.

"I'll let you guys be," her mother said and closed the door behind her.

An awkward silence followed, and I didn't know what to say, so I just spoke my mind.

"Am I missing something? I don't see you for two years, and then your Mom invites me over, takes me to your room, and shuts the door behind her. If I didn't know better, I'd think she was setting us up."

As I looked at her appearance, I realized jokes probably weren't the way to go, but she seemed to take it in stride.

"No, she just thinks I could use a friend," Evie said.

She looked up at me again, and I could see the tears coming before they hit her cheek. She was trying to hold back, to no avail, and she finally just gave up and let them flow.

"You're still a good person, aren't you Frankie?" She asked as the tears flowed down her face.

It was a surreal moment and a really odd question. "Yes, I think I am," I answered.

"Let's take a walk," she said.

"I'm guessing my Mom told you that I wanted to meet up with you," Evie said.

She said this as we walked around my old neighborhood on a brisk December day. The leaves were on the ground, and a chill was in the air. It was mid-December, and many houses were decorated for Christmas. It was almost five p.m., the sun was going down, and we seemed to be the only people on the street. Considering the state of mind Evie was in, it was probably for the best.

"Did you not want to?" I asked.

"It took some convincing by my Mom," she said.

I just nodded, sensing she wanted to say more.

"I've been home for a week, but haven't been very talkative with my parents. They always liked you and felt maybe that I could open up to you."

"I'm not really sure what's going on, Evie."

She looked up at me, and I could tell it took a lot of courage to not start crying again. She cleared her throat and then said something that must have been extremely difficult.

"Stuart Conley beat me up," she said.

This time she needed the hug, and leaned into me, not letting go for a good thirty seconds. She softly released her hold of me, and we just stared at each other. A dead end was waiting for us if we kept walking straight, so we took a right on Amito Ave.

Evie told me all the grim specifics over the next 20 minutes as we walked with no particular destination in mind. It wasn't easy hearing about her three-year relationship with Stuart Conley, but I knew how fragile she was. If I was any sort of friend, I'd be there for her, and hear her out. I did just that.

Apparently, their first two years of dating went well. He was a real go-getter, and she liked that. He thought she was attractive and was impressed with how much she read and knew about the world. Their senior year in high school and freshman year in college were going along fine. Conley was going to M.I.T. in Boston, so he wasn't that far from Providence, RI where Evie was attending Brown. They would see each other every other month or so, and more often during summer/winter breaks and the like.

She said he started taking a turn for the worse a little over a year ago, as their sophomore year was kicking off. He started asking about guys who lived near her, something he had never done before. He started holding her hand a little tighter in public, and there were many instances where Evie told him to ease up a little bit. On a trip to Brown in late November, Conley accused her of cheating on him, and Evie denied this vehemently. When he left after that visit, Evie was a little worried, but nothing prepared her for what was to come.

Conley came back to Brown early the next year, in what turned out to be the first time he hit her. It was March, and a night of drinking led to another argument once they got back to her apartment. Conley accused her of flirting with other guys at the bar. Evie explained she hardly ever drank and was just in a good mood and enjoyed talking to everyone.

"You were talking to everyone and their brother!" Conley yelled. His face was turning a bright red, and Evie just wanted to get him out of there. "Any guy who said hi to you, you smiled back and returned the hello."

"That's what normal, polite people do," Evie said.

"Don't talk back to me!" Conley fumed.

"I'm not talking back to you, I'm explaining that what I did was perfectly normal."

For some reason, this set Stuart Conley off, and he grabbed Evie and slapped her really hard to the ground. She looked up at him, and all she saw was rage.

"That's your fucking problem. You're polite to them when all they want to do is fuck you."

The tears would come in waves later, but at this moment Evie had to be strong.

"Get out of my way!" Evie yelled as she began to get up off the floor. It was as loud and assertive as Evie Somerset had been her whole life.

Conley tried to help her up from the ground, likely realizing how bad his actions were. Evie refused, and Conley started apologizing profusely, but Evie knew from that moment on that things would never be the same. She had already decided she was done with him. It took her a split second to decide that. She had heard about women who stay with a guy too long after something like this. It never ended well, and Evie wouldn't let that happen to her.

"Get the hell out of my apartment right now. You have one minute. If you don't, I will call the cops."

Conley continued to apologize, but it was falling on deaf ears. Evie was quite adamant and grabbed her phone as if she was about to call the police. Conley raised his hands in capitulation. He put his stuff together in seconds and walked towards the door. He tried to apologize a final time, but Evie shut the door in his face.

Evie broke up with him the next day via text message, and it was then that she considered that maybe she had gotten lucky. She knew that some women got it far worse. She had been slapped to the ground, and it was terrible, but she wasn't going to let herself be the victim. And that's why she ended it so abruptly.

She texted Conley that he was sick and needed to go to rehab for his temper. He responded that he would try, but rationalized his actions by saying his mind would race in their months apart, and he'd start imagining her with other guys. Evie didn't really care the reason. He had hit her, and that's all that mattered.

Once Evie was done texting him, she crumbled to the ground and balled her eyes out. She pondered calling her Mom right then and there but thought better of it. There was no reason to scare her parents from 3,000 miles away, and if the time was ever right, she knew she wouldn't be reluctant to tell her mother.

Conley tried to get back together in the intervening months, but Evie held strong, refusing to even meet up with him and let him apologize in person. Getting back together was out of the question. He seemed honest in his apologies, but Evie feared that he was just providing lip service.

She didn't see him at any time over the next six months, and their talks became less and less frequent. Conley would text her every other week or so, but Evie was responding less and less. She didn't want to text back at all, but Evie had dated the guy for three years, and she hoped that he was on the right track to getting his anger issues resolved.

Finally, he called her at the end of November and stated that he had just finished a 6-week night program for his temper and that he was a changed man. He had finished finals at M.I.T. early and was going to be in Providence the next weekend, and wanted to know if they could meet up for a bite to eat. Evie figured it would be in public, and she could say goodbye for a final time, so she agreed to the dinner.

There was no way she was going to invite him back to her apartment. This would be a public dinner where she would wish him the best but let him know that they were done. Not temporarily. Forever.

They had an early dinner in a busy part of town, and Conley was going out of his way to be nice. Evie wasn't buying it. He seemed distant, and this was not the guy she had dated for three years. The under current of violence hung over the dinner, but Evie figured the best thing was to just get it over with. If she was to walk out, who knows what would happen. *What the hell did I ever see in this guy* she asked herself several times. His excuse about being done with finals rang a little hollow as well, and Evie just wanted the whole thing over with.

The dinner mercifully ended, and Evie decided it wasn't the best time to tell him they should never talk again. He was too on edge. This would be better left for a text and not face to face. She hated using a text for what should be a person to person conversation, but he had lost all privileges when he slapped her.

They started saying their goodbyes when Randy Peters, a friend from her kickball team, saw Evie and started walking over.

"Hey, Evie! See you Thursday night, right?" Randy asked.

"Hi, Randy! Yup, I'll be there," Evie answered.

A switch seemingly turned on in Stuart's face, and Evie once again saw the furious look she had seen the night he slapped her to the ground.

"Are you dating this guy?" Conley asked and motioned in Randy Peters direction.

"I'm on her kickball team. Who the hell are you?" Peters said and walked closer.

"I'm her boyfriend," Conley stated.

"You are not my boyfriend," Evie said, and she could sense things spiraling out of control.

"Shut up you whore!" Conley yelled at Evie and pushed her to the ground.

Conley then went after Peters, and the two men swung wildly at each other, neither one connecting. People were now taking notice, and they saw Evie pick herself up and get in the middle of the two. It was foolish, but Evie Somerset was a tough young woman.

As Peters grabbed Evie and tried to get her to safety, Conley sucker punched him from behind, and Peters went to the ground, out cold. It was now Conley and Evie standing directly across from each other.

"You're a monster! You belong in jail." Evie said.

Conley punched her with a closed fist and Evie went down. He walked over to her and got several kicks to her midsection before two bystanders tackled him to the ground. They held Conley down as they waited for the police, while several other people looked after Evie. Minutes later, the police showed up. Stuart Conley was hauled off to jail, and Evie had to go to the police station to make a statement.

And that's when Evie looked up at me and said, "And that all happened 10 days ago."

I was dumbfounded, having no idea what to say, and ended out muttering something stupid about how you couldn't even notice what had happened.

"It's the scars on the inside that are going to take longer to heal," Evie said.

"Of course, Evie. I'm so sorry."

And we hugged for the third time.

7

Phillip Cokeley, a.k.a. Angry Phil, hadn't received his nickname by accident.

Unlike Darby Bowles, Angry Phil hadn't committed different crimes that repeatedly landed him in jail. He did it all in one fell swoop. His life-altering decision occurred when he was just 18 years old and a freshman at Oklahoma City University. The school, located in the uptown district of Oklahoma City, was affiliated with the Methodist Church and dated back to 1904.

While his parents wanted him to go there for the ties to the Methodist Church, Angry Phil was about as ambivalent about religion as one could be. He was a self-described redneck and would much rather be hunting or fishing than reading from the scriptures. In fact, Phil always had a gun with him, dating back to when he was 15 years old.

Al Capone was credited with saying "You can get a lot more from a kind word and a gun than from a kind word alone." It was Phil Cokeley's favorite phrase, and he lived his life by it. It would prove to be his undoing.

One night, only three weeks into his freshman year, things came to a head. He was living in the dorms, and his suite mates started blasting some loud music at one in the morning. His bullying nature had earned him his nickname back in high school, but Angry Phil could be rational and subdued when necessary. Approaching the door that connected the two rooms, he told himself he would be both those things on this night.

He knocked extra hard on the door, being sure they heard. They opened it, and Phil asked them politely if they would turn the music down. They responded in the affirmative.

As he closed the door, he heard them turn the music down, and Phil smiled, thinking maybe you could get somewhere with just a kind word.

As soon as he began to lie down, they turned the music way up, twice as loud as before. Phil jumped out of bed, and there was not going to be any politeness this time. He was pissed. He knocked on the door as loud as he could, and after the 7th knock, the door finally opened. The three guys in the room stood there, laughing at Phil. It was a big mistake.

"I'm generally not a very nice guy, but I asked you very politely to turn down the music. I'm going to ask you one last time. Please, no, pretty please, will you turn down the music? I will not ask again."

The way he said pretty please scared Anthony, the youngest of the group. He had graduated high school at 17 and was the only one in the dorms who had yet to turn 18. He looked at Charlie, the instigator of the group, pleading with his eyes to stop this. Charlie wasn't the type to bow to pressure, however, and he looked across at Phil.

"And what the fuck are you going to do if I don't turn it down?"

"I was hoping it wouldn't come to that," Phil said.

Anthony moved past Robert, the third man, and turned the music down.

"Good decision," Phil said and closed the door again.

This time he wouldn't even get to his bed before the music was turned way up again. Charlie had pushed Anthony out of the way and turned the volume up himself. People on other parts of the floor started waking up and were walking towards the room.

Phil grabbed his gun that he kept in the drawer next to where he slept. It was a semiautomatic pistol known as an ATM Hardballer. The gun had only been launched a few years previous, but Phil loved the look of the stainless steel firearm. He put the ATM Hardballer beneath his sweatshirt and walked towards the music.

This time he didn't knock, but instead kicked the door open and walked straight into the room.

Charlie stepped towards him. "What the fuck do you think you're doing? Get the fuck out of our room."

"This is your last chance," Phil said. "Are you going to turn the music down?"

The gun was underneath Phil's sweatshirt, and Charlie couldn't see it. If he had, he almost assuredly would have answered differently.

"Not a chance you fucking asshole!" He yelled at Phil. He then made a point of looking at Phil as he bent down to the Pioneer Stereo and turned the volume button up as high as it could go.

Phil raised his gun and shot Charlie three times in the chest. Charlie fell back, knocking the chord out of the speakers, and the music ceased immediately. He was dead before he hit the ground.

Phil pointed his gun at Robert and Anthony but didn't fire a shot. Phil was an ill-tempered man no doubt, but he wasn't without his morals. The other two didn't deserve to die. He walked back to his room, laid his ATM Hardballer down, and waited for the police to arrive.

Anthony would live to see his 18th birthday.

Angry Phil was convicted of murder and sentenced to 30 years, only a month after turning 19 years old. That was two decades ago, and he been transferred to different jails at different times, but Phil now found himself at Lawton Correctional Facility. It was a medium security prison and after being in much worse, Angry Phil welcomed it.

He had mellowed a bit over the years, but you still didn't want to cross him. The nickname "Angry" was still used by almost everyone, just not in front of Phil, lest you risk finding out why he had received the nickname.

Darby had been at Lawton for a few years now, so he had come to know Angry Phil a little bit. Phil belonged to the hierarchy of the jail inmates, and while Darby was just a little piss ant by comparison, he had always respected his elders and had never started shit with Phil or any of his friends. That's why Darby thought Phil might consider him for a job on the outside.

Darby approached Angry Phil as they walked in the communal area of the jail's courtyard in early October of the year 2000. Darby Cash Bowles would turn 25 years old in less than a month.

Some guys around him lifted weights, but that wasn't for Phil. He was feared due to his connections, not his physique. He didn't need to lift a bunch of weight to intimidate people.

Darby walked up to Phil. While they weren't exactly tight, Darby knew him well enough to call him Phil. As long as he didn't add "Angry" in front of it.

"Hello, Phil. Can we talk alone?"

With a flick of his wrist, Phil let two people that were hovering around him know to walk elsewhere. When they were out of earshot, Phil turned to Darby.

"What can I do for you, Cash?"

Darby was more impressed than surprised. "No one has ever called me that. How did you know my middle name?"

"I know a great many things, son, and I know you were given that middle name because your father was a huge Johnny Cash fan. I always preferred Waylon Jennings, but I can respect a Cash guy."

Angry Phil knew his stuff, Darby had to admit.

"So, what can I do for you, Cash?" Phil repeated himself.

"I guess you could say I'm here to make a little more of my middle name," Darby said half-heartedly.

"Was that a statement or a question?" Phil asked.

Darby realized beating around the bush wasn't the right course of action with Phil.

"I'm sorry. Just a little nervous. I'm asking if you'd consider me for a job when I get out of here."

"I don't do the hiring," Phil said.

This wasn't going how Darby had expected.

"Let me start over," he said. "If you hear about an open job on the outside, would you consider mentioning my name?"

"That's better," Angry Phil said.

"I'm very reliable, and I work hard. You can ask around. And I'd be up for doing any type of work you could find me. Literally anything."

"I've seen you around enough to gain an impression. I've always thought you seemed like a good, if hot-headed, kid."

"Thank you, sir, but I promise I'm mellowing."

"Sir? I didn't peg you as the type that would be so deferential."

"I imagine most people see me as an out and out prick, and they wouldn't be wrong, but that doesn't mean I don't respect authority, when necessary," Darby said.

"Authority?"

"The type that you represent. Not the pigs out there," Darby said as he motioned towards the outside world.

Angry Phil smiled. He had to admit, he kind of liked this kid.

"When do you get out?" Phil asked.

"A month."

"I'll get back to you before the month is out, but no guarantees."

"Of course not. Thank you very much," Darby said and started to walk away.

"You forget something?" Angry Phil said.

"Thank you very much, sir."

Angry Phil smiled again.

8

The day after Evie spilled out her guts to me, I spent a great deal of time thinking about her. Not in the way that most 21-year-olds thought about a pretty girl, but in a genuinely empathetic way. I felt terrible for everything she had gone through. As she said, the internal scars would take much longer to heal than the bruises. I considered calling her but thought better of it. If she wanted to talk, she could call. Unfortunately, she couldn't just walk across the street anymore.

To pass the time, I grabbed the novel that Uncle Owen had given me. I powered through the second and third chapters. It was monotonous and unexciting, hardly the cornerstone of a great novel. In fact, I was starting to think this was all an elaborate joke by Uncle Owen to get me to read the most boring book ever. Through sheer will, I managed to finish the fourth chapter. I was about to start the pivotal Chapter 5, but I couldn't keep my eyes open. If nothing else, the best novel ever might work as a cure for insomnia.

I was woken up an hour later by Fiona knocking on my door. I hated to admit it, but my younger sister was starting to blossom into a woman. It felt weird even using the word woman for a girl I had routinely made fun of over the years. She would always be the little runt of the family. Maybe only 27 months younger by the calendar, but that was a huge difference when you are growing up. And now she was an 18-year-old girl, er, woman, attending college.

I didn't like it. I preferred her as the young whippersnapper that I liked to make fun of, but also enjoyed protecting. I knew she had long been interested in boys, and living at home couldn't have been easy on her either. All the better. I would have scared the shit out of any boy she brought over, hoping he'd be too afraid to come back. I was probably more like a father than an older brother in that regard. There were some jobs I had to take on when my father had passed.

Sure, Fiona and I butted heads like every other brother and sister, but for the most part, we got along great, and she knew I had her back if push ever came to shove. Doesn't mean I didn't make fun of the little brat whenever I had the chance.

Fiona had light brown hair, was about 5'6", and had huge dimples that had somehow managed to avoid me. She was very inquisitive and loved learning things about the world. She had a real joie de vivre and was always smiling. It made her dimples even more prevalent. Fiona was cute, but most people noticed her smile and her love of life before her looks.

"Mom is taking us to dinner," she yelled, knocking on my door.

I looked at my phone. I had fallen asleep for two hours.

My mother took us to a restaurant named Rockin Crawfish, a Cajun-themed restaurant in the center of the burgeoning Oakland culinary district. They had several locations in the Bay Area, but we had staked a claim to this spot. It had become our go to place since our father had died, and we tried to eat there at least once a month.

As you walked in, you'd always notice the brick walls and red chairs. It gave the restaurant a great ambiance and was one of the reasons we liked the place so much. It was a bit of a hole in the wall, but we didn't care. The menu, which consisted of fatty, fried southern food didn't hurt either.

We were seated, and after a few minutes of small talk, we could tell our mother had something to tell us.

"My great aunt Sylvia doesn't have long to live. She's 88 years old and may only have a month left. Since we won't see her at Christmas, I am going to fly to Eugene next Friday and spend the weekend with her. I don't want to take a chance of waiting till after Christmas in case she passes. I'll send my best from you two, but you have never really known her that well, so I think it's better if just I go."

Fiona and I both nodded.

"And there will be no parties," my mother added.

"We wouldn't think anything of it," I said.

"I don't even drink Mom," Fiona said. "You know that."

"Good for you, Fiona," my Mom said, leaning in to hug her. "Your life will be better without it."

I kept my mouth shut, remembering some debaucherous, drunken nights in San Francisco that my mother didn't need to hear about.

If I said the prospect of having Evie over without my mother there didn't cross my mind, I'd be lying. I quickly eradicated the thought from my mind, however. Evie had been through a hell of a lot, and probably wanted nothing to do with another man for a long time. I kicked myself for being such an asshole.

"I leave next Friday and will return on Monday. One of you will drive me to the airport, and the other one will pick me up. There will be a few chores around the house, but it will be easy stuff. You know I trust you guys."

"Give Aunt Sylvia our best," Fiona said.

Our mother was right, we really didn't know her that well. We could have shown faux concern, but she'd see right through it. We knew what it was like to lose loved ones that mattered. Our father would always be first. Uncle Owen had been second. My mother's great aunt Sylvia came in at 323rd.

We proceeded to have a nice dinner, enjoying our heavy, southern food. I left Rockin Crawfish about five pounds heavier than when I had walked in. Seafood gumbo, with a shrimp basket on the side, will do that to you.

We arrived home that night, and my Mom floated the idea of playing a board game, but Fiona and I decided we were still too stuffed and preferred the privacy of our own rooms. I entered mine and saw Uncle Owen's book sitting on my bed. It was time. Chapter 5 awaited.

I opened the novel to Chapter 4 and leafed through the pages until I came upon the first page of Chapter 5. I looked down, and the page was full of handwriting that I had to assume was Uncle Owen's. I let out a laugh.

This crappy, plodding novel had not been Owen's end goal. He had wanted me to get to his notes. I didn't have to worry about Arthur Billingsley and his boring 18th-century love story any longer. Thank God for small miracles.

What I had instead were liner notes written in a blue pen. He had written small, but legibly, along the top, then down the margins, finishing at the bottom of the page. I imagine it couldn't have been easy in his weakened and dying state.

I read the first page, reread it, and then read it for a third time. I looked around the room even though I knew I was the only one there. I shut the window that was allowing the smallest of breezes to enter because I wanted to be alone with my thoughts. Safe to say I was a little paranoid. I read what Uncle Owen wrote for a fourth time:

Hey, Sport! If you are reading this, I'm long dead, and you are 18 years old. First things first. You can't tell your mother about this book. She'd kill me if I weren't already dead. Haha. Isn't that what you kids say when you are trying to be funny? Alright, no more jokes. These notes are for you and you only. In the pages that follow, you will be given a series of homework assignments and a possible adventure or two. If you do them all in the order I assign them, you will have a roadmap to enough money for a lifetime. You could also end up dead. Read that last sentence again, because I'm not kidding. You're going to be dealing with some awful people and real shady characters, one of which is as influential as anyone in our nation's capital. If you want to burn this book right now, I won't blame you, and it would probably be the best decision you ever made. But I couldn't die without letting someone know the secret that I hold onto. With the death of your father, I imagine your family is struggling financially, and this is your chance to get rich. I had to at least put it out there to you. It's your choice if you wish to continue. There's just one ground rule: You can only advance to the next page if you have completed the previous page. That is very important! You won't know why until later, but the final information that you will discover could potentially put you in harm's way. If you go step by step, you can ditch this at any time. But once the final puzzle piece has been revealed, you can't just walk into the sunset with the info you have. It will be too late for that. The threats

I've given you are real, so take the night and decide if you want to continue to the next page. Good luck Sport! Be safe…

9

It was now late October in the year 2000 and two weeks had passed since Darby Bowles had talked to Angry Phil. He had seen him several times in the communal area, but every time Darby thought about approaching, Phil had subtly shaken his head. Darby guessed that if Phil was going to, in fact, give him a job, he probably didn't want to be seen with him very often. At least, that's what Darby kept telling himself, as he crept within a week of his release date.

Finally, only five days from the day he was to get out, and expecting another shake of the head, Angry Phil gave a slight nod towards Darby as they saw each other in the jail courtyard. Darby approached cautiously and just as before, Phil shooed his friends away with a flip of his wrist.

"How are you doing, Phil?"

"Hello, Cash."

"I've seen you around, but could tell you didn't want me to approach," Darby said.

"I appreciate that. If we are going to do business together, the less we are seen with each other, the better. I'm sure you understand why."

Darby smiled to himself. He had been right and needn't had worried.

"I get out in five days."

"I know that. Don't forget who you are talking too."

"Of course. Sorry, Phil."

Darby Cash Bowles didn't say sorry very often, but he knew if he played his cards right there was a job at the end of this. He could play nice if he had to. He could even be charming when the opportunity presented itself. It rarely did.

Phil continued, ignoring Darby's apology.

"So here's how it's going to work. When I end this conversation, I'm going to give you a piece of paper with a time and place on it. That's where you will meet your contact. If you are even one minute late, you will never work a day for these people."

Darby nodded.

"I'm a pretty rational person in spite of the nickname I have carried for so long."

Darby looked on quizzically, trying to play dumb, not knowing where Phil was going with this.

"Don't pretend you don't know my nickname. You think I'm an idiot? Anyway, that's not my point. My point is that I'm a double fucking rainbow of happiness compared to the guy you'll be working for. He will pay you well, but from what I have heard this guy is not the type you want to fuck with. I just want you to know that up front. If you screw up or attempt to fuck him over, you'll wish you were back in this shit hole."

"I will lower my head and do my job." It was a brief answer, but it seemed to help set Phil's mind at ease.

"You're a tough kid, Darby. No question about that. You're polite to me, but I see the anger deep down. Just remember that they are tougher and angrier. Do as they say."

"Yes, sir."

Angry Phil smiled.

"Don't approach me again. It's time we part ways."

"I won't."

"Good luck," Phil said, enveloping his hand over Darby's in a handshake, leaving a small piece of paper in Darby's hand. He patted him on the shoulder and walked away.

When Angry Phil was a good 50 feet away, Darby looked down at the small sheet of paper.

> Southwest Baptist Church
> 1300 SW 54th Street
> November 4th, 7:00 am

November 4th. The day after he would be released. Darby laughed to himself. Well shit, that didn't take long.

10

I drove to Evie's parents' house on another cold December day. I had no intentions of telling her about Uncle Owen or the instructions he had left for me. I swear. She was dealing with a lot and didn't need another burden. Of that, I was sure. But I hadn't heard from her in two days, and I wanted her to know I was there if she needed me.

I knocked on the door, and Mrs. Somerset answered the door. I knew that Evie's father worked long hours at UC Berkeley, the same university which my sister now attended, and was not surprised that he wasn't there. All the better, I thought. I'm not sure he'd be too keen having a man coming around after what had happened to his daughter.

Mrs. Somerset seemed pleased to see me, however, and called back to Evie who emerged with a big smile. It was far different from the somber atmosphere only two days previous.

"Want to take a walk?" I asked Evie.

"Very much so," was her unequivocal answer.

As we headed towards the front door, we passed a television in which the President of the United States was answering a reporter's question. Evie looked at me and shook her head.

"This freaking guy," she said.

"Not a fan?" I asked.

"Furious and Nauseous!"

It took me a second to realize she had quickly come up with an acronym for fan.

"Don't get me started," Evie said.

I nodded in agreement, not knowing our lives would become intertwined with his in a few short weeks.

Evie and I walked through the same streets that we had a few days earlier, but the whole mood of the conversation had changed. Her demeanor was great, she was playful and just seemed like an altogether different woman. She looked a lot better as well, with no residual marks still on her face. She had always been very pretty, and it seemed she was only getting better looking.

"A lot of girls had it way worse than me," she said. "I was beaten up one time."

It was a weird start to a conversation, to say the least. Apparently, she wasn't counting being slapped to the ground. I took that as a good sign since it seemed like she was trying to avoid playing the victim.

I thought back to her description of being punched and then kicked several times while on the ground, and I wanted Stuart Conley in front of me so I could kick his fucking ass. He was 6'5", but I was a strong, built 6'3" and I would have rage on my side. I couldn't show Evie my true feelings, however, so I continued being the understanding friend.

"And, God forbid, nothing happened to me sexually. Those women are the ones who really have internal scars. I just prefer to think of it as one bad day."

"Wouldn't be that easy for me. You're a better man than I."

"You're right. I'm a woman!"

"You know what I mean. It's an expression," I said.

"That you screwed up."

"Hey, let me be."

We had a nice banter going, and it reminded me of our conversations from three years ago. The carefree nature of Evie had returned, at least on this day. I hoped it would last.

We talked about our respective colleges and plans we had for the rest of our junior year in college. I was somewhat surprised to find out that she was going back to Brown.

"I'm not letting him determine what I do and where I go."

She talked about how she had an internship in Washington D.C. last summer for our local congresswoman Scarlet Jackson, and just how much she enjoyed it. While most interns just did grunt work, Evie was introduced to Mrs. Jackson early on and was given more pressing matters than the other summer interns. Jackson had offered Evie the chance to return the following summer, and it sounded like she was looking forward to taking it.

"You can be the first woman president," I said.

We kept walking, and she was smiling and energetic the whole time. She was putting up a great front. After circling around the neighborhood a few times, we arrived back outside her house once again.

"So any big plans while you are home?" I asked.

"I want to get out of the house. Anything that keeps my mind off what happened. I can, and will, get over this. I just don't want to be alone too long with my feelings. That's when it gets to me. Today is a good day, but I know there are still some bad ones ahead."

I half smiled, half frowned. She really was a great girl, and it broke my heart that she had to go through something like this.

And then she said it...

"I just want to get involved in a great adventure. Take me away from reality for a bit, you know?"

I understood completely. What I didn't understand later is why I couldn't just let her comment go. But the die had been cast.

"Come with me to my house. There's something I want to show you," I said.

I drove myself and Evie to my mother's house on 26th street. We had moved from our place on Gravatt Drive late in my senior year, so Evie had never seen the place I had called home for the last three years. While it was a huge step down from our old house, she didn't seem to pass any judgment when she entered. Not that I expected it, Evie was a very grounded woman.

My mother was at work, and my sister must have been at a friend's because we were alone when we walked in the house. It was for the best, considering what we were going to be talking about. I told Evie that the walls were paper thin, so if my mother or sister returned, we really had to talk quietly.

She seemed to understand. I walked her the length of the hall, the whole 30 feet, and opened the door to my room. I was generally a clean person, and if I had known I'd be inviting Evie over it would have been immaculate. Unfortunately, I had not, and the room was a bit of a mess.

My hamper was in the left corner and clothes were lying over the edges. My sheets were disheveled, and the pillows were arranged in a haphazard way. A pair of boxers laid on the ground. I spent 30 seconds cleaning up, feeling like a jackass. Evie laughed and took it in stride.

"Not expecting company?" she joked.

"Sorry. Don't bring girls over to this house very often."

"It's fine, Frankie."

Evie looked at my desk and saw a basketball autographed by Stephen Curry.

"I remember that from your old house," she said.

"Good memory. It's one of my prized possessions. My Dad gave it to me a month before he died."

"I wish I could have met him," Evie said.

Evie had moved next to me the year after my father had passed.

"He was a great man. You would have loved him. And vice versa."

"I remember all the pictures of him at your old house. Really felt like he was still there in spirit."

I was beginning to get sad, and that's not why I had invited her over.

"Enough about the past," I said. "Let's look to the future."

I motioned to my desk.

"Why don't you sit down?"

Evie sat.

"You ready?" I asked.

"Not quite sure what I need to be ready for," she said.

"You said you wanted an adventure, right?"

Evie looked on excitedly. "I did!"

"Here goes nothing," I whispered to myself.

I proceeded to tell Evie all about Owen, how he got his "Uncle" status, his death, and what had led me to rediscovering "The Best Novel Ever." I handed her the novel and let her read the first page in Chapter 5. She sat there mesmerized, reading the thing at least as many times as I had. She was grinning from ear to ear. It was an odd reaction.

"Did you miss the part that said I could end up dead?" I asked.

"You said this Uncle Owen was your Dad's best friend growing up right?"

"I hadn't ranked them, but yeah, he was," I said, somewhat sarcastically.

"First, third, fifth. It doesn't matter. My point is, if he was one of your Dad's best friends he wouldn't put you in serious jeopardy. Would he?"

"I doubt it," I confessed. "He was a different type of guy. Rowdy. Trouble. But he had a good heart I think."

"That's enough for me. I'm not doing this to get rich. I'm sure it's just some wild goose chase anyway, but it would be nice to have some fun this winter break. You know that I need it, and I'm sure that's why you invited me back here. It will be like having our own little group of Goonies. Just you and I."

She sure knew how to press my buttons. In a good way.

The two of us going on adventures together for the next few weeks? Could be worse. More like, couldn't get much better.

Of course, we seemed to have two different reasons for wanting to continue with this. The prospect of being rich for life had piqued my interest, while the promise of forgetting her recent ordeal seemed to motivate Evie.

My reason for continuing with Uncle Owen's adventure would evolve over time, but I'd be lying if I said money wasn't the initial reason. I knew how much my mother struggled to make rent each month, and the idea of a family vacation was a dinner at Rockin Crawfish restaurant.

How nice would it be to have money to fly my mother and sister to Hawaii? Or Europe? I admit it, what was to follow started for very selfish reasons.

I looked at Evie, and she had this pleading look on her face. I had a feeling with all that was on her mind, she needed this a lot more than I did. I may have needed the money, but there are things more important than money.

"O.K. We'll do it," I said.

She clapped her hands together. "Yay! Thanks, Frankie."

"I've got a couple of rules though," I said.

"Anything," she said.

"If I decide at any point that this is getting dangerous, I can stop it. My decision is final. No ifs, ands, or buts about it."

"I can live with that."

"There's more. You can't tell anyone else. Your parents wouldn't be too happy if they knew I was including you."

"I asked to be included," Evie said.

"Semantics. No one, understood?"

"Yes, I understand. Does that go for you too?"

"For now. But I reserve the right to tell my mother if necessary. After all, Uncle Owen was my father's friend."

"That's fair."

It was time to lay down the law. "It's not about fair, Evie. It's my way or the highway."

"You sound old when you say that."

I couldn't help but laugh. "Yeah, I guess you're right. OK, how about, this is a dictatorship. What I say goes."

"No room for a woman president I guess?"

I laughed again. "Not in my dictatorship."

"So when do we start?"

"How about tomorrow morning?"

"Sounds good. And you won't read any further in the meantime?"

"No. We'll read the novel together tomorrow morning. We are a team now."

I looked at her hoping she didn't take that the wrong way. She hadn't. She was too excited about the adventure to come. I looked down at the book and didn't feel the same exuberance as Evie. I didn't doubt Uncle Owen when he said this could become dangerous. I had a hard time believing this was going to be all fun and games. What the hell had I dragged us into?

11

On November 3rd, 2000 Darby Cash Bowles raised his middle finger to the outside of the Lawton Correctional Facility.

"You won't be seeing me again," he yelled.

While some people might have preferred having family waiting for them as they exited a jail, Darby preferred the anonymity of being on his own. With no close family, he didn't have to attend some release party, vowing he was a changed man forever. He knew inmates who were released and had to deal with shit like that. He considered himself lucky.

He did have some friends he could stay with, but considering what he would be doing early the next morning, that could be problematic. There was the issue of having no money though. He had been very cash poor when he was sent to jail for his latest stint, and cash poor by Darby's standards meant he was broke.

He did have a short-term solution in mind though and it involved seeing an old friend.

After flipping the bird, Darby went old school and decided to hitch hike back to Oklahoma City. It was 90 miles from the jail to the city proper, but it was a common route, and he didn't think he would have a problem. He did finally catch a ride, but it wasn't until he had walked over a mile away from the jail. That surely wasn't a coincidence.

The man who picked him up must have been 80 years old and drove an old school Black Chevy Bronco. The car didn't seem to fit the man. He was also quite the talker. Normally, that would drive Darby nuts, but it did make the trip sail by, and the man never asked him where he was coming from. Maybe the man had assumed he had just been released and decided not to broach the subject.

Before he knew it, Darby had been dropped off in Mayfair, a suburb in the northwestern section of Oklahoma City. He didn't grow up in Mayfair, but he knew the area fairly well, and walked towards the Penn Square Mall, remembering going there as a youngster. For a childhood in which good memories were sparse, coming to this mall as a child had brought Darby some joy.

He walked parallel to the Penn Square Mall as long as he could, trying to soak up fond memories of an otherwise troubled youth, and then veered off in the direction of his friend's house, which was the reason he had come to this part of town in the first place.

Darby arrived minutes later and was taken aback at how nice the house was. It was a yellow, plantation style home with grass and beautiful shrubs scattered around the property. It was smaller than plantations homes of the

South, but it had that same feel, and the plush greens surrounding it only made it more beautiful.

There was a circular driveway that led to the front of the house, and Darby walked along it as he approached the front door. He found himself hoping it was some relative's home and not his friend's. Jealousy was starting to kick in, there was no doubt.

Darby knocked on the front door, and a familiar face opened it.

"Well, well, well, if it isn't Darby Bowles!" the voice said.

"Jake Court, how the hell are you!" Darby responded.

Jake Court was two years older than Darby and grew up as the neighborhood bully. He had beaten up Darby the very first time they met, in hopes of getting his lunch money. With Darby's ratty jeans, dirty shirt, and hole-filled shoes, Jake discovered early on that Darby was not a good candidate to be carrying loose change.

He did realize, however, that the young kid with a feminine name had an edge to him, and Jake started taking Darby under his wing. Darby's mother Mabel knew Jake was trouble, but she didn't stand a chance against the cool, older guy who had chosen to befriend Darby.

Jake Court started taking bets in high school. He wasn't known for his speed in paying out winning bets, but he was known for his rapidity in collecting money owed to him. From time to time, that collector would be Darby. The kid with the hole-filled shoes finally had some money in his pocket, albeit for all the wrong reasons.

After high school, Jake graduated to selling drugs and did several stints in local jails just as Darby did. They remained friends and occasional business partners, but inevitably one or both of them landed in jail, making it a less than an ideal partnership. One time, Darby was busted for delivering some drugs for Jake but kept his mouth shut when he was arrested. Jake never forgot about that.

Darby reached out to Jake's parents in the days leading up to his release, and much to his surprise, found that Jake was out of jail. Darby got his phone number and asked if he could come visit when he got out. Jake had answered in the affirmative, and now the two old friends stood outside his house.

"I'm great Darby, what do you think of the place?" Jake asked.

"It's great! You hit the lottery?" Darby joked.

"Hard work my friend."

"Hard work my ass. You always had the little guys like me doing the tough stuff."

"Out of that business Darby. You didn't hear?"

"No, I didn't hear. Not exactly chummy with our old friends once I got locked up."

"I got out two years ago, and with the help of some rich uncle who passed, I was able to get my own construction company off the ground."

Darby looked on dubiously. Jake reached into his wallet and handed his old friend a business card. Darby looked it over, and he had to say, it was pretty impressive.

"Court and Associates Construction. How many associates you got?"

"Three."

Darby laughed. "That's a shitload of associates!"

Jake smiled. "Sounded more official."

"And you were able to buy this home from your construction business?"

"Well, we can thank the rich uncle for most of the house as well."

"I'm happy for you. Can't say I'd ever thought I'd see the day," Darby said, trying to sound pleased for his old friend.

"That makes two of us."

"Wife or kids? You haven't become that domesticated have you?"

"Funny you should ask. I have a live-in girlfriend who is about four months pregnant."

Darby looked at the pristine house one more time. Suddenly, he wanted to get out of there. Here he was, a few hours out of jail, and his old friend, a bigger degenerate than him, had started his own company and was expecting a child.

Jake sensed the change in Darby's mood and got to the point.

"So what can I do for you, Darby? You need a place to stay?"

Darby knew that Jake would put him up, and that had been his initial plan, but not anymore. He'd just get a cheap hotel. Of course, he still needed money for that.

"Actually, I'm just looking to borrow some money until I get on my feet. I've got a job lined up, and I'll be able to pay you back soon."

"What kind of job?" Jake asked.

Darby's silence spoke volumes.

"You know what, I don't care. It's just good to see you!" Jake brought Darby in for a bear hug.

"Great to see you too," Darby lied. "We had some wild times. I can't believe you've grown up and got responsible on me."

"Crazy, right? Listen, if you ever want to come work a real job, you let me know. If I remember correctly, you know your way around a hammer and nail."

"I may just take you up on that."

They both knew he wouldn't. There was an awkward silence that followed.

"How much do you need?" Jake finally asked.

"Just a couple hundred if you've got it."

Jake took his wallet out again, and this time pulled out five crisp hundred dollar bills and gave them to Darby.

"A couple hundred extra for an old friend."

"Thanks. I'll pay you back soon, I promise." Darby said.

Jake looked on skeptically. They both knew this was where Darby would excuse himself and reconvene his previous life. It didn't even have to be said. Jake brought him in for a farewell fist bump/handshake/hug. They completed it perfectly as only old friends can do. Darby turned to go.

"You take care of yourself now," Jake said.

"Me? Always," Darby said.

Jake thought better of a smart ass retort and simply watched as his friend walked away. Darby waved a final goodbye, pocketed the five hundred dollars, and set out to find a cheap hotel for the night. He needed his beauty sleep. After all, tomorrow was his first day at a new job.

12

Evie came over for the second time in as many days, but it was the first time that my mother and sister got to see her. I was expecting a few sideways glances or mentions of us rekindling our friendship from years ago, but they behaved admirably.

The only one who seemed genuinely surprised was Evie. She couldn't believe how grown up Fiona was.

"You are beautiful, Fiona! I almost didn't recognize you."

"She's saying that you used to be an ugly duckling," I joked.

"Shut up, Frankie," my mother jumped to Fiona's defense. I realized I was thoroughly outnumbered. Three women and me. Better bite my tongue.

"Yeah, listen to your Mom, Frankie," Evie said. "She was always beautiful, but she's really blossoming."

I shrugged. My sister may have been becoming a woman, but I wasn't going to acknowledge it. That's not what older brothers do.

Fiona couldn't get enough of Evie. When you are an 18-year-old girl, getting approval from a gorgeous 21-year-old must mean the world to you.

She started following us around the house, asking questions about college and gossiping to Evie about some singers they thought were cute. I was having a tough time shaking her.

"We have some work to do," I said.

Fiona laughed. "You're both on winter break, and you don't have a job right now, Frankie. Nice try."

I was started to get flustered. I went with my go-to line with my little sister. "Stop being a pest!"

I used to say it when we were kids and she just hated it. It was my way of saying 'It's time for the adults to hang out.' I felt guilty since I knew how much it bothered her, but Evie and I had some important things at hand. Fiona glared at me with piercing eyes.

"Tell you what Fiona," Evie said. "How about the three of us go bowling sometime in the next few days."

"Really?" Fiona beamed from ear to ear.

"We'd love to have you join us."

"That would be awesome," Fiona said, smiling the whole time.

Soon thereafter, Fiona finally let us be, looking forward to a night of bowling with the two 21-year-olds. Evie and I started walking down the hallway towards my room.

"That was nice of you," I said.

"I saw her face drop when you called her a pest. I had to do something."

"Thanks. Looks like we are going bowling with the little nag. And for the record, I told her she was being a pest, not that she was one."

"You know she really looks up to you."

"What's not to love?" I said. Evie smiled and made the 'I'm about to puke' gesture.

We arrived at my door, and I pushed it open. Uncle Owen's book was lying on the bed for both of us to see. It hadn't made its way back to the bookshelf since I first took it down, and it wasn't going back up there anytime soon.

"Do you think we should make a copy of the book just in case?" Evie asked.

It was a good idea, but I decided to play devil's advocate. "What if I happen to see some of the pages from future chapters as I'm copying them?"

"You're a big boy. I trust you to avoid them."

She was getting a little more sarcastic day by day. I took it as progress; that she was gradually getting back to her old self. I remember being impressed with her biting tongue when she was younger, and it was nice to see it returning. To some people, it might have been a bit much, but she backed it up with such a fragile feminine side, and they played nicely off each other.

Evie grabbed the book and was tossing it between her two hands.

"Are you ready?" she asked.

I thought about it for a moment and grabbed the book from her.

"You know what, we aren't going to do it here."

I packed up my backpack with my laptop, a spiral notebook, a few pens, and finally, the novel.

"I don't want my sister or mother to walk by and hear us talking about Uncle Owen. Let's go to a coffee shop."

"Our first road trip!" Evie said.

Why did she have to be so cute?

Peet's Coffee opened its first store in 1966 in Berkeley, CA. Its owner, Alfred Peet, grew up in the Netherlands where his father had a small coffee shop before World War II. He is credited with introducing custom coffee roasting when most people were drinking canned coffee.

Despite all his success, Peet did make one mistake. He taught his style to Zev Siegl, Gordon Bowker, and Jerry Baldwin. Who are they you ask? They were the originators of Starbucks. They stole Peet's ideas and took them to Seattle and founded Starbucks in 1971.

Being that I had grown up about 10 miles from where it launched, my allegiance had always been to Peet's over Starbucks. My favorite Oakland location was one on Broadway street where I had spent many days studying in high school. That had transferred over to college, and I guess you could say I was a regular.

I drove us there in my new Ferrari, otherwise known as a 2009 Toyota Camry, and we walked in. I saw an open table near the back that was a little more secluded than the others. I went and set my backpack on it, marking my territory.

I rejoined Evie in line. As we approached the front, I asked her what she wanted.

"A cappuccino. You buying?"

"I am. Gotta keep my assistant full of caffeine, so her brain is in prime working order."

I ordered her cappuccino and an Americano for myself, and we looked out over the Peet's that would become our home base. The coffee shop looked like a meeting at the UN, with every race and creed represented. Oakland was an extremely diverse city. I was happy to call it home. We headed towards the back and sat down at our semi-private table.

We laid our laptops down in front of us, hung our backpacks over our chairs, and I laid the book in between the two laptops. It was all very symmetrical.

"So how is this going to work?" Evie asked.

"I'll read it once or twice and then hand it over to you to read. Sound good?"

"Sounds great."

We smiled at each other, but it didn't last long. We looked down at the book, and for the first time, I saw a hint of trepidation on Evie's face.

"Last chance to get out of this," I said. "Are you sure you want to continue?"

"Yes," She didn't even pause. The trepidation was gone that quickly.

I grabbed the book and found my way to Chapter 5, being careful not to accidentally flip too far ahead. I flipped past the page I had already read and started reading Owen's writing. It was brief and to the point.

So, I guess you are going through with this, huh sport? I figured you would. You always had that adventurous spirit. There will be 5 mandates/decrees/assignments you have to do first, and the 6th will be the big one. The one you can't turn back from. This is #1. Ready? OK. Here goes: Find out all you can about robberies, home invasions, killings, church vandalism, etc. from November 2000 to February 2001 in and around Oklahoma City. That's your first mandate.

And just like that, we were off and running. I handed the novel over to Evie and watched as she read it.

13

Darby Bowles was almost late to the first day at his new "job."

Being a frequent visitor to local correctional facilities, he knew that the first night out of jail could go one of two ways. One, you could sleep like a baby, enjoying not having a hard bed and a roommate for the first time in a while. Two, you could wake up several times in the middle of the night, unaware of your surroundings, a little anxious to be sleeping in a new place. This night had been the former, as Darby slept through his hotel alarm clock and the wake-up call he had scheduled.

When he finally woke up, it was 6:40, and after cursing himself, he called down to the front desk and ordered a cab. The year was 2000, and this was well before Uber or Lyft.

Darby didn't have time to shower, and just threw some water on his face, cleaning up as quickly as he could. Cleanliness certainly wasn't the most important attribute for his upcoming job, and he didn't worry about his appearance.

The cab arrived quickly, and the driver knew what Darby meant when he said to step on it, managing somehow to get Darby there five minutes early. The cab driver dropped him off in the front of the Southwest Baptist Church, and Darby walked around the back, not sure what to expect.

He saw a few tumbleweeds, and a squirrel, but not much else. There was no one at the church. Darby was sure that's why they had picked this out of the way church, but the stillness and quietness of the area disturbed Darby for some reason. The church was a beautiful mahogany red, but it seemed somehow sinister in the rising early morning sun.

The man who arrived a few minutes later looked much younger than the newly 25-year-old Darby. He could still be a teenager for all Darby knew. He was short and blonde, with a crew cut that looked like something straight out of the 1960's. Darby wasn't sure why, but he imagined the guy as an Opie. The nickname would stick.

"You Darby?" the young man said

"Yeah."

"Get in."

Opie, a man of few words, opened the door to a tan 1994 Lincoln Continental. He stared intently at Darby, who took an immediate dislike to the man he had nicknamed Opie.

Like the cab driver who drove Darby there, Opie knew how to put the pedal to the medal. He was taking side streets, but Darby knew exactly where they were. He had spent a good deal of time in all sections of Oklahoma City, and the southwest part of the city was no different. After five minutes, Opie pulled to the side of the road and handed Darby a bandana and told him to blindfold himself.

"Don't be scared. It's for your own protection." Opie said.

Darby did as asked.

They drove about three more minutes with several turns along the way. Darby assumed the purpose of the bandana was to prevent him from knowing where they were. Darby knew the suburbs they were in, and while he couldn't name the specific street due to the blindfold, he could definitely find his way back to the general area.

The car pulled into a garage, and Darby heard the garage door shutting behind them. A lot smarter than escorting a guy with a blindfold through the front door.

Opie led him into the house and sat him down on a couch that felt like it was lacquered daily. With every slight movement that Darby made the couch rustled and cracked. He heard a few voices talking and guessed it was Opie and two others.

Darby remained blindfolded but listened intently, trying to pick up anything he could. The men were on the other side of the room and whispering, so Darby didn't learn much.

After a few minutes of sitting in silence and relative darkness, Darby heard a fourth person enter the room. The steps he took were deliberate, and even though he couldn't see him, Darby could tell this was a man who demanded respect.

"Sorry about the blindfold. Insurance just in case we decide not to work together," the man said.

His voice was one of a kind. It was hypnotic and threatening, like no voice Darby had ever heard. He felt weird being so intrigued by another man's voice, but Darby hadn't been the first. The man's voice was that distinctive.

If Darby had to guess, the man was in his late 20's or early 30's.

"I want to work with you guys," Darby said.

"I appreciate the sentiment, but we'll make that decision," the man said. It was a perfectly reasonable thing to say, but the menace in the guy's voice was unavoidable. It was mesmerizing.

There was silence from the others as the man spoke. None of his subordinates dared interrupt him. Darby realized these guys were smart and weren't going to give away their names, so he had to come up with something to remember them by. Opie had been first. The man with the voice, the guy who was obviously the brains of the operation, would herein be known as the Ringleader.

"I'm kidding Darby. I'm sure we will like you just fine," he said.

"Thank you, sir," Darby said. It had worked with Angry Phil, and he hoped it would work with this guy.

"Cut the sir bullshit," the Ringleader said. Guess not, Darby thought. "I have selected you to work with us for a few reasons, and I can assure you that your manners are not one of them. Quite the opposite actually."

He came closer, and even with the blindfold, Darby noticed the shadow before him. It appeared the man was standing directly in front of him, taking him in.

"One of the reasons I selected you is that you didn't rat on your friend Jake Court when you went to jail back in 1995," the Ringleader said.

How the hell did he know that, Darby wondered.

"We really respect someone who knows when to keep their mouth shut."

"Thanks."

"Now Darby, you shouldn't have opened your mouth right there. You contradicted my assertion that you knew when to keep your mouth shut."

There were a few hesitant laughs from the other men in the room.

"That was funny, guys! Feel free to laugh!" The booming voice said, and the others in the room all laughed, a little more heartily this time. Darby didn't know what to do, so he kept his mouth shut. A bit late, he surmised.

The blindfold was starting to cause Darby to sweat, and he hated being in the dark. Figuratively and literally.

"Second, we know you need the money, Darby. I believe your checking account had $18 dollars in it when you went to jail."

Fuck, this guy really did his homework, Darby thought.

"Don't worry about going by the bank. That account has been closed. Believe me, we checked. The third reason I selected you is that I trust the opinion of Angry Phil. We did our research from out here, but he also monitored your behavior from inside. He said that you are a tough, hard-headed kid who could work as part of a team if necessary. He also said we could trust you. Can we trust you, Darby?"

"Of course you can trust me."

"Good. I'm going to assume you don't have a cell phone."

"No, I've been in jail."

"Have you ever had one?"

"No."

"I guess they were just starting to get popular when you last went inside. By the end of the week, I will get you a phone. Don't ever try and get ahold of us. If we want to use your help, we will contact you through the cell phone. We will give you the time, place, and any other pertinent information through a text message."

"Okay," Darby said.

The Ringleader laughed loudly. "This fucker probably doesn't even know what a text message is."

His cohorts joined him in laughing. Darby hated the bandana and felt like he was an exhibit at a freak show, with everyone pointing and laughing. He didn't dare mention it though.

The Ringleader continued talking for 15 more minutes, laying out the help that Darby would provide, along with the ways in which they would help him. To Darby's surprise, they were going to get him an apartment after the completion of his first job. The ringleader stated that it wasn't much, but they would continue to pay the rent for as long as Darby remained working for them. That worked just fine for Darby.

He was on his own when it came to transportation, except the night before a job. In those instances, he would get a text where the Lincoln Continental was, and he was to pick it up and drive it back to his apartment complex. Under no circumstances was he to drive the car again until the next morning when he went to pick the others up at the place that they designated.

As Darby had guessed, he was going to work as their getaway driver. In his knowledge of small time crime, they would often allow an outsider to come on as a getaway driver. They are not close enough to participate in the day to day operations, and by merely telling them where to pick up and where to drive, you were limiting the knowledge he had of the criminal enterprise. If something went down with the police, the driver couldn't provide much information.

They set up a time and place where they would give him a cell phone and told him they would give him the key to the apartment after the first job. Darby was on his own until then, but he could make $500 go a long way. It looked like cheap hotels or ex-girlfriends were in his immediate future. He wasn't going back to Jake's though, he knew that for sure. Fuck that guy and his real job.

What fascinated Darby most was the utter respect the other three had for the Ringleader. They didn't interrupt him one time, and they didn't even laugh wholeheartedly until they got permission. Darby couldn't be positive, he had a blindfold on after all, but he thought he noticed the other men take a step backward when the man took a step in their general direction.

"We'll have you out of here in a few minutes," the voice said.

He had been there 20 minutes at this point, and Darby was ready to get out of there and take the damn bandana off. He was starting to sweat even more, and it was dripping down into his eyes. He wasn't going to complain, but the promise that he would be gone soon was welcomed.

"No problem," Darby said.

He heard the men walk into an adjoining room. Darby could hear voices, but couldn't make out what they were saying. What he was sure of was they were in a different room with the door shut. You couldn't fake the muffled noise that he was hearing.

Darby considered taking off his bandana and looking around for a brief second. It was a giant risk, but he felt being able to know where this house was, could be a huge asset down the road. He knew the area, but he would have no idea which house it was. Unless he had a point of reference.

Darby listened intently, making absolutely sure they were in a neighboring room. When he was positive, he removed his bandana, half expecting them to be standing in the room looking down at him. They weren't. He knew he might only have a few seconds, so he had to do this quickly.

All the windows had drapes or sheets covering them. It was smart, in case someone happened to walk by and saw a man with a bandana covering his eyes. It would arouse suspicion.

Darby couldn't risk walking around, as they'd likely hear that. There was a set of windows on the wall above his couch. He swung his arms around, trying not to move his butt much since the lacquered couch could easily give away his actions. He peeled back the curtains just a few inches and looked out.

The house directly across the street had a beat up old basketball hoop sitting on the roof. It was dilapidated, with a lone string hanging from the rim. The backboard was white with a red square that had turned a rust color. There was also brown paint in the upper right hand of the backboard. Darby knew he could find this house if necessary. God, I'm good, Darby thought to himself.

He put the curtain back where it was, and gently swiveled his butt back around, trying once again not to take it off the couch. This time didn't prove successful. The swiveling had caused the leather of the couch to join together, and as Darby came back to his original sitting situation, the lacquered couch let out a squeak.

Darby's heart sunk. It sunk further when he heard a door open. He was sure they had heard him. He immediately put his blindfold back on, with barely a second to spare.

The four men walked back into the room, and Darby didn't say a word. Neither did any of the other men. Darby was blindfolded once again, but he could swear that the Ringleader was looking right at him, trying to read his mind.

The curtain was shut, the blindfold was on, and they had an over-lacquered couch that squeaked easily. There was nothing to suspect.

"You're sweating a bit there, Darby. Are you O.K.?"

Darby wanted to get the fuck out of there. The Ringleader scared him.

"A little hot under this bandana is all," Darby said.

"Of course. That must be it," the words were benign, but his tone of voice was not.

Darby started sweating more. A few more seconds went by. He knew he was still being watched.

"Welcome aboard, Darby."

"Thank you," Darby said, gratitude and relief filling his body in equal measures.

Over the next two and a half months, Darby did six jobs for the Ringleader and his cohorts. Just as promised, he had received a cell phone within the week. Cell phones in the year 2000 looked more like a car phone from the 80's, but it did its job. He was given the keys to his new apartment, and while Darby knew it wasn't going to be featured in Better Home & Gardens or any other fairy magazine like that, it did have a bed and a roof, and for a man freshly out of jail, that was enough.

Early on, he dealt exclusively with Opie, who would send him the texts about where to pick up the car and would pay Darby after the job was completed. Always cash. The job would entail picking up two people, with Darby making three. It rotated between Opie and two others. Darby assumed they had been the other two people in the house that day that weren't the Ringleader. Darby never was told any of their names, so he had resorted to nicknaming them for himself. There was Opie, Loose Lips, and Silent Bob. As he had guessed, he wouldn't be meeting the Ringleader again. He was the brains, not the brawn, of the operation.

Loose Lips was so named because he seemed the one most willing to discuss things about the operation. He didn't give any pertinent information away, and Loose Lips was an exaggeration, but he'd at least talk with Darby. If there was a weak link that Darby ever needed to exploit, it was him. The polar opposite was Silent Bob, who never said a word. Not one. Darby had driven him four times and still had yet to hear the man's voice. Darby came up with the name from some movie he had seen years before.

All three of them were likely within a few years of Darby's own age, despite his initial impression that Opie might be a teenager. They all had short cropped hair, and although it was never said, Darby knew they weren't going to be hiring minorities anytime soon. Opie and Silent Bob were good soldiers, but none of the three were leadership quality. Opie came closest, but he had nothing on the man with the voice. They were all clearly subordinates.

Of the six jobs that Darby did for his new employer, four had been home invasions. Well, technically not home invasions since no one was ever home. Robberies of unoccupied homes would be more accurate. The two people who would go inside were in and out in minutes, and Darby would wait outside.

They were very professional about the way it transpired, but that didn't surprise Darby. After all, they had known his history with Jake Court and even knew his checking account information. If they knew intimate details such as those, clearly they would have done their homework on their own crimes. These guys were nothing if not thorough. And by these guys, Darby knew he was really thinking about the man with the voice. The Ringleader.

Of the remaining two jobs Darby had done, one was a bank robbery. They were, once again, out within minutes. Darby felt like a sitting duck in the tan 1994 Lincoln Continental they used, waiting for Opie and Silent Bob to come out. And yet, he assumed things were going to work out. He was right of course, and the bank robbery went off without a hitch. This wasn't Hollywood, where one of them screams "Let's go to the vault" and everything is fucked from that point on. These guys were too smart for that.

The sixth job that Darby did for his employers would turn out to be his penultimate one. If he had his wits about him, it would have been his last, but Darby was being paid well, and it wasn't that easy to quit.

Darby picked up Opie and Loose Lips on the day in question. In previous trips, they had always carried guns, but they were merely carrying an aerosol spray can on the day in question. While this should have set his mind at ease, it seemed more sinister than when they were packing. The phrase *"The pen is mightier than the sword"* jumped into Darby's mind.

The first stop was a synagogue, where Loose Lips jumped out of the car, went to the huge front door and sprayed a swastika on it. Below that, he wrote White Power with the white paint on the Mahogany colored door. These guys even seemed to know what color of paint to bring.

The second was a black Baptist church, and this time it was Opie's turn. This church had a white front door, and sure enough, Opie was carrying a black aerosol can that he used to spray the same two things that Loose Lips had. Darby realized the irony that "White Power" was being painted in black, but thought it was probably better not to bring it up. Opie didn't have much of a sense of humor.

The third was a Mosque, and it was Loose Lips turn again. He repeated what they had done at the previous two spots and ran back to the car after completing his business. As they drove to the fourth spot, Darby thought he might have a few seconds to ask Loose Lips a question or two while Opie did his thing. He wanted to have a little dirt on these guys, in case things went to shit. With the exception of the Ringleader, he had seen their faces but didn't know their real names. And he knew absolutely nothing about the only man that really mattered.

As they pulled up on a Catholic Church that catered to Hispanics, Opie got out and headed to the front door.

This was Darby's chance. He looked in the rearview mirror at Loose Lips.

"Why are you guys doing all this? C'mon, I've been on six of these now, throw me a bone."

Loose Lips tried to resist, but couldn't hold back. What could you say, the man liked to talk.

"The boss needs seed money."

"For what?"

"To take over the world."

Darby wanted to laugh, but he knew Loose Lips wasn't kidding. He looked up, and Opie was finishing up. He only had a few more seconds.

"But he's not making any money on painting swastika's," Darby said.

"This is just to entertain him."

Darby was about to ask another question but saw Opie walking over.

"Shut up," Loose Lips whispered.

Opie got to the car and told Darby where to drive. His second to last job was over.

Darby met with Opie the next day and was paid for his services. It was his biggest payout yet, and he rustled the stack of twenties and a few hundreds in his hand. He even held them up to his nose and took a whiff. For a guy who had been in jail for years and had no discernible job skill, this money felt damn good.

Darby didn't hear from Opie for almost a month afterward. He was starting to think that they had gone in a different direction. Maybe Loose Lips had told them that Darby had asked a few questions. Maybe they only hired drivers for a few months and got someone new after that. Lots of ideas were floating around in Darby's mind when he received a text from Opie almost a month to the day of his last job.

The text read, "Are you ready for something big?"

Opie had never asked him a question, always just requesting his presence at a certain time and place. Darby knew this was something different. This wasn't just going to be a home invasion or a bank robbery.

If Darby Bowles had a father growing up, maybe he would have been taught now was the time to jump ship. Then again, Richard Bowles probably wouldn't have been a voice of reason. Darby was probably going to be fucked either way.

"I'm in," he texted back.

14

I was waiting in my car the next morning as Evie walked outside. It seemed a little less egregious than walking into her parent's house every day, and we thought they would be less suspicious. As I saw Mrs. Somerset wave to me from their kitchen, I realized that Jason Bourne had nothing to worry about. We weren't very good at this whole covert operation thing.

I drove us to the Peet's coffee we were at the previous day and was happy to see that our secluded table was free once again. I told Evie to go ahead and sit down, and I'd bring back our coffees.

We had allocated a few months for each of us. I had given myself November and December of 2000, leaving January and February of 2001 for Evie. We still hadn't decided exactly how we were going to do this, so we had done our research independently for our first assignment.

"You want to start?" Evie asked.

"Sure."

I told her I had found over 50 internet articles on home invasions, robberies, killings, and church vandalism around Oklahoma City in the months of November and December of the year 2000. I had no doubt there were many more, but these are what I could find from Google and from the newspapers *The Oklahoman*, *Oklahoma Gazette*, and the *Journal Record*, which was mainly a legal paper but came in handy as well.

I had summarized the major ones and handed Evie a page of the most egregious cases.

"It's hard to know exactly what we are looking for, but to summarize every single crime I came across would take too long. Here are eight cases where it was murder or some serious home invasions, basically things I'd expect Uncle Owen to want us to look for."

"I like how you still call him Uncle Owen after all these years."

"My Dad would like that," I said.

"Would he like what we are doing?"

It was a question I hadn't really asked myself, probably because I knew I wouldn't be happy with the answer. My Dad would never, ever want me to put myself in harm's way over money. Not for a million dollars. Not for 10 million.

If there was a heaven and he was looking down, he was probably just happy at how close me, Fiona, and his beloved Sally Waters were. Sure, he'd hope we could move to a nicer home, but not at the expense of putting ourselves at risk.

"No, he probably wouldn't," I said.

"Well, I'm sure he wouldn't mind this research we are doing. And we can always get out of this later if we feel it's too risky," Evie said.

"You're right," I said.

She could tell I didn't want to talk about this subject, so she changed it.

"So, why don't you do a quick rundown of the big crimes you found," Evie said.

I took a few minutes to explain each of the cases that I had decided were important enough. There was a home invasion of a rich lawyer who claimed they got away with $10,000 dollars in cash from a safe he had. There were three deaths in a biker bar when a fight turned into a melee, and someone took out a gun and started shooting. The final one I relayed to Evie was a woman who poisoned her husband, hoping to get his life insurance. The only life she got was a life sentence.

"People who commit crimes amuse me sometimes," Evie said.

"And that was only the big ones. One guy swung a knife at his wife, and on the follow through managed to sever his penis."

"All the way?"

"I don't know. I stopped reading after the word, sever."

"Serves him right. Trying to stab his beautiful, angelic wife." Evie said.

"I'm sure she was a saint."

"Am I sensing sarcasm?"

"No fooling you."

She smiled and pushed my arm away playfully. I had feelings for her dating back to high school, but I couldn't act on them because of what she had recently been through. Plus, it probably wasn't the best idea if we were trying to be detectives together. It's not like one of the Hardy Boys ever dated Nancy Drew. At least, I didn't think so.

We sat there staring at each other for a few seconds.

"Are you doing alright?" I asked.

She paused for a moment but put up a strong face. "Getting better every day thank you very much."

"Glad to hear it."

"What we are doing is really helping me. Until someone, I won't say who, decided to bring up my recent past."

I raised my hands in surrender. "I'm sorry. Just want you to know I care."

"Thanks. How about we go over the findings that I have made?"

"Let's hear 'em," I said.

Evie went through a similar litany of bank robberies and home invasions for January and February, but I could tell she was holding on to something good. I listened intently, knowing that she was just going through the appetizers and the main course would be served soon. It arrived about 10 minutes later when Evie had finished recapping the smaller stuff.

"And then there's this," she said.

She started to slide a copy of a newspaper article across the table to me. I looked at her, surprised.

"I thought this was important, so I made a copy," she said.

"Where?" I asked.

"At my parents."

"I thought we were going to keep this on the down-low?"

"I just used their printer. I connected through my laptop, so you have nothing to worry about."

I was a little perturbed but tried not to get too riled up.

"We don't know exactly what we've gotten ourselves into, so I'd just prefer if we don't do anything to bring other people's attention to us."

"I get it, Frankie. I won't do it again."

"Thanks," I said. "Now let's see what you got."

She pushed the copy of the newspaper article the rest of the way across the table towards me. There was a headline and then a picture with two bodies covered by body bags. I looked over to gauge Evie's reaction and saw a very serious look on her face.

I started reading.

Oklahoma Tribune, February 27th, 2001.

The Headline read: **"Two killed in racist murders. Three suspects dead."**

"Early yesterday morning, there were two brutal murders in Oklahoma City, and it appears the police may have prevented more. It started at 8:00 a.m in….."

15

On February 25th, 2001, Darby got a text telling him where to pick up the car. He did so, drove it to his apartment, and left it there for the night, just as he had been instructed to do. The tan 1994 Lincoln Continental was about as inconspicuous a car as you could hope for. No one would ever remember it. That's why it made such a good getaway car.

Darby tried to fall asleep early that night, but it wouldn't come. He wasn't sure if he was just being paranoid, or whether he had some things to be truly worried about. He started thinking about what would happen if he got pulled over alone in the Continental, and imagined the conversation with the police:

"I'm just the getaway driver......You see, I met this guy named Opie who gave me a cell phone and gave me places to pick them up......Well no, I don't know their real names......I've nicknamed them Opie, Loose Lips, and Silent Bob after a movie I saw........No, I'm not being sarcastic......No, I don't know where they live, but their boss has a memorable voice, and they fear him....I've nicknamed him the Ringleader.....I said I'm being serious.....Check the car's owner......Oh, it's been stolen the night I got out of jail?.....I swear that wasn't me.....I'd like to see an attorney."

Darby recreated this potential conversation in his mind several times. In reality, what information did he have on these guys? Absolutely nothing. He knew Angry Phil wasn't going to say shit if it ever got back to him. He didn't know these guys names or really anything about them. He was sure the car had been stolen, and they easily could have done it the night he was released, just to make it look like he stole it.

Darby felt like he was fucked if he was arrested without them. Maybe they would even leave a silent tip, and Darby would get arrested and blamed for everything. Calm down, Darby told himself! There was no proof of any of this, and the guys had been very professional with him. Distant and discreet, but professional.

After several hours of beating himself up and fearing the worst, Darby finally fell asleep at 1:07 a.m.

He woke up at 6:30 the next morning, took a shower, got dressed, and was ready to go by 7:00. The previous day's text had said to pick them up at 7:30 in the alley behind the Southwest Baptist Church, the place where he had originally met with Opie. It was all coming full circle.

The church was only 10 minutes away, so Darby started pacing around to pass the time. This didn't help as he started recreating the conversation he had with himself the previous night. He went to the ground and started doing pushups in an effort to get his mind to stop racing. It didn't work.

He left his place, and when he arrived at Southwest Baptist Church, his fears were only enhanced. For the first time since he had begun working for them, Opie, Silent Bob, and Loose Lips were all there waiting for him.

Opie took the front seat as he always did, Loose Lips sat behind him, and Silent Bob sat behind Darby. Darby felt uneasy with Silent Bob behind him and wished Loose Lips had sat there. He didn't really have a reason, just a feeling he had.

"The whole group is here," Darby said, trying to bring some levity to the situation.

"No talking," Opie said. "Not today."

Darby wanted to jokingly reiterate to Silent Bob what Opie had said, but thought better of it.

"Where are we going?" Darby asked instead.

"Head to the northeast part of the city. Going to a Tinker Federal Credit Union." Opie said.

Tinker Federal Credit Union was a very popular credit union in Oklahoma City. What garnered Darby's attention was that they were going to one in the northeastern section of the city when there were plenty of them closer. The northeastern part of the city was predominately African American, and this fact wasn't lost on Darby as he took Interstate 35 going north.

He noticed that the three passengers had gone back to the Glocks that they had carried on previous occasions. He reprimanded himself for thinking the aerosol cans were more menacing than the guns. He was mistaken. The sword was mightier than the pen.

They arrived at the Tinker Federal Credit Union in less than 15 minutes. Opie told him to pass it. Darby did as instructed, and after passing the Credit Union was told to make a U-Turn at the next light.

Darby passed the bank a second time, and Opie pointed to a spot in front of a Jack in the Box, two blocks up from the bank.

Opie put the gun in his jeans and grabbed a nylon mask from his sweat-shirt.

"Keep the car right here," he said.

Opie got out of the car and ran back towards the credit union. Darby adjusted his rear view mirror and tried to look where Opie was headed, but Silent Bob popped his head up so Darby couldn't see past him. Darby then looked out of his driver's side mirror and adjusted it so he could follow Opie. He saw him crossing the street in the direction of the credit union.

Darby was then taken completely by surprise, hearing Silent Bob speak for the first time.

"Why don't you just look straight ahead there, champ?"

It ran a shiver through Darby.

Darby didn't have to look straight ahead for long. Less than a minute later, he heard two gunshots in rapid succession.

"Start the engine," Silent Bob said.

Darby was reminded of a story from the movie *GoodFellas*. A guy who never speaks is prompted to speak, to which he says, "What am I going to say, that my wife two-times me?"

His wife responds by saying, "Shut up! You're always talking."

That's how Darby felt about Silent Bob at that moment. He wished he'd keep his mouth shut.

Darby looked at his rearview mirror, this time with no rebuff from Silent Bob. He saw Opie running towards the car like a bat out of hell. He was removing his mask as he approached the car.

Opie jumped into the car and yelled "Go! Go!"

The second Go was unnecessary, as Darby had the car moving the instant Opie jumped in. Darby raced ahead towards the freeway, his heart rate seemingly outpacing the rate of the car.

"Don't speed," Opie said.

Darby lowered his speed until he was going exactly the limit. The freeway on-ramp was a quarter mile ahead. This was the most nerve-wracking part as Darby knew once they made it to the freeway, they were likely home free.

They saw no police and made it back to the freeway without issue. Darby finally had time to think. This was fucking crazy! He hadn't signed up for murder, and he had to assume that's what happened back there. He couldn't wait to ditch the car and get the fuck away from these psychos. For good.

Not that Darby Bowles was a saint. Far from it. He had been in many fights, had sold drugs, and put a guy in a coma. He had been a nuisance his whole life. But this was different. A guy calls you out at a bar, or he hits on your girlfriend, then violence is warranted. That isn't what happened here.

This was straight up murder, and likely based on someone's skin color. That's the only assumption that Darby could make. Why else come to a predominately African American part of town?

Darby was a great many things, but a racist wasn't one of them. You should judge people by whether they are an asshole or not, not on the color of their skin. It was one of the moral qualities that Darby Bowles possessed, and it differentiated him from the three other people in the car.

"Where am I dropping you off?" Darby asked.

Opie laughed. "Nice try. Remember you agreed to join something big today."

"That wasn't big enough? You fucking murderer."

Darby regretted saying it almost immediately. If he didn't watch himself, he might be the next one killed.

Opie turned around and looked at Silent Bob. They never called each other by name, and that wouldn't change on this day.

"Why don't you let Mr. Bowles know who is in charge here."

Darby heard Silent Bob moving around, and moments later, felt the nozzle of a gun shoved up against his back. Silent Bob was taking his gun and pushing it through the seat in order to touch Darby's spine. Darby didn't dare move. In part, because he was afraid he would accidentally set off the trigger of the gun, but even more so, because he was scared stiff and couldn't move a muscle.

"You are going to do as I say, right?" Opie asked, although it was the furthest thing from a question Darby had ever heard.

"Yes," Darby answered.

"We are going to a Chelino's. I'll tell you how to get there."

Darby did as he was told, even though he shuttered about what was to come. The painted swastikas were just a warm up. If Darby had his guess, they had now graduated to killing certain races or religions. It was his own fault, he told himself. He should have bailed on this group after the swastikas were painted. But he never thought it would come to this.

Darby Bowles was no hero, but he knew how wrong this was, and if he could think of any way to try and stop what was coming, he would. As he took in his surroundings and the weapons that his passengers had, he knew there was nothing he could do. At least not yet.

They got off the freeway after a five-minute drive and approached the Chelino's, one of many in Oklahoma City. Their clientele was, for the most part, Hispanic. Another point not lost on Darby.

On the morning of February 26th, 2001, Bart Saxon was in his office. As usual, he had his door ajar. He thought it served as a reminder, not just anecdotally, that his door was always open. An important meeting or phone call would necessitate that it be shut, but the majority of time Bart Saxon had his door open for his fellow officers to walk in and ask any questions they might have.

Bart Saxon had been the Chief of Police in Oklahoma City for nine years by 2001 and was respected by everyone he worked with. There were people who didn't like him, but at the very least, he had earned their respect. That wasn't always easy to do in a field as nuanced as law enforcement.

A white man in his mid 50's, Saxon treated everyone with the same amount of respect that they treated him, race or sex be damned. He was a God fearing man who enforced the law instead of breaking it and was basically the polar opposite of Darby Bowles. On the issue of judging a man by his character, however, they were on the same page.

Lieutenant Ronald Bowe was the first one at police headquarters to hear about the shooting outside of the Tinker Federal Credit Union. Preliminary reports from inside the bank indicated that one person was likely dead on the scene, having been shot twice. There were no witnesses and thus far no description of the suspect. Not that Ronald Bowe was surprised. If you heard someone shooting from outside of a bank and you were inside, you were likely to stay there.

Bowe went to the Chief's office and walked through the open door. He relayed the information to Saxon, who put both of his hands together on his desk and rested his chin on them. This was Saxon's deep in thought pose. Every member of the force who had come in contact with the Chief knew it well.

After 20 seconds of deep thinking, Bart Saxon raised his head towards Lieutenant Bowe. "Put 30 officers on standby."

"Chief, that seems a bit much. It was just a shooting outside of a bank. Most likely a robbery gone wrong."

Bowe then remembered who he was talking to and added, "Don't you think that sounds logical, Chief?"

"Do as I say, Lieutenant."

"Yes, sir."

Bowe walked out of the office. He knew the Chief was renowned for his gut instincts, but he seemed a bit presumptuous in this case. Still, he respected the Chief immensely and wouldn't write off his judgment. Bowe had been on the wrong side of that more times than he cared to remember. He went about his job of getting 30 officers ready in case something else happened.

Alone in his office, Chief Saxon remained in thought, his head back resting in his hands. I hope I'm wrong about this, he thought to himself.

Darby was once again amazed by the precise planning that these guys had made. They must have taken weeks to set up the targets, freeways to take, places to park the car, etc. He now realized why they hadn't asked him to be on a job for a month. All of their focus had been on setting up this one.

Opie had him drive past Chelino's, take a left, and then proceed down a back alley parallel to the restaurant. The car was now facing the main street, with the freeway entrance less than 200 yards away. The restaurant was only one street over, but the car was in a secluded back alley, and it would be extremely unlikely they would be seen. It really was the perfect place to commit a crime if your goal was a quick getaway.

Opie got out of the car first, but instead of heading towards the restaurant, he walked to the back of the car. Silent Bob got out, and Opie slid into the seat behind Darby.

"Easier to keep an eye on you from here," Opie said menacingly.

Opie whispered a few words to Silent Bob who nodded and headed in the direction of the restaurant. Darby looked in the rear view mirror and focused his eyes on Loose Lips. He hadn't said a word the whole time, and by the nervous look on his face, he looked like a man who would rather be anywhere else in the world. That makes two of us, Darby thought.

Lieutenant Bowe received another call 15 minutes after leaving Chief Saxon's office. There had been another shooting, this one outside of a Chelino's, a Mexican restaurant in a Hispanic part of town. He rushed down to Saxon's office.

Chief Saxon listened to Bowe intently. When he finished, the Chief spoke very deliberately.

"I want you to send an APB out immediately. Tell all officers to gravitate towards synagogues, mosque's, Jewish deli's, or Muslim eateries."

"You think this is related to the spray painted swastika's, don't you?"

"I'm pretty darn sure it is," Saxon said matter of factly. "The first murder could have been a robbery, but then you get a second murder of a minority 15 minutes later? Sorry, but I don't believe in coincidences like that."

"I hope you are mistaken, Chief."

"So do I. But, I'm not."

Silent Bob sprinted back to the car approximately 15 seconds after two more gunshots had pierced the Oklahoma City air on that February morning. Darby headed off towards the freeway as soon as Silent Bob jumped into the Lincoln Continental. He wanted to believe this was going to be the end of it. Unfortunately, Darby knew better. He decided to try and throw one last Hail Mary.

"You guys don't have to do what he says," Darby said, and everyone knew the HE that Darby was referring to.

Opie, who had remained in the back seat to save time, responded. "If you say one more word, I will not just put the nozzle of the gun to your back, I will squeeze the fucking trigger. This is your last warning."

Darby bowed his head ever so slightly. "Where to?" he asked.

"Temple B'Nai Israel. It's on North Pennsylvania Avenue."

Peter Lassiter had been a police officer for all of 19 days when he received the All Points Bulletin over his radio. As a young candidate in the police academy, his senior officers raved about his instincts. He hadn't had the chance to put them to use in a real life scenario, but he constantly made the right decision over the course of his training. He had graduated first in his class, and everyone thought he was going to be a fantastic officer.

Lassiter was a well-known name in Oklahoma City police circles. His father had served for 30 years. Peter Lassiter was the third of four brothers, and his two elder brothers were officers as well.

He had light brown hair that was often confused with red. He was unmarried but had been dating a beautiful woman named Lori who he was considering proposing to. He tried not to think about her when he was busy working, but that was becoming tougher to do. He might be building a life with this woman, after all.

The APB said there had been a black woman shot outside a Tinker Federal Credit Union, and a Hispanic man shot outside a Mexican restaurant. Chief Saxon had said they feared it was the same people who had spray painted the swastikas' on two churches, a synagogue, and a mosque approximately a month ago. The officers were told to park their cars in places where Jews or Muslims were likely to hang out. Chief Saxon expected the offenders to try and strike there next.

Oklahoma City didn't have a very big Jewish population, but Lassiter knew that he was close to two synagogues or temples. He didn't understand the difference, but he knew they were both Jewish and that's what mattered. Most cops would have set up camp at one of them, and that would be the logical thing to do. Peter Lassiter liked to think outside of the box, however.

He reviewed the limited information as quickly as he could. Considering the killer or killers had struck at the Credit Union first and then proceeded to that specific Chelino's, Lassiter knew they would be traveling from the north and the east. That means if they were headed this way (and Lassiter had to prepare as if they were) they would likely be approaching from Interstate 44, known as the Will Rogers Turnpike in Oklahoma City.

In his eyes, it would be much better to catch them early, before they arrived at their destination with weapons drawn. Lassiter decided to leave his location near the synagogues and try to meet the perpetrators when they exited the freeway.

Lassiter executed a U-Turn and headed towards the Will Rogers Expressway. He arrived and drove up the gravel of the off ramp, but realized that from that vantage point the cars would be going too fast to get a good look inside. At the base of the off-ramp, there were two stop signs, where you could either turn left or right. They would have to slow down for the stop signs, so that is where Peter Lassiter would park his car. He drove back down the off-ramp and parked on the gravel, 20 feet from the stop signs.

He started to go over a checklist of what he was looking for. He guessed it would be between two and four men, but he leaned towards three or four. He found it unlikely that two people would try to do a job this big. It could also be a lone wolf situation, but Lassiter's instincts told him it was something more ominous. It seemed too coordinated.

He would be looking for white males under the age of 35. Likely younger. He didn't want to get too specific in fear of missing a prospective suspect, but Lassiter guessed they would have short hair. Especially after the swastika incident, he didn't expect a long-haired hippie to be conducting these crimes. This wasn't concrete in any sense, but in a situation like this, sometimes you had to play your hunches. Lassiter would be playing his, looking for crew cuts or short cropped hair.

Lassiter knew, for obvious reasons, that the car wouldn't be flashy, and would likely be an older model. A getaway car wasn't one you recently drove off the lot.

Finally, since Lassiter was parked on the right side of the two stop signs, he knew the car in question would head towards the left-hand lane once they saw his police car. Human nature was a bitch, and Lassiter would use that to his advantage.

He put his police car in park and started waiting. He would be looking for multiple, young white men with short hair driving an inconspicuous, older car that headed towards the left lane upon seeing Lassiter's car. His senior officers had been right about Peter Lassiter. He was one sharp cookie.

He started watching the cars exiting the Will Rogers Turnpike.

Darby was filled with dread as he drove towards the third destination. The first crime was an easy one to get away with. No one saw it coming, and there was no expected police presence. The second crime was almost as easy. Yes, there had been an original crime committed, but the police had no idea it was related to anything else. To them, it was a singular event.

However, after a second crime, the police now have two criminal activities that, if they are astute, they can tie together. It increases the risk tenfold. Darby would have liked to explain this to his passengers, but with a gun pointed directly at him, he decided against it.

These guys had been so safe and well prepared up to this point that it shocked Darby that they would try to go through with three or four separate murders in the span of an hour or so. Sure, their getaways and murder locations had been intricately planned out, but they still seemed to be taking a huge undue risk. The Ringleader seemed like an individual who would recognize that. What the hell was going on here? Darby had a fleeting suspicion that something more sinister was occurring. Something far above the three passengers he was escorting around.

He looked at the rear view mirror and found Opie staring back at him with an icy glare. Darby realized he hated the nickname he had given him. Opie was the nickname of a playful, fun loving, innocuous person. This guy was a hateful, racist murderer.

Darby exited the Will Rogers Turnpike, and as they got on the off-ramp, they all noticed a police car sitting on the right side about a quarter mile ahead.

"Get in the left-hand lane when it becomes two lanes," Opie said, quietly but intensely.

Darby couldn't resist. "But the Temple is to the right."

"We're going to have a nice talk when this is over, you smart ass. Plans have changed obviously."

Darby got in the left lane as instructed. They were 100 yards from the police car.

"Everybody look straight ahead," Opie said.

They approached the police car. 50 yards. 30 yards. 20 yards. 10 yards. Darby pulled even with the police car but didn't dare look to his right. He thought of times where he was looking straight ahead but just knew the car next to him was looking right at him. This was one of those times.

Peter Lassiter had an eye on the tan 1994 Lincoln Continental almost immediately. After the car straightened out on the off-ramp and had a view of Lassiter's police car, it headed towards the left lane. This could be it, Lassiter thought.

When the car entered the left-hand turn lane and approached him, Lassiter saw there were four people in the car, all white, and at least the driver and front seat passenger had short hair.

The thing that really did it for Peter Lassiter, however, was the rigidity in which they stared straight ahead. It was obvious there were doing everything they could to not look his way. These guys wanted nothing to do with the police officer to their right. They all had stone faces.

In a court of law, this would all be considered circumstantial evidence, but Peter Lassiter was trying to prevent another murder, not try a case. Let the courts figure that part out, but he wouldn't be able to sleep at night if something happened that he could have prevented, and he thought there was a pretty good chance these were the guys. The Lincoln pulled up a few feet ahead of his police car, and that's when Peter Lassiter turned on his siren.

There was about a two-second window where Darby thought everything might just work out. They had pulled ahead of the police officer who had made no move in their direction, and Opie had just made it clear that Temple B'Nai Israel was no longer in their plans.

Maybe, just maybe, they could go home now and Darby could ex-communicate from these guys forever. But then the cop turned his sirens on.

By the time Peter Lassiter had started heading towards the left-hand turn lane, the Lincoln Continental had already taken off. Lassiter did a quick semi-circle to get behind the now fleeing car, and following protocol, picked up his radio.

"In pursuit of a mid 90's tan Lincoln Continental. Could be the perpetrators of today's murders. They are about to turn left on North Pennsylvania Avenue."

While a bland 1994 Lincoln Continental is ideal as a getaway car because it's so forgettable, it is less than ideal when it comes to evading a police officer. The horsepower isn't in the same ballpark, nor is the traction or overall handling. Not even close.

The 5-10 second head start that the Lincoln had was gone in no time, and Lassiter found himself within 20 feet of the car almost instantly. It was his 19th day on the job, and Peter Lassiter was poised to become a legendary cop, just as all his senior advisers had expected.

But things are never quite as easy as they seem, and just as Lassiter was imagining a medal being thrown around his neck, the rear window of the Lincoln was shot out, and he saw what looked like a Glock being pointed directly at him. It was then that Peter Lassiter realized if he weren't extremely careful, he'd end up not a legend, but dead.

When the sirens of the police car were turned on, Darby's instincts kicked in, and he was going to do whatever he could to get away.

He pulled up to the curb, where no cars were, and sped towards the stop sign. He drove right through it and took a left on North Pennsylvania Avenue, barely avoiding two cars slowly driving through the intersection. As he took the left, he looked in the rearview mirror, and the police car had just got in the left-hand turn lane and was accelerating towards Darby.

Opie was yelling something, but Darby didn't pay it any attention. They were all relying on him now, and he didn't give a fuck what they were saying.

He soon realized Opie wasn't yelling at him, but instead at his two partners. "Shoot that mother fucking pig!" he said.

The police car had caught up in what felt like a millisecond. Opie shot out the back window, and Loose Lips and him started firing at the police car from the back seat. Darby knew this was all sorts of fucked up, but he had no love for cops, and if this helped them get away, then so be it.

As the shots rang out, Peter Lassiter had two choices. He could hang back, follow in distant pursuit and wait for backup, or he could continue following them.

He chose the latter. At least for the moment. He loved Lori, and he knew she would hate this, but he had a job to do.

Lassiter stayed in close pursuit, zig-zagging to make himself a much tougher target. A bullet blew through the front windshield on the passenger side, and Lassiter looked over, thanking his lucky stars. He also thanked God he didn't have a partner with him.

His intentions were still to stay in hot pursuit, but then Lassiter saw something that changed his mind. He looked ahead, and there was a packed four-way intersection approaching. Lassiter could deal with the suspects shooting at him without other people around. A police officer was a dangerous job, and he had signed up for that. But, he couldn't deal with them shooting randomly with civilians around. That was way too dangerous.

Against all of his instincts, Lassiter decided to slow down and follow from a further distance.

Darby saw the police officer drop back, but he had no delusions of grandeur. He heard the sirens of other officers coming, and he knew despite this particular cop dropping back, there would be no getting away in a 1994 Lincoln Continental. He looked up to the sky and saw a Helicopter approaching from the west. There was no doubt why he was headed their way.

At that moment, knowing they would never outrun the police, Darby formed a plan in a matter of seconds. It was dangerous and could kill him, but considering he saw no other way of escape, he thought it was worth the risk.

Darby knew he needed a diversion in order to get away. There was enough room between him and the cop car that he began to think his plan might just work. By the time the officers would have arrived on the scene, hopefully, Darby would have time to flee. Assuming he could walk.

Lassiter dropped back, but they continued shooting. There was no point in dropping back if they didn't stop shooting, so he dropped back further. He radioed in again, saying shots were being fired and he was going to follow protocol and shadow them from a safe distance.

He looked ahead and barely saw them, realizing they were getting too far ahead. Lassiter increased his speed. He thought he saw the Lincoln take a right and enter the approaching strip mall, but he couldn't be sure since he had dropped too far back.

Fifteen seconds later, he heard a loud bang.

Darby thought if he crashed the car into something, with the passenger side taking the brunt of the punishment, he might have a chance to get away before the cops arrived on the scene. Even though the cop had dropped back after being shot at, it would still only be a matter of seconds until he arrived. Thirty seconds if he was lucky. Any more would be gravy. That wasn't a very big window to get away from the crash scene.

Darby looked ahead and to his right, seeing a massive Home Depot in the upcoming strip mall. He veered quickly into the right lane and entered the strip mall via a little inlet, avoiding the packed four-way intersection they were approaching. It was a precise, svelte move and he wasn't sure if the cop, who had now drifted quite a bit behind them, could have seen it.

Opie didn't suspect anything and was actually impressed with Darby's maneuver into the huge strip mall. They weren't going to out pace the officers, so blending into a crowded mall area sounded a good idea as any.

Darby looked around at his possibilities. There were other cars he could hit and some big concrete posts, but there were people around all of them. He needed something a little more discreet. He saw a thick pole that was the base for a streetlamp, and it was about 100 feet from the Home Depot entrance.

It was blocked by the entrance so the people walking in the store would be unable to see the pole. It was perfect.

It was now or never. If this worked, he could walk into the Home Depot, and blend into the crowd. If he was off by a few feet, he might end up dead, or at least so badly injured that he'd be a sitting duck when the police arrived.

Darby decided it was worth the risk. He increased his MPH from 15 to 20 to 25. He straightened his car out so that the poll was lined up directly with the passenger side of the car.

As he hit 30 miles per hour, he heard Silent Bob say, "What the fuck, man!"

It was the last words he'd ever say…

Darby hit the pole of the street lamp at 34 mph, perfectly splitting the passenger side of the car in half. Silent Bob had no chance as the pole went through the car and collided with his head, killing him instantly. The collision knocked Loose Lips up against the roof of the car, knocking him unconscious immediately.

Although the left side of the car took far less of the brunt of the collision, Darby and Opie were still thrown against the left side of the car like laundry in a dryer. They were then both pinballed back to their original positions, having been heavily concussed. Opie was bleeding out of his left ear, and his shoulder bone was protruding from the skin.

They had both remained conscious, however. If it was any other time, Darby might have passed out from the pain, but he knew time was of the essence and willed himself to stay conscious. He began to get out of the car, and hearing sirens getting closer, he knew he only had seconds.

Darby looked over and saw the pole cemented in Silent Bob's head. He was as dead as a doornail. He looked back at Loose Lips who looked like he may be dead, but Darby couldn't be sure. At the very least, he was badly injured. He then saw that Opie was conscious, but bleeding from his ear, and then Darby saw his gruesome shoulder injury.

"You did this intentionally you fucker!" Opie screamed.

Despite being in severe pain, Darby smiled at Opie, exiting the car. He would have loved to stay and gloat but every second mattered. Silent Bob was dead, Loose Lips may have been, and Opie wasn't going anywhere. His plan had worked to perfection thus far.

Darby walked towards the Home Depot, as three people came around the corner walking towards the accident. It was time for Darby to play dumb.

"Three people are really badly hurt. I'm going to call 9-1-1," Darby said.

They seemed to buy his bullshit story, and the three of them continued walking in the direction of the accident.

Darby arrived at the entrance of the Home Depot and looked back one last time. To his amazement, Opie was getting out of the car. He had propped his body up against the door, and Darby could see the gun in his right hand. The bone protruding from his left shoulder was clearly visible as well.

A police officer was pulling up right then, and as much as Darby wanted to watch what transpired next, he had to get the hell away from there. He walked into the Home Depot and started moving as briskly as he could without drawing attention to himself. A few seconds after entering the store, Darby heard a series of gunshots.

Darby felt this might buy him some extra time, as the officers would make the car a crime scene. Hopefully, it would be a few minutes until they noticed there were only three people in and around the car.

Darby ignored the pain in the left side of his body and his light-headedness, setting off towards the opposite end of the Home Depot.

As Peter Lassiter heard a loud bang, he turned his sirens back on and noticed a police car coming right behind him. As he looked in his rearview mirror, it sped right by him.

Shit! This was supposed to be my collar, Lassiter thought. It was my ingenious move to sit by the freeway that prevented more murders, and now some asshole who heard my call on the radio was going to get all the credit.

Lassiter increased his speed and headed off in the direction of the noise. He looked up and saw a plume of smoke coming from that general direction.

Darby continued towards the back of the Home Depot and was pretty sure he had heard a few more gunshots. He couldn't be sure, however, as his mind was starting to play tricks on him. He was getting more and more lightheaded, and he needed to get off his feet.

He made it to the back entrance of the Home Depot and walked out through what appeared to be a loading area. He was hoping this would open into another strip mall that he could get lost into, but he had no such luck. He had been spit out onto the curb of a parallel street.

Darby needed to get the fuck off the main streets. The shooting had bought him some time, but when the cops realized that there are only three people in the car, they would start searching the area.

He looked around, not sure what he was going to do. He looked to his left and saw a bus stop about a quarter mile up. There were a good 20 people waiting in line. Despite all the pain, he managed another smile and walked off in that direction.

The police car that passed Lassiter turned into the strip mall and drove towards the mangled car. There was smoke now billowing from it.

Lassiter had a car change lanes right in front of him, and he had to hit the breaks. He was now a good 10 to 15 seconds behind his fellow officer. He finally entered the strip mall just as the cop ahead of him pulled up behind the Lincoln Continental, which Lassiter could now see was wrapped around a street lamp.

There was a man standing outside of the car, with something visible in his right hand. Lassiter was too far away to tell if it was a gun. There were three people a mere 20 feet away, and Lassiter knew this was a dangerous situation.

Lassiter saw his fellow officer get out of the car and brandish his gun. He pointed it at the man outside of the car, and not wasting any time, fired five or six rounds into the perp, who dropped to the ground immediately. Lassiter finally arrived at the scene, his car screeching to a halt. He watched as his fellow officer approached the mangled car.

Lassiter looked towards the car, and heard the officer yell, "Don't move!"

A split second later, the officer fired two shots into the back of the Lincoln.

Lassiter had been the early bird. He should have gotten the worm. But this officer had bypassed him and was sure to get all the credit. Lassiter cursed his luck.

The officer turned around and started walking back towards Lassiter, who saw it was Officer Derek Plough, a newly minted police officer as well. Of course. It had to be one of the biggest assholes who gets his collar, Lassiter thought. *Just my luck!*

Lassiter looked at the man on the ground, outside of the car. There was a gun by his side. Lassiter realized that he was just being a selfish asshole. It's a good thing that Plough got there in time, or this man might have shot the three bystanders.

Lassiter ran to the car, where he saw the pole embedded into the head of the man in the front seat. In the back, there was a man with two bullet holes in his chest. There was a gun sitting by his side.

Derek Plough turned to Lassiter.

"Hey, Peter. I heard your call over the radio. You did all the work on this one. I just happened to get here first, but you'll get all the credit, and you deserve it." Plough tapped Lassiter on the shoulder.

Maybe Plough wasn't such a bad guy, after all, Lassiter thought to himself. And then it hit him...

"There were four people in this car."

As Plough and Lassiter looked around the car, wondering if they had somehow missed someone, they heard a loud noise emanating from the engine. The police academy had recently taught them about the danger of smoking cars blowing up. They both seemed to think the same thing at once.

Lassiter and Plough started running from the car and then jumped as they heard the sound of the car exploding. They landed safely on the concrete, and besides a few scrapes and bruises, they would be fine. The same could not be said of the Lincoln Continental, which had been blown to smithereens.

16

A day after the murders, Darby Cash Bowles sat at a Super 8 motel in Oklahoma City reading a newspaper. And counting his blessings. He could have tried to implement his plan 50 different times, and it wouldn't have been as successful as it was on its first and only attempt.

The other three people in the car were dead. He was alive, and not in jail. The odds of that were astronomical, and yet, it had happened.

As if things couldn't get any better, he had read that the car had exploded, likely taking with it any evidence that may have been left. Fire and smoke had a way of doing that.

Angry Phil and the Ringleader were now the only two people who knew Darby was related to these killings, and neither one of them was going to be volunteering any information. Of that, Darby was positive.

After getting on the bus the previous day, he had considered going to his apartment to get his money, but thought better of it for two reasons. First and foremost, if the cops had somehow found something on him, he certainly didn't want to be there when they arrived. Second, there was a lingering thought that he should be less scared of the police, and more worried about the Ringleader.

The only people that the Ringleader had dealt with outside of jail had been Opie, Loose Lips, Silent Bob, and Darby himself. With the three of them dead, Darby knew he was the lone link back to him. If he was willing to set up murders as gruesome as yesterday's, Darby had no doubt that he would kill him if he had the chance. And since the ringleader had put him up at his apartment, Darby knew that was the first place that he would look.

That's why on the morning of February 27th, 2001, Darby was stuck at a shitty, fleabag ridden Super 8 Motel reading the Oklahoman. The article was very detailed for a crime that had occurred only a day previous, but it made sense considering the whole thing ended by 10 a.m. Darby found out some things he hadn't known, including the names of his three passengers that day. There were pictures and a little biography of each.

Opie was, in fact, Charles Wade Leonard. Leonard was only 23 years old. He had attended Southeast High School in Oklahoma City, but there was no record of him ever graduating. He had worked a few odd jobs over the last few years, including as a delivery driver for Domino's, but it didn't appear he had worked in the last 6 months. He had no rap sheet. He was identified as the man killed while pointing his gun at three good Samaritans.

The man who Darby had nicknamed Silent Bob was Jared Wilder. He had also attended Southeast High School. Wilder was 25 years old. He had started college at a local JC but had dropped out after his first semester. He had been arrested for burglary, but the charges were dropped. The paper reported that they believed Wilder was killed in the collision and then burned posthumously in the resulting fire and explosion, but an autopsy would be conducted soon.

Elliot Walden, a.k.a. Loose Lips, was the youngest of the three at 21 years old. There was very little information on him, but the article said he attended Polk Valley High School for a time. There was no criminal record for Walden. He was in the back seat and was shot two times by the responding officer. A gun was found next to him.

Darby read each of their mini-obituaries and was initially surprised that all of their rap sheets were so small. When he thought more about it, it began to make more sense. If you were going to hire people to carry out horrible crimes, it might be better to start with a blank slate. To mold them into the criminals that you wanted. At least, that's how Darby envisioned the Ringleader choosing his subordinates.

Even though he didn't believe in God, Darby said a quick prayer for Loose Lips. He seemed like he had a soul somewhere down there, and had just ended up in the wrong place. The other two could rot in hell for all Darby cared.

There were a few paragraphs on each of the victims, but Darby skipped over that. Not that he would readily acknowledge it, but he knew he bore a small responsibility for what happened. He didn't know he was signing up for murder, but he knew something bad was going to go down, and he didn't get out of it. He felt too guilty to read the obituaries of the two people murdered.

Two rookie officers were praised to close the article. Peter Lassiter had the brilliant idea of cutting the criminals off at the freeway, not allowing them to get to any of their possible destinations. He was praised effusively in the article for his quick decision making.

The other officer mentioned was Derek Plough. He had been down the street guarding a synagogue when he heard Officer Lassiter over the radio. He headed in that direction and passed Officer Lassiter who had followed protocol and dropped back. Plough was first on the scene and likely saved innocent lives when he shot and killed Charles Wade Leonard, who had brandished his weapon in the direction of the three bystanders. Plough then went and shot Elliot Walden twice, who was found with a weapon near him. Plough was praised for his quick actions as well, but he was quoted as saying that Peter Lassiter deserved all the credit.

The article said that police are going on the assumption that these were the same people who committed the crimes on the churches, synagogue, and mosque a month previous.

All of this information was interesting to Darby, but it was something in the second paragraph that caught his attention most of all.

It read "Although three people died at the scene, the police believe there may have been a fourth involved and are asking for any help from the public."

Darby knew it was time to get the fuck out of dodge, but he had something he had to do first. He knew the general area of the house where he was blind-folded, and thanks to the house with the basketball hoop, he knew he could find it. It was time to get a few pictures of the Ringleader. Would be his own little insurance policy.

Early on February 28th, two days removed from the murders that had rocked Oklahoma City, Darby Bowles went to a local convenient store and bought a disposable camera and a newspaper. Cell phones wouldn't be equipped with a camera for a few more years, and Darby saw no reason to buy an expensive camera he'd only use once.

He took a cab to the suburbs where Opie had driven him the first day. Darby told the cab driver the general area he was looking in and had him go up and down streets, hoping that the basketball hoop with the single thread of net and the decomposing backboard would jump out.

The cab driver was suspicious of him, but Darby knew it was too big a risk to get out and walk. There was a good chance the Ringleader would see him. So Darby told the cab driver that he was looking for the house he grew up on, saying he couldn't remember the name of the street. The cab driver didn't seem to buy it, but he stopped asking questions after awhile.

Finally, after 10 minutes of driving around aimlessly, Darby spotted the basketball hoop.

"Stop!" he yelled.

The cab driver brought the car to a screeching halt, and Darby looked out at the basketball hoop. There was no doubt that was the one he had seen. The lone strand of the net still hung down from the rim. He looked across the street and saw the house that surely was where they had brought him.

Realizing a cab in the middle of the street was pretty suspicious, Darby told the cab driver to keep driving and had him drop him off on the next block.

Darby grabbed the camera along with the newspaper and headed off in the direction of the house.

He knew he didn't want to get too close. This was just insurance in case he ever came into contact with the Ringleader again. He didn't want to get him-self killed over something that he may never use.

Two houses over, there was a huge oak tree that Darby felt he could hide behind. The problem was that while the Ringleader's house couldn't see him, cars driving up and down the street could. That wasn't going to work.

Darby knew he was going to have to get closer to the house. Anywhere else and he was too far out in the open and neighbors would surely start asking questions. Darby walked up to the Ringleader's house, being sure to avoid any large windows. The side of the house was actually the garage where they had parked, and Darby thought that would be the best place to hide. There were enough trees to cover him.

He made his way to the side of the garage and set up shop there. To his surprise, he heard a couple of voices coming from inside the house, although he couldn't make out what they were saying. Had there been other people in on this? Darby didn't think so, or he would have met them. Maybe it was just some old friend, although he would have thought the Ringleader would have been laying low.

Darby was afraid he was going to be stuck there for hours, but after hearing the men's voices talk for 5-10 minutes, the front door open opened. Darby grabbed the disposable camera, making sure to be terribly quiet. Darby held the newspaper out so that the date was clearly visible. It had been his idea to have a newspaper in the foreground, thus showing the picture was taken two days after the murders. It had been a brilliant idea in a lifetime littered with poor ones.

The two men who left the house started walking towards a car parked on the street, and Darby snapped three quick pictures in rapid succession. One of the two was a young, hulking 6'3" man with broad shoulders who towered over the other one. The second man was just under six feet and going prematurely gray with what looked like a bad, Caesar haircut. At least, that's what it looked like from Darby's angle. He was skinny, almost fragile, and yet Darby could tell it was the big man who was following the smaller man's lead.

If you knew that one of these two men possessed the voice that had so infatuated Darby, a huge majority of people would have guessed the big man. But Darby knew better. The big man was reverential towards the skinny one. There was no doubt of that. Darby's premonition proved correct, as the big man got in the car and the smaller man started walking back to the house.

Darby ducked back behind the corner as the man headed back in the direction of the front door. Obviously, a picture of him now would be perfect, but he'd almost assuredly see Darby peeking out of the corner of the house. He knew he couldn't take that chance. The side profile pictures would have to do.

Darby heard the front door shut, and walked away from the house, hoping he'd never see the man ever again. Somehow, the fact that he was diminutive in stature made him even scarier to Darby. People wouldn't be scared of him physically, so that meant he must have packed a wallop mentally and with his personality. Those were the guys who truly scared Darby.

"Good riddance," Darby said and walked away from the house forever.

Oklahoma City and Oklahoma, in general, had run its course for Darby Cash Bowles. What had he ever really achieved here? Nothing. Actually, less than nothing. He was an ex-con who was now wanted by the police for the most infamous crime in Oklahoma City since the bombing of the Alfred P. Murrah building back in 1995.

As he sat in bed at the Super 8, Darby pondered where to go and the phrase *"Go west young man"* kept entering his mind. It was pretty pathetic, but the most West Darby had ever been was going to Colorado and New Mexico as a teenager.

California, Darby thought. Where the girls were all blonde. Wasn't that what the song by David Lee Roth had said? Whatever, it didn't matter. What did matter is that he got the hell out of Oklahoma City as quick as he could. The police were looking for him, and as unlikely as it was that he be found, there was no use hanging around. The fact that the Ringleader might be out there looking for him hung over his head as well.

Billy Gullicksen, an old friend of Darby's, had sent him a few letters while he was in jail. He had moved from Oklahoma City to a sleepy, quiet, little town named Eureka, in northern California. Billy was making decent money as a longshoreman and told Darby to look him up if he ever made it out that way.

Darby had saved up $3200 from his jobs over the last several months. He wasn't exactly a millionaire, but it was plenty of money to get to California and then figure things out. After all, Darby was only 25 years old and had the rest of his life to look forward to.

If the demons from his past didn't catch up to him first.

Darby left the motel at 4 a.m. of his third day. His mission the previous day to get pictures of the ringleader had been a success, and he knew the disposable camera he had was his most important possession. He looked down at his cell-phone and knew the quicker he got rid of that, the better. He didn't want any ties to the horrific crimes. He broke the phone in five pieces and threw it into the dumpster outside the Super 8.

There was an Amtrak train leaving the Oklahoma City station at five that morning, and Darby was going to be on it. His destination was Denver, CO with the intention of catching a new train there that would take him to Northern California.

Darby called for a cab and told them he was headed to the train station with one stop along the way. He had to risk going to his apartment so he could grab the rest of his cash. He couldn't imagine that anyone would be staking out his apartment at 4 a.m., but that didn't mean he didn't have some butterflies.

Turned out he had nothing to fear, the area around his house was clear. He entered the apartment, grabbed his cash, and walked back out to his waiting cab.

He arrived at the train station at 4:20, bought his ticket, and then picked the most out of the way corner to wait. It would be just his luck if some cop saw him and got suspicious. That didn't happen and at 4:52 Darby boarded the Amtrak train destined for Denver. His new life was about to start.

After stops in Denver, Salt Lake City, Las Vegas, San Francisco, and Sacramento, Darby Bowles finally ended up in Eureka, CA. He stepped off the train and smelled both the ocean and the exhaust from the factories. It was hardly the "California Girls" persona that David Lee Roth had exalted on the MTV, but he was 1900 miles away from Oklahoma City, and that was what mattered.

Eureka was the most well-known city in Humboldt County, known most for their redwoods and their marijuana. The redwoods towered over the region, while the stigma of the weed-growing hovered over it as well. The main exports, besides weed, were timber and the fishing industry. It was very much a blue collar town.

The city hugged the Pacific Ocean along Highway 101, so it really should have been a more desirable place, but the exhaust from the factories didn't lend itself to a beach town. The average annual temperature was in the 50's which didn't help either. It was a coastal city in California, but that's about all it had going for it. Women in bikinis were not the norm.

Darby flagged down a cab and asked to be dropped off at the cheapest hotel in town. The place he was dropped off was just that, and at $39 a night you got what you paid for. It was a step down from the Super 8 he had left in Oklahoma City, if that was possible.

He got settled in, but it was already 6:00 p.m., so he decided to wait until the next morning to head down to the docks and see what the life of a longshoreman consisted of. He knew they worked their asses off, but that didn't matter to Darby. Any job with a little structure sounded just fine to him.

William Gullicksen, a.k.a. Billy had met Darby Bowles when they were back in high school. Billy owed a gambling debt of $20 to their mutual friend Jake Court. The first time they met wasn't a courtesy call as Darby had been sent to collect the $20 by any means necessary. This rarely meant more than a threat, and there would be no violence this time either. Billy Gullicksen delivered the $20 to Darby a few days later, who in turn gave it to Jake Court.

Billy got the impression that bookies were successful for a reason, and stopped his betting career at the ripe old age of 16. He and Darby remained friends, and when Darby wasn't getting in trouble, they would go play pool at some of the seedier bars around Oklahoma City.

When Darby landed in Lawton Correctional, Billy was one of the few friends who kept in touch. He had described Eureka and his job. He didn't paint it as any Utopia but did tell Darby it was a good place to stay out of trouble once he got released from jail.

Darby appreciated his old friend reaching out. At the time, he had no intention of going to Eureka, wherever the fuck that was.

Obviously, plans had changed after what happened in Oklahoma City, and without many options, he remembered his old friend's offer. That's why Darby had taken the Amtrak to this small Northern California town of 26,000 people, and it's why he ended up at the docks of the Pacific Ocean the next morning.

A huge freight ship was harnessed to the docks, and what seemed like hundreds of men were unloading it. The docks themselves were as dirty as you'd expect, and the longshoremen themselves weren't much cleaner. They were a tough, rugged looking group and they eyed Darby as he approached the ship.

Darby saw someone who looked like he might be the manager.

"Do you know a William Gullicksen?" Darby asked.

"Don't know no William," the portly man replied. "We've got a few Bills, though."

A longshoreman who looked like he was 80 years old, but was probably more likely in his early 50's, walked by. He had been listening to their conversation.

"I know Gulllicksen is a William," he said.

"That's him," Darby said.

"Thanks so much for your help, Jones," The portly man said sarcastically. "Now get back to work."

Jones left, and the man turned to Darby.

"This better be important!" he yelled.

He forcefully grabbed Darby by the arm and led him down the wharf to the huge freighter that they were helping to unload.

"Gullicksen!" the man yelled.

"Gullicksen!" he repeated.

Out of the shadows stepped a face that Darby knew well. Billy Gullicksen was 25, the same age as Darby, but looked like he was still in high school. His dark brown, wavy hair looked the exact same as it had years earlier. He stood out next to the weathered longshoremen around him. A young, fresh-faced longshoreman wasn't the norm.

"Boss, I have no idea who this asshole is!"

The charade didn't last long as Billy walked over to Darby and gave him a big bear hug.

"You got five minutes, Gullicksen," the portly boss said and walked away.

"Sure hope I get to work for that kind man," Darby joked.

Billy laughed. "Darby Fucking Bowles! Good to see you. Let's walk this way."

Billy Gullicksen wasn't back to the docks in five minutes. He walked Darby along the boardwalk and pointed out some local watering holes and good seafood restaurants. He asked Darby what brought him to Eureka and Darby told a half truth, saying he just wanted to try something new. Darby didn't divulge any of what had happened in Oklahoma City, and Billy didn't seem keen to know.

They told stories of how they met, and how Billy had been a terrible sports bettor. He asked how Jake Court was doing and Darby told him about going by the house and finding out that he owned a contracting business and was expecting a baby. Billy seemed to be surprised by this and was happy for his old friend. More so than Darby had been.

Darby took in the scenery and the people walking around this quaint little town. He could honestly say he could see this being home. It was low maintenance people who just went about their daily lives. Which, besides his stints in jail, is how Darby viewed himself.

Of course, he needed a job and a place to live if he was going to make that happen, so after 15 minutes of small talk, he turned to Billy and asked the all important question.

"Do you think you could get me a job working on the docks?"

"You kidding me? The boss loves you."

Darby laughed loudly, just imagining how the rotund boss was going to react to them coming back well after their allotted five minutes.

"Yeah, I'm not so sure about that," Darby said.

Billy waved off Darby's apprehension. "We're understaffed as it is. Even if he thinks you're an asshole, he'd still hire you. And he thinks everyone is an asshole anyway. Don't think you're special."

"It's that easy? I meet you 20 minutes ago, and you've already got me a job?"

"Anything for an old friend. And like I said, longshoremen are always in demand here."

Darby smiled at his buddy. "Thanks so much, Billy. One more thing. How about finding a place to live here?"

"Piece of cake. There's plenty of decent apartments. Dirt cheap too. Nothing like living down in the Bay Area where they charge you an arm and a leg for rent."

"I owe you big time."

"You can buy me a drink. Got a few good bars around here, and got some cute girls rolling around occasionally. You don't have a girl, do you?" Billy asked.

"Well, I did have my eye on that old lady who just passed us." Darby joked. "No, I don't have a damn girl. I just got here."

"Let's go back. I'm going to tell the boss that I'm taking a few hours off, but to make up for it, he'll have a new employee starting tomorrow morning."

Darby couldn't believe his luck. He was looking forward to getting settled down and starting to forget what happened in Oklahoma City.

"We'll go grab a beer. You still drink, right?" Billy asked.

"Of course."

"Why don't we take it easy on the bar fights here though, alright buddy."

"I'm a changed man. No more of that shit. Don't want to end up dead in a bar like my old man."

"Damn, you really have changed."

"Something happened to change me," Darby said.

"I don't want to know about it."

"Don't worry, I wasn't going to tell you."

Billy and Darby drank beers that night till 10 p.m. Darby behaved himself and the only hitting that happened was him hitting on some cute girls who walked in the bar. He spent the night at Billy's, a clean, but unspectacular apartment. Billy woke him at 4 a.m. sharp.

"Get up buddy. You can shower first."

"Damn, you longshoreman start early," Darby said.

"Have to be there ready to work at 5 a.m."

"Glad we didn't stay out till 2 a.m.."

"Been there, done that. The next morning is no fun. Now get up and get in the shower. There's a towel in there. And we'll get you your own place within the week."

"Thanks for everything," Darby said.

Darby's first week as a longshoreman went by in the blink of an eye. He worked six consecutive days before getting his first day off. It was hard damn work, but when Darby looked around and saw guys in their 50's doing the work, he wasn't about to complain. He made friends rather easily. People didn't ask too much about his past, and Darby was sparse in his responses. There was no need for them to know he had spent most of his adult life in jail.

True to his word, Billy helped Darby find a one bedroom apartment in a place they called Old Town Eureka. Darby actually preferred it to the newer parts of town. It had some charm which Darby didn't think the corporate strip mall of the downtown area did. Old Town Eureka looked like something out of small town America in the 50's. Or at least how Darby envisioned it would have looked like.

His rent was $500 a month, which he found to be very reasonable. He still had $3000 saved up from Oklahoma City and was now going to have paychecks coming in. And longshoremen were paid fairly well. Things were looking up for Darby Bowles. He bought a cell phone and put Billy in as his first contact.

His phone rang on his seventh day in Eureka, and he picked it up without looking at it. When you only had one contact in your phone, you could get away with things like that.

"Billy, what's going on?"

"Why don't you come over to my place?"

Darby could tell something was wrong. His voice didn't sound quite right.

"Everything okay there?" Darby asked.

"No. I'll show you when you come by."

Darby walked the half mile to Billy's house. He did not have a car yet, but that was his next order of business. He wouldn't be driving much, so he figured he'd just get an old beat up car. Just not a 1994 Lincoln Continental.

Darby knocked on the door and saw tears in Billy's eyes as he walked in the house.

"Have you ever used the internet, Darby?"

"Not really. I know what it is, but I haven't had the chance to learn it since I got out."

Billy walked him over to his computer screen.

"Read this article. You can use this little mouse to scroll down."

Darby looked at the computer screen and instantly recognized the picture of his old friend Jake Court. Then he saw the title: LOCAL BUSINESSMAN KILLED IN HOME INVASION.

Jake Court, 26 years old, was found shot to death in his Oklahoma City home on Thursday. It appeared to be a home invasion gone wrong as things were stolen, and a broken window had been the point of entry. Court had attended high school in Oklahoma City and had just started his own contracting company. Neighbors have said that Court lived with his girlfriend and that they were expecting their first child. Authorities have no leads at this time and are asking the public for any help."

Darby turned to Billy. "How did you find out about this?"

"My old friend from Oklahoma City, Cecilia Fields, sent me an email telling me what happened. She linked to this article."

Technology sounded like Greek to Darby, but he got the gist of it. He took a moment and bowed his head for his old friend.

"And you said you had just seen him, right?"

"A few months back. Actually, the day I got out of jail."

"So terrible. I could have seen this happening to him years ago, but it sounds like he had turned his life around. Who the hell would do something like this?" Billy asked rhetorically.

Darby had an idea.

Darby left Billy's house as quick as he could. He didn't want his friend noticing that something was on his mind. The less anybody knew about what happened in Oklahoma City, the better. He told Billy he wanted to go home and grieve alone, and like many things in Darby Bowles life, there was some truth to it.

Darby started thinking that Court could have been killed for a myriad of reasons. He used to be a bookie who put out collectors on people. After that, he had become a drug dealer. People like that had enemies, and even if Court had quit the game, that didn't mean someone from his past hadn't come back to seek revenge. Or maybe it was just a home invasion gone wrong. After all, the Ringleader didn't have his three subordinates to do his work any longer.

Unfortunately, every time Darby almost convinced himself it had nothing to do with him, he remembered what the ringleader had said: "We know you didn't rat on Jake Court when you had the chance."

So he absolutely knew who Court was. And wouldn't it make sense that the ringleader would go to him if he was trying to locate Darby? Of course.

As much as he didn't want to believe it, Darby had a sinking feeling that it was his involvement as the getaway driver that had led to his friend Jake Court's death.

Darby didn't know much about the internet, but he realized that you could search for things that you never could have in years past. If his premonition was right that the Ringleader had killed Jake Court, then surely he would do anything he could to find out where Darby was. This meant using the internet to his advantage.

It also meant that a name like Darby Cash Bowles would be a pretty easy one to search for. Not many of those around. Why couldn't I have been named Joe Smith, Darby thought to himself.

He decided then and there that he needed to keep a low profile. First and foremost, no arrests. Landing himself in jail was probably the easiest way they would find him. If he was arrested, he would be found. Darby was sure of it.

The longshoremen's association had his full name, but there wasn't much he could do about that now. Plus, they were as tight on security as the Teamsters, and Darby thought that would be a pretty unlikely way to find his whereabouts. Also, he was all the way in Eureka, CA. The Ringleader certainly wasn't going to stumble upon him there. Stay out of jail and keep your name out of the news and you'll be fine, Darby told himself.

Just keep your head down and go to your job every day. That's what you need to do.

And that's exactly what Darby did for the next nine years...

17

Evie and I had finished the first mandate in Uncle Owen's book, and it had only made me more secure in my opinion that we were in way over our heads. I didn't know yet what some racist murders from 16 years ago had to do with 2017, but I knew this wasn't some game. And yet, that's how Evie seemed to be approaching it. She was enjoying this.

We went to the Peet's on Broadway for a third straight day. The table we used each day was vacant again, and I was starting to take it as a sign. Of what, I wasn't sure yet.

As had become tradition, I started reading Uncle Owen's writing first.

"*Congrats on finishing your first mandate*," Uncle Owen had started the next page in his now familiar blue handwriting. "*Just a reminder not to share this information with anyone.*"

I looked across at Evie as I read it. She was wearing a tan sweater that would occasionally cling to her body and give my blood pressure a quick jolt. It was the middle of December, and I wasn't going to be getting her in a bikini or a pool anytime soon, so the tight sweater was a nice reminder of the curves I remembered so well.

She seemed to be in better spirits each and every time I saw her. I was happy. I was tired of just being the shoulder she cried on. If she needed me, I'd be there for her, but I preferred not discussing what she had gone through.

We got along great and had developed a fun back and forth banter. We were discussing heinous crimes, but since they happened 16 years ago, we were able to talk about them with a detachment, and not have to be deathly serious the whole time.

She looked over at me, realizing I wasn't reading the second mandate. I quickly returned to the book, not wanting her to know what I was really looking at.

"*For your second mandate, I want you to go be a teenager! Go have sex with a beautiful girl. Go get drunk. Go watch a ball game. Go and do something fun, because I can assure you that the last three mandates are only going to be grown up stuff. So go have fun today. That's an order. Don't turn the page sport, I mean it. Go enjoy your day.*"

It was going to be hard to be a teenager now that I was 21. I also knew that it was going to be hard to have sex with a beautiful girl, considering it was probably the last thing on the mind of the one sitting across from me. It didn't help that I blushed when I read that part, and she would soon know why.

"Do you want to go get a huge bowl of ice cream with a bunch of sprinkles?" I asked.

"Is that the next mandate?"

I laughed. "You know what, in a way it is."

Evie grabbed the book and read what Uncle Owen had written.

"Is that what teenagers do?"

"Besides getting drunk and having sex," I said. I awaited her response.

"In that case, let's go get that ice cream," she said.

"That was my second choice," I said.

She laughed and playfully tapped me upside the head as we got up from our table.

That night also happened to be the night we were to take Fiona bowling. It hadn't been my idea, but it seemed like a nice thing to do, so I went along with it. The only thing I wasn't looking forward to, was Fiona's questions that were coming about Evie and I's friendship. They were inevitable.

I drove the three of us to Plank, a bowling alley/beer garden with a view of the San Francisco Bay, located down by Jack London Square. That's right, a bowling alley with a view. They also had bocce ball and sporting events on Jumbo TVs. It was a great spot.

We got our shoes and were assigned Lane 18, the age of my younger sister, and the age when I was supposed to have started reading The Best Novel Ever. I hadn't thought of it as that in a while since I now realized reading the novel had been a ploy to get me to Uncle Owen's writings that started Chapter 5. I wondered why he hadn't just told me to start there. I'd get my answer eventually, but not on this night.

Fiona inputted our given names on the screen, using none of the nicknames she had bestowed on me over the years. Not a Buttface or a Douchebag to be seen. My guess was that she wanted to be on her best behavior to ensure more outings with Evie and myself.

I was first and started with a gutter ball.

"Hey, do you want us to put in those bumpers for you?" Evie asked. Fiona reacted like she was seeing Richard Pryor, circa 1977. She thought it was the funniest thing ever.

I was a competitive SOB when I wanted to be, and two girls making fun of your bowling ability could bring that guy out. I responded by knocking down all 10 pins on my second roll for a spare. I walked towards the girls and blew on my hand as if it was a gun that needed to be put out. Fiona smiled at this, but it was no Pryor in 77' kind of laugh. It was more like Dane Cook in 2009. A courtesy laugh.

The competitive SOB in me didn't last long as the three of us proceeded to have a great time. I won every game and the girls alternated getting second place. None of that mattered though. What did matter was that it looked like Fiona had found a friend for life. I didn't know what they were talking about as

I would go to roll, but every time I turned around, they were laughing it up. I was happy for both of them.

In the final of the four games, Fiona finally broached the subject that I had been expecting.

"So are you guys' just friends or what?" she said.

Evie and I looked at each other. Not in a sordid way since we had nothing to hide, but more in a who is going to answer kind of way.

I took the lead.

"We're just friends, Fiona."

"Then what are you always doing together? I have a friend who works at Peet's, and she says you guys keep going there. It's like you are hiding something. Don't worry, Mom hasn't said a thing."

"We're not hiding anything, we...." I said, but was interrupted mid-sentence by Evie.

"I had to deal with some bullshit from my last boyfriend, and your brother is helping me get through it," she said.

I didn't know if it was Evie's intention, but it definitely got Fiona to forget about our little escapades. All of her concern was now directed at Evie. Fiona, as was her custom, had a hundred questions. Evie didn't get into particulars, but she did say that she had been abused. Fiona cried when she heard this, and in turn, Evie started crying too. The people in the neighboring lanes must have been surprised to find out bowling could be such an emotional sport.

It must have been nice for Evie to talk to a young woman about it. As helpful as I thought I had been, I'm sure there are some things that she'd rather discuss with a fellow female. I didn't mean anything sexual, but just the underlying fear living as a woman must sometimes bring. I kept my distance for a few frames and let them talk amongst themselves.

After a few minutes, I saw them looking in my direction, and I realized they were done with that part of their conversation.

I felt like we needed a little comic relief, so I bowled the last few frames though my legs while looking back at the girls. It was a gift that had no practical value unless you needed to loosen up the mood a little bit. It appeared to have done its job as the girls started laughing once again, and we left Plank on an upbeat note. We exited the bowling alley, glancing out onto the bay as we left, and headed home.

Evie sat in the front seat on the way back. If she was truly just a friend, shouldn't family, i.e. my sister, get the coveted shotgun position? I looked over at Evie as we drove. I could swear she was smiling at me as more than just a friend. Of course, this was the same girl who I had misread several years ago, and found myself falling off a lounge chair, ending up in the pool as her Mom looked down at me; both figuratively and literally.

I was certainly not going to make that mistake again. If this truly was a blossoming romance, it was going to have to be Evie who made the first move. And considering what had happened to her, that wasn't likely to happen.

Looked like our adventures would be a strictly platonic undertaking...

I saw Fiona the next morning, and she was still riding high after the bowling excursion of the previous night. As she had the previous night with Evie, she had a million questions for me. Most of them centered around Evie having been beaten up by her boyfriend and why I wasn't trying to date her. I tried to explain to her that those two were inextricably tied together. The reason I wasn't trying to get too close to Evie was because of the heartbreak she had just recently endured. Fiona finally seemed to get the point.

"I guess," she said. "I'm just saying she's very pretty and she's really cool."

"I'm not going to disagree with either of those," I said.

"You know Mom is leaving in two days."

We hadn't really discussed it much, but I knew why Fiona brought it up now.

"Stop playing matchmaker you little pest."

"I'm just saying it's a good time to bring Evie over. Mom being out of the house and all."

"If you keep this up, I'm going to tell Mom she should take you along with her. You know I can be convincing."

"You wouldn't!" Fiona looked genuinely worried.

"Don't tempt me," I said.

"Fine. Hey, I'm going to go get some lunch later, let me know if you want me to pick up something for you."

My plan had worked. She had quickly changed the subject away from Evie and went out of her way to offer me food. She was going to be nice to me until our mother left. I laughed. Little sisters were so easy sometimes.

I didn't see Evie at all that day. Her father had just finished grading finals, so the Somerset's had a day to themselves. Evie was texting me as they went from lunch to shopping to dinner and then back home. I could tell she wanted to see me, but I thought a day with her family was a good idea.

Plus, from the gist of Owen's last writing, it was going to be all business from here on in. A relaxing day was in the cards for both of us. I finished watching Chapter 12 of the show I had been watching on Netflix and was somewhat let down by the ending. Twelve hours invested in a show and a bullshit ending like that? I was pissed. I then realized if they had been called Episodes instead of Chapters none of this would have transpired, and I wouldn't be spending all this time with Evie. I quickly forgave the show.

I texted Evie early the next morning and told her my mother was leaving the following day. We could study at my house for a few days. I tried to make it abundantly clear that it wasn't a plan to get her to my house alone, and in the process of doing that, I made it sound like that was precisely what I was doing.

I couldn't help myself sometimes.

With my mother still around, we went back to our favorite table at Peet's. We were becoming regulars and got a smile from one of the barista's who had served us a few times. Her face was familiar to me, but I couldn't quite place it. I thought that maybe she had been in Fiona's class. And then I realized she was probably the one who had told Fiona that we had been going there.

"How was the day with your parents?" I asked Evie. She had seemed a little quiet on the drive there, and we hadn't talked much.

"Pretty boring, I guess. That's why I kept texting you," she said.

"Oh, I'm so privileged. I feel like a fire extinguisher. In case of boredom, break glass, and text Frankie."

Evie laughed. "That's not what I meant. It's just the same old thing with them. They want to handle me with kid gloves after what happened, and I've told them I'm already over it and ready to move on."

"I don't think they realize how tough you are," I said.

"You really think I am?' she asked, a very earnest look in her eyes.

"Unquestionably. I think a lot of girls in your situation would sit in their room for months on end. And you really couldn't blame them. You are getting out of the house and seem to be enjoying whatever this thing is we have going."

"You mean our friendship or our adventure?"

She was quick, I had to give her that. I hadn't even realized my faux pas.

"Our adventure," I said.

"Speaking of which, let's open up Uncle Owen's book. This is where things are going to start getting pretty serious, right?"

It was my turn. "Are you talking about us or the book?"

She laughed a full belly laugh and leaned over and kissed me on the cheek.

"You got me! Touche," she said, continuing to laugh.

I removed Owen's book from my backpack and carefully leafed through the book, making sure not to jump too far ahead. I came on the chapter telling us to go be teenagers, and I apologized internally to Uncle Owen for not getting drunk or getting laid.

I turned the page and came upon our third mandate. It was brief and to the point. **"Research a man named Darby Cash Bowles. He was born in Oklahoma. I think the year was 1975, but I could be a year or two off. Find out everything you can about him. Good luck, sport."**

18

On July 16th, 2010, Darby Bowles had been in Eureka, CA for over nine years. He was now 34 years old. He had a live-in girlfriend by the name of Patricia Page who was 10 years his junior. He had stayed out of jail and had led a quiet, unassuming life. He rarely thought about the murders in Oklahoma City. They seemed like a lifetime ago.

Lately, his thoughts had turned to the idea of having a child of his own. He and Patricia had recently started trying, and Darby was very excited by the possibility. Billy Gullicksen was still living in Eureka and was married with two kids to a pleasantly plump woman named Tina. Darby was still close to Billy, and at times he felt like he owed his life to him. Darby had reinvented his life in Eureka, and while maybe it wasn't an idyllic postcard type life, it was a lot better than being in and out of the jails in Oklahoma.

July 16th, 2010 was a Friday, and after a long week of working on the docks, it had become tradition that Darby and Billy would go out and grab some beers. Patricia and Tina would often go out on their own on Friday's knowing the boys wouldn't be back till nine or ten. The ladies considered themselves lucky as they knew a great many women whose boyfriends or husbands would stay out much later than that.

Darby was still intense, but he had definitely mellowed over the years. He liked to read history books and considered himself something of a renaissance man. Others would have said that was a huge stretch. Regardless, he was not the same angry young man that he had been in his youth.

He'd still get in the occasional argument when he was drunk, but it was always limited to something verbal. Billy hadn't seen Darby get in a single physical altercation since he moved to Eureka almost a decade ago. There were times he could tell Darby wanted to, but something always held him back, almost as if he knew he couldn't go to jail. Billy couldn't explain it.

On this Friday night, they hit up their favorite local spot, a dive bar called The Long and Shore of It. It was a cheesy combination of the phrase *The long and short of it,* and its constant patrons, the local longshoremen. Despite its less than stellar name, the longshoremen loved to frequent the spot. They were constantly fed shots, and they were handed the occasional free pitcher of beer. There were not many places where a longshoreman was treated like royalty, but The Long and Shore of It was one of those spots.

Everyone knew Darby and Billy, and they got a hero's welcome as they walked in. Billy got a table in the corner which surprised Darby and ordered two pitchers of beer and two shots of their best tequila. This surprised Darby even more.

"Did you hit the lottery?" Darby asked. He had asked this same question to Jake Court years ago when he saw his beautiful home. It was a go-to line of sorts for Darby.

"In a matter of speaking, yes..." Billy said.

"What does that mean?"

"Tina is great, isn't she?"

"Yeah, she's the best. Patricia and I love her. Why?"

The shots arrived, and Billy handed one to Darby.

"Raise your glass," Billy said.

Darby raised his glass, not quite sure where this was headed.

Billy leaned his shot glass forward, and as they clinked glasses, he said, "Tina is pregnant again."

They looked at each other, and both quickly finished the shot.

"Wow, that is some great news! Number three? Damn, you almost have a basketball team" Darby said.

"I know, I can't believe it. You got here nine years ago, and I had no girl-friend. Now I'm married with a third child on the way. Who would have thought?"

"You know, not to take anything away from your special night, but Patricia and I have decided to try to have a child too."

Billy was beaming from ear to ear. "Oh shit, I'm almost as happy to hear that as I am about my own."

"Figured you could use a point guard or power forward for the basketball team you are building," Darby said.

Billy laughed.

He saw Christy, the sexiest waitress at The Long and Shore of It and called her over. Billy and Darby would always flirt with her, knowing it wasn't going to go anywhere. Christy enjoyed the banter as well.

"What's up guys?"

"It's a celebration here tonight, Christy! Please bring me two more of your top shelf tequila shots."

Christy started walking away, but Billy wasn't done ordering. "And a few Jagermeister shots to back them up!"

"So it's going to be one of those types of nights?" Darby asked.

"You're damn right it is!"

Billy and Darby ended out consuming two pitchers of beer each and ap-proximately eight shots apiece, although Darby had lost count at five. Darby had become a better man since moving to Eureka, avoiding bar fights alto-gether, and generally being less angry at the world. Unfortunately, he had not given up the terrible habit of drinking and driving.

Patricia had gone out with Tina that night, as she had on so many previous Friday nights. She was back by nine p.m. and patiently waited for Darby to make it home. When 10 p.m. passed, she wasn't surprised he hadn't arrived. Tina had told Patricia the good news about her pregnancy so she knew that the guys would probably be out celebrating a little later than usual. Patricia went to sleep around 11:00 p.m., assuming she'd be woken up by a drunk Darby stumbling in. That didn't happen.

If Billy had been in a normal state of mind, he would have grabbed the keys from Darby, but he was no better off than his friend. He was smart enough to have a bartender at The Long and Shore of It call him a cab though. For months to come, he'd try to remember if he asked Darby to come with him in the cab, but he could never quite piece together the end of the night.

Patricia woke up at 12:30 a.m. and rolled over in bed, but there was no Darby. She started to get a little worried at this point and decided to call the bar. She was hoping they just decided to stay really late tonight.

Abraham Adams, a bartender that they all knew well, answered the phone and informed Patricia that Darby and Billy had left at least an hour ago. Patricia started getting nervous and debated whether to call Billy or the local hospital. As she spent five minutes debating, her phone started ringing. It wasn't Billy or the hospital. It was the police.

"Hello?"

"Hi, Ms. Page. Are you the girlfriend of Darby Cash Bowles?"

"I am."

Patricia knew she shouldn't be happy, but at least it wasn't the hospital calling. She could deal with a drunk in public. Hopefully, it was that and not a drunk driving charge.

"I think you should come down to the police station."

"Was he drunk in public?"

The officer didn't answer. Patricia got a little more nervous.

"Was he drunk driving?"

Patricia heard the officer clear his throat, and she knew what he said next was going to be bad. She never could have guessed just how bad.

"Ms. Page, I don't think you understand. Mr. Bowles ran over three people. Two of them have already died."

Patricia Page set out for the police station upon getting the crushing news. She would have to head in the direction of The Long and Shore of It, so she knew that she was likely to pass the scene of the accident. Sure enough, about a half mile after she got on Interstate 101, she saw some lights up ahead.

Although it was technically a highway, Interstate 101 slowed down in Eureka and acted more as a lazy street or boulevard. There were crosswalks where people could walk across the highway, and it was one of these crosswalks where Patricia saw the lights ahead. She looked ahead, and she saw Darby's Chevy Tahoe facing her, its back up against a small tree.

Traffic slowed to a near standstill, and people were driving only 10 mph as they passed the scene of the accident. Patricia tried not to look but couldn't stop herself. She looked across at Darby's gray Tahoe, and she could see that there was a red color all over the grill on the front of the truck. She started crying and looked away as quickly as she had seen it.

The police station was only another mile up, and Patricia was still in tears as she entered. There was an older, graying police officer sitting at a small, mahogany table as she walked in.

"I'm the girlfriend of Darby Bowles," Patricia said.

"Right this way," the officer said. He shot her a frown and escorted her towards the jail cell.

Eureka was not a big city, and the police station only had eight cells. They had a county jail not far away, but they had taken Darby to the local station for booking. Darby looked up as Patricia approached, and she noticed that his eyes were completely bloodshot. She wasn't sure if this was the alcohol or whether he had been crying.

Patricia walked up to the cell and put her arms through it, grabbing Darby's hands. He started crying. Patricia could tell he was still drunk as well.

"I fucked up," he said.

There was no doubt about that, Patricia thought.

"It's going to be alright," she said. She didn't believe it but figured he needed to hear it.

"No, it's not. I hit a bunch of people in the crosswalk. I didn't even see them. God, I hope they are okay."

Jesus, Patricia thought, they haven't even told him that two of them had died. She couldn't break the news to him.

"I'm fucked anyway. Once I go to jail, the Ringleader is going to kill me."

"What the hell are you talking about?" Patricia said.

"For what I did. He'll kill me. Only surviving witness."

"You're drunk and making no sense. And I think you should stop talking anyway. There are cops all around, and you don't want to say anything you'll regret."

Darby started sobbing even louder now. "I'm so sorry, Patricia. Looks like you're going to have to find someone else to have a baby with."

The thought hadn't even crossed Patricia's mind, but it was impossible to avoid it now. If you killed two people while drunk driving, you were going to be put away for several years. Patricia looked across at the man she had loved for the last few years and had hoped to have a baby with. That wasn't going to happen now. Patricia Page started crying as loud as her boyfriend.

Darby Bowles hired an attorney, but he never had a realistic chance of getting off. He had hit three people trying to cross the highway and blew a .21 blood alcohol content when arrested. After hitting the pedestrians, Darby swerved and hit a small tree. The police were on the scene in less than five minutes, followed by several ambulances. While the ambulances were loading the three people who had been hit, the police were arresting Darby. He offered no excuse and merely said he was drunk and had not seen them.

Greg Fisher would escape with only a broken leg, but his friends Jonathan Pitt and Isabelle Fuentes were not as lucky. They both were declared dead on arrival at the hospital. Fisher was 21 years old, while Pitt and Fuentes were only 20. They had been coming from a party and had smoked a little weed, but they were in the crosswalk legally and would be alive if it weren't for the gross negligence of Darby Bowles.

The trial was postponed several months, and then two weeks before it was to begin, Darby's attorney came to him telling him that the prosecution had offered him a deal that was fair, seven years in prison. Darby accepted it without even hearing all the specifics. He deserved to go to prison for what he had done, and he knew it. He accepted the deal, signed the papers, and privately apologized to the families of the victims via a letter from his attorney. Darby Bowles's roller coaster of a life had landed him back in jail.

After being sentenced, and held at San Quentin, Darby was transferred up to the prison in Susanville, located in Lassen County, about five hours east of Eureka.

In Darby's first several weeks in prison, he had a very fatalistic view. He figured he'd been living on borrowed time since Oklahoma City and it was only a matter of time until the Ringleader found out he was in jail and would have him murdered. He spent his times in the shower and in the yard expecting to feel a shiv in his back at any time. It never came.

The days turned into weeks which turned into months, and Darby became pretty well acquainted with the prison at Susanville . It had been nearly 10 years since Darby had been in jail, but he managed to get to know the right people, and he flourished in jail. At least, as much as you can.

The visits from Patricia which were once a week when he was first sentenced, occurred less and less often as time went on. Finally, 14 months into his seven-year stint, Patricia came to him and said she had a new boyfriend and she was pregnant. Darby was happy for his girlfriend who he had loved dearly, and sad for himself because if he hadn't fucked up again, that child could have been his.

2010 became 2011 and Darby had gone through three different cell mates in total. There was his first cellmate, Rich Bowers, who was amused that his name was so close to Darby's father, Richard Bowles.

Bowers was transferred and in came Aaron Netherton, an 18-year-old who had a lifetime of trouble ahead of him. He reminded Darby of his younger self, and he tried to impart some wisdom into the young man. He didn't think it had worked.

Next was Felix Ortega, a man in his 60's who like Darby had killed someone while drunk driving. He hated sharing a cell with Ortega as he was reminded of his own crime every time he looked into Ortega's face. Darby wasn't sure if it was the fact that he had a better attorney or only killed one person, but Felix Ortega only served three years in jail, the last several months as Darby's cellmate.

Ortega was released in August of 2011, and Darby enjoyed the next two days of having no cellmate. On the third day, the guards brought in a man who was probably a few years older than Darby. He had a lot of tattoos on his arms, and he certainly looked like a tough guy.

The guards frisked the man one last time and then exited the cell. One of the guards who Darby had come to despise, left by saying "I'll let you two lovebirds get to know each other."

The tattooed man spoke first. "What an asshole!"

"My thoughts exactly," Darby said. "That's McGraw, stay away from him."

"I will. Thanks."

Despite the tattoos and gruff exterior, Darby could tell that this guy wasn't some overt asshole. He actually smiled and seemed like a pretty polite guy.

"I'm Darby Bowles."

"Nice to meet you. I'm Owen Harding."

Darby's new cell mate was none other than Uncle Owen.

19

What Evie and I had done to that point certainly didn't feel like some great adventure. It felt more like something that was required, like San Francisco State had sent winter break homework back with me. Part of that feeling was because nothing exciting had happened yet, but it's also because we were doing our work separately.

Did Woodward and Bernstein do all their work away from each other? No. Did the Goonies outfox the Fratelli's individually? No. They did it together! And that's when I decided that I didn't care if we sat at Peet's all day, Evie and I were going to do this together. Starting the next day, of course. We had already gone our separate ways for the day, and I was sitting on my bed googling "Darby Cash Bowles."

My Google search led me to an article about a case of vehicular homicide in which Darby Cash Bowles was the perpetrator. The crime had occurred on July 16th, 2010 in Eureka, CA. I knew Eureka was up north and surrounded by beautiful Redwood trees. Our family had been up that way a few times as children, and my fondest memory was of driving through a hollowed out Redwood tree. That's how big these things were.

I also seemed to remember that Uncle Owen had spent some time up there. At least, I thought so. It had now been over five years since Uncle Owen had passed away, and I found myself remembering less and less of him as the years went by. It didn't help that my memories of him were all from when I was 16 years old and younger.

As I reminisced about the man who had me googling some guy with a feminine name, my phone rang. I looked over, and it was Evie.

"Hey. What's up?"

"Can you come over?" she asked.

"Sure, did you find something?"

"I'll tell you when you get here."

I drove over to the Somerset's and was greeted by Evie's mom.

"How are you doing, Frankie?"

"I'm fine, Mrs. Somerset, just came over to see Evie."

"You guys are spending a lot of time together. I think it's nice."

"Mom!" Evie was walking down the hall. She grabbed my arm and saved me from having to respond to her mother.

We walked down to Evie's room, and she slammed the door. I think her Mom got the point that Evie wanted some privacy.

She motioned for me to sit down on her bed, and for the briefest of moments, I thought my dreams were coming true. It would not be for a roll in the hay, however. Her laptop was on her bed, and it was easier to show me what she intended.

I joined her, and we both leaned back against multiple pillows.

"How much do you know about Darby Cash Bowles?" she asked.

"Not much. I just started reading an article about a fatal drunk driving case.

"Yeah, that's the first thing I came across too. But I've been digging a little deeper since then," she said this ominously, and I could tell she was a little nervous.

"What is it, Evie?"

"Your Uncle Owen gave you the book five years ago right?"

"Yeah, when I was 16."

"Well, I think we need to read the rest of what Owen wrote to you. Now. Today."

"Why?" I said. Evie sounded anxious, and I wasn't sure why.

"Because things have changed and there's no way that Owen could have foreseen it."

"Slow down Evie. I'm not sure what you are saying."

"First off, I think Owen and Darby were either cellmates or met each other in jail. You had said that Owen Harding was in and out of jail all the time and Darby Bowles was the same. Well, thanks to the internet, I was able to find that your Uncle Owen was in the Eureka jail at the same time as Darby Bowles."

"That's amazing, Evie," I said.

"That's just a side note. I'm sure we would have found that out soon. The other thing I found is the one that really worries me."

I noticed Evie looking a little nervous, which in turn made me nervous.

"What is it?" I asked.

She looked at me, and I knew I was going to have to wait.

"Darby Cash Bowles was sentenced to seven years back in 2010. Owen gave you what he called the greatest novel ever back in 2012. Right?"

"Yeah, Uncle Owen gave me the book in 2012. I still don't follow."

"You were supposed to read his book in 2014 when you turned 18, right?"

"Yeah, that's right. You know all this Evie."

"Just making sure."

"So what does this all mean?" I asked.

"Well, when you were supposed to start reading the book, Owen still thought Darby Cash Bowles was going to be in jail for three more years."

My heart sank.

"He's out of jail?" I asked

"He gets out in four days."

PART 2:
DARBY'S PLAN

<u>20</u>

Darby Cash Bowles and Owen Harding struck up a friendship almost immediately. It was late 2011 and Darby was 16 months into his seven-year sentence. They both knew they had done some terrible things, but that deep down they had good hearts. They weren't irredeemable like so many of their fellow inmates. Darby confessed to Owen that he asked forgiveness daily for what happened in Eureka.

Owen made Darby laugh by telling him of scams he had pulled off. Taking money from old ladies for aluminum siding, or getting down payments to shingle a roof, and then getting the fuck out of dodge with people chasing him down rural highways.

Darby knew that Owen Harding was no saint, but he enjoyed the way he told stories, and he had never hurt anyone. Financially yes, but not physically. After what had happened in Oklahoma City and then Eureka, Darby couldn't help but consider Owen Harding's crimes extremely minor in comparison to his own.

Owen talked about beautiful girls he had screwed and long chases he had taken cops on. He had made it on CNN with his latest joy ride. That's what he called it when the cops were chasing him. Joy rides. Darby couldn't help but laugh at this.

It didn't appear that Owen had ever been married, but he talked about his best friend's kids all the time. They were living down in the Bay Area, and that's where Owen said he was heading once he was released. His latest joy ride had landed him a two year sentence, but he'd be up for parole in a year. Regardless, he'd be getting out well before Darby.

Owen was the first guy that Darby had considered telling about what happened in Oklahoma City. Billy had been a great friend and helped him start a new life in Eureka, but he was a friend of Jake Court's, so there was no way Darby could let him know about what went down in OKC.

Owen was different. He seemed like the type of guy who could keep a secret, and if Darby was being honest with himself, he needed to tell someone. He had carried this awful burden for way too long, and he thought a confession would do him some good. Catholics were absolved of their sins after they confessed. That sounded like a pretty good deal to Darby.

Darby debated back and forth about whether to tell Owen but eventually decided against it. He just didn't know Owen well enough yet, and there were a million jailhouse rats out there who would love to reduce their sentence if they had some dirt on a fellow inmate.

Darby continued enjoying hanging out with Owen, but after nine months as cellmates, he still hadn't told him anything about Oklahoma City. That changed in July of 2012.

The prison in Susanville was fairly modern, and because they were dealing with generally agreeable inmates, there was a TV in the common area. There was no HBO, or shows depicting violence or sex, but there was news channels and ESPN.

Most of the time, the inmates would have it on ESPN, watching how their favorite teams were doing. On this day, one of the inmates wanted to watch the Fox Business Channel. He said he had a bunch of stocks that were going to make him rich when he got out of jail. No one believed him, but it was a slow day in sports, so no one protested when he changed the channel to the Fox News Business Channel.

They were interviewing some guy who was rattling off all the perceived failings of President Obama, and all the inmates got bored and left the communal T.V. area. Darby and Owen were walking by without any plans of stopping in.

"And then the old lady came running out after me, wearing only her bra and panties. Keep in mind she was like 80 years old," Owen said. He waited for the oncoming laugh from Darby who would have him repeat these stories again and again.

Instead, he got the Shhh sign from Darby, and as Owen stared at him, he knew he meant it.

Owen watched as Darby closed his eyes and walked towards the T.V. It appeared that Darby wanted to hear, but not see, the man on T.V. Owen thought it was extremely weird.

"Everyone shut up," Darby yelled, even though there was only the future stock millionaire and Owen in the room. They could both tell Darby was quite serious, so they remained silent.

Darby listened to the guy on T.V. talk for a good 30 seconds. Owen looked up at and saw an extremely intense man being interviewed. He had prematurely gray hair, but he didn't look a day over 40. He spoke with an air of confidence, and the authority in his voice was something to behold. Owen had no idea who he was, however, and wasn't quite sure why Darby was so intrigued.

"My God, it's fucking him," Darby said and finally opened his eyes to look at the T.V.

The man being interviewed was named Howie Doss, and the graphic said he was the founder and C.E.O. of a website named alwaysright.com. Owen knew it was a political website that leaned, not surprisingly, to the right. He was hardly a political buff, but the site was a well-known one. But he still wasn't sure why this intrigued Darby so much.

Owen looked over, and Darby was still absolutely fixated on the T.V. Darby sensed that Owen was about to say something, and he raised a finger and waved it at him, telling him to be quiet. The interview ended a few minutes later, and still, Darby didn't speak for several seconds. Owen had had enough.

"What the hell is going on, Darby?"

After much deliberation, Darby turned to Owen and said, "I just became a multi-millionaire."

Darby returned to his cell that day and couldn't believe his luck. If he played his cards right, he had literally just been handed millions of dollars. The CEO of one of the most influential websites in American politics had authorized the murder of people in Oklahoma City. Of this, Darby had no doubt. He would recognize that voice anywhere.

Owen couldn't get much out of Darby over the next few weeks, as Darby mulled his options. He knew he couldn't blackmail the guy from jail for obvious reasons, and he kept coming back to the fact that Owen was due to get out in three months. If Darby was willing to take Owen on as a partner in this, it would be much, much easier since he'd have someone on the outside. It was necessary, in fact. Still, Darby had to be positive this is what he wanted to do, so he wasn't forthcoming with Owen.

Darby researched as much as he could about alwaysright.com and their founder Howie Doss. Susanville had limited internet access for the inmates. Darby went there as often as he could and had gone from an amateur to average when it came to navigating the internet. It was heavily regulated for the inmates, but Darby was able to get enough information to confirm his suspicions. Or more accurately, to not disprove them. He couldn't find a whole lot of info on Howie Doss in and around 2000 and 2001, but there was nothing proving he wasn't in Oklahoma City at that time. That was enough for Darby.

Howie Doss appeared to be a very private man, and when Darby went to YouTube, he could only find a few other videos he was in. None were very helpful other than to reiterate that this man was very conservative, and ran a hugely popular website. Doss's Wikipedia page wasn't much either. It said he had started alwaysright.com in 2001 and talked a lot about his website. There wasn't much personal information except that he grew up in Missouri, went to college at the University of Missouri, and had worked on some small congressional races before launching his website.

Darby knew he couldn't go googling "Howie Doss racist" or anything close to that. He didn't know just how closely they monitored the inmates'

Google searches, but he didn't want to do anything that could potentially draw their attention.

It didn't really matter because Darby already knew this was the guy he had come to call the Ringleader. He knew it from the first word out of his mouth as they walked by the T.V. room. And he knew Doss had to be extremely wealthy from the website he had launched. That made him prime for extortion. Darby didn't like the words extortion or bribery, but he preferred them to the words broke and penniless.

After much internal debate, Darby concluded that he had to include Owen. Darby wasn't scheduled to get out for five years, and that was just too long to wait. And he knew he couldn't very well bribe Doss from jail. If Doss knew where he was, he'd find a way to have him killed. After all, this was a guy who had ordered murders, and now he had a huge enterprise he could lose. Of course he'd do away with Darby if he had the chance.

Darby knew that he would potentially be putting Owen in harm's way, but he didn't lose any sleep over that. He was giving him the opportunity of a life-time. You couldn't steal enough aluminum siding in a lifetime to make the money Owen could make if this went right.

After answering most of Owen's questions monosyllabically for two weeks, Darby decided it was time. A half hour after all of the lights went out on his cell block, he finally spoke to Owen.

"Owen, are you awake?"

"That's like four words you just said to me. Are you sure you're okay?"

Darby laughed. He had missed talking to his friend, but he had needed to wait until he had finalized his plan.

"Can I come down?"

"Trying to cop a feel?" Owen responded.

"Shut up, this is serious."

"Fine."

Darby came down from his top bunk and sat on the bed next to Owen.

"Sit up," Darby said.

Owen got up and faced Owen.

"Do you remember when I told you that I had just become a multi-million-aire?" Darby asked.

"How could I forget," Owen said.

"How would you like half of that?"

That got Owen's attention. He sat up straighter and listened intently as Darby laid out his plan for the next 20 minutes.

21

Owen Harding had his first cigarette when he was 10 years old. His best friend, Eddie Waters, had stolen a pack from the local pharmacy and they each smoked one. This was back in the day when no one saw the irony of selling cigarettes in a place like CVS. While Eddie would grow up to be a responsible father to Frankie and Fiona, he was a bit of a troublemaker at the time.

They went out to the backyard of Eddie's parents, who had gone to church, and Eddie brought out an old school Bic lighter from the house. Owen went first, and not knowing what he was doing, coughed up a lung on his first attempt. Eddie couldn't stop laughing, not realizing he was going to have the same reaction a few seconds later. Needless to say, they hardly looked like the tough guy smokers that they had envisioned when Eddie had stolen the pack.

As with many events of their childhood, Eddie would try things once while Owen would have a harder time giving them up. Eddie quickly realized that stealing was wrong and the cigarettes he stole would be his last foray into theft. He also didn't enjoy coughing and feeling light-headed, so the cigarette fetish didn't last long either. The same could not be said of Owen, who started a lifelong addiction to nicotine.

Eddie and Owen grew up in the same city, Sacramento, CA, but the parts of the city they grew up in were drastically different. In fact, they likely never would have crossed paths if Owen's mother hadn't taken him across town to a day care when he was just seven years old. It was a bit out of the way, but when Owen seemed to enjoy it there, his mother decided the 15-minute drive every day was a small price to pay for her son's happiness.

Eddie Waters had already been at Discount Day Care for a year or so, and even at seven years old could tell Owen was a little different. He had a little edge to him, or as much as you could at that age. He dressed differently, and Eddie had no way of knowing it was merely because all of Owen's clothes were hand me downs.

They bonded originally over the game of basketball. While the other kids were inside playing board games, Eddie and Owen would go outside and constantly shoot baskets on the 6-foot high rim. It was hardly Madison Square Garden, but two seven-year-olds didn't mind. They'd spend hours upon hours shooting balls at the basket.

Unfortunately, their hoop dreams wouldn't come to be. Owen would grow up to be a strong, well-built kid, but at 5' 10" he wasn't headed to the NBA anytime soon. He had also developed an affinity to the cigarettes as well as getting in trouble. The basketballs they had shot as kids were a distant memory as they entered high school.

They stayed close through their teenage years, despite Owen being a lost soul and Eddie becoming a straight A student. They really were an odd couple, but they had been inseparable since they were seven years old, and that bond is tough to break, no matter how different they may have become.

When they finished high school, they went their different ways. Eddie went to college at Stanford, while Owen started his schooling at the Sacramento County Jail. He pretended to be doing a fundraiser for the school baseball team, and people would pledge money. The problem was Owen wasn't on the high school baseball team, and they weren't doing any fundraiser.

Owen was hardly a criminal mastermind and was caught less than a day after collecting hundreds of dollars. He was sent to county jail, having turned 18 years old only a few months previous. He continued smoking cigarettes when he went to jail. His affinity for poker made it easy to get a lot of free cigarettes in jail, and he smoked them all. This was back in the day when most jails allowed smoking, and cigarettes were used as a form of currency, with people using them to barter for various amenities.

Eddie knew that Owen was in and out of jail in his 20's, and they did lose touch for a while. Eddie graduated from Stanford and became an engineer. He met a beautiful woman named Sally Anderson and moved into a house in the Oakland Hills. The beautiful home had three bedrooms, so Eddie and Sally made good use of their time together, and filled the two rooms with a son named Frankie and two and a half years later, a daughter named Fiona.

One year when they were in their early 30's, Eddie got a phone call from Owen saying he was going to be down in the Bay Area. He wanted to know if he'd like to meet up. Eddie agreed to it, and they had a great time rehashing their childhood memories, including their love of basketball and that first time they had a cigarette. As they walked outside after the lunch, Owen immediately lit up a cigarette and Eddie felt a bit guilty for stealing that pack so long ago.

Owen told Eddie he was heading back to Sacramento in a few days and wanted to know if he could crash on his couch until then. Eddie agreed and went home that day to tell Sally the "good" news. Sally was a gracious and accepting person, but she wasn't too keen on having a guy who was in and out of jail spending time with two young children.

Sally knew how close Eddie had been to Owen as kids, so she gave it her approval. Eddie promised it wouldn't be for long and he was right. Owen was gone two days later, on his way back up to Sacramento.

But now that Owen had his foot in the door, he would periodically drop into the Waters' home. Sometimes he'd stay a few days, sometimes he'd stay a few weeks. At some point, the moniker Uncle Owen had been adopted, and much to Sally's chagrin, it stuck.

While he was a criminal with shady morals, Owen was always good with the kids. Even Sally had to admit that. He would babysit when necessary and take them about town when Eddie and Sally needed a little break from the monotony of raising young children. And he was respectful with the smoking. He'd always go outside when he smoked, filling up Coca-Cola cans with the butts of the cigarettes.

He never was able to kick his long-standing addiction to nicotine. Still a relatively young man, he told himself that at some point he would quit. That day would never come.

He even flicked a cigarette out his car window years later as the police were following him on his joy ride through Eureka, CA. They added a few charges of littering to the much more serious crime of evading police. The police sure had a great sense of humor.

Midway through his short prison term, Owen got a letter from Sally saying that Eddie had died of a heart attack while playing basketball. Owen was crushed. Selfishly, because he had lost his best friend, and also because he felt terrible for Sally and the young kids. Sally said the kids could use a father figure if Owen wanted to come down when he got out of jail.

Owen knew Sally Waters didn't think too highly of him, so this was a touching gesture. Owen wrote back, expressing his sorrow to the fact that Eddie had passed away, and he promised Sally that as soon as he got out, he'd come down and hang out with the kids.

As his release date became closer, Darby mentioned that Owen had been coughing a lot. Owen didn't think much of it. He was still only 45 years old, and lung cancer was an old man's disease. He'd periodically remind himself that he had started smoking at 10 years old and 35 years was a long time, but he wouldn't worry about it for long. That wasn't Owen's style.

Owen was released from the Eureka County Jail in the fall of 2012, after agreeing to be partners with Darby Cash Bowles. It hadn't taken long, as Owen Harding was seeing dollar signs in his sleep.

He had some business he was supposed to deal with in Eureka that pertained to Daby's plan, but Owen decided that could wait a week. He needed to go down and see his best friend's family. He owed Eddie that.

Owen arrived down in Oakland and tried to comfort the Waters children as much as he could. It didn't last long.

The coughing was really starting to bother him. He still wasn't that worried, but it was becoming a nuisance. Sally thought the same, and after two days of constantly coughing around the kids, she ordered him to go to the doctor. She said they would pay for it.

Owen went through a series of tests and was asked to come back two days later. When the doctor walked through the door, Owen knew from the expression on his face that it was bad news.

"Is it terminal?" Owen asked.

The doctor was not one for false hope when it came to his patients. Telling them the truth was the only way.

"You have weeks to live. I'm so sorry."

Owen bowed his head and started sobbing.

Darby Cash Bowles got only one letter from Owen Harding after he was released from jail. It had UCSF Medical Center as its letterhead.

It read: *"Darby, I've got some bad news, my friend. I'm dying. The cough that you remarked on was actually lung cancer, and I'm sitting at the UCSF Medical Center down in San Francisco with days to live. You probably think this is bullshit, and I'm going to use your plan to make myself rich, but I can assure you it's not. I'm rotting away and will die soon. Maybe that old lady in the panties and bra will get her revenge in Heaven. Take care, my friend. Owen."*

Owen was right, Darby's first inclination was to believe this was all bullshit and Owen was trying to screw Darby over. He soon found out that wasn't the case.

There were certain people in jail who had cell phones, and for the right price, you could use one for a minute or two. Darby had always been good at handling the politics of jail, and he knew a few guys who could help him out in this regard.

Darby got his hands on one and called the UCSF Medical Center three different times asking if Owen Harding was a patient there. All three times, Darby heard back in the affirmative. Darby pretended to be his estranged brother and was able to get one of the nurses to admit that he wasn't going to make it much longer. Unless he had everyone from the hospital staff in on the charade, Owen Harding really was dying.

A week later, Darby got the sad news via the internet. He went searching for Owen Harding on Google and found a few obituaries that confirmed that his friend had indeed died. Darby said a prayer for his former cellmate and then went to read Owen's letter again. He laughed at the comment on the old lady, remembering the stories that Owen would tell him.

Darby was truly sad. He had liked Owen Harding and felt like they were similar in many way.

He bowed his head for his friend and said a final prayer. And then he vowed to try and forget about Owen. Darby had business he had to attend to, and it needed all of his focus.

Darby had asked Owen to do one thing immediately upon getting out of jail. It was crucial to the plan that Darby had set up. There was no mention in the letter of whether Owen had done this, so Darby had to assume that he hadn't.

Darby decided that he would not be taking on any more co-conspirators. He could wait it out. In fact, as the years went on, he thought he was just making more money as he sat in jail. The website alwaysright.com got bigger and bigger in the intervening years. He'd often look for his "old friend" Howie Doss on T.V., but the guy appeared to be camera shy. Or maybe, he just didn't want to be in the public eye. With your history, I don't blame you, Darby would think.

He was relishing the chance to take the murdering scumbag for millions of dollars.

Darby would occasionally remember Doss's voice, and it would run a shiver through him. He thought back to their first and only meeting, when he noticed, albeit with a blindfold on, that Opie, Loose Lips, and Silent Bob were deathly afraid of him. If he noticed this blindfolded, Darby knew the men's real fear of Howie Doss was even more palpable.

Over his last five years in jail, there wasn't a day that went by where Darby didn't think about Howie Doss.

There were a few times that Darby thought he was going to be released early for good behavior but it never came to be. Apparently, killing two young adults while being extremely drunk wasn't a crime that led to an early release.

Finally, after serving his full seven year sentence, Darby Cash Bowles was set to be released from the Eureka County Jail on December 21st, 2017. He was 42 years old.

As he waited to be a free man again, Darby went over his plan for the 426th time. He smiled at the thought of being rich for the rest of his life.

22

"How the hell do you know he's getting out?" I asked.

"I called the Susanville prison," Evie answered.

I was impressed.

"How'd you think of that?"

"I had read the original articles, and they said he was scheduled to serve seven years. That will be December 21st. The crime took place in July, but he started his jail sentence in December. I called the jail, and this is all public information, so they informed me that he will indeed be released on the 21st. They don't often keep inmates in for their full sentence, but they'll make an exception if you kill some kids while driving drunk."

"Great detective work," I said.

Evie continued. "That's why I think we should go ahead and read everything that Owen wrote. When he gave you this five years ago, Owen thought this Darby Cash Bowles guy was going to be in jail. The fact that he's getting out may well have changed things."

She was right after all.

Unfortunately, I couldn't stay long. My mother was leaving the next morning and had requested a going away dinner with Fiona and I. If she thought anything suspicious was going on, she'd cancel her trip in a second, so I knew I had to go to the dinner. I explained this all to Evie.

"How about I come over tomorrow morning?" Evie asked.

"That's fine. I drop her off at Oakland airport at 7:30 a.m. I'll be back before 8:00."

I grabbed the book from my backpack, deciding we could read the next two mandates together. She could start up on them when I was at dinner and could tell me about them in the morning.

I was holding out on the 6th and final mandate. Owen said there would be no turning back after reading it, so I wanted to read that myself, away from Evie. This had been my "assignment" from the beginning, so I wanted to read the most important thing myself, before deciding whether to share it with Evie.

Most likely I would, considering she had shown more interest and done more research than I, but I didn't want her reading something that she could potentially never un-see.

We read the two mandates consecutively. For the fourth mandate, Uncle Owen asked me to find out everything about Howie Doss, a man whose name had made my skin crawl on the rare occasions I had read about him. For the fifth, he wanted me to research alwaysright.com, the website that Doss had created, and its eponymous company, Always Right, that Doss ran.

Always Right was the company and alwaysright.com was its featured website, although there were rumors that Doss owned thousands of smaller websites. When people talked about Always Right, they were generally talking about alwaysright.com, however.

I knew very little about Doss personally, but you'd have to be living under a rock to not have heard of his website. It was the furthest right of all the well-known conservative websites, making the Drudge Report, Breitbart, and Fox News look like MSNBC. Its readership was increasing every day, and it was becoming the go-to site for young conservatives. It may not have passed Fox News or Breitbart as far as readership, but there was no doubt that Always Right was the future.

Doss had been on the occasional political show, but he seemed to keep a low profile. To that point, we had discussed Always Right on numerous occasions in my Poly-Sci classes, but never once had Howie Doss been mentioned. He had my attention now, however.

I thought the website was a disgusting, propaganda-filled hit machine against good honest people. And that included middle of the road Republicans. The more extreme right the candidate or cause, the more Always Right went out of their way to extoll its virtues.

"And you really aren't going to show me the final mandate? The thing that ties them all together?" Evie asked.

"Tomorrow morning," I said. "You've been awesome Evie, but remember what Uncle Owen said. There's no turning back after this. Let me read it first, and then I'll let you read it."

"Fine," she said, her lips purposely pouting.

She looked cute doing it, but she wasn't going to get her way.

"Nice try. I'll see you tomorrow morning," I said, taking the novel with me.

I drove back to my mother's and left Evie there to research Howie Doss and Always Right.

The going away dinner with our mother was a casual ordeal. After all, she was only leaving for three days, and when she got back, Christmas would almost be upon us. There would be plenty of time for family bonding then. We went to a local burger chain known as Nation's. It was the Bay Area equivalent of In-N-Out for Southern California. I was a Bay Area kid to the core, but I had to admit that I'd take a double-double from In-N-Out over a Nation's burger any day.

That didn't mean I wasn't going to devour my double bacon cheeseburger, and that's exactly what I did. The women got single cheeseburgers, and I looked at them with faux disdain.

The discussion with my mother had reverted to chores to be done and parties not to be had. I reiterated to her that there would be no party. I saw a little twinkle in Fiona's eye, and I just knew she was going to say something. I gave her a quick glare, but it was too late.

"Frankie just wants a two person party with him and Evie!"

My Mom almost coughed up her burger.

"What did you say, Fiona?"

"I think you heard me," she said.

My mother composed herself. "I take a little exception with the way your little sister said it, but now that the cat is out of the bag, what is going on Frankie? You guys are inseparable all of a sudden."

"We're just friends, Mom. And Fiona knows that. She went bowling with us, ask her if anything was going on," I said, knowing I was on the defensive.

"I said that you wanted to, not that you had," Fiona said.

I couldn't argue with that.

It was times like these where I really missed my father. I could just hear him saying, *"Evie is a great looking girl. You're 21 years old Frankie, I have no problem with you hanging out with her so much. Go get her son!"*

I loved my sister and mother very much, but I was always outnumbered. I know my father would have had my back. I missed him so very much, even though it was approaching six years since he had passed.

My Mom's voice brought me back from daydreaming about my father.

"It just seems all very secretive to me. Closing doors, going back and forth to each other's houses. If I didn't know better, I'd say you guys were acting like spies," my mother said.

"Waters. Frankie Waters." I tried to do it in my best James Bond voice.

That got a laugh from the table.

"James Bond wasn't a spy, Frankie," Fiona said.

I had managed to change the subject, which should have been considered a win, except now I had left them thinking Evie and myself were spies. I couldn't let them think that. I hated doing what I did next, but I couldn't let this conversation end with them imagining me as James Bond.

"Fiona knows what I'm about to tell you, but you can't tell anyone else."

My mother listened intently, anxious to hear what I was going to say.

"Evie's last boyfriend beat her up a few times. The last time was earlier this month. Mrs. Somerset came over to me because she thought Evie could use a friend and maybe get out of the house a little bit. That's how this all started."

My mother gave me a hug. "Oh, I'm so sorry Frankie."

"She's getting better all the time. Sometimes, I think she's forgotten about it entirely."

"That's probably not the case, Frankie."

"Yeah, I know," I said.

"You've got a good heart Frankie," my Mom said.

Fiona wasn't as convinced.

"I'm most impressed that you are doing this out of the kindness of your heart Frankie, and it has nothing to do with the fact that she's a beautiful girl," she said.

We all laughed, and gladly the subject was changed after that. The rest of the conversation was mostly small talk, and I welcomed the change. We left Nation's and headed home.

On the road home, I started to think that the next three days with my sister were not going to be a picnic. She had a good sense that something was going on, and we'd have to be extra stealth to avoid detection.

"Waters. Frankie Waters," I thought to myself.

I was only missing a martini. Shaken, not stirred, of course.

I arrived home that night and wasted a solid two hours on the internet. I checked scores on ESPN, looked for new music on Pitchfork, and even read a disgusting article about immigration on alwaysright.com The website made me nauseous.

It was amazing just how easily I could waste two hours surfing the web. What did people do back in the day to pass the time? Read novels? Certainly, not if they were as boring as the story of Arthur Billingsley, the agrarian widow. The first four chapters of "The Greatest Novel Ever" seemed so long ago, but it had actually been just over a week.

I grabbed the novel, and just for kicks, I shuffled to the very last page of the book. More precisely, the last paragraph. *"And with that, Arthur Billingsley was able to close his eyes and die in peace. All he had wanted to hear from her was that it was all worth it. She had said exactly that and his life was now complete. Arthur Billingsley closed his eyes for a final time and died with a smile on his face."*

What the hell! That was beautiful. Much better than those four crappy chapters I had to endure to start. Well, I'm glad Arthur Billingsley died in peace, that chance does not avail itself to everyone.

I shuffled the novel back to where Uncle Owen had been writing his notes. I scanned through the pages where he had mentioned Howie Doss and the website that I found so repulsive.

Pausing on that page, I knew full well I was going to turn the page eventually. So, this was it. Uncle Owen had said that there would be no turning back if we looked at the final mandate and then the follow-up. And here I was, a flip of the finger from reading it.

I closed my eyes and said a silent prayer for Evie and myself. I wasn't very religious, but I didn't mind saying a prayer when I thought it might do some good. At the worst, saying prayers or sending good vibes do nothing, but I was kind of convinced they did do some good. I didn't think there was a God, but maybe there was some sort of good-vibes angel out there. That was about as religious as I got, but it certainly wasn't nothing.

Okay, here goes, I told myself. I turned the page, and read what Owen had written.

"You need to find a woman named Patricia Page and get a photo album that Darby Bowles left at her house when he went to jail. She was his former girlfriend but may have a different last name by now. Her last known address is 778 Dakota Street, Eureka, CA 95501. She isn't going to know who you are or why you are trying to pick up some of Darby's stuff, so you better think up a good story. Do not give Ms. Page your real names and don't mention my name just in case Ms. Page gets in touch with him. I made the mistake of telling Darby who you and Fiona were. I'm sure you have figured out by now that he was my cellmate. If you are 18 right now, he has three years left in jail. I'm glad you won't have to deal with him. After you get the photo album, you can turn the page, and everything will come into focus. Stay safe, sport!"

I cursed Uncle Owen after reading it. What the fuck! He had told some felon who Fiona and I were. He probably rationalized it at the time because Darby was going to still be in jail. Well, guess what Uncle Owen, he's getting out in a few fucking days! And he knows who I am? And now I've got Evie involved. I threw the novel across the room, and it hit the wall.

I started thinking that maybe I should stop picturing Uncle Owen as my big-hearted, crazy "Uncle" anymore. He was having us research some, at the minimum, unsavory people, and I didn't even know why yet. It was time to consider that maybe he didn't have my best interests in mind.

And yet, just as I had turned the previous page, I knew I was going to try and find out where Patricia Page was. And that's exactly what I did.

My mind was racing as I dropped my mother off at Oakland Airport the next morning. Luckily, she didn't seem to sense anything was wrong, and I gave her a goodbye kiss and sent my condolences to her dying aunt.

And then I started concentrating on my business at hand. With Darby Bowles getting out of jail in a few days, I thought we should try and get the photo album as soon as we could.

I was able to locate Patricia Page. It had taken minutes, or maybe it was seconds. I googled her name and the previous address that Owen had given me. Three websites popped up with her history of addresses. Her latest address was in a city named Ukiah, about halfway between Eureka and the Bay Area. The website said she had moved there in November, so I was going to assume she was still there.

Ukiah was about a two and a half hour drive from my mother's place in Oakland. I hoped Evie was game for a road trip.

I texted her, asking her if she was up for it. She texted back in the affirmative. I told her to try to sell her parents on a whole day just in case we had to stay overnight up there. She said that was fine.

When I arrived home, I starting packing an overnight bag. Evie was at her house doing the same.

We were fully immersed in whatever the hell this adventure had become. It looked like there was no turning back now.

The drive to Ukiah sailed by pretty quickly. There was a knot in my stomach, but I couldn't decide if it was anxiety or excitement. Probably a little of both. Evie looked a bit more excited than anxious, but there was definitely a little less exuberance than when we had started. She was starting to realize that this was real life and not some mystery novel.

She spent a good deal of the first half of the drive explaining everything she had found out about Howie Doss and Always Right. For a website that had millions of hits every day, there was surprisingly little information about the founder.

Howard Anthony Doss was born in Columbia, Missouri in 1972, although as far back as Evie could find, he's always referred to as Howie. He graduated high school in 1990 from Rock Bridge High School in Columbia, and then stayed local and went to the University of Missouri from 1990-1993, graduating in computer science.

I looked over at Evie as she said this.

"What did Computer Science majors do back in the 80's and 90's? Reprogram Pong?" I asked.

"Exactly."

Evie continued, saying he was pretty well-known on campus as being a bit of a shit disturber. He helped chair the Young Republicans and arranged for conservative speakers of the time to come on campus and make speeches. There was a picture of a young Howie Doss in the University of Missouri campus paper, *The Maneater,* with William F. Buckley in 1993.

"That was quite the catch to have him speak," I said.

"I've heard of Buckley, but don't know much about him," Evie said.

"He was a conservative hero for many dating back a long time. He launched the National Review sometime in the mid-50's and was probably the most famous conservative voice for decades."

"Wow, you know a lot about him," Evie said.

"Remember, I'm majoring in computer science, but I'm minoring in political science. I know my politics too."

"Well, you share the computer science major with Howie Doss."

"Gross. I read Always Right the last few days, and it gives me the Heebie-jeebies."

"You're using the phrase Heebie-jeebies, and you know conservative politics of the 1950's? Are you sure you are 21 years old, Frankie?"

"I'm an old soul, what can I say," I said.

And then she kissed me. It was quick and impulsive. It was partly on the cheek and partly on the mouth since I was facing the road, but the intention was obvious. This wasn't a kiss amongst friends.

"I'm sorry," she said.

"Don't be sorry," I said. "I just want you to be sure this is what you want."

"I don't want to hate men forever, Frankie."

"I understand that Evie, but I don't want to be a one-time thing so you can get over what happened."

"I promise it's not that. I really like you."

I leaned over and showing no regard for the road ahead of me tried to kiss her on the lips. It wasn't very glamorous.

"No more kissing. Let's try to get to Ukiah in one piece," I said.

She smiled and continued telling me about Howie Doss. I tried to pay attention as much as I could, but let's just say, something else was weighing on my mind now.

The time between graduating college and when he launched Always Right late in 2001 was a little hazy. He worked on a few local congressional races in Texas from 1996-1998 and then the trail goes cold until he launched his website in 2001. That was before Facebook and Twitter, and it wasn't as easy to track what someone was doing back then.

Howie Doss did very few interviews and the ones Evie had watched on YouTube never touched on that time period. He didn't seem shy talking about his time as the leader of the Young Republicans in college, so Evie wasn't sure why he was so reticent to talk about the time period between college and launching his site.

Maybe, like many people in their 20's, he was out finding his way in the world, not doing a whole lot. Or maybe he was partying too much. There were many reasons that there wasn't much info on Howie Doss during that period, and Evie told me she didn't put much stock into it.

"Of course, there is a lot of info about him since Always Right launched," Evie said.

I looked over at her. Was it really just a few minutes ago that she had leaned over and kissed me? She sure was good at compartmentalizing things. She looked like she was making a speech, and her face didn't give away what had happened between us.

"So, let's hear all about alwayswrong.com," I said.

"You have been working on that joke for a while?" Evie was unimpressed.

"Better keep my day job, huh?" I asked.

"If you had a job that is,"

"How dare you," I joked. "I'm working as a private investigator this winter break."

"Can't argue with that," Evie said.

"Waters & Somerset. What we lack in experience we make up for in doggedness."

"Perfect!"

We stared at each other, but there would be no more kiss. That would have to wait.

Evie continued. "The Always Right website, or as you called it, Always Wrong, was launched in 2001. The company got off to an up and down start. It had much more traffic than your typical new website, but it didn't have anywhere near the numbers that it would enjoy later. In 2001 and 2002, it wasn't even in the top 10,000 most popular websites in the United States. In 2003, it was the 6,642nd most popular website in the U.S. according to the website Alexa, which keeps track of this stuff. In 2004, it was 4,128th, and in 2005, it was 2,871th. It was trending upward, but certainly not a household name yet. That changed in 2006."

"What happened?" I asked.

"In February of 2006, Dick Cheney shot his friend while quail hunting."

"I know about it. So what's it have to do with Doss's website?"

"Always Right started a daily poll where readers could pick a Democratic politician that they wished had gone quail hunting with Dick Cheney instead. The site made it clear that the man wasn't killed, and tried to make it a playful game, but it created a firestorm. It was one of the first times that people said the internet had crossed the line in politics, with the public choosing a politician they wish had been shot. It was considered beyond the pale at the time. While many standard media companies crushed Always Right for the poll they were conducting, the site's readership went through the roof. They had their best month in readership for five consecutive months after launching the contest. They ended 2006 as the 88th most popular website in the United States, and they have only become more popular since. They are currently the third biggest conservative news site in the U.S. behind only Fox News and Breitbart."

"This company is a monster!" I said. "Anything else?"

"Doss launched the site in New York, but in the mid 2000's, the company officially relocated to Washington D.C.," Evie said.

"I'm not surprised. Although I find it funny that all these conservative companies that rage against the left and the blue states, almost inevitably are based out of New York, California, or D.C."

"If you can't beat them, join 'em," Evie said.

"Are you sure they aren't beating them? Look who is in office." I said.

"Let's not talk about that man," Evie said.

I agreed and changed the subject.

"We need to come up with a good reason why this Patricia Page will be willing to give us Darby's photo album. I've thought of a few ideas. Let me know what you think."

"Shoot."

"We could be from Vermont and have an emerging maple syrup conglomerate."

"Wedding Crashers! Very nice."

Evie seemed to get all my cheesy pop culture references.

"Okay, this one's for real. Our father was Darby's cellmate last year, and he is picking up Darby from jail in three days, so he sent us to go pick up his stuff."

"Not bad, but are we sure that Patricia Page hasn't talked to Darby Bowles and might know that's bullshit?"

"It's doubtful. Owen wrote that she was dating someone else and that was five years ago. I can't imagine they still talk."

"You're probably right. That one sounds promising. What's next?"

"I could say I work for the jail, and Mr. Bowles asked that we come to Ms. Page's house and pick up his photo album. I brought a suit just in case, and I'd try to look a little bit older."

"I don't like it. She could keep you there and call the jail and ask if this is standard protocol. Doesn't sound too legit. Plus, that wouldn't include me and you know I'm in this 100%," Evie said.

"It wasn't my favorite either. I've got one more. We work for a sort of halfway house, and we are taking all of Mr. Bowles properties there since he's going to live with us for a bit. Since he killed people while driving drunk, I think it sounds legit."

"Don't like that one either. We are only 21 years old, and I'm not sure we are going to pass as employees of a jail or a halfway house. You can barely grow a beard!"

"How dare you," I said, laughing just the same.

"Saying we are the children of an inmate makes more sense with our age. I think we can sound pathetic enough to have her hand it over. We can say our Dad isn't a great father and sends us on these fool's errands sometimes. We'll have her eating out of our hand."

"It's settled then," I said. "We are going to be playing brother and sister. What are our names going to be?"

"Gina and Matt Meyer."

"Your neighbors in Oakland. Good thinking cause it's easy to remember, but I don't want to use anyone's real names. Just in case, you know?"

Evie nodded. "Yeah, I guess you're right. Why don't you pick the names."

I just said the first thing that came into my head. "Jane and James Simpson."

"The Simpsons…" Evie said, trying to sound like the voiceover from the T.V. show.

Ukiah was a small, rural, slow moving town located on Interstate 101 halfway between Oakland and Eureka. It was known for producing wine and, like Eureka, having some of the biggest redwoods around. Despite its proximity to the San Francisco Bay Area, it felt completely different. The locals, for the most part, weren't involved in the rat race and valued the slow lane in life, something that was often lost in the hustle bustle of the Bay Area.

Evie and I decided to get some lunch and map out our plan before we headed to Ms. Page's house. We found a Chinese restaurant named Anna's Bistro and I ordered a chicken fried rice while Evie was fine with just a small order of spring rolls. Neither one of us mentioned the kiss that had happened on the drive up.

The petite, older Chinese woman brought our food to the corner table and walked back behind the register. There was only one other couple in the whole place, but I still kept my voice down.

"We'll approach the house, and I'll introduce us as James and Jane Simpson. We live in Eureka at our parent's house and were sent down here by our father who was too busy to make the trip himself. I'll say that our father, Harry, was Mr. Bowles's cellmate last year and they became good friends. Our father agreed to put him up when he gets out. That should hopefully bring us a little gratitude from Ms. Page."

"Wow, you are good at this," Evie said. "A little too good. She may start asking questions, so you need to have an answer for most things. How long was our Dad in for? What did he do to get imprisoned? How old are we? Things like that."

"I was thinking about that on the way up. Our Dad was also in for a DUI that killed someone. I'm 21, and you are 19. I even researched Eureka for an hour last night in case she starts asking me questions about growing up there. The mall is the Bayshore Mall, and they have the oldest zoo in California, the Sequoia Park Zoo. I also have a fake address that we live at, and it's the opposite side of town from where she last lived. The less questions, the better."

"Wow, you really are prepared."

"Probably better if I do most of the talking. Remember, I can do this myself if you want," I said.

"No," Evie said quickly. "I'm part of this."

She took out her phone and googled something. "Did you know Eureka, CA has hundreds of significant Victorian Homes, and the city has retained its original 19th-century commercial core as a national recognized Old Town Historic District."

I smiled. "Okay, Miss Wikipedia, you can join me. Just let me do most of the talking."

"Yes, sir," Evie said.

"Hopefully she will be there, but if something comes up, we should be ready to stay up here if necessary. No reason to drive back and forth from Oakland."

"Sounds good. So when do we go?"

"Right after I finish demolishing this Chicken Fried Rice."

I reached my fork down, grabbing a huge scoop and bringing it up to my mouth.

Patricia Page's address was 184 West Clay street, a stone's throw from South State street, one of the busiest streets in town.

I approached the address and passed by it. I went up a block and pulled over.

"What are you doing? It was back there," Evie said.

"All things being equal, I'd rather she doesn't have access to my license plate number."

"You've thought of everything."

"I think I 'm just taking this a little more seriously than you. This isn't a game, Evie."

"I know. I'm just enjoying the cat and mouse of it."

"We haven't even started that part yet. But we are about to. You ready?"

"I am."

"Alright, put your game face on, Jane Simpson."

She smiled and then leaned in and hugged me.

"Glad you didn't kiss me again," I said. "Not sure that would look believable seeing that we are brother and sister."

Evie laughed.

"Alright, time to get serious," I said.

We put our game faces on and walked down the street, ringing the doorbell at 184 West Clay Street.

I didn't hear anyone approaching for a few seconds, so I pressed the doorbell a second and then third time. Finally, I heard someone walking, or what sounded more like waddling, towards the direction of the door.

The woman who opened the front door and then the screen looked to be about 50 but was probably more likely in her mid-thirties. She looked like someone who life had beaten up, and had entered older middle age way earlier than she should have. She was too heavy, and her frame looked like it struggled to carry all the weight. Her face was still pretty, but you could tell that was going too. She scanned over Evie and me, not sure what to make of the two young people standing on her doorstep.

"Can I help you?" she asked.

"Hi, Ms. Page, my name is James Simpson, and this is my sister Jane," I said, and immediately realized the names sounded ridiculous.

Luckily, Ms. Page didn't seem to notice. She didn't look to be a very insightful woman, and unlike us, she wasn't trying to solve a puzzle.

I continued. "Our father was the cellmate of Darby Cash Bowles last year, and we were sent here to pick something up."

"I'm not quite sure I follow," she said. She was still holding the screen door open, not sure what to do.

"Could we come in?" I asked.

She paused for a moment, but it didn't last long. "Sure, come on in." She smiled, showing she was a few teeth short of a full set.

Patricia Page opened the screen door, and she motioned us to sit on a couch. A couch is being generous. This thing looked more like a trash receptacle with all the garbage on it.

"I'd offer you coffee or something, but I don't get visitors much. I don't have anything made."

"We're fine," I said.

Evie hadn't said anything yet, and I thought it was smart of her. The less talking, the better. Let's try to get in and out as quickly as we can.

"So I don't know if you heard, but Mr. Bowles gets out of jail in a few days. Our father had become pretty friendly with him before he was released, and when he heard Mr. Bowles was getting out, he offered to put him up until he gets back on his feet. Mr. Bowles took him up on the offer and asked my father to go get a few things he had left at different friends' houses. He had mentioned that he left a photo album with you."

Patricia Page looked on, but I still wasn't sure she was processing everything. "So why isn't your Dad here?" she asked.

Evie/Jane thought it was time to jump in. "He sends my brother and me out on missions like this sometimes. James and I will do anything to get out of the house," she said sadly. It was pathetic, and Ms. Page ate it up.

"Not the best home life?" she asked.

"No, it's not. I'll leave it at that." Evie/Jane played her role perfectly.

"I'm sorry kids. I know a little about shitty home lives," Ms. Page said. I knew we had her.

"So do you still have a photo album that Mr. Bowles gave you years ago? I know it's random, but it must have meant something to him since he asked my father to get it."

We paused as we waited for the answer. This was our first big moment.

"I wouldn't call it an album, but yeah, I got it."

I gave myself an internal fist bump.

"What do you mean it's not an album?" I asked.

"Well, it's an album I guess, but there are only a few pictures. And none of them are of Darby. Never quite sure why he kept the damn thing, but when he was arrested and all, I held on to it. Not my place to go tossing things away."

Good for you, Ms. Page. She started walking towards a room, but turned around and paused.

"You know, Darby was the love of my life. You tell him that. We were going to have a child together, but then he went and wrecked his life. And mine. I found a new boyfriend, had a few children, so Darby and I stopped talking. My babies' Dad was a real scumbag, and the state ended out taking our children. I think Darby and I could have done way better. You tell him that too."

"I will, Ms. Page," I said. It was heartbreaking.

"The saddest part of all is that the night he killed those kids, he was out celebrating the pregnancy of a good friend of ours. And then because of what happened, we never got to get pregnant ourselves."

Ms. Page started to tear up and wiped her eyes with her sleeve. "Let me go get that album," she said.

She went into one of the back rooms and Evie looked over at me, sadness written all over her face. Patricia Page returned a few minutes later, with a small photo album made of cheap leather that could only fit 4 x 6 photographs.

"Here it is," she said.

She started to hand it to me but instead flipped to the middle of the album where the three pictures were. The pictures showed two men walking across a little lawn in the direction of a car. One man was at least four inches taller than the other, and probably 50 pounds heavier. The other man had a slight build and was prematurely graying.

Evie and I looked at each other. We couldn't be sure, but it looked very much like a younger Howie Doss.

Darby had put an Oklahoma City newspaper in the foreground with the date February 28th, 2001 clearly visible. It was a very smart thing to do. I think the intelligence was lost on Patricia Page, however. She never mentioned the clearly visible newspaper.

"See what I'm saying," Ms. Page said. "The pictures ain't even Darby."

"Well, they must mean something to him," Evie/Jane said.

Patricia Page was tired of talking about Darby. "So how is Eureka? Same dump as it used to be?"

"It's home, "I said. "But you can only hang out at the Bayshore Mall so much."

Patricia Page laughed. "I remember the Bayshore. Probably the one nice thing in Eureka. And it ain't that nice."

"What about the Sequoia Park Zoo?" Now I was just showing off.

"Never did get to see that. Tell you what, I did actually enjoy my time in Eureka, but mainly because of Darby. Once it happened, there were only bad memories."

She didn't have to specify what "it" was.

"Thanks for everything Ms. Page. We should probably get going. We've got to drive back to Eureka right now," I said.

She opened the door for us and let us out.

"How did you guys know where I lived? Last I talked to Darby I was still living in Eureka."

"We're kids, Ms. Page. We just Google things to find out information."

Patricia Page smiled, but it was more a resignation than anything. She was still a young woman, but the world had already passed her by.

"I really should get better at the whole internet thing," she said.

Somehow, I guessed that wasn't going to happen. We thanked Ms. Page for her time and walked back up the street to our car. Evie and I didn't have to say anything. We were both happy to have been given the album but were sad for what a pathetic life Patricia Page was living.

The trip back to Oakland was exciting. We started to forget about the sadness that was Patricia Page and realized that we had our first real piece of evidence. This was no longer just a research paper; we were out collecting information, like real detectives.

We vowed to both look at the final words of Uncle Owen when we got back to Oakland. There was no need for me to read it first anymore. Evie and I were both equally involved. We were a team.

Waters & Somerset.

When we were five minutes away from Oakland, I tried to get down to business. Yes, the other type of business.

"You told your parents you might be gone all day, right?"

"Yup," Evie said.

"Why don't you come stay over tonight?"

"Yeah, that's a possibility I guess. To work on the case, right?"

She wasn't going to make this easy.

"Of course," I said. "Why else?"

She leaned over, and just like on our drive there, Evie kissed me on the lips. I was relieved to know it hadn't just been an impulsive thing. It was at that moment that I knew I was going to make love to Evie Somerset, something I had dreamt about it since I was 17 years old.

When I fell off the lounge chair in front of Evie and her mother, I thought my chance would never come to pass. And here we were, four years later, and it was going to happen. I wanted to release the biggest smile the world had ever seen, but Evie was sitting next to me, and I had to play it cool.

I arrived home at my mother's house, and we walked in. There was a letter pinned to the wall right as you walked in. You couldn't miss it.

It was from Fiona and read, "*Let me guess, you and Evie went somewhere together? Well, have fun tonight because I'm staying over at Addison's.*"

Addison Chrome had been Fiona's best friend since they were little kids. I was delighted to hear that she was going to be gone. I think I knew why.

"Your sister is a little matchmaker, isn't she," Evie said, echoing my suspicions.

I grabbed Evie's hand and led her down the hall to my room. I sat on my bed and looked at Uncle Owen's book laying next to me. I knew it could be a distraction and I was hoping it didn't ruin the moment.

Evie wasn't going to let that happen.

She walked over towards me, grabbed the book, and threw it in the general direction of my closet.

"Uncle Owen and his novel can wait," Evie said.

I grabbed her hand and lowered her down to the bed. I cupped her head and kissed her for a good 10 seconds. This was my first true kiss with Evie Somerset. Four years ago, I had leaned in for the infamous kiss that led me to falling off my lounge chair and into the water. Then there were the two earlier today, hardly true kisses as I was concentrating on the road.

This was a real kiss though, and a wonderful one at that. Evie had put on a tough front lately, trying to show she could get over the terrible experience she had endured. But beneath the exterior, Evie was still very feminine, and that showed as she kissed me delicately.

There are many different types of kisses, and I was fine keeping them soft and delicate. I knew not to rush things and played off the beautiful woman across from me.

Our lips stayed locked for several minutes, me consciously letting her decide when and how it would proceed. She went for my shirt and started taking it off, and then set her hand near my groin. She had made her inclinations obvious, and I started taking off her clothes as well.

"Please be gentle," she said.

I had every intention of doing just that.

We finished taking each other's clothes off, and she gently glided me inside her. I'm not going to say it was groundbreaking sex, but for what it was, and with her recent travails, it was perfect. I was gentle, tender, and everything she wanted me to be. I knew we'd have plenty of time to be more lustful in the future, but this wasn't the time.

She rolled over when we were done, and I saw her flush cheeks smiling before her teeth even showed themselves. I figured I had done it right.

"That was perfect," she said.

I didn't want to screw up the moment, so I just replied, "Thanks. You were great too."

She put her head on my right shoulder, which meant both of us were looking in the direction of where she had thrown Uncle Owen's book. Neither one of us said anything, but we were both thinking it.

We could have just enjoyed lying in each other's arms for the rest of the night, but the book being in our line of sight made that impossible. It's almost like it was calling to us.

After an uncomfortable minute, I said, "Should we get it over with?"

"Yes," Evie said.

I grabbed the novel and opened it to the last few pages of Uncle Owen's writing.

"First off, I'd like to congratulate you on getting this far, sport. I'm sure it hasn't been easy keeping all these secrets to yourself."

I was reading Uncle Owen's writing out loud and looked over at Evie as I read it.

"I'm going to assume you now have researched Oklahoma City in and around 2000 and 2001, Darby Cash Bowles, Howie Doss, and alwaysright.com. Also, hopefully, you have a few pictures in your possession. OK, I guess you deserve an explanation of how this all came about. It started with a little joyride I took in Eureka, CA a few years back. I led the cops on a high-speed chase, and it landed me in the Susanville prison. My cellmate was none other than Darby Cash Bowles. What a name, right? Apparently, his Dad wanted to give him a female name like in the Johnny Cash song "A Boy named Sue" so that's how he was stuck with Darby. It's also why his middle name is Cash. His Dad sounded like a bit of a wacko. Anyway, Darby and I became friendly pretty quick. He's made a lot of mistakes in his life, but he's an alright guy. And in jail, having friends can help, but I digress. Things changed one day when we randomly walked into the communal T.V. area, and Darby heard a voice he recognized from his past. I'll get back to that. A few weeks after he heard this voice, he opened

up to me and told me everything. Darby grew up in Oklahoma City and lived in the city or in the local jails until he headed to Eureka in his mid-20's. His Dad had died when he was really young, so he fell in with the wrong people and was in foster homes or Juvie as a kid. That became jail when he turned 18. During his last of several stints in jails around Oklahoma City, he met someone who offered him a job when he got out. He took it and worked as a getaway driver for several months. He said they were mostly home invasions and bank robberies, but then things changed."

I was still reading aloud. I looked over at Evie, and I could tell that she was getting a little tense. That made two of us. I turned the page.

"The second to last job he ever did was painting swastikas on some churches, a synagogue, and a mosque. Then things got really out of hand. He was the getaway driver in the murder of the black woman and Hispanic man in Oklahoma City in February of 2001 that you have surely read about. He was being chased by the cops, and he came up with the idea of intentionally crashing the car in order to get away. Quite brilliant, actually. He was able to evade the police, while the other three people in the car either died on impact or were killed by the cops who responded to the crash. Now, back to the voice Darby heard on the T.V. He swears that the voice he heard was the same man who ordered all of the crimes in Oklahoma City. He only met him once, and he was blindfolded, but he said he would recognize the voice anywhere. I've heard the guy talk, and his voice is pretty unmistakable. You have probably guessed it by now, but the man that Darby heard on the T.V. was Howie Doss, the founder of alwaysright.com. The website is a monster, and if Darby was right about his identity, he felt he could blackmail Howie Doss for millions of dollars. I imagine he is right. Darby doesn't get out of jail for five years, so he decided to include me in on his plan. If you waited the two years I asked you to, Darby still has three years left in jail. He outlined how everything was going to go down, and I was going to be his point man on the outside, but as you know, I was given a terminal cancer diagnosis."

I turned the page.

"You are probably wondering why I told you to wait a few years. First off, at 16 you are not ready for something like this. I doubt you will be at 18 either, but at least you will technically be a man at this point. I made you promise to read to Chapter Five because if you just opened the book and saw my writing immediately, Sally may well have seen it, or you would have been tempted to tell her. I had to ensure that didn't happen, so I made you read four chapters of this terrible book before you got to the good stuff. The book really is bad, isn't it? Sorry, I had to put you through that, but this is the only book I have in this godforsaken hospital room. I don't even know how it got here, but it really doesn't matter. You may also be wondering why I didn't just give all this information to another adult, but I think you know the answer to that. Your family is going to struggle financially without your father. When you read this, I'd be surprised if you still own the place in the suburbs. So I'm giving you the chance to get rich again. But if you do go forward with blackmailing this guy, just know that you are entering a dangerous world. Howie Doss is a very important man now, and I doubt he would take kindly to blackmail. Tread lightly, sport."

I turned the page again.

"Once your father died, I knew when I got out of jail, I'd come down and see you guys immediately. I was supposed to go and get the photo album from Patricia Page, but I postponed it. As usual, I fucked up. Never was great at this thing called life, and now I'll be dying young to boot. Sorry sport, just a brief moment of feeling sorry for myself. Anyway, I never saw the pictures, but Darby says there are three of Howie Doss in and around Oklahoma City in the days that followed the murders. And for your final piece of information, turn the page!"

I turned the page for a final time, and there was a piece of paper that was taped to the next page. It prevented the paper from falling out if someone shook the book or was leafing through it. Above it, Owen had written his last sentence. "Darby sent this to me when I got out of jail. He arranged to have a letter notarized and then sent it down to me."

I opened the paper. It had been notarized by a law firm named Bollinger & Yearn, based out of Eureka, CA.

"I, Darby Cash Bowles, am 100% certain that Howie Doss is the man who ordered the infamous murders in Oklahoma City on February 26th, 2001. I only met him once and didn't see his face, but I would never forget his voice. I did, however, go back to the house where I met him and took pictures 2 days after the murders. The newspaper I am holding backs up the date.

I was the getaway driver for Charles Wade Leonard, Jared Wilder, and Elliot Walden on the day in question, and also participated in some home invasions, bank robberies, and the painting of the swastikas on multiple churches. I was scared for my life and took the pictures as a bargaining chip if it ever came to that. I can give a rundown of each of those men and even tell you the car that was used in the murders or any other information that you need. To summarize, Howie Doss, the owner of alwaysright.com, is the man who ordered the racially motivated killings in Oklahoma City in February of 2001."

I looked over at Evie, and we both just stared at each other, too scared to say anything.

The next few days were some of the weirder ones of my life. I had a beautiful girl who liked me, and because of my sister, we had the house to ourself. I should have spent 24 hours a day between the sheets with Evie. And we did spend a good amount of time doing just that. It wasn't pure bliss though, because we now had the full shadow of Howie Doss hanging over our heads.

I also didn't know if Evie really was falling for me or whether she was just trying to feel normal after Stuart Conley, but I didn't fight whatever it was. I figured I should just enjoy the ride.

"Well if Darby Bowles comes down here and kills us, I'm glad I'll be dying in your arms," Evie said to me, after sex the following night.

"That's not even funny, Evie," I said.

"Once Darby Bowles locates Patricia Page, don't you think he'll suspect it was you, with your connection to Uncle Owen? You said he mentioned you and Fiona to Bowles."

"Yeah, he did."

"Why don't we call Ms. Page and make up a story? We could say this was all going to be a surprise and ask her not to tell him."

"Wouldn't work," I said. "We told her that Darby asked us to go there. Can't backtrack on that now. He may well come down here, asking if Uncle Owen told us anything five years ago. But if he came down, under those circumstances, he would just be fishing. That's a lot different than if he knew we got the pictures from Patricia Page."

"Huge difference. How about we get ahold of him and tell him we will take Owen's role and ask for half?"

"You want to try and bribe Doss?"

"Of course not. I don't want a penny from that asshole." Evie said. "But if Darby looked at us as partners, maybe he wouldn't hurt us."

I was happy to hear Evie say she didn't want a penny of Doss's money. When Owen had first written that I could make life-changing money, it obviously had intrigued me. But now that I knew it would be coming from Howie Doss, the money no longer mattered. Like Evie, I wouldn't take a penny from the man. His website had proved he was a scumbag. We now likely had proof he was much worse than that.

"Darby may be sitting on millions of dollars, but he is sitting on something much bigger as well," I said.

"What do you mean?"

"Howie Doss is one of the most influential people in the world right now. Our president, the one you don't want to talk about, lives and dies by what Doss publishes. His readership is right up there with Fox News and Breitbart. If it was proven that Doss ordered the murders in Oklahoma City, it would be one of the biggest stories this country has ever seen."

"You really think it's that big?"

"Bigger," I said. "A lot of people think Doss is, with the exception of the President, the most powerful man in Washington D.C. I just read that he had a one on one meeting with the President at the White House last weekend. Media types don't get those types of meetings. But Howie Doss does."

"So what does this mean big picture? Do you want to go to the media? The cops?"

"That's a long way off. We don't even know if Darby Bowles told Uncle Owen the truth. He could be some crackpot just trying to get attention."

"Is that what you think?" Evie asked.

"No. My gut tells me there is something here. I'd like to talk to Darby Bowles to get an impression of him. See if he seems honest or if he's just some guy out to make trouble."

"But we can't exactly just wait for him outside of jail."

"Nope. He might try to kill us."

"You don't really think that, do you?" Evie asked.

"We're talking millions of dollars in bribe money and one of the biggest stories in decades. Yes, I think people would kill for this."

"So, what do we do?"

"We spend the next two days reading up on Howie Doss, Always Right, and Darby Cash Bowles. Let's see if we can find a connection that's a little more concrete than recognizing someone's voice or some pictures from 16 years ago. Nothing much is going to happen until Bowles gets out of jail, so let's be prepared for when he does."

"Okay, Frankie."

Evie leaned her body into mine. It wasn't a move to instigate love making, it was one saying she wanted to be protected.

23

Darby Cash Bowles walked out the Susanville prison on December 21st but didn't throw the bird at the gates this time. He was now a mature man of 42 and knew he had to own up to all of his shortcomings. It had been his fault that those two young people had died in Eureka. It was time to stop hating the world and blaming others for his mistakes.

Darby may have been more reflective, but that doesn't mean he was a relaxed individual. Howie Doss was on his mind at all times.

He had spent seven years in jail, and the last five mapping out what he was going to do when he was released. He had planned it so many times in his head, he had no doubt it would be successful. He was already imagining himself on a Caribbean island beach with an umbrella drink in his hand. A beautiful, tanned, island girl was always lying next to him.

Billy Gullicksen knew Darby was getting out of jail and had agreed to pick him up, despite the fact that Susanville was five hours from Eureka.

They had talked periodically over the years, but Billy made it to see Darby less and less as time went by. Over the last three years, he had only visited twice. It was a meeting that they had both come to dislike, for different reasons. Billy knowing full well that his wife's pregnancy had been the reason for the excessive drinking on the night in question. Darby hated the meetings because he'd have to see Billy, who had a nice wife and three children he would get to return to. Darby would be going back to his 6 foot by 8 foot prison cell.

Still, Billy was there waiting for his old friend as Darby walked out of jail a free man. He gave him a big hug, but both of them knew things were never going to return to how they used to be.

"What do you want to do Darby? Anything you want?"

"I want to go see Patricia."

This was not the answer that Billy was expecting.

"Gotta say, I'm a little surprised by that. Do you know she moved to Ukiah?"

"I didn't know that. Haven't thought about her in a long time though."

"And yet, that's the first person you want to see?" Billy was sure he was missing something.

"She has something of mine that's very important."

"It's been a long time, Darby. Are you sure she still has it?"

"Only one way to find out."

"And you'd rather do that than go get laid or," Billy was going to say get a beer but stopped himself short. Darby knew what he had intended to say.

"Exactly," Darby said.

"Sorry," Billy said.

"I've told you every time I've seen you, it's not your fault. I was a grown man and made my own decision."

"Thanks," Billy said. It meant a lot to hear him say it.

"So how do we get ahold of Patricia?" Darby asked.

"I think Tina still has her number. We'll drive back to Eureka and call her from there."

"Fine," Darby said. "But I need to see her soon. It's very important."

Billy had no idea what Patricia had, but he could tell that it was something that Darby needed. He knew he would help him out. Billy still felt guilty as shit about the night in question, despite Darby admitting his own culpability.

Billy felt like Darby was a walking contradiction. He had mellowed undoubtedly, but about going to see Patricia Page, he was as hard-headed as ever. Billy figured it was better not to ask any questions, and they headed off towards Eureka in silence.

They made the drive in four and a half hours, much quicker than expected. Tina was home, just like Billy knew she would be. They had bought a new house since Darby had last seen them, needing another room for the third child they had. It was in a more prosperous part of town, but it was still Eureka. It was a four bedroom, gray house that was inconspicuous and uninspired, but it was home to Billy's family, and that's what mattered.

He was still working as a longshoreman, and Tina had been a wonderful stay at home mother. She wasn't very pretty to begin with, and the years hadn't been kind to her waistline, but she was the mother of his children, and Billy still loved her very much.

Timmy was now 10 years old, Bridget was eight going on adulthood, and Ben was six and a half years old. Billy knew that Darby would probably have mixed emotions on meeting their youngest.

Billy's fears appeared unfounded as Darby went out of his way to greet all of the kids, and he saved the biggest hug of all for Ben. Billy looked at Darby and couldn't figure him out. He was obviously very tense, but he also seemed to have a childlike happiness to him that hadn't been there before he went to jail.

"They are adorable, Tina," Darby said. "Of course, I remember Timmy and Bridget, but they were just little kids back then. They are all grown up now."

"You look good Darby," Tina said, and Darby could tell she meant it.

"Hard to get fat on the crap they serve you in there."

Tina shrugged. "I'm sure."

Darby was happy to see Billy, Tina, and the kids but there was something that took priority.

"I wanted to call Patricia. Billy said that you have her number."

"I do. A heads up though Darby, she's had a rough time since you went in. She had two kids, but the guy was a real piece of work. He was a deadbeat dad, and she wasn't much better. Child protective services were called and took their kids away. She recently moved to Ukiah, living but not really living. If you know what I mean."

"I know what you mean. You just described jail."

Tina gave Darby a pat on the shoulder. "Let me get that number."

Tina retrieved the number and Darby went outside to call the woman who was supposed to be the mother of his first child. Of course, that never came to be. He dialed the number and waited five rings until a voice he barely recognized picked up.

"Hello?"

"Hi Patricia, do you know who this is?"

There was a long pause. "Oh my God. Darby, how are you?"

"After the hell I've been through over the last seven years, I'm surprisingly good. How about you?"

"I'm thinking the last seven years may have been tougher on me than on you," Patricia sadly said.

Darby wasn't even sure if he would have recognized Patricia's voice if he didn't know it was her. She sounded old, resigned to her fate.

"Listen, Patricia, I'd love to come down there and see you soon, but I need to ask you a question first."

"What is it?"

Darby thought that Patricia sounded nervous.

"Did you save that photo album that I had at our apartment in Old Town Eureka?"

"Oh shit."

"What is it, Patricia?"

"You don't know about the kids?"

"What kids?" Darby asked.

Darby heard some heavy whimpering coming from the other end. Darby imagined a wounded hyena. It was a terrible way to think of his ex-girlfriend, but that's the visual that came to mind.

"Patricia! Get ahold of yourself."

"Some kids came and picked it up a few days ago. They said they were the son and daughter of your cellmate."

Darby's last several inmates had been in their 20's. Before that it was Owen, and he didn't have any children.

"How old were they?" Darby asked.

After a few more muffled cries, Patricia managed to compose herself. "You know I loved you. I think we could have had a great life together."

This wasn't what Darby had in mind. He had to get Patricia back on track. "We would have, honey. It was my fault, don't blame yourself."

The intentional use of the word honey seemed to work. Patricia answered Darby's previous question.

"Early 20's I'd guess."

"And you gave it to them?"

"I'm so sorry, Darby. They said they were picking it up for you."

"It's alright. I know you wouldn't do anything to hurt me. I'm going to call you later, honey."

"I'm so sorry, Darby."

Billy walked out just as Darby hung up the phone.

"Let's get you some more time with the kids," Billy said. "They'll be calling you Uncle Darby before you know it."

Of fucking course!! The proverbial light bulb went on in Darby's mind. It had to have been Owen Harding's friends' kids. The ones who had taken to calling him, uncle. Darby remembered how highly Owen had thought of those kids. He must have told them about the photo album before he died from cancer.

But why would they have waited five years to go and get the photo album? Darby had no answer to that one.

"I'll be inside in one second," Darby said to Billy, not so subtly telling him he needed a little more alone time on the phone.

Billy walked inside the house, and Darby called Patricia back.

"Hello?"

"Patricia, it's me again. Listen, honey, can you tell me everything you remember about them."

"Like I said, they were probably college age. The boy was handsome, and the girl was very attractive. They were brother and sister, and they said their Dad had been your cellmate."

Wow, they were pretty honest for the most part, Darby thought.

"OK, thanks. Stay close to the phone the next few days."

Darby hung up before waiting for a response. What were those kids' names? Owen talked about them all the time. Darby racked his brain until he got it. *Frankie and Fiona Waters.*

"I think it's time I come and pay you a visit, Frankie and Fiona," Darby said to himself.

24

I was starting to think I was going to meet Darby Bowles sooner rather than later.

Evie had called Patricia Page under the guise of thanking her, and Ms. Page had told Evie within seconds that she had told Darby Bowles about their visit. It didn't appear Ms. Page could keep a secret to save her life.

It was time that Evie and I had a serious conversation. A convicted felon was possibly headed down to Oakland with millions of dollars dangling in front of his eyes. I didn't imagine he'd be treating us with kids' gloves.

We had to decide what to do. And fast.

With the return of my mother, everything was getting more complicated. We couldn't just sit in my room and discuss the case all day like we had the last three days. Okay, maybe that's not all we did in my room, but you get the point. I didn't want to talk at Peet's either. This was not anything that was meant for other people's ears.

I texted Evie and told her I was picking her up, and we were going to find somewhere to park. We could talk then.

I picked her up, and we drove further up into the Oakland Hills, far above where her parents lived. You could see San Francisco and the blue of the Pacific Ocean beyond that. When I was in high school, the spot was somewhat of a lover's lane late on weekend nights. I had been there three times. Twice I had struck out, and once I ended out making out with Gillian Rhodes. Batting .333 was good in baseball, but it was pretty pathetic for Lover's Lane.

Evie Somerset blew the other three girls out of the water, but that's not why we were there. We needed to talk about our next move. This was all coming on so fast, and although I was a smart, mature 21-year-old, I knew we were slowly getting in too deep.

I shut off the engine, and we looked out upon San Francisco.

"Quite a view," Evie said.

"My favorite in the Bay Area."

"I see why."

"Let's discuss our options," I said.

"Let's do it!" she said.

Her response was too enthusiastic. She wasn't still enjoying this, was she?

"As I see it, we have three options," I said. "The logical and most sensible is to go to the police right now. They will likely stake out my mother's house, and we won't have to deal with Darby Bowles ourselves. Our families will probably disown us, and I doubt they will want us seeing each other anymore, but it's the only way we guarantee our safety. And our families. Second, we try to join forces with Darby Bowles. Hardly an ideal option. I don't want to be running around with a guy responsible, in one form or another, for several people's deaths. The third and final option, and the one I like best, is agreeing to meet with Darby Cash Bowles and giving him the pictures back. We can tell him we are out and we don't care what the hell he does from here on in. After all, this was his gig to start with, and as long as he leaves our families out of it, I'm happy."

"And you think he's just going to let us go?" Evie said.

"We don't have to tell him how much we know. We just claim that Uncle Owen told us to go pick up a photo album years ago, and we finally got around to doing so."

"You think he's going to buy that bullshit?"

"It's partly true. When I started reading his novel, I had no idea Darby Bowles was getting out of jail soon."

"I don't think he's going to buy it. And like you said, he has so much at stake, I don't know if he's going to want to leave two 21-year-old kids around to potentially fuck everything up."

"I get all that Evie, but what's our option? To roll around with him, collecting information? Two 21-year-olds and a dangerous felon." I said

"Your Uncle Owen said he was a good guy."

"Not exactly. He said he was a bad guy with a decent heart somewhere down there. After all, he is partly responsible for at least seven deaths."

"That's not quite fair. The DUI, yes. But he didn't order the death of those people in Oklahoma City, and he helped kill the murderers. That's more a hero than a villain to me. And, if we are really talking about millions of dollars I'm sure he'd include us."

"I don't care about the fucking money," I said, making my opinion abundantly clear.

"Nor do I," Evie said. "I told you that. But I wouldn't mind being a part of taking down Howie Doss, assuming this is all true. He ordered the murder of two innocent civilians strictly because of the color of their skin. Doesn't that bother you?"

"Of course it does, Evie. I'd love to nail Doss too, but not at the expense of the safety of you or my family."

"I want to go after Howie Doss. You have explained to me just how powerful this guy is. Do you know how many of his articles are fake news? How he destroys the marriages and families of people he doesn't like? He's the scourge of good, honest people everywhere and if I can help bring him down than that makes this all worth it. I should show you some of the articles about how he treats women politicians. Just disgusting."

"I agree he is a terrible man. I just don't want these people showing up on our doorsteps," I said. "I just thought of a fourth option."

"Let's hear it."

"We go to the press. Or better yet, to that Congresswoman you worked for. Get the story out there and let the real detectives and reporters see where it leads. If there's something there on Doss, they will find it."

"That's probably your best idea yet Frankie, but I still don't like it. We stumbled on this story, and I want to follow it a little longer. Plus, we really don't even know if any of this is true yet. Let's meet with Darby and make sure he's not some crackpot, and there's actually some teeth to this thing. It will be a public place, and we'll make sure it's safe."

She made a convincing argument.

"Well if that's what we are going to do, I want you to call Patricia Page back right now. I want to meet Darby before he comes down here and knocks on my mother's door. If that happens, I'm calling the cops right away."

"That's fair. We are sitting on something huge, Frankie. I don't want to just give it up."

I hated to admit it, but I agreed. I had been playing devil's advocate, but deep down, I didn't want to give up just yet. The allure of going after Howie Doss was on my mind.

"Call Ms. Page," I said.

"I'll call her right now," Evie said, excited I had come around.

A voice on the other end answered, but all I could hear was Evie. "Hi, Ms. Page, it's me again…..we need you to pass along a message….I'm sorry we put you in a bad spot……we just want you to call Mr. Bowles and have him call us……then call Tina, whoever that is…..he can call us at (925) 702-2331…..thank you Ms. Page."

"My number?" I said.

"Would you rather I gave your mother's home line?"

"Of course not. Now let's hope he calls back and isn't already on his way down here."

On that, we could both agree.

We sat at Lover's Lane for another hour but didn't get a call-back, so we decided to head down to our favorite coffee shop and get our usuals. A little jolt of caffeine would do us some good.

Our favorite table was taken, and we had to sit at a community table, which turned out to be a blessing. It forced us to partake in trivial conversation since we couldn't talk about what was really on our minds in front of others. It was nice, and we remembered, if only for a minute, that we were still only 21 years old. Pop culture, the Golden State Warriors, LCD Soundsystem, and our upcoming Christmas plans were all topics of conversation.

We even broached the subject of what was going to happen when winter break ended. That conversation ended before it began, as we realized we didn't want to talk about what we had become personally. It was more than a fling, and we both knew that, but we weren't sure if it was something sustainable with us on different coasts. It was a conversation altogether suited for a different time.

We were joined by a great couple who engaged us in conversation immediately. Their names were Bryce and Elise Connor, and they had been married for two years. He was probably in his mid-30's, and if I had to guess, she was approaching 30. They had a beautiful child and seemed a genuinely happy couple. Elise was from Paris and had the most beautiful accent you could imagine.

They lived in New York and were back visiting Bryce's parents. Bryce was a writer and had just published his first book.

"What's it about?" I asked.

"It's about a little adventure that Elise and I ended up on a few years back. It started as a series of articles in the New Yorker," Bryce said. He talked in the matter of fact way of someone who was confident in his own skin. "Eventually, they became quite popular, so a publisher came to me about putting it in novel form."

"What type of adventure?"

"You wouldn't believe it if I told you," he said. "Being chased by killers across Europe and in New York. We were lucky to get out alive."

He leaned over and kissed Elise. I could tell that Evie really liked this couple as well, but the irony wasn't lost on her. She seemed to want to change the subject from the notion of being chased around by killers.

"So what's the baby's name?" Evie asked.

"Hugo Leroy Connor," Elise answered. "He's named after a French guy we met in Normandy and a black guy who helped save our life in New York."

"I was going to say, it's quite the eccentric name," I said.

Bryce laughed.

"Yeah, we almost went with Leroy Hugo Conner, but we thought he might have an identity crisis," he said.

Everyone laughed this time.

"Well, he's absolutely precious!" Evie said.

She started tickling Hugo Leroy under the chin, and the baby responded with a huge smile and a great laugh. Bryce reached into a beautiful leather satchel that he had and handed me a novel. "Love in Paris, Death in New York" was the name of it, and it had pictures of the Eiffel Tower and the Statue of Liberty on the cover.

"Here's a copy of my book."

"Thank you so much. How much do I owe you?" We all knew it was a gift but figured I'd still offer.

"Nice try, Frankie. This one is on me."

Bryce and Elise started to get up.

"You guys have to go?" Evie asked, although it sounded more like a plea to stay.

Bryce took this one. "My parents get mad if we keep the little one from them for too long."

"I don't blame them. He's a charmer," Evie said.

We got up to exchange handshakes and hugs. Bryce had turned around to leave when Evie asked him one last question.

"What would be your advice to someone who had gotten themselves in a bad situation with the wrong people?"

Bryce looked at her, not sure of what to make of the question. There was a brief pause as Bryce considered the question.

Evie let out a huge laugh.

"Because I have gotten myself in a situation with this guy named Frankie and I just don't know how to get out of it…"

Bryce and Elise started laughing.

"You had Bryce scared there for a moment," Elise said.

"Just pulling you guys' legs."

This time we did say our goodbyes. Bryce slipped me his business card. Bryce and Elise had left a great impression on us. With their great attitude and that adorable baby, I knew they had a great life ahead of them.

When they left, I turned to Evie. "What was that all about?"

"It sounded like they were in a pretty precarious situation once, and thought maybe they could help us."

"What changed your mind?" I asked.

"I didn't think it was right to get anyone else involved. That includes Fiona, your mother, and my parents. This is our problem, and we should figure this out together. Just us two."

I hugged Evie and then kissed her. "I agree," I said.

And then my phone rang.

25

"I think you have something of mine," the voice from the other end said.

Darby Cash Bowles sounded pissed off.

We were still in Peet's Coffee, and that wasn't going to work. "Call me back in two minutes, please. I'm in a public place."

For some reason, this phrase hit me like a ton of bricks. I'm in a public place? What the hell had happened over the last several days? I was starting to sound like a spy out of a World War II novel.

Evie could tell I was a little shaken, and she patted my shoulder as we walked outside.

"Are you alright?" she asked.

"I'm fine. I just don't want to talk to him in here. Let's go to the car."

We walked to the car and got in. Another car hovered behind me, waiting to pull in, but I gave him a wave of the hand, alerting him that I wasn't leaving. He sped off.

The phone rang.

"Thanks for calling back. I figure this is a conversation that is better kept between you and me."

"Your sister isn't there with you?" Darby asked.

I wasn't sure if he was referring to Fiona or the fictitious Jane Simpson, but I had to assume it was Fiona. After all, Uncle Owen had told him about us.

I thought it better to leave him in the dark about Evie. Maybe we could use his lack of knowledge to our advantage at a later date. Of course, that meant letting him think my sister was involved. Some choice.

"No, she's not part of this. She just went up to Ukiah and played a role for me."

"What a sister," he said sarcastically. "Regardless, she is part of this now. Keep that in mind when you decide how you want this to proceed."

"Don't threaten my sister!" I was furious. "If you threaten her again, I will burn everything we have and go straight to the cops."

I heard a deep breath on the other end of the phone. "I'm sorry. Now, what do you want?"

"To meet with you."

This seemed to take him by surprise. "When? Where?"

"Tomorrow. Some public place that I will decide on. It will be somewhere up near Ukiah or Eureka. I don't want you anywhere near my family."

I realized my mistake immediately. So did he.

"But I thought James and Jane Simpson lived in Eureka?" Darby asked sarcastically.

I didn't know how to react and didn't say a thing. Darby spoke again.

"If it makes you feel any better, I already figured out who it was. Owen had a big mouth sometimes. Or should I say, Uncle Owen?"

There was no point in denying it now.

"Do you want to meet or not?" I asked, changing the subject.

"Tomorrow? You do know tomorrow is Christmas Eve, right?"

So much had been going on, that I had barely remembered that Christmas was fast approaching. I felt a tinge of guilt for being gone from my family so much.

"I don't want this hanging over my head during the holidays. I need to find out whether we can work together or if I should just go to the cops. Or the media," I said.

"Work together? That's precious."

"You were going to cut Owen in. Just pretend we are taking his spot."

"He used to tell me how much he loved you and your sister, Fiona. I'll be honest. You sounded a lot cuter back then."

I couldn't help but laugh.

"Do you think we can make this work, Mr. Bowles?" I asked.

"Call me Darby. I guess I don't have much choice, do I?" He then paused and added, "Frankie."

"I get it. You know my sister and I's names. Just remember that I hold the cards right now."

Darby seemed to realize he should play nice. "I understand. Just remember, I'm not the bad guy here. Consider that when you think about going to the cops or the media."

"You're referring to Howie Doss?"

"You guys know a lot, don't you?"

"I want you to stop referring to "Us" or "You guys." It's me and me only. Just remember, if you involve my family in any way at all, that's a deal breaker. Do you understand?"

"Yes."

"OK, here's how it's going to work. I'm going to call you tonight at five sharp. I'll tell you when and where we are going to meet tomorrow."

"I understand."

"Talk to you soon," I said and hung up the phone.

I buried my head in my hands. It was almost too much to handle.

"You were fantastic," Evie said. "And trying to keep your sister out of it is so admirable."

I looked at her quizzically. "You do realize I was doing that for you. You are the girl who is involved, not her. And by the way, you can drive with me to meet Darby, but I'm not letting you meet him."

She looked like she was going to protest, but I think she understood why this couldn't happen.

"Fine," Evie said.

The next several days were going to include meeting a felon, Christmas with the family, and possibly a plan to blackmail one of the most influential men in the United States.

Just your normal, everyday 21-year-old stuff.

I called Darby that night at exactly five and told him that we would be meeting at a place called Anna's Bistro in Ukiah at 11 a.m. the next morning. It was the same place that Evie and I had lunch at the day we went to see Patricia Page.

Anna's Bistro hardly sounded like a Chinese Restaurant, but it was, and it had been excellent. I had called ahead, and they were open until 2 p.m. on Christmas Eve, so it seemed the perfect place to go. It had been quiet which was key, and the women who worked there couldn't care less about any customer's conversations.

Darby protested for a bit, saying he was in Eureka and wasn't sure how he'd get down there by tomorrow. I told him to borrow a car, take the train, the bus, any damn thing. He acquiesced and agreed to meet me there.

I picked Evie up the next morning, and after a quizzical look from her mother, we pulled away from her parent's house. When we were out of her mother's eyesight, she kissed me long and passionately.

"You know kisses while driving are literally the hardest kind," I said.

"Take what you can get!" Evie said.

I laughed. "Don't think your Mom was too happy."

"Imagine if she had seen me kiss you."

"Just add it to our list of worries," I said.

Evie smiled reluctantly, and then changed the subject.

"Exactly what are you going to tell Bowles? Things have been so frantic the last few days, I feel like I don't even know our plan anymore."

"I'm not even sure I have a plan. I'm playing this by ear, and just addressing each new piece of information as it comes."

"Do you still think we should just go to the police?"

"For now, I'm with you. I was thinking about it last night and what exactly do we have anyway? The word of an ex-con and a photograph that looks like it was taken 50 years ago. Do you think the guy in the picture is Howie Doss? Yeah, it looks like him, but I wouldn't….."

I was about to say bet my life on it but thought better of it.

"Bet on it," I said.

"We're in agreement then."

"I mean, if this was a court of law, they would laugh us out in a matter of seconds. There's absolutely zero proof that Darby Bowles knew the three people killed in the car that day. Only his word. And all we have in that notarized statement is Darby Bowles saying he was ordered to do the crime by Howie Doss. No proof of that either. It was genius putting the newspaper and the date in the photo, but that isn't really evidence. There was a lot of people in Oklahoma City in the days following those murders."

"You're very rational about all this, Frankie."

"Thanks."

"And what is the exact plan for today?" she asked.

"I'm going to park the car two blocks down from the restaurant. I'll have my phone with me, and I will text you 9-1-1 if something starts going down."

"And what do I do if that happens?" she asked.

"Meet me in the back of the restaurant. They have those side streets that we saw last time, and we could get lost in them."

"Okay," Evie said sheepishly.

"I don't think anything is going to happen. We have what he wants after all, and the first thing I'm going to tell him is that I don't have the photos on me. That should stop him from getting any crazy ideas. And I won't even mention the notarized letter. I don't think he knows we have that."

"I'm starting to feel like this is all my fault. I pushed you to keep reading Uncle Owen's novel, and to go down this road."

"I didn't do anything I didn't want to," I said. "I might have enjoyed the time with you a little too much early on, but my head is screwed on straight right now."

"I don't know how to take that."

"I'm sorry, I didn't phrase that too well. Part of me may have started this because I liked spending time with you, but there was never a point where you persuaded me to do something I didn't want to. Is that better?"

Evie laughed. "Not really."

It was my turn to laugh, and I leaned in to kiss her this time.

"OK, no more kissing on the highway. We're worse than people texting," I said.

We were pretty quiet for the rest of the drive. Two hours later we were in Ukiah, and we took our exit off the freeway.

I went over our plan again.

"So, I'll park the car two blocks down the street, and just obviously be checking your phone in case I text you 9-1-1, in which case you drive to the back of the restaurant immediately. Got it?"

"Got it. It's only 10:30 you know."

"I know. Haven't you seen any spy novels? You have to go in early and scope out the scene."

She smiled, but I wasn't sure she found the humor in it that I had.

"How long do you think you will be?" she asked.

"Assuming he gets there at 11, I would expect to be out by 11:30 or so. More than anything, I'm trying to see what type of guy he is. Is he believable? Do I think he could make all this shit up? Does he have any other evidence? How do we continue from this point? Etc., etc."

"I get it," Evie said

"And if I don't show up by 11:30....."

"Yeah?"

"Just wait longer."

"Asshole," Evie said, but in a playful manner.

I turned on to State Street and passed Annie's Bistro to make sure I didn't see anything out of the ordinary. Everything appeared normal, and I parked two blocks down from the restaurant.

"I'll be back as soon as I can. Just stay here and don't move unless I text you."

"Be safe," she said.

I smiled, shut the door, and walked towards Annie's Bistro.

I knew I didn't want to be seen first by Darby Bowles. I wanted to be the one watching him enter and making sure he didn't have anyone with him. And most of all, I couldn't have him see me with Evie. At all costs, I had to keep her out of this.

A block before the restaurant, I crossed the street and walked up to a Starbucks that was across the street from Anna's Bistro.

I bought a coffee, put my sunglasses on, tightened my baseball cap, and grabbed a newspaper to cover my face. I looked ridiculous, like the Inspector from those old Pink Panther movies that my mother loved. She used to tell me Peter Sellers was the funniest guy around. Give me Bill Murray any day.

I sat there for the next 15 minutes, looking across the street at Annie's Bistro. Not a single soul walked in. I'm glad I had called ahead, or I would have been thinking they were closed for Christmas Eve. At 11:04, a beat up SUV entered the restaurant and parked in the back. Shit! That was where I was going to have Evie pick me up in case of emergency.

Why didn't he just park in front where there were plenty of spots available? Maybe he was as jumpy as I was. I guess I couldn't blame him.

When he walked to the front of the restaurant, he was alone. Two minutes later, I left the Starbucks and headed towards Annie's Bistro.

I opened the front door and wasn't surprised that Darby Bowles was the only person in the place. Evie and I had found inmate photos of him, and while he was certainly older now, there was no denying it was him. I walked to the table, he stood up, and we shook hands. A couple of old friends getting together for lunch is what it must have looked like.

"You're just a kid," Darby said.

He was about six feet tall and skinny, but you could tell he was wiry strong. I was bigger and taller than him, but he didn't look like the type of guy you fucked with. His veins popped from his forearms, and he didn't look to have an ounce of fat on him. He had a few tattoos, but certainly not as many as Uncle Owen. He was wearing jeans and a white t-shirt that was tucked in. He was relatively young, but also weathered, if that makes any sense. He was wearing a hat tight on his head just like I was. Two guys trying to hide their faces.

"I started taking anti-aging cream at 14," I said.

It caught him off guard, and he laughed quite loudly.

"Not bad," Darby said.

"How old are you?" I asked.

He looked me over, deciding it was a harmless question.

"Forty two. But it feels like yesterday I was 25 and living in Oklahoma City. A decade in Eureka and seven years in jail just sailed by."

"Time flies when you're having fun," I said.

"Don't be an asshole," he said.

I had intentionally been trying to keep him off balance, knowing the more I controlled the conversation, the better.

"So I'm going to assume you and your little sister have my photo album?"

"I said not to mention her," I said.

I made a brief move like I was getting up, but it was one of the worst bluffs in history.

"I'm sorry," he said. "Let's try to get along before this spirals out of control and we both get ourselves killed."

That sobered the situation quickly. The same waitress that had served Evie and I came over and handed me a menu.

"No need. I'll take the chicken fried rice again."

That was a mistake.

"I remember you. You in here with girlfriend last week," she said in broken English.

"My sister, actually," I said, hoping my quick thinking had worked.

She looked at me dubiously and then took Darby Bowles's order. As she walked away, he looked me in the face.

"Girlfriend, huh?"

"I was with my sister," I said, but he wasn't buying it. This wasn't something I could have foreseen.

"I could find out quite easily. Just find your sister online and then go ask Patricia if that was the girl who came to her house."

"Let's change the subject," I said.

"I'll forget about it for now. But that info is going to stay up here," he said, tapping his head.

"Let's get down to business, Darby. Can I call you Darby?"

"You sure can, Frankie. Or should I call you Sport? That's what Owen used to say he called you."

Damn, he knew a lot. "Frankie is fine."

"So you said you wanted to get down to business. What do you want to know?"

"I want you to tell me about that day in Oklahoma City."

"You really want to know? Once you know everything, Howie Doss would undoubtedly kill you for it."

"I understand."

"I'm going to need something from you in return. After all, you would now have information that could land me in jail."

"The statute of limitations is up on being a getaway driver," I said.

"Not if they wanted to charge me with murder," Darby said.

"What do you want?"

"I want a promise that you won't go to the police or the media. At least, not yet. I need a smoking gun, and I'm in the process of getting that."

"How are you going about doing that?"

Darby smiled devilishly.

"I'm getting the rooster to come out and play."

"What does that even mean?" I asked.

"Let's just say, I sent Doss a letter. I need him to make a mistake, talk to me, admit something."

"I hope you didn't use a return address," I was half serious/half kidding.

"I'm not that dumb," Darby said.

I wasn't sure what to make of him in the intelligence department. It was obvious that he had street smarts. Being in and out of jail almost ensured that. But I didn't think he realized just how important a guy Howie Doss was.

"He's going to put that envelope through every test there is," I said.

I looked over at Darby and saw him flinch for just a second.

"Please tell me you were wearing gloves," I said.

I was starting to feel like the only adult at the table.

"Of course I was, kid," he said, but I didn't believe him. The fact that he had added "kid" showed that this line of questioning was getting under his skin. I wanted the upper hand but didn't want him completely rattled.

"I'm sure it's fine," I said. "I wouldn't go calling him though."

"Enough about that. So, do you promise not to go to the cops or the media if I tell you about that horrific day?"

"I promise," I said.

"Good, because I'd prefer to not have to make a house call in the Bay Area."

Safe to say, I was going to keep my promise.

Darby started talking and I didn't interrupt for a full five minutes. The only reason he stopped was when our food was brought over. He told me of picking the three others up, parking down the street from the bank in which the black woman was killed. Then driving across town and parking in a back alley as the Hispanic male was killed.

Darby spoke in an emotional way, and I could tell it was tough for him to recollect that day. He had to pause a few times to gather himself. It made me like him more and take pity on being in such a shitty situation.

When the police officer ID'd them at the stop for the third murder, everything changed. Darby summarized the ensuing chase, and his brilliant idea to crash the car into the light post. He said he never would have gotten away if it weren't for that. I had to agree.

Next, he holed up in a hotel for a few days, leaving one day to take pictures of Howie Doss. At that point, he had to backtrack and tell me about the one and only time he had met Doss, and how he had quickly turned around to see his surroundings. The guy had balls of steel, I had to give him that. Taking off his blindfold in that situation could have been suicidal.

He said he knew with the other three dead, that Doss could try to have him killed, so that's why he wanted some insurance and took the photos.

I told him adding the newspaper was a brilliant idea. He seemed pleased.

When he finished talking, I was halfway through my chicken fried rice. He looked at me, letting me know that was it.

"Unbelievable," was all I could muster.

"So you see, this is personal to me. I'm not a racist, I didn't want those people killed," he said.

"But hadn't you been the driver when they had painted swastikas all over town the week before?"

Darby nodded, impressed with my knowledge. "You're pretty fucking good. Yeah, I was, but I never knew they were going to graduate to murder."

"I believe you," I said.

I wanted to believe Darby. He was rough and tough, but I kind of liked the guy, I had to admit. He reminded me of Uncle Owen in that way, and I could see how they became friends.

"So what's next?" I asked.

"I want to see if the rooster comes out to play," he said. "Give me a week, and then we can talk again. If something happens, and I need those photos, I'll call you."

"And what do we do?" I asked.

"Nothing. Are you trying to get your girlfriend killed?"

I didn't even deny it anymore. "No," I said.

"Give me a week, and then we can discuss money, amongst other things," Darby said.

"You keep mentioning the money, but I'm not even sure that's why we are in this."

"Then why are you?"

Because I liked spending time with Evie? Terrible answer.

"Because my Uncle Owen asked me to," I came up with. It wasn't a great answer, but it was somewhat believable.

"I liked Owen," Darby said. "We were two peas in a pod. Until he told you all about my plan. Don't think I can forgive him for that. Which brings me to a question I've been meaning to ask. Why the fuck now? He died five years ago. Why wait until I'm getting out of jail to go and get the pictures?"

"You wouldn't believe me if I told you," I said.

"Try me," Darby said.

"He had written all of the information in a book. I put it on my shelf and forgot about it. It only recently came to my attention again."

Darby shook his head. "Just my fucking luck."

"That's yet to be decided. For you or I," I said.

"Or the girl you've now involved," he said, but raised his arms to show it wasn't malicious. "Truth be told, you seem like a nice young man, Frankie. Maybe we'll all end up doing okay by this. With the exception of Howie Doss that is."

"Amen to that," I said.

Darby started to get up. "Are we done here?"

"I'll still be able to reach you at the same phone number?"

"Yeah. It's my friend's landline, and I'll be staying there awhile. I'll call you if I get a cell phone in the meantime."

"O.K. So that's it? This is a "to be continued " basically?"

"Exactly. And you promise not to go to the police or the media in the meantime, right?"

"I promise. And you will not go anywhere near the Bay Area?"

"You have my word. I don't want to do anything to you or your loved ones. You're alright, Frankie."

It was a mutual admiration society. Me, a 21-year-old college student getting along swimmingly with a felon twice my age.

"I'll leave first, Frankie. Talk to you in a week," he said.

I watched Darby walk out of Annie's Bistro. I waited a minute and walked down the block towards Evie.

In the short walk towards Evie, I realized that I had got us out of harm's way, at least temporarily. And somehow, it didn't feel like a total success. It was hard to explain, but we had been on this adventure together, and now we were handing the reigns over to Darby. At least for a week.

But it wasn't like we were out of the game forever. We were just giving Darby a little time, and then we would meet with him again.

I approached the car, and a brief moment of panic set in. Evie had been bending over, and for a second I didn't see a body in the car. She appeared soon thereafter, and I was able to breathe. She saw me and looked at her watch.

"11:35. Only a few minutes late," Evie said.

"We decided to split a dessert."

"Very funny. How did it go?"

"You want to drive?"

"Sure."

I got in the passenger seat and let Evie drive us home. Probably for the best, as I spent the next 10 minutes explaining what had happened in the meeting. Evie took turns smiling, frowning, and looking perplexed.

She took the fact that Darby knew I was with someone besides my sister in stride. She said if we were doing this as a team he was going to find out eventually anyway. I told her about his idea of needling Doss.

"So how exactly is he going to get the rooster to come out and play?"

"He wasn't very definitive about that."

She was hard to read. I couldn't tell what she was thinking.

"So, what do you think?" I asked.

"I have mixed emotions. I kind of feel like we are handing the baton off mid-race. I also realize that this could get dangerous the longer we are involved, and as tough as I've been acting, I think a week off could do us some good."

"Those pretty much sum up my feelings," I said. "We have Christmas Eve tonight and Christmas Day tomorrow. It will be nice to just enjoy our families without all of this hanging over our head. And it's not like we are jumping off the ship. We are just giving him a week to do his own work. After all, this was Darby's thing well before ours."

"Darby? Wow, you guys are on a first name basis now."

"Mr. Bowles," I said in a very official sounding voice. "Is that better?"

"What was he like?" Evie asked.

"Like Uncle Owen was reincarnated. Rough around the edges, charismatic, street smart but not a Mensa candidate. Probably a rough childhood, but I think overall I could like the guy."

"So you believe him?"

"Yeah, I do. If not, he's the best bullshitter I've ever met. He knew details, names, places, etc."

"So one of the most important men in the country right now is a racist murderer?"

"It looks that way."

"Wow."

"You can say that again. Anyway, we'll give Darby his week and then we'll see where we stand."

"I feel like a weight has been lifted," Evie said.

"Me too," I said.

I grabbed her shoulders and started massaging her as she drove. She moaned in exaggeration, but I wasn't complaining.

"Nice to have this Frankie back," she said.

"You want to go to our respective family's Christmas Eve dinners tonight?"

"As what?"

"As close friends," I said.

"Is that all we are?"

"No, you know we are more than that."

Evie smiled, and I leaned over and kissed her. We really had to stop kissing in cars.

26

Christmas Eve had always been a bigger deal than Christmas Day in our family. It's the day we had relatives over, made the house look really nice, and my mother would spend hours cooking. It had lost a lot of its luster when my father had passed, unfortunately.

We used to have 15-20 of my father's relatives over, but that had faded over the years. My mother was an only child, so our Christmas Eve's had become pretty much a three-person affair over the last several years.

Upon arriving back from Ukiah, I broke it to my mother that we were going to have a fourth that night.

"Evie is going to swing by later," I said.

"What time is she coming?"

"I have to call her. She'll probably just come over for 30 minutes or so when she has a break from her family."

"And you are going to stop by there at some point too?"

"That's' the plan," I said.

"Meet the Fockers," my sister said, and obviously I knew what she meant. My mother apparently did not.

"Fiona, how many times have I warned you about swearing."

"It's a movie, Mom. Jeez, so far behind the times."

Fiona and I looked at each other and started laughing. My Mom couldn't help but join in.

Christmas Eve was really nice at our respective places. My house was easy as Evie got along so great with Fiona and my mother, that the hour she spent there just sailed by. She was having 20 relatives over, so I knew it would be a little different.

I was definitely run through the wringer, but the relatives seemed to like me. Most importantly, I could tell that Evie's parents really appreciated how polite and charming I was around their family. They never mentioned my relationship with their daughter, but they had to assume we were becoming more than friends.

There was an awkward moment where a political debate broke out, and one of the more conservative members of Evie's family, professed that she thought Howie Doss was a national hero. Evie and I glanced quickly at each other, knowing neither one of us would say anything

The political talk ended quickly, thankfully, and Evie's parents went out of there way to engage me in conversation. After what had happened to her,

I'm sure they enjoyed seeing her hanging out with a bright, presentable, man. Me.

Of course, if they knew the adventure I had her mixed up in, things would have been a little different.

Christmas Day came and went just as quickly. My mother's spinach and roquefort soufflé was as good as I remembered it. She literally made it once a year, and it had taken on a life of its own since we knew she wouldn't be serving it again until next December.

I was given a gift certificate to Gary Danko, a high-end restaurant in San Francisco. I went out on a limb and guessed that was a gift bought recently. After all, you don't buy a gift certificate to dinner for a guy who is single.

I called Evie, but they had to go to a relative's for Christmas dinner. I was happy to just chill out with my family after being in and out of the house so much the previous two weeks. If I had known what was to come, I would have cherished it even more.

The next day went by without much fanfare either. Evie and I went back to spending a lot of time together, and things were different, but in a good way. Her parents came out of their way to greet me when I came over, and my mother did the same. It was almost as if spending time with the respective families on Christmas Eve had given us carte blanche to come and go as we pleased.

We went to Peet's early that morning and found our favorite table was empty. It made it much easier to talk when we weren't surrounded by other people.

She sat down, and I went and ordered our respective coffees. We had this down pat. When I arrived back, Evie dove right in.

"I've been reading about Howie Doss a little bit at night," Evie said. "If he really was in Oklahoma City in 2001, how can that just disappear from the internet?"

"Easy answer is he got lucky. The three people he used to commit these crimes were all killed. Darby has been afraid to say anything and is selfishly doing this just to get rich. The only other tie he had was the guy Angry Phil, and the guy ain't talking, if he's even alive. And I'm sure once Doss became a public figure, he was careful not to include anything that could tie him to Oklahoma City in any of his interviews or biographies."

"Yeah, I guess you're right. This would just be so much easier if we could prove that he was in Oklahoma City during that time. I don't think that picture is definitive."

"In a court of law, you're right. But if you are just trying to extort some money, it could be enough."

"For Darby Bowles?" Evie asked

"Yes. We're not doing any extorting. We've discussed this."

"I know. Just making sure we are doing this because Doss is terrible for America, along with being a murderer."

"We are," I said. "I saw that Scarlet Jackson, your old boss, is going to be in Oakland tomorrow. She's speaking at a local high school."

"With the students on Christmas break?"

"Might be more for the community. Not really sure."

Evie seemed excited. "You want to go see her with me?"

"That's why I brought it up, silly. I'd love to subtly ask her about Howie Doss and see how much pull this guy really has in Washington."

"I bet she'd have a coffee if she's not too busy. She likes me and wants me to spend another summer interning for her."

"Invite me on the coffee date. You can tell her I'm thinking about interning for her as well."

"Frankie, I don't want to lie to a congresswoman."

"Who said you'd be lying?"

"You're really considering it?"

"A summer with you in Washington D.C.? I could think of a lot worse."

Evie beamed from ear to ear. I told her that Fiona and my mother were going to a Cal basketball game that night and I had the house to myself for a few hours. Her smile got even bigger.

We put the three hours that my family was gone to good use. I lost count at three times, but I'm pretty sure we got a fourth love making session in there. I had to open up the window to my room and the door to the hall. The room smelled like sex, and I'd just rather avoid the ammunition it would give Fiona when she got home. I knew my mother would be too embarrassed to mention anything.

I drove Evie over to her house and gave her a hug at her front door. There was still a little hesitancy around her parents, so I decided a kiss in public wasn't in the cards just yet.

Fiona and my mother had just got home when I arrived back, and they didn't mention any funky smells from the house. I excused myself to my room and turned on my laptop. I googled 'Always Right Website' to see if I could find out any more information on Doss or his hate-filled site.

An hour in, I hit the mother lode. I texted Evie that I was coming to pick her up. This was something that had to be said in private.

"This better be good," she said, waiting for me when I arrived.

"It's a game changer!" I said excitedly.

I drove out of her parents street, took a right, and pulled up about 100 yards to the right. It was silly, but I just preferred talking out of the view of her parents.

"Alright, let's hear it," Evie said.

I was going to give a big lead up and tell her how I had stumbled on the information, but instead, I just blurted out, "Derek Plough is Howie Doss's director of security at Always Right."

Evie looked at me with a blank face. Obviously, the magnitude hadn't registered with her. "Who's Derek Plough?"

"That's what I said at first. But the name meant something to me, so I went back over all of our information."

I paused for dramatic effect.

"Derek Plough was the first arriving officer when Darby intentionally crashed the car. He was the man who shot two of the guys who had been in Darby's getaway car."

Evie looked at me, letting the information sink in.

"So maybe him and Doss met during the course of the investigation," she said.

"If you were Howie Doss and you had just orchestrated these murders, you'd want to get close to the investigation?"

"Well no, probably not. I guess I'm not sure what you are saying, Frankie."

"I'm saying that Howie Doss already knew Derek Plough. He didn't arrive first on the scene by accident. This wasn't random. Derek Plough had been there to assassinate all of the people who had ties to Howie Doss. He was mostly successful. Jared Wilder was dead from the crash, and he shot Charles Wade Leonard. The papers didn't say if Elliot Walden died from the crash or at the hands of Plough, but I'm willing to bet he was alive until Plough shot him. Darby's quick thinking allowed him to get away, but I have no doubt he would have been shot by Plough as well."

Evie covered her face and didn't say anything for at least a minute.

"Howie Doss is even more of a psychopath than we thought. He had an officer on the inside that he sent to assassinate his associates?"

"That would be my guess. But there is some good news," I said.

"What's that?" Evie asked.

"We now have our link between Howie Doss and what happened in Oklahoma City."

"Holy you know what. Does this mean we are back on the case?" Evie asked. Her face was a mix of nervousness and excitement.

"I'm afraid so," I said.

27

Derek Plough was born in 1979, weighing 11 pounds at birth. His family moved from New Orleans to Oklahoma City when he was less than a year old, and he would grow up in a middle-class family in the suburbs, the only brother amongst four sisters. He was an active kid and tried to get out of the house any time he could. Easy bake ovens and playing dress-up were the furthest things from Plough's mind, and he found it tough to relate to all his sisters.

He grew into his own body at a young age, towering over boys his same age. He showed an interest in football and was a third team all-state tight end in high school in 1997. He'd always dreamed of playing college football at Oklahoma State, and you'd think being all-state would be enough to get a scholarship, but Plough came from a small school, and the level of competition was pretty weak. He decided to enroll in a junior college instead, working on his strength so he'd be ready when Oklahoma State came calling.

Plough finished one year and then a semester at the JC, but the Cowboys didn't come calling with a scholarship. Instead, the Oklahoma State football team only offered him a try out for the team. It wasn't exactly what he envisioned, but he accepted, confident he would show the coaches he was good enough.

He enrolled at Oklahoma State University in Stillwater, Oklahoma, about 70 miles northeast of Oklahoma City in early 2000. He arrived at the huge campus with stars in his eyes and football in his heart.

6'3" and 220 pounds, Plough was a big man no doubt, but when he arrived on campus for freshman football practice, he realized that he was just another guy out there now. There were guys who were bigger, there were guys who were stronger, and there were guys who were faster. And the majority of the other tight ends were bigger, stronger, and faster. Thirty minutes into his first practice, Derek Plough knew he wasn't going to be playing on Sundays in the NFL.

Turned out he wasn't even going to be playing on Saturdays for Oklahoma State. He was hit going across the middle in his third practice and had recurring headaches for days. It was before all the attention that is now paid to concussions, and his coaches tried daily to convince him to get back out there. He knew he was in no position to play, but rather than be called a pussy by his coaches and fellow players, he got back out on the field way too early.

Five days after his concussion, Plough returned to the field. He didn't last long this time either. He was hit so hard that teammates practicing on the other side of the field heard the sound. This time, along with another brutal concussion, he had three broken ribs. He had been sandwiched between two defenders, taking massive hits from both.

Plough still had a love for football, but he just wasn't big enough or good enough, and he knew it. The broken ribs took weeks to heal and even when he was given a clean bill of health, he knew he was done. He never participated in another practice for Oklahoma State.

Without his love of football to fall back on, Plough struggled to keep motivated in school. His grades suffered, and he lived his first year below the magical 2.0 grade point average line. He was finding Oklahoma State tougher than junior college. He drank too much, and although that wasn't rare for a college student when you are 6'3", 220 pounds and have a bad temper, it can be a problem.

Plough got in a few fights his first year at Oklahoma State and was a menace to be around. He never got arrested, however, which would have put his future profession in doubt, and for that, he was lucky. He was constantly broke and never had any money to take any girls out. He drank Natural Light, and he ate dorm or fast food. He didn't know how college students did it for four years. Derek Plough wanted money, not an education.

His life changed when his old high school acquaintance Elliot Walden, who Darby Bowles would later nickname Loose Lips, invited him to a party one day. Walden and Plough weren't all that close, so the invite surprised Plough. It was spring break, and Plough was back in Oklahoma City visiting his parents. He decided he was going to go back and finish his first year at Oklahoma State, but he already knew he wouldn't be returning for a second. Derek Plough wasn't meant for college. He drove over with Walden to what he thought was going to be a party but turned out to be a get together with a few guys. There was beer at least.

It was when Derek Plough first met Howie Doss. The man across from him was going prematurely gray, and under different circumstances, Derek Plough would have bullied him. Once he heard him speak, he was immediately under his spell, however. Doss was several inches shorter and 40 pounds lighter than Plough, but there was no doubt who the boss was. There would be no bullying, at least not by Plough.

Doss's voice was booming, and he held a command over the English language that Plough wouldn't have attained with 50 years of college. He was also more charismatic than Plough could have ever been. This skinny, graying twenty-something had power over Plough almost immediately.

At the time, he did not know him as Howie Doss, however. He was Lester to everyone there. No last name, just Lester. They all knew it was a fake name, but no one dared press the man.

Plough wasn't a natural leader, and he preferred to follow strong willed people, and Doss was certainly one of those. Doss talked of setting up their own little criminal enterprise with the five people who were there. It was Doss,

Plough, Elliot Walden, and two guys named Charles Leonard, and Jared Wilder. Plough liked these guys, they seemed like his type of people.

Doss spoke in generalities and never specifically said what they were going to do, but he did drop a few ethnic slurs, and the four people there had a general idea what Doss had in mind. Plough knew now why Walden had invited him. Derek Plough had always felt more comfortable around white people. He wasn't sure if he'd call himself a racist, but he certainly wasn't going out of his way to befriend any people of color. His room at home had a confederate flag much to the dismay of his sisters.

The "party" lasted two hours, which meant about nine beers for Plough. He left with a promise to come back the next night. He was already infatuated with the man they called Lester. Derek Plough wasn't homosexual, and he loved women, but there was something about the charismatic individual he had just met. He understood how people could fall under the spell of a man like that.

Plough and Walden drove over to the same house the next four nights in a row. The man Plough knew as Lester began to slowly outline what he had in mind. They would rob some banks and raise some money, and with that money, they would start a criminal enterprise, with the end goal being to enrich themselves and the white way of life. *The white way is the right way,* Doss said more than once.

On the final night before Plough was to return to Oklahoma State, Doss asked him to stay a little longer than the others. He had Walden wait outside.

"So what do you think about what we've got going on here?"

"I dig it," Plough said.

"I think we have a chance to do some big things. Some great things. But there's one thing I need that I don't have."

"What is that?" Plough asked.

"Someone on the inside," Doss said.

"On the inside of what?"

Doss stood up from the table, and circled around Plough, making him nervous. He walked 360 degrees around the table, ending up where he started. He looked at Plough with unbridled intensity and asked, "How old are you?"

"I'll be 21 in a few weeks."

"How would you like to become a police officer?"

Plough went back to Oklahoma State for his spring quarter, but his mind was clearly elsewhere. His grades suffered more than they already had been and he was considering dropping out. That's when a call came from Howie Doss.

"You don't need a four-year degree to become a police officer, but they aren't going to take a guy who just flunked out of college. You need to go back to school and suck it up for this quarter. Get passing grades at the minimum. You can drop out to join the police academy after that, but they might not take you if you flunk out. Do you understand?"

It was a less a question, and more of a declaration.

"I'll get passing grades," Plough said, and he did just that.

During his final semester in school, he would text with "Lester" several times a week, who'd always start by asking if Plough had gotten his grades under control. The guy exuded confidence and Plough had no doubt that this guy was headed for greatness. Derek Plough knew that he would never achieve greatness on his own, so he had no problem hitching his wagon to someone who would.

If Plough didn't necessarily believe in the degree of hate that Doss would sometimes spew, he wasn't entirely devoid of those feelings either.

Doss hadn't outlined exactly how he would use Plough, but he assured him that when he did use him, it would be of the utmost importance. He told Plough that he should just be a cop first and foremost, and he was to do his job well. That would allow him the necessary standing that he would need when Doss called on him to do something a little more sinister.

Plough finished the semester, enrolled in the police academy and excelled immediately. While he wasn't the biggest or strongest guy on the football field, he was precisely that in the police academy. His athleticism served him well in all the physical tests that becoming a cop entailed. And while Plough was no Rhode Scholar, he was plenty bright to understand the intricacies of becoming a cop. It was something that he actually enjoyed learning, unlike the remedial classes he was forced to take when he was at junior college and then at Oklahoma State.

Plough graduated the police academy near the top of his class and got a job as an Oklahoma City police officer in late 2000. The police force was understaffed, and Plough became an officer quicker than he probably should have. During this time, he was still talking to Doss several times a week and had fallen completely under his spell. Plough had no doubt that this guy was going to change the world; one way or another. Obviously, his five-person network in Oklahoma City wasn't the end all, be all.

The last few months of 2000 were Plough's first few months as an officer, and he graded high on all of his superiors performance reports. He was physically fit, proficient, and handled adverse situations well. Doss never asked Plough to do anything untoward until December of 2000, and even then it was just to make sure that the cops didn't have any leads in some of the home invasions going on around town. Plough informed Doss that they were safe, the police had no leads.

Elliot Walden had introduced Plough to "Lester," but after Plough became a cop, Doss asked the two of them to stop hanging out. He was using Walden and the others for illegal activities, and it just didn't make sense for them to be seen together. They both agreed it could be problematic and stopped hanging out altogether. They had never been that close anyway, and neither one of them lost any sleep over it.

By the end of the year 2000, Plough knew that Doss had taken on a getaway driver who they used in all of the home invasions. If truth be told, he thought it was beneath "Lester" to be doing things so remedial. He told him so on one Friday night as they enjoyed a few beers together.

"Don't worry Derek, this little Mickey Mouse shit will all be ending soon," Doss said.

"What do you have in mind, Lester?" Plough asked.

"I'm going to tell you something that none of the other guys know."

Plough was excited, in spite of himself.

Doss continued. "My name is not Lester, which I'm sure you've probably already guessed. My name is Howie Doss."

Plough smiled. He was delighted that Doss had shared his name with him. Plough had felt that he had reached a friendship with Lester/Doss well above the other guys, and this only furthered that opinion.

"I'm still Derek," Plough said, and they shared a laugh. "What do you mean this Mickey Mouse shit is going to end?"

Doss got up from the table and started walking around. This was his go to move when he was about to say or discuss something important. Standing above you coupled with his commanding voice made it hard to say no to Howie Doss.

"How much do you know about the internet?" Doss asked.

"I know about it obviously. The department is having people set up email addresses, but I don't think anyone really uses them yet. Is the world wide web going to be huge?"

Doss laughed again. He wasn't prone to laughter, but he found this one of the funniest things he'd ever heard. This amateur in front of him was still calling it the world wide web. He composed himself, not wanting to offend Plough.

"The internet is the biggest invention of all time."

Plough looked dubious. Doss continued.

"This shit we are doing around Oklahoma City is peanuts. With the internet, we are going to be able to reach millions with just one website. It's going to be bigger than anyone imagines."

"So what does this have to do with us?" Plough asked.

"It means all of these little things we are doing around here are going to end soon. I'm too big for this shit, and it's time to make my stake in the world."

This was the confidence that seduced Plough in the first place.

"So how does everyone else fit in? No offense, but I don't see them as the computer types." Plough asked.

Howie Doss laughed for the third time in a minute. That didn't happen often.

"You're right about that Derek. And I can't really take them with me either."

Plough didn't like the ominous way that Doss said it. "What do you mean?"

"We'll deal with that soon enough. Are you ready to move on to bigger and better things with me?"

"Of course, Lester."

"Howie."

"Of course, Howie."

"And I want you with me. But that means you may have to do something you might find distasteful when the time comes."

Plough nodded. Howie Doss sat back down. His standing above Plough had worked its desired effect.

The time for Plough to do something for Doss came only a few months later, in February of 2001. Doss had managed to slowly work his way up to requesting Plough do the ultimate backstab of Elliot Walden and the other men. They met in late February, and Plough knew this was going to be a hellish meeting.

"It's time Derek."

Plough knew it was coming but still bowed his head.

"What's your plan?"

Plough had put up all his objections over the last few months, and Doss had shot them all down. Doss had said it was just too risky to include the others in the next phase of his plan. They were becoming too visible, and Doss was losing faith in them. Especially Elliot Walden, who had a big mouth, Doss said. Plough tried to forget that he and Walden had grown up together and had been acquaintances, if not friends. Walden had even introduced him to Doss, and now Plough was going to kill him? Some friend.

"On February 26th, Oklahoma City is going to be hit by a few racist murders. And you, my friend, are going to be the hero...."

Plough doubted he would be canonized for his actions.

The morning of February 26th, 2001 didn't go as expected, as an Oklahoma City officer named Peter Lassiter almost ruined Howie Doss's plan all by himself. When Lassiter intercepted Bowles, Leonard, Wilder, and Walden before they got to the Temple B'Nai Israel, everything changed.

The original plan was to have Plough waiting behind the Temple in a secluded alley where Doss had told them to park. Plough would approach them as friends, and they would figure something had gone wrong. When Plough got close enough, he was supposed to empty his weapon into the four of them.

It may have sounded difficult, but these guys knew Plough so they wouldn't be pointing their weapons at him when he approached. It was an evil, treasonous plan, but Plough thought it would work. He would say they pulled a weapon and when it came out that they were the people who had committed the earlier murders, Plough's actions would be thoroughly justified. No one knew that Walden and Plough worked for the same man, and the fact that they went to the same high school would just be a coincidence.

When Plough got the call on his radio that Peter Lassiter was chasing the suspects, he had to adapt. Plough knew he was close and headed off in the direction of Lassiter. Plough often thought about what would have happened if Lassiter had arrived at the car at the same time. It would have been much tougher to kill the others. Luckily for Plough, when Lassiter dropped back, and Plough raced by him, that wasn't an issue.

He shot Charles Wade Leonard first, and no one could have blamed him. After all, Leonard had his weapon raised and pointed in the direction of three bystanders. It all happened so quick that Leonard never realized that the officer shooting at him was Derek Plough.

That was not the case with Walden. After killing Leonard, Plough quickly ran to the car. Lassiter was arriving, and he knew he had to finish this quickly. He immediately saw that Jared Wilder was dead as a doornail, with a pole sticking out of his head. He looked in the back and saw his old friend Elliot Walden, badly injured but very much alive.

Plough didn't have time to reminisce as Walden looked up at him. He shot him three times and killed him instantaneously.

Before he died, Walden was able to say his parting words to this world. "HE really is the devil, isn't he?" Plough knew the HE that Walden was referring to.

After Plough killed him, he looked down and saw a gun right next to Walden on the back seat. Plough knew Howie Doss was right. He was going to be hailed a hero. It hadn't gone down exactly like Doss had outlined, but the end results were going to be the same. That was until Lassiter walked over and Plough realized what he was going to say before he said it.

"There were four people in this car."

Thirty officers were on the scene within minutes, but despite all the manpower, they were unable to find Darby Cash Bowles. Plough guessed that in the frenzied minutes after he shot Leonard and Walden, Bowles had escaped through the Home Depot. It was the building right next to where the crash occurred, so it made the most sense. By the time they set up a half-mile perimeter, precious minutes had been lost, and Plough knew they were not going to find Darby Bowles.

After a long, long day, Plough called Howie Doss that night to update him on all that had gone down. He wasn't sure how he was going to take it.

When he finished explaining everything, he heard Doss sounding relaxed on the other end.

"You've done very well Derek," the familiar voice said.

"But Bowles got away."

"That's fine. He's not going to be turning himself in, and even if they found him, he knows less than nothing. He met me for a total of five minutes, and he never saw my face. He was blindfolded and has no idea where my house is. Don't worry about Bowles."

"OK."

"I'm very impressed with all you did, Derek. Driving towards the chase when you heard it on the radio. Disposing of Leonard and Walden as quickly as possible. That's called thinking on your feet."

"Thanks, Howie," Plough said.

He felt like a child who had just gotten high praise from one of his parents. The praise was overshadowing the horrible actions Plough had committed. There was no turning back now. Derek Plough was going to be with Howie Doss from here on in. For better or worse.

"There is one more thing I need before we put this whole episode to bed," Doss said.

Plough knew he wasn't going to like it, but also knew he was going to do whatever Doss asked.

"I need you to go see a friend of Bowles. His name is Jake Court, and he may know where Bowles is. Again, I'm not scared of Bowles, but I'd still rather find him before the cops."

"Yes, boss."

"If Court becomes suspicious, you have my permission to use any means necessary to shut him up."

"Alright."

"And one more thing. Do it at night and don't go dressed as a cop."

For better or worse.

The police continued looking for the fourth man in the car for months, but nothing ever came of it. The explosion had done away with any fingerprints, and none of the friends of the men killed had any idea who the fourth man was. The case was still active, but after months of no leads, it eventually was pushed to the back burner. Plough still kept his eye out for Darby Bowles but never heard anything. Howie Doss figured he had moved and they would never hear from him again. He was half right.

In 2006, Doss recruited Plough to come work for Always Right, Doss's company named after the website of the same name.

They had kept in touch in the intervening years, and Plough had often told Doss that he'd like to come join him, but Doss thought it would be better to have Plough in Oklahoma City in case the February 2001 murders ever got renewed interest.

Five years had passed, however, and the website had become huge after the silly Dick Cheney game. Doss came to the conclusion that Plough would be of better use in Washington D.C. Doss's website had blown up in popularity, and they needed a Director of Security. Doss knew he could trust Plough implicitly and started to work on getting him to the nation's capital.

Doss had to make sure that they had a nice cover story as to how they knew each other. Obviously, it would be best not to include any mention of Oklahoma City, just in case people ever started poking around. Doss had been very careful not to leave a blueprint in Oklahoma City, and only six people really knew him. Three were dead, Darby Cash Bowles was either dead or deathly afraid of the police, Angry Phil knew him as some shadowy figure named Lester, and Plough was indebted for life.

The rent that Doss paid was always done with cash, including the shitty one bedroom he put Darby Bowles up in. He had used a fake ID for the initial paperwork, and the slum landlords were just happy to rent the places out. Needless to say, Doss knew that Oklahoma City wasn't going to be his last gig, and took measures not to leave a trace.

Doss told Plough he should plan a trip to D.C., and they would "randomly" run into each other at a bar. The talk would turn to police work, and Doss would talk about his need for a director of security. It was all very elaborate, and it didn't seem all that necessary to Plough, but he certainly didn't tell Howie Doss that.

Derek Plough officially joined Always Right in early 2007. His title was Director of Security, and he handled threats to Doss and other things security related.

His first job was to try and do anything he could to find out where Darby Cash Bowles was. One last attempt to find the man.

Plough came back to Doss and told him that he hadn't found anything about his whereabouts. Over the intervening years, Doss began to forget about Darby Bowles. He figured he was either dead or didn't want anything to do with his past. It made perfect sense. He once again assumed that Bowles was out of his life forever.

From 2008-2017, Doss had said nary a word about Darby Cash Bowles to Plough. That would change on December 26th, 2017.

Plough was called into Doss's office, which raised a red flag right away. Plough had a secured cellphone that Doss had given him specifically for phone calls with him. It was encoded, and no one would ever see or hear what they had talked about. However, on this day, Doss texted him and asked him to come to his office.

Plough knew something was up.

Doss's company, Always Right, named after its eponymous website, now had 37 employees, which might sound like a small number of people for a company with so much influence, but Doss was such a hands-on CEO, that he did everything he could. He also didn't trust many people and tried to keep his employee level as low as he possibly could.

Of the 37 employees, 36 were straight, 35 were white, and 33 were men. Two of the four women employees were secretaries, and the third secretary was the only gay employee. Plough knew what the numbers would be if Doss had his choice, but he knew to further his agenda, he couldn't make it look like Always Right was a workplace for white males only.

There are two K streets in Washington D.C., but if you are talking about K Street in the generic way that people have come to call it, you are always referring to the northern side of the street. K street had long been known as the location of the big lobbying firms in Washington D.C., even though most of the big firms had moved off of K Street over the years.

The reputation has persisted, however, and it's become the generic term for lobbyists in Washington D.C. While it may not consist of many lobbying firms anymore, it's still a desirable address for a business, and Always Right was surrounded by Law Firms, PR Firms, and the International Finance Corporation.

Plough entered the building of Always Right, took the elevator up, and made his way towards Doss's office. He saw Gloria Flores, the lone non-white women working for Doss. She was the most virulent anti-immigration writer they had at alwaysright.com and calling her a pistol would be a royal under-statement.

Plough nodded to her. Everyone in the office had heard of Plough, but none of them knew him well. Flores, being one of Doss's prized employees, had been introduced to Plough a few times and was one of a few who knew him by his face alone. What the other employees did know was that Plough was Doss's right-hand man, so if you pissed off Plough, you'd have to deal with Howie Doss. That meant no one ever fucked with Derek Plough.

He nodded to Virginia Hale, Doss's longtime private secretary. Plough had now acknowledged two of Always Right's four female employees in a minute. A bastion of feminism it was not. Hale called into Doss, and a few seconds later, the huge doors to Doss's office opened.

Derek Plough was not a man interested, or impressed, with design, furnishings, or anything of that nature. As a child, he had avoided his sisters playing house, and considered any type of interior design a feminine thing. That being said, Plough had always been amazed at just how beautiful the office of Howie Doss was.

The highlight had to be the huge bay window that looked out on, or more precisely, down on K street. It covered the whole of Doss's office, which Plough guessed was probably 60 feet long. Doss had often joked that it had allowed him to look down on his enemies, although Plough never thought he was joking when he said it.

The interior of the office was no slouch either. There were two beautiful wood pillars that went up on each side of his huge mahogany desk, something that looked like it was from the 18th century. It may have been old, but it always shined like it was bought yesterday.

To Plough, it seemed like the chair where Doss sat was elevated ever so slightly, so whoever was sitting across him had to look up at him. It would be a small psychological fuck you, but something that Plough could absolutely see Doss doing.

He had come to despise his boss over the years. And yet, he still feared him and knew he would never turn against him. He had gotten over his school girl like reverence of him years ago, but he still idolized him for all he had become. It was a complicated relationship where Plough alternately held his boss in the highest possible standing while hating everything he had done to get there.

As Plough entered the office, he could tell that Howie Doss was a bit nerv-ous. This didn't happen often, and Plough tried to rack his brain for the last time he had seen his boss like this. He couldn't remember a time. Pissed off? Absolutely. Doss had one of the biggest tempers he had ever seen, and he had ruined many a person when his rage took over. But nervousness? That was something new.

He motioned Plough to sit down, and as he did, he once again felt like he was looking up at Doss. Plough wondered if maybe it was just in his head, and that 17 years of feeling beneath Howie Doss had manifested itself in this way.

Howie Doss's hair was already prematurely graying back in 2000, and he now had a full head of silver hair, despite only being in his mid 40's. He always seemed to have a red tint to his skin, which had led more than one liberal pundit to refer to him as the Albino Devil.

"I think one of our old friends is back," Doss said.

Plough's stomach suddenly felt uneasy.

"We have a lot of 'old friends,'" Plough said.

"The oldest of the old," Doss said, and it was clear who he was talking about.

"Darby Bowles?" Plough asked.

"It sure looks that way."

"But how?"

"I don't know how yet. I've been doing some searches today, and it looks like he had been in jail from 2008 until earlier this month. It was 2007 when I last had you try to locate him, and I'll be honest, I had kind of sworn him off after that. But he's back alright."

"Did he contact you?"

"Sort of. He sent this," Doss said and handed Plough a piece of paper.

He grabbed it and started reading it aloud: "Hey Howie! This is your favorite old getaway driver. It looks like the years have been kind to you. They have been pretty shitty for me, but I think the money you are going to pay me will make my latter years quite enjoyable. I'll be in touch, but why don't you keep your checkbook handy. This is going to cost you!"

Plough looked down at the paper in disbelief.

"He put like five post it notes on the outside, saying 'For Howie Doss's eyes only.' It made its way up to me pretty quickly. Smart thinking actually."

"How did he find out who you are?" Plough asked.

"I don't know. We only met one time and he never got a look at my face."

"He heard your voice though. And that hasn't changed," Plough said.

Doss looked at him in amazement. It was one of the more insightful things that Plough had ever said.

"Fuck, you're probably right. I never should have agreed to any fucking interviews. Should have been like the Wizard of Oz and just remained behind the curtain."

Howie Doss was pissed, and Plough subconsciously leaned back in his chair, getting ever so slightly further away from Doss.

"So what do you want me to do?" Plough asked.

"I think you know. I have you on a flight to Eureka, California later to-night."

"Where the fuck is Eureka?"

"Eureka is where our favorite getaway driver was released from prison last week. Northern California. You catch a connector through Sacramento. Check your secured phone. I'll be sending all the relevant information to it."

Doss motioned for Plough to stand up, which he did.

"You have a right to carry a firearm, and I'd suggest bringing it with you."

"I understand, Howie."

"And this probably doesn't need to be said, but I don't expect you to return to D.C. until we know that Mr. Bowles no longer poses a threat to me, " Doss said.

"You're right," Plough said. "That didn't need to be said."

28

Darby Cash Bowles had spent Christmas with Billy, Tina, and their three children. Billy's only family was back in Oklahoma and Tina's family was in Virginia, so it was just the six of them for Christmas. It was Darby's first proper Christmas dinner in many years, and he savored every bite of ham, scalloped potatoes, and anything else Tina put in front of him. He entered a food coma later that day and spent the rest of the day on Billy and Tina's couch.

His first letter to Howie Doss was sent out on December 22nd, only a day after getting out of jail, but due to the logjam around Christmas, Doss didn't receive it until the day after Christmas. Which was, coincidentally, when Darby sent out his second letter.

He read it three times before he finally mailed it. It read: "Howie, my old friend! I hope this letter finds you well and you didn't drop dead of surprise when you received my first. We're going to start small, and I'm going ask you for $9,900. I'm sure that's a drop in the bucket for a man like you. But don't worry, I'll be upping the ante soon. I've listed below the account # of my local credit union, and I'll be expecting the money before January 1st, or I'll go to the police and the media. Good to talk to you again."

Darby had told Frankie Waters that he needed the week to find further evidence on Howie Doss, but that wasn't the case. What Darby really wanted was to try and get paid without Frankie or his girlfriend getting in the way. He couldn't have them going to the cops or the media, getting Doss arrested, and fucking everything up. Darby would enjoy the hell out of Doss getting arrested, but that could wait. He wanted to get paid first.

But he also knew he couldn't just ask for a huge sum right off the bat. He knew the IRS wasn't notified for deposits under 10k, so that's why he asked for $9,900. He could then give the Waters' kid a taste of the money and be sure they wouldn't go to the cops.

His next demand would be different. Obviously, a few hundred thousand or a million couldn't be deposited in a local credit union. Darby wondered if he should have it delivered by money order or set up an offshore checking account.

"First world problems," Darby said aloud and laughed to himself.

A few thousand miles away, Howie Doss was laughing to himself as well.

As Derek Plough was in the air heading to Sacramento and then on to Eureka, Doss was able to accomplish his goal of locating Darby Bowles. Doss had no doubt that some of his better programmers and computer geeks could have found him in minutes, but he didn't want them knowing the name of Darby Bowles. If they later came across the fact that he had been murdered, Doss would have some serious questions to answer. So even though he had some of the best internet wizards in the world working for him, he had to do this himself.

He googled "Darby Bowles" and "Darby Cash Bowles." It was how Doss had originally found Darby had been released in Eureka, CA, but now Doss was looking for something more specific. He had googled "Darby Bowles Facebook," but nothing had come up, but in a moment of brilliance, Doss decided to try something different.

While Darby Bowles didn't have a Facebook account, Doss thought that maybe someone might have tagged him or posted about him since he had been released from jail. He typed in "Darby Bowles" in the search area of Facebook, and something popped up.

A man named Billy Gullicksen had posted something saying "Merry Christmas everyone! Our old friend Darby Bowles is back and staying with us for a while." The photo consisted of Darby, whom Doss recognized right away, along with Billy Gullicksen, his wife Tina, and their three kids. Although Darby Bowles had been wearing a blindfold the one time they met, Howie Doss very much knew what Darby Bowles looked like.

A short Google search later and Doss was able to find out that Billy Gullicksen lived at 481 16th Street in Eureka, CA. He texted Derek Plough the information, knowing he'd get it when he landed. Doss smiled, leaned back in his chair, and said his goodbye to Darby Cash Bowles.

29

Early on the morning of December 27th, Evie and I walked into Oakland Technical High School. Our local congresswoman Scarlet Jackson was speaking to students and local voters about following their dreams, and not getting sucked into the gang culture that was prevalent in the poorer parts of Oakland. The turnout was solid, if unspectacular, as it's hard enough getting 14 to18-year-olds to go to school when they have to, much less when it's optional.

Congressmen and women lived in Washington D.C. obviously, but the good ones came back to the communities that elected them as often as they could. Scarlet Jackson was one of the good ones and came back to Oakland as much as her schedule permitted. She grew up in the poor part of Oakland and was an example to all those who were stuck in that shitty environment that they could rise above it. She was a beacon of light locally and well-respected in D.C. as well. Scarlet Jackson was 47 years old, and there were rumors she might be running for the open California Senate seat in a year.

Evie and I weren't that far removed from high school, but we still looked like we were in our 40's compared to some of the pimpled-faced kids that we saw. There were also a great number of parents and local citizens, and we looked young as hell compared to them. We were lost between two worlds, too old to pass as high school students, and way too young to pass as parents.

Jackson spoke for about 30 minutes, and it was probably more personal than any of the speeches she had ever given in Washington D.C. After all, these were the streets she grew up on, and some of these kids were the same at-risk kids that she once was. You could tell how important making the inner cities safer was to her, and her energy was contagious. Jackson may have been 47, but she had the energy of some of these high school students.

When her speech ended, she was quickly surrounded by students and parents alike. Evie and I slowly walked in that direction, and I looked forward to the moment when she recognized Evie. That came almost immediately.

"Evie Somerset," she said, with a big smile on her face. "What the hell are you doing here?"

Scarlet Jackson was a thin, but not frail, African American woman. She looked very stylish, not something you'd imagine from a congresswoman. She was quick with a smile and seemed very likable.

Evie went and hugged her. "Hi, Scarlet! I'm home for Christmas break, and my boyfriend Frankie here saw that you were speaking here today. I had to come."

It was a surreal moment for me. For the first time, Evie had referred to me as her boyfriend, and at the same time, I was meeting a United States Congresswoman. It was a lot to digest, but I managed it fine.

"Nice to meet you, Ms. Jackson," I said.

"Please, call me Scarlet."

"Nice to meet you, Scarlet."

She smiled at me and turned to Evie. "He's a lot cuter than that boyfriend who came and visited in D.C."

I knew from that point on that I was going to like Scarlet Jackson. Evie smiled as well, but for obvious reasons, didn't want the conversation to head in that direction.

"Is there any way we could sit down and have a coffee with you?" Evie asked.

"I'm really rushed for time, but I can give you 10 minutes after I say hi to all these people?"

"Perfect."

Once Scarlet Jackson was done with her obligatory greetings, she asked the principal if there was a room we could have some privacy in. She led us towards an unoccupied schoolroom and Scarlet, Evie, and myself sat around a teacher's table. There was a World Map right behind us, a few globes scattered throughout the room, and a remedial drawing of Europe on the drawing board.

"So what's on your mind, Evie?" Scarlet asked.

Evie and I had talked about what we were going to say on the way over. We had to be delicate, and couldn't get her suspicions too aroused. She was a U.S. congresswoman after all, and if she knew what we knew, this would be out of our hands in an instant. Evie and I had agreed that we would give Darby the week, and while we were back doing our own research, we still hoped to keep that promise.

We decided to say that a cousin of mine worked for Howie Doss and claimed he had some dirt on him. It was close enough to the truth where we could hopefully get some information, but it certainly wasn't anything that Scarlet Jackson could run to the press with. It was way too general, and we weren't going to get any more specific.

"Do you know who Howie Doss is?" Evie asked. The answer was obvious, but it would get the conversation headed in the right direction.

"You mean the Puppeteer," Scarlet said, more a statement than a question.

I looked on quizzically.

"What do you mean?" Evie said.

Scarlet laughed. "Just a little inside joke between Howie and I."

"Didn't know you knew him that well," Evie said.

"I don't. Only met him one time."

This conversation was becoming a one on one exchange, but I wasn't just going to be a wallflower. Was time for me to speak up.

"You call him the Puppeteer because he pulls all the strings?" I asked.

"Well yeah, that's the reason why, but it was a nickname he gave himself," Scarlet said.

She reached for her cell phone, and we knew to stay quiet. She pulled the phone out and scrolled through it.

"I was at a function in D.C. about four months ago. Evie, you had probably just left to go back to school. Anyway, it was some media get-together, and all of the big political bloggers were invited, along with some Congressmen and Senators. To my surprise, Howie Doss was there. Everyone knows about Always Right obviously, but he's generally a recluse, doing things behind the scenes, so everyone was shocked to see him there. There were no cameras or media allowed, so I imagine that's why he came. Pretty ironic, right? A shindig for the media where outside media wasn't allowed."

Evie and I looked on in expectation but didn't say a word.

"So about an hour into the event, I decided to go up and introduce myself. He's got a commanding presence, and I'll be honest, he was intimidating. This despite the fact that he's a slight man with Andy Warhol's hair and a red tint to his skin. But he could also be very charismatic, and he was to start our conversation. At some point, our discussion went downhill, and he became a bit aggressive. At least with his words. So that's when I realized I had my phone in my hand, and I subtly pressed video and recorded a bit of our conversation."

Scarlet put the iPhone on the classroom table and pressed play. The video was all blurry, probably a view of Scarlet's hand. The words were very clear, however, and you could hear Scarlett and Howie Doss just fine.

"Boy am I glad you aren't in the White House," she said.

"Oh, you are so naive. I can put up an article on my website and drop the president's approval rating 10 points in a day. I could release a story about a cabinet member that would get everyone so up in arms he or she would have to resign within days. I can make a war sound necessary and inevitable. I can make an enemy sound sympathetic or a long-time ally sound conniving. I have dirt on some of the biggest people in Washington. And if I don't, I'll make shit up! No one cares what the truth is anymore. They only care about what will advance their cause."

"Not everyone is as cynical as you," we heard Scarlet Jackson say.

There was then a pause before Doss continued.

"I know you deal with all those politicians and statesmen all the time, including the President, but you know what?"

"What?"

"I'm the one pulling all the strings. I'm the fucking Puppeteer!"

No one said a word for several seconds, as we soaked in what we had just heard. It was chilling for a few reasons. First, the sheer intensity of Howie Doss's voice. Evie and I had watched the few YouTube videos available, but it was different hearing him angry. I could understand how Darby would never forget that voice. It was one of a kind. Second, were the words themselves. Howie Doss really believed he was as influential as the president. You couldn't fake the authenticity he spoke with. He was a true believer.

What Scarlet said next was probably the most chilling of all.

"Do you think what he said is true?" I asked.

"Up to a point, yes. There are two different ways to look at it. Can Howie Doss press a button and launch nuclear weapons? No, so in that way, he doesn't have the true power of a president. But he can absolutely affect policy. In fact, he can shape the president's viewpoints on just about any issue. If Always Right conducts a poll, and 3/4 of conservatives say burning the flag should be a jailable offense, you can be sure the President will take note and adopt that position. The scariest part is that Doss can post articles or even makeup polls if he wanted, just in order to affect policy. Always Right is such a mammoth website that the President would be foolhardy to ignore it. There's also the rumor that Doss has paid out millions to get dirt on the biggest people in Washington. It hasn't been proven, but most people think he was behind the leaks that cost two cabinet members their positions. Is he as powerful as the president? I don't know, but he's right up there."

Scarlet then turned and looked at us. "Well, how's that for the longest winded answer ever? All you did was ask about Howie Doss!"

Evie laughed. "So what do you really think of Doss?"

This time, it was Scarlet Jackson's turn to laugh. "I think that's pretty clear. So why do you ask about him?"

I hated lying to my local congresswoman, but this was no time to tell the truth. We could always get to that later.

"I have a cousin that works for Doss, who thinks he might have some dirt on him."

A huge smirk came across Scarlet Jackson's face. "Christmas is coming 363 days early. Or maybe two days late," Scarlet Jackson said.

"We aren't sure exactly what he has, and I'm not prepared to tell you anything yet, but I just wanted to make sure we could come to you when the time is right," I said.

Scarlet shrugged her shoulders just a little bit. I had gotten her expectations up, and she was hoping for more.

"Of course you can come to me. Your girlfriend is one of my favorite all time interns."

"Frankie was thinking about doing an internship in D.C. next year. Are you hiring Scarlet?" Evie asked.

"If there is some truth to what Frankie's cousin told him, I will put you guys on payroll!" Scarlet said enthusiastically.

"Does Evie have your cell phone number?" I asked.

"No. She just had the official officer numbers. I'm going to give both of you guys a phone number. This is a safe number to dial, and no one can listen in or record, so feel free to talk about anything."

I stood to go, not wanting to say anything else.

"There's nothing more you can give me for now?" Scarlet asked.

I wanted to throw her a bone, but we couldn't risk it at this point.

"Not right now, but you'll be the first to know when we do," I said.

We parted company, with a promise from Evie and I to be in touch.

30

Darby Bowles woke up on the morning of the 27th in his best mood in years. He started imagining spending the rest of his life on a white sand beach with an umbrella drink and a tanned woman doing her native dance in front of him. He would buy a little bungalow on the water and live out the rest of his days drinking and screwing. Couldn't get much better than that.

He would never need a car so he could drink as much as he damn well pleased. And he could slowly forget about the first half of his life. He had a rough childhood, spent many years in and out of jail, and played a slight part in an infamous day in Oklahoma City history. He had then unfortunately killed some young people while drunk driving. Darby knew he'd forever regret the last one, that was on him, but the others were bad circumstances and a shitty childhood. At least, that's how Darby rationalized it.

He told Billy and Tina that he wanted to go walk along the docks and say hi to some old friends. Billy laughed, knowing the hero's welcome that Darby would get when all his former longshoremen saw him.

Darby turned down Billy's offer of a ride and headed off to the docks alone. He wanted some time to be by himself and ponder his future. Every time he thought about laying on the beach for the rest of his life, he got a little giddy. For a guy growing up in Oklahoma City, the ocean always seemed like such a distant thing. Not too distant for this guy, Darby thought to himself.

He realized the irony of thinking about spending his life by the ocean as he approached the docks. After all, the Pacific Ocean was right next to him as he walked along the Eureka boardwalk. But really, it was a boardwalk in name only. It had nothing on beautiful boardwalks like the ones in Venice Beach or Coney Island.

The water below the docks had been so contaminated by the exhaust of boats and ships over the years, that the formerly blue water was now closer to gray, and with a shiny, oily substance on top to boot. It looked like a slime that would envelop you if you ever had the misfortune of landing in it.

The drop off from the docks to the water was about 10 feet, and yet, Darby had only seen a few people ever in that water, and it was never on purpose. The longshoreman knew how dirty and contaminated that water was and would never push one of their friends in there. Even as a joke. A few had accidentally fallen in and probably needed an hour long shower just to feel themselves again.

As he walked up towards a huge freighter ship that was docked in the murky waters, he looked out towards the Pacific in hopes of seeing the bluer water that he would be living on soon. He sure had become a sentimental fool lately.

The first person who saw Darby approaching was Yancy Taylor, one of the toughest longshoreman he had ever worked with. That was saying something as there were a whole bunch of rugged guys Darby had worked with over the years. Taylor came over and gave him a big bear hug.

"Darby! When did you get out?"

"Almost a week ago now."

"You been avoiding us?"

"Can you blame me?"

That got a laugh out of Taylor. Several other longshoremen saw Darby and started to walk over. There wasn't much turnover in the longshoreman business, and Darby recognized several faces even though he hadn't worked there for almost a decade.

"You picked the wrong day to come down. Not many guys working today," Taylor said.

"Yeah, I know. I've been staying with Billy, and he has the day off."

"Billy really likes you, I hope you know. He was broken up for years about what happened."

This wasn't what Darby wanted to talk about and tried to change the subject.

"That's all in the past, Yancy. I'm thinking about the future."

Darby looked out at the Pacific once again. Taylor caught him doing it.

"You going out to catch a white whale, Moby Dick style?"

Darby liked the comparison. Moby Dick was one of the many books he had read in jail. He was Captain Ahab, and Howie Doss was his Moby Dick.

"In a way, I am!" Darby said.

"Well, you look good. You haven't aged 10 years or whatever it's been, I'll tell you that. Still got that baby face."

"Might be a first in this business. Look at all these leather faces," Darby said.

The longshoreman sense of humor could be tough, but they all liked a good leather face joke. The men who had gathered behind Yancy Taylor laughed and came over to give Darby a hug.

Darby recognized Greg Weatherly, Hank Style, and Art Baker. Others he recognized by face, but not by name. Clearly, they were all happy to see Darby. Even though his crime had been terrible, and they had all prayed for the lives lost, Darby had been one of them, and they all welcomed him back. They had all shared drinks with Darby at The Long and Shore of It over the years, and many of them had driven home drunk. *There but for the grace of God (go I).*

Hank Style came up and gave Darby the biggest bear hug of all, probably because Hank was built like one. He was 6'5, " and over 300 pounds and his strength was legendary. Darby felt at least six bones crack as Style hugged him.

"So here's what I'm thinking," Style said. "Tomorrow, we got a big ship coming in. Why don't you work a day for old times' sake and we all take you out to a nice steak dinner after?"

All of the men gathered smiled in unison, and Darby heard a couple people say "Hear, Hear." It sounded like a swell idea to Darby, and truth be told, it would have been tough to turn down Hank Style even if he hadn't.

"I'm in! I'll be here at 5 a.m. sharp." Darby said.

"And we are going to work you like you haven't been worked in years," Art Baker said.

"I've been in jail with guys 10 times as tough as all of you," Darby said, smiling the whole time. "You guys look like a bunch of pansies by comparison."

"Speaking of which, you've been surrounded by dudes for a long time, how about we get you a beautiful girl after dinner tomorrow night."

"I wouldn't complain," Darby said.

"A big steak for dinner, followed by some tuna for dessert," Hank Style said, and all of the men laughed.

Darby laughed hardest of all. "You guys haven't changed one bit, and I mean that in the best possible way."

"It's great to have you back Darby," it was Greg Weatherly's turn to chime in. "Are you hanging around Eureka?"

"Actually, I'm not Greg. I've got some big plans," Darby instinctively looked at the ocean again.

"He's going to catch Moby Dick," Yancy Taylor said.

"I thought that's what he got in jail," Hank Style said, and this time the longshoreman really lost it, laughing hysterically.

"You wish big guy," Darby laughed it off. "I still love the fairer species."

Style bear hugged Darby again.

"I won't get emotional until tomorrow night, but just wanted to say it's great to see all of you guys," Darby said.

Longshoremen were not an emotional group by nature, but they were all touched by the moment.

"We're longshoremen, stop trying to prove we have emotions, Darby," Art Baker said.

"Touche, Art. I knew I couldn't get you robots to show anything."

This was all in good fun, and the people surrounding Darby were enjoying it as much as he was. Unfortunately, the fun was about to end as a bell went off and they had to get back to the ship.

"Listen, Darby, you know what that sound means, but we'll see you here tomorrow," Yancy Taylor said.

All of the men came over and hugged Darby a final time. He was smiling from ear to ear.

"Thanks, guys! Sure know how to make an old friend feel welcomed," Darby said.

They waved their goodbyes, and the longshoremen started walking back towards the ship they were unloading. Darby was reminded of the iconic final scene of *On the Waterfront.*

When people talked about the boardwalk in Eureka, they are really referring to the more touristy section, but to Darby, the whole long row of walking along the ocean was the Boardwalk. After all, if you just took it as its word, it was walking on boards, and by that definition, the boardwalk was a lot longer than most people would acknowledge.

Darby was in a walking mood that morning and was already buoyant after a much better than expected trip down to see his old longshoremen buddies. It couldn't have gone any better than it had.

He also hadn't taken a long walk since he got out of jail, and you certainly didn't get any of those opportunities when you were inside.

Darby never had much time for self-reflection when he was young, but he found himself doing a lot more of it lately. Walking around the docks and looking out at the ocean, had brought out the most introspective Darby.

He had conveniently excused himself for most of his fuck-ups over the years, but he could never get over those kids he had killed when he was drunk driving. Even he couldn't forgive himself there. For that, he would need the forgiveness of a higher power.

Darby had seen a lot of churches around Eureka and considered stopping into one and baring his soul. He knew that Catholics were allowed into heaven if they apologized and were absolved for all of their sins. Maybe that's what he'd do. Apologize for every single thing. Even the ones he had found a way to excuse himself of blame. Like Oklahoma City for example. He knew that being a getaway driver wasn't admirable, but he had never condoned the racist murders the others had partaken in. If there was a higher power, he hoped he wasn't lumped in with the killers.

An hour in confession would do him some good. He was pretty sure that priests had the same sort of attorney/client privilege that lawyers had, but he'd have to check up on that. The last thing he wanted was the police to show up at Billy's door just as he was starting to get paid from Howie Doss.

Darby kept walking down the boardwalk, taking his leisurely time. When he passed through the more touristy area, he paused and looked at the shops, and the families coming out of them. There were times he regretted never having kids. This was one of those times.

He was so close to having them with Patricia before his fateful decision to drink and drive. It was obvious to him that it had fucked up Patricia's life as well. She sure had bad luck with guys. Darby thought they would have been pretty good together, but his decisions had cost them those opportunities.

Maybe one of the native girls he'd dreamt of would want to have one of his children. Johnny Bowles if it was a boy, in honor of his late father's favorite singer, and Grace Bowles if he had a daughter. He always thought Grace was an elegant sounding name, and Lord knows elegant was something Darby's life could use.

Passing by the end of the shops, he looked in at a few bars and restaurants that sat just off the boardwalk. In the old days, Darby might have stopped in for a drink or two, but he didn't feel like it on this day. He was enjoying this walk too much and was appreciating this introspective side of himself.

As he finished walking through the touristy area, the beautiful boardwalk now started to grow a little dirtier and grimier. Eureka had become home to a lot of meth heads in the last 15 years, and they would sometimes sit down in this section of the boardwalk. Darby looked around and not seeing any shadowy figures, kept walking.

He laughed at himself. He had dealt with criminals and lowlifes of the highest order, and he found it funny that he was now worried about a few meth heads. Was he getting old? No, just smartening up, he told himself.

Darby remembered fishing with Billy a few times in this general area. He looked down at the water and thought maybe it was better they never caught anything. The fish would probably have had three eyes.

It amazed Darby how they could keep the water relatively blue in the touristy area, but the further down you walked the dirtier it became. Maybe they policed the littering there much better than where he was now. He could throw a trash can in the water right now, and there would be no one to raise a finger. There was no one down this way, and certainly no police officers to prevent you from littering. He hadn't seen a soul for at least a quarter mile.

The end of the board planks was about 500 yards ahead. That would be the end of Darby's walk, and then he'd turn around and start walking back. No need to climb up on the grass and the smallish bluffs above the ocean. He was just fine staying on the wooden planks.

There was a man sitting on a bench about 50 yards from the end of the board planks that caught Darby's attention. It was a weird spot to be sitting, but he was dressed nicely and certainly didn't look like a tweeker. Darby approached the guy and waved at him. The man waved back and seemed perfectly normal. Any apprehension Darby had was gone.

He walked past the man and towards the end of the planks, and once he got there, he grabbed a wood pillar that was the last piece of wood. After that, it was just grass and marshland above the Pacific. Darby smiled. He had just walked the length of the Eureka boardwalk. He wasn't sure how long it was, couldn't have been more than a mile or a mile and a half, but for some reason, he was really happy with himself. It probably had more to do with the general contentment that he was feeling that day, but he truly was proud to have made it to the last plank.

At the ripe old age of 42, Darby was becoming a better man. He was willing to accept his mistakes from the past. It had started as he awaited release from jail and had become more prevalent in recent days. He wasn't above trying to bribe Howie Doss, but hey, nobody's perfect. Plus that terrible man deserved anything he got, Darby reasoned.

His blood pressure rose as he started to think of Howie Doss, so he calmed himself down by thinking about the umbrella drink. And the native girl dancing. And maybe a child by their side. Darby smiled again. This had been a great day, and he was really looking forward to his day on the docks tomorrow, followed by a great steak and a greater woman.

Darby took a deep breath and exhaled. If he didn't watch himself, he might start crying. He pulled himself together and patted the wood pillar for the last time as he decided it was time to head home.

His back was now to the boardwalk, and as he began to turn around, he saw someone briskly walking towards him. It was the guy who had been sitting down, and he was reaching for his jacket. Darby knew something was seriously wrong. It was happening so quickly, and Darby had to decide what to do.

He looked around but had nowhere to run. On one side he had the Pacific Ocean, and on the other side were the grass and marshland that was wet from winter. He would slough through it, and it wasn't a realistic escape route.

When the man's hand hit his jacket, and Darby saw the butt of a handgun, he knew he had to decide a plan of action immediately. He knew he couldn't run at him, he'd be shot before he ever got there. There was only one thing that he could do, and Darby knew it. It was now or never. He took two big steps and hurled himself through the air, knowing he was going to land in some of the dirtiest water on earth.

Derek Plough had woken up at 5 a.m. and drove his rental car to Billy Gullicksen's house and set up his own little stakeout. The Glock-19 he had brought with him was at his side. He knew his goal was to take Darby by himself if at all possible. He didn't want to involve any innocent people, and more importantly to Plough, the more people you had to kill, the less likely you were to get away with it.

Ideally, the family would leave by themselves, and Darby would be left at the house by himself. That was wishful thinking, and Plough knew it was unlikely. If Darby left with Billy, the man of the house, Plough was ready to kill both of them if necessary. The wife and kids were off limits; unless he had no other choice.

Around 7:30 he saw movement in the house, but he was too far away to make out faces. About a half hour later, Plough hit the jackpot as Darby Bowles left the house by himself. This might be easier than I thought, Plough hoped.

All things being equal, Plough didn't want to kill Darby on a public street, but it all depended on the circumstances.

Darby walked out of the house and started heading towards the ocean. Plough knew this because he had driven in from the direction of the ocean and was now doubling back. Plough trailed behind Darby at a safe distance and would pull over ever so often just so Darby didn't get any ideas he was being followed. He never turned around, and Plough was pretty sure he hadn't been seen.

He considered just gunning the car and trying to run Darby over, but decided against it for a few reasons. First off, Darby was walking on an elevated curb. It was only a foot higher than street level, but when the car hit the curb, there's no guarantee it would continue in the exact same direction. Second, he'd have to hope that Darby didn't hear the car approaching. If he heard it early, he'd have plenty of time to run away or dash into someone's yard.

And above all else, he couldn't have Darby survive an attack. He'd undoubtedly know who had arranged it, and he'd be singing to the cops within minutes. It would be the end of Howie Doss, and by extension, Derek Plough. No, trying to run him over was too risky, so he just kept back at a healthy distance.

Darby made his way down to the docks where a big freighter ship was docked. Plough parked the car and made his way in the direction of the dock. He stayed back and tried to pretend he was just casually walking around. He started walking down and away from the ship, knowing there wasn't any reason for Darby to go the other way unless he could walk on water.

After about five minutes of talking with friends, Plough saw Darby start to head down the boardwalk in his direction. Plough walked faster, looking to find a place where he could intercept Darby. He still didn't know what he would do when he saw him since the area was quite populated. Plough had his gun by his side, but he couldn't exactly shoot him on a crowded boardwalk.

Plough continued to move quickly, not wanting Darby to catch up to him or see his face. He didn't think there was any chance Darby would recognize him as the hero cop from the Oklahoma City papers so many years ago, but he still didn't want Darby to see him. There's only so many times you can see someone in your vicinity without getting a little suspicious.

Plough continued down the boardwalk, bypassing the shops, restaurants, and bars. He knew that area was way too populated. He kept walking down the boardwalk, and the scenery began to change. The planks became dirty, as did the surrounding area, and there were fewer and fewer people walking around. Plough kept on going, hoping to get as far away from other people as possible.

He saw a little table that was 50 yards from where the boardwalk ended. He sat there and waited. Now he just had to hope that Darby wasn't going to turn back before he reached him. Plough waited for what seemed like 20 minutes but was actually less than half of that. He looked up every minute or so, and finally, he saw Darby Bowles walking in his direction.

Plough waved at Darby as he walked by, thinking politeness was his best course of action. He subtly watched as Darby passed him by and walked towards the last remaining section of the boardwalk. Plough looked forward at Darby and then looked behind him one last time, making sure they were alone. There was no one to be seen, so Derek Plough got up and started walking briskly towards Darby.

He approached, and with Darby's back to him, it should have beeen easy. Plough got within 40 yards and then 30 yards. He started to reach for the Glock-19 he had in his jacket pocket, and as he did, Darby Bowles began to turn around. They stood, facing each other, with a shrinking 25 yards between them. The recognition in Darby's face told Plough that Darby knew he was reaching for a gun.

There was no need to continue the charade at this point, and Plough grabbed the butt of the Glock and pulled it out of his jacket. He saw indecision on Darby's face, as Plough raised the gun, readying himself to fire it. As he did this, Darby took two steps toward the end of the boardwalk and leaped into the ocean.

Plough was shocked. The ocean was right there, but somehow he hadn't considered it. It looked more like a sewer than an ocean and Plough couldn't imagine why a man would voluntarily jump into it. Maybe one who was about to be shot, he realized too late.

There was no time to beat himself up, and Plough walked to the edge of the boardwalk, firing a few shots where it looked like Darby had entered. Darby didn't resurface, and Plough was starting to get a sick feeling in his gut. If Darby was able to swim further away from him, popping up for small breaths, he might be able to get away.

Plough considered jumping in, but he didn't know which way Darby had swum once he entered the murky ocean. He decided it would be better to try and wait till he popped up on the surface and try to shoot him then. Plough waited 5 seconds, and then 10.

Finally, about 30 feet away, a head appeared above the surface, but only for a second. He saw Darby rise up to get a big breath of air, and then went back under just as they locked eyes. Plough took his gun and fired three times in the direction of Darby. He didn't resurface, and Plough assumed that he hadn't hit him. At that moment Plough realized that he couldn't just stand idly by and let Darby swim away.

Plough ripped off his jacket and shoes and jumped off the boardwalk in the direction of Darby.

When Darby leaped in the direction of the water below, he made sure to close his mouth as he entered.

As soon as he hit the water, he felt seaweed, plankton, and who knows what else hit him in the face as he sank below the surface. The smell of dead fish was unmistakable, and he knew he wouldn't be able to last long under water. Darby thought he heard a gun being fired, but there was so much shit circling around his ears, he couldn't be sure.

He tried to swim as fast as he could because he knew he wouldn't be able to hold his breath much longer. The best plan would be to get air for just a split second, and then he'd go back down underwater.

If he kept popping up above the surface, he was just waiting to be shot. He had to think of a plan, but he was so disoriented under water, he wasn't sure which way he was facing. When he went up for his first breath, he would look at his surroundings and then head away from the boardwalk.

Darby couldn't wait any longer and rose to the surface for the briefest of breaths. He was facing Plough as his eyes and mouth protruded from the surface. He didn't have time to take a full breath as Plough raised the gun to shoot. A split second later, after he lowered his head and was back under water, Darby felt a brutal pain shoot through his left side.

He had been shot, but Darby was pretty sure it was a through and through, meaning it had entered but then quickly exited his body. It felt like it was the very outer layer of skin on his flank, which meant it wouldn't have hit anything vital. It's something he could survive from if he was lucky enough to get out of the water. The shot had disoriented Darby, however, and as he started to swim again, he mistakenly swam in the direction of the dock instead of away from it.

A few seconds later, as Darby continued swimming as feverishly as he could, he swam right into Derek Plough. The water was so dark that there would be no chance to see the other one coming, and they collided mid stroke. In the instant their bodies met, Darby could tell that the other man was much bigger than him. He tried to kick him away, but there was so much crap in the water that the kick lost any momentum before it connected.

Darby did have the advantage, as he was nearer the top of the water, and this gave him some leverage. Plough had dove in and was rising through the water as he hit Darby, leaving him below him and at a disadvantage.

Darby's immediate concern was the gun, so he slashed his arms down towards the man's hands. Darby felt something in Plough's right hand, so with all his strength, Darby hit down on it several times, causing Plough to drop it in the dark sea.

The upper hand was still Darby's at this point, as his body was a little above Plough, but that wasn't going to last long. Plough was the bigger man and started pushing Darby away from him. If he could get Darby off of him, he could rise above him in the water and have all the leverage.

Darby knew what Plough was trying to do, so he shoved Plough's head down further into the water. Darby thought if he could hold the man down long enough, he could drown him, but if the man got away, he was in deep trouble. Darby continued to push Plough down, and Plough knew he needed to get a breath. And soon.

Plough felt the seaweed and gunk throughout out the water but felt like if he could just connect a blow to Darby's chin, he could knock him back just enough to get up for a breath. He brought his right fist from underneath Darby and rose up with as much force as he could muster. The uppercut's velocity was slowed by the water and everything in it, but it connected with enough of Darby's chin to knock him back just a bit.

It was all Plough needed. He went up for a quick breath and then was on top of Darby, with the leverage now on his side.

Darby would continue to fight as hard as he could, but he quickly realized he was overmatched. In a split second, he had gone from having the upper hand to knowing he was going to die. Plough was above him in the water and squeezing the life out of him. Darby fought back, trying to throw a few haymakers, but they had no chance of connecting as Plough had him by the neck and Darby couldn't muster any strength.

As Darby started to feel the breath leaving his body, he wasn't sure if he was drowning or being suffocated to death by the man's hands. In the end, it didn't matter, Darby realized. He was going to die in this armpit of the Pacific Ocean, not on a white sandy beach. There would be no native girl dancing for him while he sipped on an umbrella drink. There would only be a dark, stinky grave.

In his last few seconds on earth, Darby realized this guy must have been a goon for Howie Doss. He cursed himself for sending a letter to him. Darby tried one last time to hit the man across from him, but he had no more strength and the punch never had a prayer. Darby felt his breath leaving his body for a final time. He apologized for all the pain he had caused people in his life. Derek Plough tightened his grip around Darby and felt his body go limp.

Darby's arms gave way, and he stopped breathing a few seconds later. Darby Cash Bowles was dead.

31

Derek Plough swam away from the shore carrying Darby Bowles's lifeless body with him. The closer Darby's body was to shore, the quicker it would be found. There was so much gunk in this part of the ocean that Plough hoped that if he took the body out far enough, people wouldn't be able to see it from the shore. Or maybe it would sink. Regardless, the further away from the shore, the better.

Plough was able to drag Bowles's lifeless body about 60 yards before he realized he needed to head back soon or he wouldn't have enough energy to get back himself. He wrapped all the seaweed he could around Darby's head and pushed his body under water. Plough then swam back to shore, exhausted beyond belief when he finally made it.

The drive back to the hotel was a solemn one for Derek Plough. He had killed people before, but never with his bare hands. It had affected him more than he thought it would. It was dark and nasty in the water, but he had seen Darby Bowles's eyes go buggy in the moment where Plough squeezed the final breath out of him.

Assuming this was the final straw that tied Howie Doss to Oklahoma City, Plough was going to ask Doss for a few weeks off. He knew he had earned it.

Plough called Howie Doss on his secured phone when he got back to his hotel room, telling him everything that happened. Doss was quieter than usual, and Plough had a tough time judging his reaction. He should have been ecstatic, as the final connection to Oklahoma City had been eradicated. Plough then had a quick, piercing realization that HE was the actual last link to Oklahoma City.

He tossed out that notion as quickly as it had entered his mind. Howie Doss needed him and would never touch him.

"Can I head back, Boss?"

"I need you to do one more thing. Can you get supplies to tap a phone?"

"Yeah, it's pretty easy."

"When Billy Gullicksen and his family leave their home, I want you to tap their phone. I'm going to assume a family of five has a home line. And since Darby just got out of jail, he may not have a cell phone yet, and people may try to get ahold of him through the Gullicksen's."

"Seems logical. I'll do it."

"Call me after you have set up the tap," Doss said and hung up the phone.

Derek Plough had become an expert on phones, taps, bugs, etc. over the years. Howie Doss would do anything to get dirt on an enemy and tapping their phones had become par for the course.

He was able to get all the equipment he needed at an electrical and hardware store in town. He headed back over to the Gullicksen's residence for the second time that day.

He parked his car on a different street, facing the house from a different angle. The odds that Darby's body was found already were astronomical, but if it somehow was, Plough didn't want some nosy neighbor remembering a car that had been around that morning and then later that day. As he parked his car and looked out, the Gullicksen's pulled up to their house and walked in.

Plough sat in the car for an hour. He hoped they weren't in for the night. Finally, at about 4:45, the Gullicksen's all loaded into their family car. Plough looked at Billy Gullicksen, and although he was far away, he could tell Billy looked nervous. He kept looking around. He had to be wondering why Darby Bowles hadn't come back to their house yet. Hopefully, he just thought Darby was taking a day for himself, and Gullicksen hadn't called the police yet.

If there were any hints of police activity, Plough would be out of there as quick as you could imagine. He wasn't too worried, though. Plough knew the police wouldn't do much on the first day a guy was reported missing, especially once they found out he was an ex-con just recently released. They'd probably think he was up to no good somewhere.

After the Gullicksen's left, Plough waited 15 minutes. The sun was going down, and he wanted to do this without some neighbor seeing him hop the fence to the back door. Plough didn't have any kids, but he knew the odds of getting to a store and back within 30 minutes while having to deal with three kids was highly unlikely. Plus, he only needed a minute or two once he got into the house.

Plough got out of his rental car, walked over towards the Gullicksen house, jumped a small fence, jimmied the back door, broke in, and installed the tap into the back of their phone. It was all over in a matter of minutes.

32

We hadn't talked to Darby for several days now, and his week-long grace period was up in a few days. I told Evie I thought we should call him, and tell him our discovery that Derek Plough worked for Doss. Evie thought it was better if we didn't tell him, thinking he might just get more brazen with information like that. She was convincing, but I won out. I didn't like being in the dark this long.

I called the phone number he gave us, but there was no answer. I didn't think anything of it, and we went back about our day.

Evie and I got some lunch and talked about our next course of action. We went over all of the information we had and how everything fit together.

At one point, a bright light bulb lit up over my head

"I just thought of something."

"What?" Evie looked on expectantly.

"I'll bet the other guy in the picture in Darby's picture is Derek Plough."

Evie smiled.

"Of course! The one guy who Doss would need to see in the days after the murders. To be updated on the investigation. Great thinking, Frankie."

"Thanks. Plough looks like a big guy in the few pictures I saw, and the guy in the picture is much bigger than Doss."

"I have no doubt you're right," Evie said.

"This is all coming together," I said.

"Thanks to you."

"You're just as big a part," I said. "I'm going to tell Darby if he wants to blackmail Doss to go for one big lump sum. I'm not condoning it, but it's not like I can stop him. I'll tell him he better get it while he can because we can't sit on this too much longer."

"Agreed. Let's call and tell him that right now, so he knows he better expedite this."

I picked up my cell phone and dialed the number for the second time that day. Once again, there was no answer.

I looked over at Evie.

"I don't like this," I said.

The rest of the day was Evie and I doing nothing of importance, but the fact that Darby hadn't answered was hanging over our head. Our conversation was veiled with a hint of foreboding.

We had put it off long enough.

"Why don't you try Darby one last time?" Evie asked.

I picked up my phone, and for the third time, I dialed the number he had given me.

On the third ring, a man's voice answered. I smiled at Evie, just happy that someone had picked up.

"Hello," the voice said.

"Is Darby there?" I asked.

"No, he's not. Who is this?" the voice said. He was perturbed or worried, it was hard to tell. Maybe a little of both.

"A friend of his."

"I know all of Darby's friends," the voice said, but didn't seem too sure.

I knew that I wasn't going to get any more information from this man if I didn't give him a little myself.

"I met up with him several days ago in Ukiah," I said.

I wasn't sure if I had said too much, but this guy was holding something back, and I had to know what it was.

"I remember. He borrowed my truck. Well like I said, Darby isn't here right now."

"Listen, it's very important I talk to him," I said. I was trying to sound older than my age.

The man shrugged, or at least that's what it sounded like from the other end of the phone.

"Truth is, Darby went out this morning and hasn't come back."

My body tightened, and Evie noticed it. She looked at me, knowing something wasn't right.

"He just got out of jail, maybe he's just out blowing off steam," I said, not sure I believed it myself.

"I hope you're right," the voice said. "Was he in some sort of trouble?"

It was time to cut my losses and end this call.

"Not that I know of," I said. "Listen, I have to go, but I'll give you a call tomorrow."

With that, I hung up before he could respond.

"What is it?" Evie asked.

"Darby hasn't come back since he left this morning."

"Shit," Evie said. "Do you really think he's just blowing off steam?"

"No," I said succinctly.

"There's always that chance though, right?"

"Sure, there's a chance, but I'm starting to think that maybe Darby really shouldn't have mailed a letter to Howie Doss."

"You mean the Puppeteer, right?"

I let her rhetorical question hang in the air.

PART 3:
THE PUPPETEER

33

Howie Doss's life nearly ended before it actually began.

The year was 1972, and Spencer Doss's junior prom was approaching so he and his fellow juniors rented a cabin on Cedar Lake in their hometown of Columbia, Missouri. Spencer Doss had been working up to this night for weeks, telling his girlfriend Jan Tillerman that almost every other junior had already lost their virginity. He slowly wore her down, and she agreed that prom night would be the night.

Having helped reserve the cabin, Spencer Doss made sure that he got a room overlooking the lake. Not that he or Jan would see it when they were beneath the sheets, but it certainly was a romantic spot to lose your virginity. Neither one enjoyed prom itself, as Jan was nervous as hell leading up to what was to occur later. Spencer was equally petrified.

Despite their misgivings, they did have sex that night, not wearing any protection as it was the first time for both, and they had no STD's to contract. The other outcome of sex without condoms hadn't crossed their minds. They were both just relieved to have it out of the way. Spencer wasn't impressed with his stamina, while Jan thought it was slightly painful and agreed it ended quickly. She told Spencer that it was better to get the short sessions out of the way when it was still painful for her. Spencer didn't find this funny.

Junior prom was six weeks before the school year ended, and by the time summer came around, Jan knew she was pregnant. She had been as subtle as she could be, going to a friend's father who was a doctor, and avoiding the doctor her parents knew about. She had convinced herself she was going to go through with an abortion. When she told Spencer, he agreed that was the best course of action.

Unfortunately, Spencer's mother had a keen ear and one day when she was walking by Spencer's room, she heard Spencer mutter the dreaded A word. She knew that her son had been dating Jan Tillerman, so she called her parents and told her what she had overheard. Jan's parents, Allan and Bev, were extremely religious and as soon as they heard Jan was pregnant, abortion was no longer an option.

1972 was nothing like 1950, but it was still rare to see a girl in high school walking the halls while pregnant. Jan had wanted to drop out of school due to embarrassment, but her parents wouldn't allow it. You have to own up to what you've done, and ask for Jesus's forgiveness, her parents would tell her. Spencer was there by Jan's side, but her parents didn't want him in the picture long-term.

As their senior year began, Jan and Spencer stopped dating, and Spencer realized he was being shut out from the child's future. He hated to admit it, but he didn't want to make sacrifices for a one-time mistake. He was actually relieved that the Tillerman's seemed willing to raise the baby themselves.

And that's what happened. Howard Anthony Doss was born on February 10th, 1973, and while there were eight Tillerman's in the waiting room, there were zero Doss's, with the exception of the young baby. Allan and Bev Tillerman were very old school, and that included thinking that the young boy should keep his father's surname, even if he wouldn't be a part of the boy's future.

Howard was called Howie within weeks, and the nickname would last. He grew up being raised predominately by his religious grandparents, with his mother rarely in the picture. The elder Tillerman's wanted their daughter to live a normal life, so they paid for her to go to college and to live the life she wanted, while they raised young Howie. They were strict, and Howie was not above a beating when it warranted. Allan Tillerman was in his 50's and 60's in Howie's formative years, but that didn't mean he was grandfatherly and fragile. He was a very strict disciplinarian around the house, and Howie was taken to church every Sunday.

Howie Doss's life changed when he was 10 years old, and his father came back to Missouri for a protracted period of time. Spencer Doss had held a few odd jobs after high school, and then entered the military, but was accidentally shot twice in a training exercise and had received an honorary discharge. His left leg had undergone many surgeries following the accident and he never fully recovered. He walked with a prevalent limp and used a cane at times.

Spencer Doss was still in his 20's when he returned to Columbia, but he was already a broken man. He had a child that was his, but who he could rarely see, and a lifetime of walking with a limp ahead of him. He became depressed and started doing drugs to try and cope. He was always sober when he visited young Howie, but people around town knew Spencer Doss was fucked up.

Like any 10-year-old, Howie looked up to his father like he was a God. To Howie, his Dad couldn't visit because Allan and Bev wouldn't let him, while his biological mother chose not to visit. It was a huge difference in young Howie's mind and one that helped harbor the resentment towards his mother.

When his father had been in the military, Howie Doss would tell friends that his father was off fighting in wars, and that's why he wasn't around. When he was told there weren't any wars going on, Howie Doss took out his encyclopedia and read all about something called the Cold War, the only current war he could find. The next time a friend said there wasn't a war going on, Howie Doss would recite 25 facts pertaining to the Cold War.

When his father did return a few months after his 10th birthday, little Howie was almost happy to see that his father had been injured. He now made up stories about how his father was in the Soviet Union and took down 14 Russians before he was shot. It wasn't true of course, but Howie didn't care. It got a sympathetic reaction from his friends, and that's what matters. Early on in life, Howie Doss realized that the truth was often less important than the impact it caused.

Howie Doss was very intuitive as a young man, and even though his father was sober when he visited, young Howie knew he was going downhill. He'd tell his father that they would start a business together when Howie got out of high school. Even as a 10-year-old, Howie Doss was responsible and had an eye for the future. Unfortunately, his father would not be a part of the future.

Spencer Doss applied for some jobs around town, but the cane and the limp ruled out any blue collar job, and Spencer Doss wasn't exactly meant for a white collar job. He was amazed how intelligent his son was, knowing the smarts hadn't come from him. Jan Tillerman was no dummy, but she was hardly a Mensa candidate either. Young Howie was just special, Spencer assumed.

Howie would often ask his father how the job hunting was coming, and not wanting to sound inept, Spencer Doss would do what some poor whites do; blame minorities.

"Only hiring Niggers, Spicks, or Jews," he told his son more than once.

Howie had heard these types of words on the school playground, but never from an adult. Certainly not from his religious grandparents, and his mother, when she would come visit, would never talk like that.

Howie Doss knew that the jobs that never came were more likely due to Spencer's flaws than any reverse racism practices, but that didn't prevent him from starting to hate minorities. Whenever his father was going through tough times, Howie could be heard on the playground blaming his father's failures on a darker skinned person. Howie's grandmother Bev heard him say the N-word one time, and took him upstairs and wiped his mouth out with soap.

"Good, the soap will make me even whiter," Howie said.

Bev Tillerman looked down at the child she had helped raise and broke out in tears.

Of course, it wasn't just his father's racist comments that influenced Howie Doss's world view. He would see that most minority communities were in poor areas, and he'd blame them for not rising above it. When told about racism, a problematic police force, or judicial bias, Howie would just laugh it off, and say that those things didn't matter, or even better, didn't exist. Howie would often argue with his teachers about such heavy subjects even as a young man.

At the age of 13, Howie Doss came home from school one day, and he saw his mother Jan Tillerman at the front door with tears in her eyes. She was visiting less and less, and for all intent and purposes, Howie was Bev and Allan's son. But she was here on this day, and Howie thought he knew why.

"My Dad is dead, isn't he?" Howie asked.

"How did you know that?" Jan replied.

"Well, I see your parents back there, so I know they're alive. And I'm not sure why else you would be home and waiting for me with tears in your eyes."

Jan Tillerman was both impressed and perplexed. This young man, who had just become a teenager, was both really smart and really cold at the same time. She thought that generally, the smartest people were some of the warmest people. That didn't seem to be the case with her son.

"He had a drug overdose, Howie," she said.

"Maybe if you guys had stayed together or all the damn foreigners hadn't taken his jobs, he'd still be alive today."

Howie had already found other people to blame for his father's death.

Jan's parents walked over. Howie thought they were coming to comfort him, but they went to comfort Jan instead. She was in tears over what Howie had said. Howie didn't apologize and ran towards his bedroom in tears. They probably think I'm crying because of what I said to my mother, Howie thought. But he wasn't. He was crying for his father. Screw his mother and her desk job in St. Louis.

Allan and Bev Tillerman knew that Howie was their obligation, at least until he turned 18. Their relationship with Howie only got worse over the years, and they were counting the days until he was on his own. Every time Bev Tillerman was at her wit's end, her husband would have her read passages from the Bible and remind her that they had made their daughter keep him. He was their responsibility.

Howie Doss turned 18 during his senior year of high school and moved out of his grandparent's house the next day. He was working an after school job and had earned enough to pay the minuscule sum for a small one bedroom in a cheap part of town. The town's reaction to this was mixed. Some thought of him as a pretentious little asshole that was disrespectful to his grandparents, while some thought he showed a maturity rarely seen at that age.

Another change happened when he turned 18. Doss decided to stop using racial slurs when talking about minorities, except around people he trusted implicitly. He realized there was no benefit to it, and would only get him labeled as a troublemaker or a racist. Howie had big dreams, and he wasn't going to let something like that derail his plans. He would start arguing against minorities by using reason, and if that failed, by using persuasion. As with his belief that facts were often overrated, a young Howie Doss also knew that persuasion often worked better than reason.

Howie Doss graduated from high school in 1991 from Rock Bridge High School, and neither his mother nor his grandparents attended the ceremony. He did send them a letter, however, that read: *"Thank you for convincing your slutty daughter to keep me. I'm going to make my mark in this world, and it couldn't have happened without you. For that, I'm very appreciative. This is where our correspondence will end, however. I'm on to bigger and better things."*

Howie Doss flourished in college at the University of Missouri and was a visible campus Republican. He had managed to get William F. Buckley to speak on campus, and the picture of the two of them in the college newspaper was one of Doss's proudest achievements. After college, he moved to New York and got a job for the National Review, writing bylines and the occasional article. His hero, Buckley, had started the magazine in 1955 and Doss just knew he was going to love working there.

He thought the authors at the National Review were brilliant when it came to policy, but over time he realized they lacked any sort of persuasion. Doss just knew there were millions of Americans out there ready to be convinced to come to their side, but the National Review wouldn't attract them. They looked at themselves as above Middle America, but that was exactly the people they would need to attract. The first party that stopped looking down on the flyover states would have all the power. Doss knew this as a fact, but the people at the National Review failed to recognize it. Doss quit the National Review, chalking it up as a learning experience, and moved to Texas next.

He spent his next several years in Texas and Oklahoma. He knew he would return to either New York or D.C. at some point, but he wanted to get a feel for the people he would be trying to attract when he finally had consolidated some power of his own. Which he knew was inevitable. He was going to change the world.

In Texas, he worked on some local congressional races in both Dallas and Fort Worth, and when people learned he had left the National Review to come work in Texas, they couldn't understand why. Most of the people who worked for the Republican Party in Texas had an ultimate dream to write for the National Review. Doss would tell them that they could actually get more done on the ground, working on local races than the writers of the National Review would ever do. Despite his obvious intelligence and booming voice, people thought Doss had some crazy opinions, and that was one of them.

As always, Doss knew he was right, but it was lost on the idiots he was talking to. If he could get all of his opinions out to the masses, he could tilt the country in the direction that he wanted. It was too hard trying to talk to people individually.

Doss moved to Oklahoma City in 1999. He had now worked at the National Review and taken part in numerous political races. He had a good gauge on the Republican Party, and its strengths, and its flaws. The flaws were numerous, but they did have some advantages. Things like abortion and gun rights were so important to a lot of America, that if they could pound those issues into the heads of voters, they could easily win the majority of elections across the country. The one-issue voters could be easily manipulated, and the Republican Party had much more of them than the Democrats.

Howie Doss's life changed once again in July of 2000. His grandparents had died in a car crash, and he decided to attend the funeral. He had not spoken to them since he wrote them the vitriolic letter after he graduated high school, despite living in Columbia, Missouri all through college. Although his letter was gratuitous, he didn't despise his grandparents and thought overall they had done their best in trying to raise him. Their slut daughter, now that was a different story.

Close family stood near the casket, and although for all intents and purposes he was their son, Doss stood on the other side of the casket, facing the family. There was a black man sitting with his mother, and Doss was curious to find out who this man was. He didn't remember him from his childhood, and he certainly wasn't family. Doss's blood boiled.

After the brief ceremony, Allan and Bev Tillerman were lowered into the ground. People there were encouraged to throw a little dirt on their coffins, but Doss didn't take part. His eyes were fixated on the black man on his mother's arm. He could tell this was more than just friendship, and his suspicions were proven correct a few minutes later.

Doss approached his mother, who had seen him in the crowd, and it was obvious she was not looking forward to this encounter.

"Hello, Jan," Doss said.

"Hi, Howie. How have you been?"

"Oh you know, just getting ready to take over the world."

"That will be the day," she said.

Doss's blood started to boil even more. He couldn't wait to show her.

"And who is this gentleman on your arm?" Doss asked, sarcastically accentuating the word gentleman.

"This is Robert, my boyfriend."

Robert was a distinguished looking man with a graying beard. He was 15 years older than Jan, but they looked happy together. He extended his hand to shake Doss's, but Doss just let it sit there, outstretched.

"Your mother has told me a great deal about you," he said.

"My mother is in that grave over there," Doss said, pointing to the holes in the ground. "A real mother wouldn't want to have her son aborted."

Jan Tillerman started crying. She had already been crying at the loss of her parents, and then she had to deal with her asshole son. It was too much.

"You've always been a jerk, Howie. I don't defend what I did, but my parents did a great job raising you. You got much more than you would have if Spencer and I had raised you."

"Don't talk about my father like that," Howie said.

"What did he ever do for you? Nothing. And yet, you always took his side. I sent money and made sure you had a good upbringing, and he didn't do shit," Jan said, still holding back tears.

"Maybe if people like this didn't take his jobs he wouldn't have resorted to drugs," Doss said, looking at Robert when he said "this."

Robert was a much bigger man than Howie, and he was about to confront him when Jan looked at him as if to say no.

"You're despicable, Howie. I don't want to ever see you again," she said.

"You won't have to worry about that."

"You just think you are always right about everything, don't you?"

Doss sat there for 10 seconds as Robert and Jan waited for his next vulgarity. They wouldn't get one.

"Always right.....I like that," Doss said and walked away.

When Howie Doss arrived back in Oklahoma City after the funeral, he was more motivated than ever. He had always been a man with a plan, but he had felt he had been floundering a bit in recent years. The home invasions and robberies that he had orchestrated had given him enough money to where he didn't have to work, but Oklahoma City was not his endgame. Not even close.

He started to think how best to get out of his situation in Oklahoma City. Charles Leonard, Jared Wilder, and Elliot Walden had been good soldiers, but he couldn't take them with him to New York or Washington D.C. These were simpletons who he had recruited from local bars. They were country hicks and had no aspirations like the ones Doss had. There was also the problem of them knowing too much. Sure it was only home invasions and the occasional bank robbery, but that would be enough to sink Doss before he had his chance to make it big.

Doss started to think of ways that he could eliminate the three of them. He would keep Derek Plough in his employ. Having someone in the police force was way too valuable.

When he returned to Oklahoma City, Doss also started studying everything he could about the internet. He initially had the idea of enrolling in night school to learn how to code, but he was nearing the end of his time in Oklahoma City and didn't want anyone to remember him. Instead, he learned how to code at home, reading book after book. He knew the Internet was the wave of the future and it was time he got involved. Better to get in on the ground floor.

Darby Cash Bowles joined Doss's little group as a getaway driver in November of 2000. It was a risky move by Doss, but since he was planning on upping the ante a little bit, he felt he needed one more person.

Doss formulated his brilliant plan to kill off his associates in late January of 2001. He had become more aggressive ever since returning from his grandparents' funeral, and he knew this was a recipe for getting caught. So he began orchestrating his final two missions and then he was getting the hell out of Oklahoma City. He would spend the days setting up a foolproof plan, and the nights studying the internet and tinkering around with different domain names and looks for the website he planned on launching once he got out of Oklahoma City.

Always Right started to stick out in his mind as a potential website name. He liked the double meaning of always being correct and the political reference to always being on the right side of the political landscape. The fact that his Mom had said those words while standing with her black boyfriend made it perfect.

Doss spent more and more time on his plan. The man he would have to convince was Derek Plough. He had the most to risk, and he was also being asked to murder some acquaintances who bordered on being friends. Doss knew that Plough was wrapped around his thumb, but killing people would be a major obstacle for anyone. Doss kept emphasizing that if Plough didn't do this, eventually this would all come crashing down, and Plough would spend time in jail for being affiliated with Doss and his friends. And cops don't last long in jail, Doss would remind him.

Taking far less time than he anticipated, Doss was able to convince Derek Plough. After going over the plan probably 40 times, Plough did ask one question that Doss should have expected.

"Why not just have them go to the Temple first?" Plough asked. "I could kill them there."

It was a great question, and Doss was backed into a corner, but as always he was able to use his intelligence to talk his way out of it.

"There would be no reason you would be at the Temple if they went there first. We need a couple of murders first, so the police will send their officers to watch Jewish and Muslim spots. That's why I am having them paint swastikas on some churches, mosques, and synagogues next week. That will lay the groundwork, so the police will then realize what is going on when the two people are killed that morning. I assure you after the first two murders, your superiors will tell you to watch out for Jewish and Muslim places, and that will give you your reason to be near the Temple."

Derek Plough couldn't argue. It was a brilliant plan.

Of course, Howie Doss could have found a way for Plough to be at the original crime. But he wanted to send a big fuck you to minorities, so he altered his plan. He knew he was going to be a white-collar racist from here on in, and this was his last chance to get his hands bloody. Well, not precisely his hands, but close enough.

The plan didn't go off as expected, but all things considered, Howie Doss was happy with the result. Plough had done some quick thinking, and he was being heralded a hero by the local press. Doss would watch the T.V. and laugh, knowing he had orchestrated the whole thing. Derek Plough was no hero, just a pawn in Doss's game to kill off the people who knew too much.

The fact that Darby Bowles escaped caused Doss a few sleepless nights, but he was less worried than he thought he would be. First, Darby had taken part in many crimes, and Doss couldn't see him turning himself into the cops. Second, if he was caught and arrested, he knew less than nothing about Doss. He didn't know Doss's name or where he lived. Doss had paid Darby's rent, but it was cash, and the lease was signed with a fake name.

Of course, Doss didn't realize that Darby had been able to narrow down where he lived, and that Darby took pictures of him two days after what transpired in Oklahoma City.

Doss would look for information on Darby over the next several years, but would never find anything. Darby was in Eureka, CA living a quiet life, and Doss couldn't find him. Derek Plough was commissioned by Doss to do an exhaustive search for Darby in 2007, but it turned up nothing. After that, Doss was so busy with his flourishing website that he began to forget about Darby Cash Bowles.

Of course, Darby was arrested and thrown in jail a year later, but at that point, they weren't really looking for him anymore.

Following the murders, Doss spent the next four months in Oklahoma City, fine tuning his coding and internet skills. Doss was a borderline genius, and it came naturally to him. He knew, in the end, that the stories and links are what really mattered, but he also knew how important it was to have an official looking website.

He left Oklahoma City and moved to New York in June of 2001, launching alwaysright.com to little fanfare and even less daily visitors. When September 11th occurred, Doss was in a tiny apartment in Midtown Manhattan. His hate for people of color only became more pronounced. When he saw the amazing outrage (all of it deserved in his eyes) towards Muslims, he knew that maybe he should curb his articles towards anti-Muslim pieces. That would be an easier sell than articles that bad-mouthed African-Americans. It was a major change and one that worked well for Doss. He still had no love for African-Americans, Hispanics, or Jews, but most of all he wanted to increase viewership on his website, and he guessed Muslim bashing would work best.

Doss was very active with alwaysright.com in the months following 9-11, but he wasn't attracting all that many visitors to his site. The internet was just taking off, and he wasn't sure the best ways to get people to keep coming back to the site. As with anything, Doss would get better over time.

He teetered around the next few years, with the site progressively getting a little bit more popular. He started making a little money from advertising, but Doss was still struggling financially, as his rent in Manhattan was highway robbery. He had come to New York City with a tiny nest egg from his robberies in Oklahoma City, but that nest egg was slowly dwindling.

He moved to Washington D.C. in 2005, thinking he wanted to be even closer to the politicians he was covering. Despite its liberal leanings, Doss loved New York, thinking that bigger was always better. He was one of those hardline conservatives who nonetheless never wanted to live in a fly over state. He had tried that. Never again. I want them to vote with me, not live next to me, Doss would think.

The move to Washington D.C. turned out to be a lucky charm.

Everything changed for Always Right in 2006, when Dick Cheney shot his friend while quail hunting. Doss came up with one of his most brilliant ideas, taking daily polls asking his readers which Democratic politician they wished had gone hunting with Cheney instead. His site went through the roof that first day, and that night his small little server couldn't take all the hits and crashed. Doss upgraded and paid for a much bigger server a few hours later, and cursed himself for allowing his site to go down at all.

Sometimes, being offline for three hours can be crushing for a website, and Doss was worried as he hustled to get his back up and running. To his relief, the site was still getting record traffic when he got it back on the grid. His site went from a few thousand daily visitors to over 100,000 in the days that followed his quail hunting polls.

He ended out running the polls for six weeks, and by then alwaysright.com was a big time website. Doss was able to move out of his rinky-dink apartment a few months later and got a small office on K Street, the fashionable Washington D.C. street that was best known for lobbyists. It would be the first time he'd upgrade to a new office, but it wouldn't be the last. He would remain on K Street, but his offices got bigger every few years.

Back then, the website worked mainly by accumulating articles from different sources, so it's not like he had to hire 20 writers. That would come over time, but early on what he needed was people who had a keen eye for conservative articles. Anti-Muslim and anti-immigration articles were encouraged. When Doss interviewed prospective employees, he'd make his conservative views clear, but his racial tendencies would never be mentioned. It wouldn't take a genius to infer them, however.

He hired two interns whose jobs was to look for articles that fit the mold of alwaysright.com. They would verify with Doss that they were good to go, and when they received the go ahead, they'd post them on the site.

Around this time, Doss also hired his first social media manager, a young, conservative man from of all places, Southern California. His name was Brad Milner, and he was a natural. Doss knew how big social media was going to be. Facebook was already getting attention amongst people in the know, and Twitter would launch later that year. Doss was very ahead of his time when it came to social media. He made sure that alwaysright.com had one of the first Facebook business pages, and Doss was all over Twitter during its infancy.

He would have Milner set up 40 Facebook pages dedicated to Always Right. There was the one official page, but he knew the more ways people could find links to Always Right, the faster it would spread. Doss likened it to a fire. If you could start little embers all over the forest, it would spread a lot quicker than with just one initial starting point.

When Twitter launched, he had Brad Milner set up 500 accounts, all with conservative-sounding names. He'd tell him to follow all of the conservative papers/websites/organizations and then follow all of the people who followed those sites. Doss knew Twitter was just a big popularity contest. If you had a lot of followers then people would want to follow you back, so he got in early and built a huge following.

He'd tell Milner that any time that the official Always Right twitter account tweeted something, that he wanted all of the other 500 accounts to Retweet it, thus sending it out to tens of thousands of people. Doss would look at his computer screen and watch his social media presence grow and grow. He'd sit back and think just how accurate his forest fire analogy really was.

Doss also started buying up domain names with the words "American" "Conservative" "Far Right" "News" "Network" "Truth" "Conspiracy." These little websites he built were nowhere near as big as his eponymous website, but he would set up a template where these little sites would take the articles from alwaysright.com and post them on their site.

So while Howie Doss was known for alwaysright.com, he had scores of other websites that would post the same articles. These websites all had their own Twitter Accounts and Facebook Pages, and worked as their own entity, although everyone knew they were Doss's websites as well. It just helped him mass produce the junk that alwaysright.com was producing.

After the Cheney poll, Doss knew he was sitting on a monster, and he called his old friend Derek Plough with a plan for him to come to D.C. and work as his director of security. People on the right were getting a little jealous of Doss and his no longer little website, and people on the left were constantly threatening Doss. He needed some security, and he knew he could trust Plough. Plough officially joined in 2007.

From 2007 to 2017, Always Right and all its affiliate websites only got bigger. It continued rocketing up the charts of the most viewed websites. It was a longtime critic of President Obama, being one of the first to post articles related to the Birther movement. The Tea Party started during the Obama presidency, and they had found their website in alwaysright.com. Fox News may have had the best TV ratings, but they were no longer the source of news for the far right. Breitbart and Always Right had cornered that market.

Starting in 2015, Always Right started paying close attention to a longshot Republican nominee. He didn't come from the world of politics, and Doss viewed him as an empty suit. He knew if he played his cards right, however, that he could fill that suit with whatever policies/opinions he wanted. The guy had a bunch of liberal views and statements from his past, but Doss knew he could use that to his advantage. He was now an empty slate and Doss would fill him with anti-immigration, anti-abortion, and pro-NRA viewpoints.

And how would Doss go about filling him with viewpoints? He would post articles on his websites stating that those were the three biggest issues for Republican voters. Maybe they were, and maybe they weren't, but if Doss/Always Right stated that, then the man in the empty suit would listen. While the empty suit's viewpoints were for sale, he was no dummy. He knew that when Always Right spoke, he better listen.

And the empty suit did, in fact, listen. He reached out to Howie Doss, knowing how important Doss was if you were trying to get the Republican nomination and eventually the White House. The empty suit would often call him for the next day's stories so he could tell his constituents things what would be "proven" true the next day.

"We need to turn even more virulent anti-Muslim!" the empty suit would say.

"I think we should focus on jobs," an adviser would respond.

And the next day Always Right would have an article highlighting all the ways Islam was festering in the United States and how another terrorist bombing was inevitable. Doss would often add a poll, and the result would be that a huge percentage of people believed radical Islamic terrorism was the core issue of our time. The adviser would then agree with the empty suit, and they would go in that direction. It worked like clockwork.

When the long shot candidate came out of nowhere to win the presidency, he called Howie Doss and offered him a job in his cabinet. Doss rejected the empty suit's offer for two equally important reasons. First, he knew that he would have to go in front of congress and he really didn't want people shining a light on his background, especially his time in Oklahoma City. Second, he knew that he could do a lot more to change the country in his present position. He had millions of daily visitors to his website, and he knew he could publish an article on almost any issue, which would in turn necessitate a change in the president's stance. He had as much power as anyone, and certainly more than he'd ever have in a cabinet position.

Interest in Howie Doss began to rise, especially after he was considered for the cabinet position. The man who had taken a website he started in his small apartment to national prominence. It was a huge story, and many reporters tried to find out more on the Howard Hughes-type recluse. They covered his time in college, his writings for the National Review, the congressional races he worked, and his years in New York and now D.C. But no one ever mentioned his time in Oklahoma City. It was like he had never lived there, and that was just fine with Howie Doss.

For many reasons, not the least being Oklahoma City, Doss had ignored the spotlight over the years. He would occasionally do a question and answer session for a magazine, but rarely did he allow himself to be interviewed for television. He had only three interviews up on YouTube, the least of any big time CEO/Founder.

One of those videos was the interview Doss had done with Fox Business News, the one in which Darby Cash Bowles had recognized his voice.

Doss sat back in his chair, recollecting his unlikely rise to the top. He was awakened from his daydream by the sound of his phone ringing. Derek Plough informed him that Darby Cash Bowles was no longer a threat.

Howie Doss kicked off his shoes and put his feet up on his mahogany desk, smiling the whole time.

There were a few articles that Doss particularly liked for that day. One told the story of how people living within 50 miles of a predominately African American community were 5x more likely to die in a drive-by shooting. There was no link or mention of where they got this stat, but Doss knew that didn't matter. The day of honesty in journalism had passed. The people wanted their Meat and Potatoes, and they didn't care if it was served up on a bed of bullshit.

Howie Doss was not just some knee-jerk racist, and he did spend time contemplating how he had come to this point. He knew he tended towards racism, but no more than a lot of people he knew. To him, it was a means to an end. He knew his readership went up the more virulent the article. Anti-Jew: Good. Anti-Hispanic: Better. Anti-Black: Great. Anti-Islam: The Best.

So while Howie Doss was a racist, a good portion of the reason he posted these articles was because it brought more eyes to his websites, which led to him consolidating more power. He liked to think of himself as a sophisticated racist, not some hick who drove a truck with a confederate flag draped over the back.

There were a whole lot of overt racists out there, and Doss used this to his advantage. He wasn't exactly like them, but he needed their daily visits to his sites, and most of all, he needed their votes. And thanks to them, his power had grown and grown over the years to where he now had the ear of the President of the United States.

And Howie Doss was about to come into some information on the POTUS that would give him the ultimate power.

34

I rolled out of bed the next morning and went down to grab some breakfast. Originally, the first thing I was going to do was call Darby's friend and see if there was an update, but I figured that could wait until I went over to Evie's. For now, I was just going to enjoy some time with my family.

My mother served some Belgian Waffles with strawberries and whipped cream, topped with a large amount of maple syrup. It was one of my Mom's favorite breakfast's. It was also the tryptophan of breakfast's, because you couldn't move for hours afterward.

"Are you and Evie battling the Russians or the Iranians today, Frankie?" Fiona said.

"What are you talking about, Fiona?" my mother said.

"I told you, Frankie and Evie are doing some clandestine operation."

"We prefer covert to clandestine."

Always go with humor. It helps.

"Frankie's right," my mother said. "Clandestine sounds like you are trying too hard to use big words."

"How dare you take his side Mom!" Fiona said. "Ask Frankie where him and Evie go every day. Almost missing Christmas Eve dinner? I could never get away with that."

Well, this had escalated quickly.

"I've got a new girlfriend, and it's not exactly that easy to get alone time when we are both staying at our parents," I said.

It wasn't exactly the full truth, but there was enough to make it believable.

"Sounds good, Frankie, but I'm not buying it," Fiona said. Fiona was very insightful. We probably could have used her skills.

"He's got a new girlfriend and a beautiful one at that. Let him have his fun, Fiona," my mother said.

"She goes back to school in early January. Aren't you going to miss her, Fiona?" I asked.

"Yeah, I guess so," Fiona admitted.

"Well, I'm going to miss her a thousand times more. So don't be too hard on me if I choose to spend time with her before she heads back to school."

Fiona looked at me intently, as if to say she didn't believe me, but she'd stop the battle for now.

"Have you guys discussed if you are going to stay together when you go your separate ways?"

"It's a good question, Mom. What do you think of Scarlet Jackson?"

"Well, there's a non-sequitur if I've ever heard one."

"Actually it's not. What do you think of her?"

"I like her. Seems well respected in D.C. and she's always looked after our district. Why?"

"I met her yesterday, and there's a chance I might go work for her this summer. With Evie."

"So much to digest! You met a congresswoman yesterday and didn't tell us?"

"Sorry, I was busy most of the day."

"I'm starting to believe your sister may have a point," my mother said.

"Oh stop," I said, and pivoted away from that subject. I was starting to sound like a politician. "Evie has interned for her in D.C., and she was speaking at Oakland Tech, so we went and met her."

"That is really cool!" My mother said, but it could have come from Fiona too. I could tell she was impressed.

"Evie was one of her favorite interns, and she mentioned my name to Scarlet who said she'd definitely love to have me," I said.

"An internship for a congresswoman would look great on your resume," my mother said.

"Oh Mom, you're so silly sometimes. He's doing it to be with Evie," Fiona said.

"You're both right. Sure, I came up with the idea because Evie and I could spend the summer together, but I also think working for the government would be fascinating."

"I think it's a great idea," my mother said.

"I'll keep you updated."

"I'm your mother. Of course, you will keep me updated."

I had no response to that one. I guess I hadn't been the best son since I had reopened Uncle Owen's book. I excused myself soon after breakfast and told them I was going over to Evie's. My mother smiled, imagining me spending the summer with her, surrounded by the Lincoln Memorial and the White House. Fiona just shrugged her shoulders.

"I know something is going on," she whispered to me.

Evie walked out of her house and met me as I pulled up.

"I thought I was going to come in and get you," I said.

"My parents like you, but they think we're spending a bit too much time together. They are starting to get a little suspicious."

"Fiona is the same way. My Mom doesn't suspect a thing, though."

"Just be forewarned. Next time you come into the house, you might get a little grilling."

"I'll be prepared."

"Have you called Darby yet?"

"No, I was waiting for you."

I drove the car out of the Cul-de-sac and parked the car less than 100 yards from her house. Our surveillance was just like those out of a Vince Flynn novel. Only the exact opposite.

I dialed the number and the familiar voice who answered yesterday picked up.

"Hello?"

"Hi, this is Darby's friend. Any word from him?" I had decided not to use my own name. I knew this guy really was a friend of Darby's, but the fewer amount of people who knew my name the better.

"No, we still haven't heard back. I called the cops last night, but they have some bullshit rule that you have to wait 24 hours to report someone missing."

He certainly was more talkative than yesterday.

"Thanks for the information," I said and tried to get off the phone, but he was too quick.

"Was Darby in some sort of trouble? I know he was talking to his ex-girlfriend Patricia about some things and then he went to meet you. What's going on?"

This guy may be a useful ally in the future, but it was too early to tell him anything.

"Let's just wait and see if Darby shows up," I said.

"Do you want me to call you when he does?" he said.

I thought about it but decided I'd rather be the one doing the calling.

"I'll call back later today."

I hung up and looked over at Evie. She understood what I had been told.

"You know," Evie said, "If one of Doss's friends got to Darby, they might know who we are."

"What do you mean?" I asked.

"I don't know. They could have tortured him."

"Seems a bit unlikely," I said.

"Say you are Howie Doss. If you are going to try and eliminate someone who has information that could end your career, wouldn't you make sure he hadn't told anyone else?"

Evie was right as usual. Of course, kidnapping someone and torturing them for information wasn't an easy undertaking. It seemed to me far more likely they would just kill Darby when given the chance.

I thought Evie's suspicions were a long shot, but that didn't mean they weren't plausible. They were certainly in play.

Evie read my mind.

"Is it time to count our losses and end this thing?" she asked.

I sat there, trying to come up with a good reason why we should continue.

35

Employees at Always Right had often speculated that Howie Doss was into some kinky shit when it came to sex. They would see him around town with beautiful women, but the relationships would never last. A month was a long relationship for Doss. And while he had almost completely white hair and was just short of six feet tall, he was still powerful and extremely confident. There was no shortage of women who found that attractive. And yet, he was rarely with the same woman twice, which led to people talking.

In reality, Howie Doss enjoyed a pretty normal sex life. It was dealing with women for a protracted period of time that he wasn't very good at. Along with his racism, Doss was a sexist as well. It wasn't overt and rarely made it into the pages of his websites, but he tired of women quickly.

He thought that they were simple creatures and he couldn't think of any female political pundits that he cared to listen to. Washington D.C. had some of the brightest women in the country, and Howie Doss couldn't find them compelling, so you know what his overall opinion of the fairer sex was.

Doss had once told a well-known female senator that women were lucky the Bell Curve hadn't included a judgment on the respective intelligence of the sexes, or everyone would know they truly were second class citizens.

"Unless you want to include fashion and playing house," Doss had added. "I concede that you girls rank above men in those categories.

The senator didn't say a word. She was too stunned.

The women that Doss dated learned pretty quickly that he felt this way, and that's why you wouldn't see Howie Doss with the same woman for very long. This would just cause him to resent the fairer sex even more. It became a vicious cycle. Doss was no Freud, but he guessed that his distaste for women lied predominately in his hatred of his mother for trying to have him aborted, and then not being there to raise him.

Doss had never married and knew he never would. It pained him to even have to employ four women, thinking they were good for sex and nothing more.

That wasn't entirely true. There was one woman he employed who was fantastic at what she did, better in fact, than all of her male colleagues. Doss had tremendous respect for her. It was the woman he respected most in the world, not that that was saying much.

She had asked Doss for a meeting, and his secretary told her to go in.

Gloria Flores, his resident pit-bull, walked into the office. She was tough, unsentimental, and actually, quite vicious. While Doss would never admit to having a female counterpoint, if there was one, it was Gloria Flores.

She had started in the male-dominated business of lobbying, and being a woman and a Hispanic helped her get her name out there. Conservatism can often be a sea of white males, and the chance to get a woman and a Hispanic in photo ops was something that looked good to their constituents. For this reason, Gloria Flores became highly sought after in Republican circles.

The predominately older, white lobbyists were using Flores, but she was using them as well. She rose up the lobbying business faster than most and was on the board of some extremely powerful ones. People were surprised when she left her plush, high-paying positions to go write for Always Right, feeling it was a demotion.

She had her own reasons, as Gloria Flores saw something in Howie Doss that the others didn't see. She knew he was going to change the world. He was ruthless and would do anything to push his agenda forward. Flores had found him charming at times and a boor at others. But in the end, she knew they wanted the same thing, so she took the job at Always Right. And stayed there.

She had now been there for ten years, was 51 years old, and they were indeed changing the world. It was the most influential conservative website and only getting bigger. Doss had accomplished all that Flores knew he would, and she was probably the most iconic writer at Always Right. She was as ruthless as Doss, and her core issue was to limit immigration. Her parents had illegally immigrated from Mexico, and she had been called a traitor, the Uncle Tom of Hispanics, and much, much worse. She paid it no mind.

On this day, Gloria Flores had some information that would make Howie Doss the most influential man in the world. This was not hyperbole. Gloria Flores knew it to be true.

She approached Doss and shook his hand. Gloria had short brown hair to her shoulders, and was wearing a beige pantsuit, something similar to what Hillary Clinton might wear. It was the only thing that these two women would ever have in common.

"Nice to see you, Howie," she said.

"Oh, Gloria, when did I ever give you permission to call me by my first name?"

"I figured being your first and favorite female employee gave me that right."

"You'd be wrong. But at least I can tolerate it with you. I wouldn't allow it from any of the other women who work here."

"I'll take that as a victory."

"You know I hate small talk, Gloria. What are you here for?"

"I see a great opportunity in your future, Howie."

"I'd love to hear it, Gloria."

The tit for tat of calling each other by their first name only underscored the stubbornness of both Flores and Doss.

"We all know you have about as much sway as anyone in the world, with the possible exception of our President."

"Flattery will get you everywhere," Doss said.

"What if I told you I had some dirt on the President that would basically make him so neutered that you could become the de facto Commander-in-chief?"

"I'd assume you were joking. This president has been racist, misogynistic, and all my other favorite words, but nothing has stuck. He's the true Teflon Don, with all respect to John Gotti."

"This is different," she said.

"I'm really not sure what you could possibly have, but please indulge me. I don't think there's anything that his dumb ass voters could hear that would change their minds on him."

"Those dumb asses are your readers."

"I know. Isn't it great? So impressionable and hard-headed."

Doss and Flores shared a quick laugh.

"Alright, I'm filibustering. What do you have?" Doss asked.

Gloria Flores grabbed her cellphone and pressed play.

Doss was as skeptical of this as anything in his life. He literally couldn't think of a single thing that could harm the President. He had been bulletproof through everything that had been lodged against him.

And yet, much to his surprise, Howie Doss noticed himself smiling and then laughing as he listened to the President's voice, obviously unaware he was being recorded. He had Gloria Flores play it again, and it was even sweeter the second time. Doss was speechless for several seconds.

"My God," he said.

"Can you believe it?"

"No. Do you realize how catastrophic what you are holding would be to the President?

"He wouldn't last a day," Gloria Flores said.

"He wouldn't last a minute!" Howie Doss yelled with child-like exuberance. "And you are 100% sure this is legit?"

'Yeah, I'm pretty sure. He's talking to my daughter after all," Flores said.

"I don't even want to know how she was able to get him to admit that," Doss said.

"She's a believer in our cause," Flores said.

"That still doesn't explain it."

"My daughter is drop dead gorgeous."

"Still doesn't explain it. I mean how could the President be that big of a fool?"

"Is that rhetorical?"

Doss and Flores smiled, enjoying the inside joke.

"And we have nothing to worry from your daughter?" Doss asked

"She's more vicious than I am."

"Somehow, I doubt that," Doss said.

"When she gave it to me, I assure you she knew I'd end up here."

"You've raised her well."

Doss asked her to play it for him one last time. What the President admitted on the tape got more amazing each time Doss heard it.

"This is pure gold," Doss said.

"More like plutonium."

"Touché. And what do you want, Gloria?"

"Well, I'm getting what I want. A country so conservative that liberal snowflakes will melt from the heat."

"Stop trying to hit on me. Those are beautiful words," Doss said.

"Hit on you? And be seen around town for a few months before we break up? No thanks."

"Tread lightly, Gloria," Doss said.

She realized he didn't enjoy her attempt at humor.

"I'm sorry. Although my main goal will be achieved by you having this information, I wouldn't mind a raise in salary as well."

"It's just been doubled."

"Thank you."

Doss walked around his desk and gave Gloria Flores a huge hug. She had never seen him so happy.

"This is truly beautiful, Gloria. The empty suit is going to get more and more conservative. He'll have no choice if he wants to stay in office. The strings are going to get a little tighter on our little marionette in the White House."

"You truly are an evil bastard," Flores said.

"Thank you," Doss said, taking it as a compliment.

He went to his mirror and looked out on K Street. Flores could see the shadow below his white hair and knew he was smiling. Doss said nothing for several seconds, and Gloria Flores took the hint and let herself out of Doss's office.

Once he heard Flores leave, Doss returned to his chair and pondered his good fortune. When he eventually contacted the president and told him what he had on him, the president would have to do whatever Doss asked. If he didn't, Doss would threaten him with turning over the tape to the media. The President had nine lives, but even he would realize he couldn't escape the furor that this would cause. The President would have to play ball with Doss if he wanted to remain in office.

Doss would have loved to continue sitting there and soaking up the good news, but he got a call on one of his secured cellphones. It was Derek Plough.

"Any news on the phone tap?" Doss said. There was no greeting.

"The Gullicksens' have received several calls, but most of them were from friends and benign. There was one number that has called Billy Gullicksen twice and was highly suspicious. It was a young guy on the other end, and he asked both times about Darby. Apparently, he met with Darby within the last week."

Howie Doss took his phone and slammed it on his ridiculously expensive desk, causing it to chip.

He covered the phone and yelled "Fuck" so loud his secretary heard it from outside the office. He took a second and calmed himself down.

"Have you found out where the phone calls are coming from?"

"Yes, that part is easy. It's the cell phone of a 21-year-old kid named Francis Edward Waters. Looks like he goes by Frankie judging from his social media. I've been able to find out that he's a junior at San Francisco State, but the calls are coming from Oakland, where he is originally from."

"That's good work Derek," Doss said, trying to calm down.

"Thanks."

"Find out any more information you can on this Frankie Waters kid, and I'll do the same. I'm going to have you stay in Eureka one more day to monitor the Gullicksen's as well as their phones. Depending on what we find out, you'll either be flying to Oakland or back to D.C. next."

"Got it," Plough said. He waited for Doss to hang up, and when he did, Plough hung up himself.

Doss looked down at his desk and cursed himself again. He had just been handed, for all intents and purposes, the keys to the White House, but now there was a chance Darby Bowles wasn't the last link to Oklahoma City. It was quite an up and down morning for Howie Doss.

He picked up the phone and called his secretary.

"Virginia, find a woodworker who can come fix a chip on my desk."

"I'll get right on that, Mr. Doss."

Howie Doss hung up the phone and googled "Frankie Waters Oakland."

36

When Evie had put me on the spot about ending this thing, my response had been more emotional than pragmatic.

"Because we are this fucking close, and I don't want to give it to someone else to finish. It's like we are pitching a shutout and they want to bring in a closer to finish it. No thanks, I want us to close this thing ourselves."

Evie smiled and kissed me. I didn't know if it was because she agreed with me or just liked my intensity. I didn't really care. I had made up my mind that we were going to follow this to its conclusion. There would be no more flip-flopping. We had done enough of that.

I started to think about Darby. I really hoped he wasn't dead. He was full of rough edges, but I had liked him. Deep, deep, down I think he had a good soul, and I hope that light hadn't been extinguished. Unfortunately, every hour that he didn't go back to his friend's house made me think he was likely dead. It looked like it may truly be just Evie and I from here on in.

I went back over the evidence. A notarized letter. An old photo. A big coincidence. A missing man. It wasn't nothing, but it was hardly concrete evidence either. We needed more.

Arriving home that night, I went to bed, but couldn't sleep. I tossed and turned, but nothing helped.

I sat up in bed and started to think everything over. I knew we needed more evidence against Doss, but I wasn't sure how to get it.

Nothing came to mind, so I logged onto Facebook to pass the time. I saw that Parker Gates, a friend since high school was currently on Facebook Live, a tool that allows you to broadcast live to the world from your smart phone. It was 3:30 in the morning and very few people were watching, but Parker was going off about how great the Golden State Warriors were.

I laughed for a bit and then started to get the inkling of an idea. I sat up in bed and thought about the tool that was Facebook Live.

After two hours of research, I thought I had come up with a plan that just might work. I started looking at flights. I could afford two tickets and a cheap hotel for a few days, but my checking account would be on life support after that.

Evie had loved my enthusiasm the previous day, but it hadn't lasted through the night.

"It's December 29th, Frankie. I'll give you to January 1st, and then I'm calling Scarlet Jackson."

Those were the first words out of her mouth when I arrived the next morning.

"Oh wow, you are giving me until 2018. Thanks," I said.

"This isn't a laughing matter, Frankie," Evie said.

I turned serious.

"You're right. Let's get down to work," I said.

"I'm not sure what more we can do right now. We have a bunch of information, we just don't know what to do with it."

"I've come up with something."

The plan had been percolating since the previous night. It wasn't fully formed, and I really could have used a few more days, but one thing we didn't have was time. If Darby had given away our identity, we needed to move fast.

"I'm not going to like this, am I?" Evie asked.

"Probably not," I said. "As Darby said, we need to poke the bear a little bit."

"Yup, I don't like it. Were you thinking about sending letters? Doesn't look like that worked out too well for Darby."

"I had something different in mind," I said.

"And what might that be?"

"What do you think Washington D.C. is like this time of the year?"

37

When I got home from convincing Evie to fly to Washington D.C., I began to write my mother a letter detailing everything that had happened. I began by telling her how it had all started when I had mentioned Chapter 5 of a Netflix series and her odd reaction to it. If not for that, "The Greatest Novel Ever" would still be sitting on my bookcase.

From there, I outlined what Uncle Owen had written to me, how I had come to take Evie on, and all the investigating we had done since. I included Patricia Page and our escapade up to Ukiah. I wrote extensively about our dealing with Darby Cash Bowles and how he was the impetus that started this all when Uncle Owen became his cellmate.

I talked about Howie Doss and just how big Always Right was, and mentioned that Darby had written a letter to him and was now missing. I left out the Derek Plough connection, thinking it would just be too much information. I told my mother that I had considered telling her and Fiona many times, but decided against it. I knew that would be her biggest bone of contention, but I explained my reasons why.

To close the letter, I told her why I was flying to Washington D.C. and included how I planned on taking down Howie Doss. I then asked for her forgiveness. I doubted I would get it, at least not right away.

Of course, I wasn't going to give my mother this letter before I left, or she would never let me get on the plane. My plan was to give it to Fiona before we left, and have her swear to wait until January 1st. That would give us enough time and then she could give it to my mother.

When I felt the letter was satisfactory, I folded it up and enclosed it in the envelope, including copies of Darby's notarized letter and the photos we got from Patricia Page. I wrote "Dear Fiona, please open on January 1st," on the outside of the envelope.

I told myself I had written the letter to inform my mother why we had left Oakland and were rendezvousing in Washington D.C. Another part of my brain knew the full truth. If I somehow got myself killed in Washington D.C., I wanted her to have all the information that I had. My mother would get it in the right hands.

Regardless of what happened to me from here on in, the truth about Howie Doss would get out.

Or so I thought.

I called Evie at 10 p.m. that night.

"Hello?"

"Haven't changed your mind, have you?" I asked.

"Waffling? Yes. But changed it? No."

"Good. I need you for the most important thing."

"What's that?"

"I'll tell you on the flight."

"Such a tease…"

I smiled. It was a rare moment of levity over the last few days.

"But I do need you to pack a ruffled skirt or something that could hide a phone. Jeans or a straight skirt would be too obvious."

"I know where this is going," Evie said.

"We'll talk about it. By the way, I wrote a letter to my mother outlining everything that happened."

"Read it to me," Evie said.

"I can't risk her walking by right now. I could print you out a copy if you want to leave one for your parents."

"Won't she just call the cops when she reads it?"

"I'm going to give mine to Fiona before I go to sleep tonight. I'm going to ask her to wait till the 1st to give it to her. I think Fiona will do that for me. I'll tell her that she was right that we were up to something, and I just need a few more days to see it through."

"But when your Mom realizes you're gone, won't she go crazy and ask Fiona if she knows where you went?"

"I'm going to leave a separate note to my mother saying we decided to go to Lake Tahoe for New Years. I'm going to leave my car at the airport, so when she sees my car is gone, she'll believe it. If she thinks I'm up there with you, she won't be mad."

"I should probably just leave my parents a letter saying we are going to Tahoe. If they had two letters, they'd know something was up."

"Yeah, I guess you're right. You don't have the luxury of a little sister to do your dirty work," I said.

"What time are we leaving in the morning?"

"Flight is at six, so I want to get to the airport by 4:30. I'll pick you up at 4:15. Make sure your parents don't hear you leaving. That would end this before it even gets started."

"They are sound sleepers. You don't have to worry about it," Evie said. "Same goes for you obviously."

"I know. Fiona is my only worry, but I'm going to talk with her tonight."

"We're really doing this aren't we?"

"Against all better judgment, yes we are," I said.

"Do you want me to call Scarlet Jackson?" Evie asked.

"No, not yet. But we will be using her at one point."

"You better have this all thought out."

"We just have to make sure that Doss will meet with us," I said.

"You make convincing one of the most influential men in the world to meet us sound like a foregone conclusion."

"When I tell him that we are going to the press if he doesn't, he won't have much choice."

"Somehow, I thought winter break was going to be a bit more mellow."

"You're the one who wanted an adventure."

My attempt at humor fell on deaf ears.

"Are we in danger, Frankie? And is Darby dead?"

"The answer to both questions is likely yes. But we are also on the verge of being involved in one of the biggest political stories of all time."

"Maybe they'll write that on my tombstone," Evie said.

"Don't say that, Evie."

"Sorry, just a little nervous is all."

"I am too. But I can see the finish line."

"I hope you're right. I'll be outside at 4:30 tomorrow morning. Don't turn your lights on."

"I won't...."

I started to continue, but Evie had hung up.

38

FRIDAY, DECEMBER 30TH:

Friday, December 30th started early for both Evie and I. I was up by 3:45 and made sure to make as little noise as I could. I had showered and packed the night before, trying to eliminate any prospective noise I'd have to make that morning. At 4:10, I quietly walked downstairs, getting ready to leave the note for my mother saying that I had gone to Lake Tahoe. I hoped she'd assume I left right before she had woken up. If she knew I had left at 4 a.m., she'd certainly have some questions.

The talk with Fiona the night before had ended well, but there were a few times where I feared she might go tell our mother right then and there. She wanted more and more information about what Evie and I were doing. I told her that it was a national story, and she laughed at me, but as she looked closer, she could tell I wasn't joking.

She asked me if it was dangerous and when I didn't shoot the question down right away, she became a little scared and said maybe she should just tell our mother. I was able to talk her down from that.

I told her all I wanted was two full days and then she could open the envelope I had given her. Just until the 1st. And she could hold this over my head for the rest of our lives, and I'd owe her a lifetime of favors. She liked this idea.

She asked what she should say to our mother. I told her that I was leaving a letter for her saying I was going to Lake Tahoe for the New Years' Eve weekend, and she should just play along with that. And then if I wasn't back on the 1st, Fiona could give her the letter.

Fiona knew she was lacking some information, but she agreed to do what I asked. I told her she was the best sister ever, and that I would owe her big time. I also told her she just might have a famous brother when this was all over.

Or a dead brother. But I didn't include that.

I wasn't sure if she grasped the magnitude of what I was doing until I saw a little tear in her eye, and then I knew she had. She had gone to bed shortly after.

The next morning I left the note for my mother, and made my way towards the front door, and sure enough Fiona was there. I guess our talk hadn't been such a success.

"What the hell are you doing?" I whispered.

"I'm not sure I can lie to Mom for the next few days," she said.

Not fucking now.

"Fiona, we finished this conversation last night. You agreed to keep my secret until the 1st."

"I didn't sleep well. I have a feeling you are in over your head, and something big is going on."

As usual, Fiona was right. The two young ladies in my life, my girlfriend, and my sister, were equally intuitive.

"Fiona, I could have just left and never told you. I told you because I love you and I trust you."

"You love Mom, too."

"Of course I do. But she's our parent. A brother and sister have to stay together even if they have reservations," I said, barely getting above a whisper.

"You haven't even told me where you are going to be."

I thought about it. Looked like I might have to throw her a bone to keep her on my side.

"We're going to Washington D.C."

"Are you fucking crazy?" Fiona's voice rose above a whisper, and I put my finger to my mouth.

"Shhh." I stared at her intently. "Fiona, I'm going to go now. If you want to run upstairs and scare the shit out of Mom, you can, but I'm going either way, so it's better to just let her sleep. You can hold a secret for a few days, and then I'll be in your debt for the rest of my life."

I saw the look on her face soften. "Okay, Frankie. Just promise me you'll be safe."

"I'm sure we'll be fine," I lied.

She had one final question. "What the hell are you doing in D.C. Going to try and take down the president?"

Turned out she wasn't far off.

"You have a healthy imagination, sis."

She grabbed me and hugged me, and I did the same with her. The tears from the previous night had returned.

"Thank you for this," I said.

She smiled through the tears, and I walked out the front door.

I drove to Evie's, turning off my lights as I entered the Cul-de-sac. I saw her sitting on the curb, and as I approached, she stood up and walked to the car. I helped her put her bag in the trunk, and she sat down in the front seat. I leaned across and kissed her.

"Are you ready?" I asked.

"Ready as I'll ever be," she said, hardly a ringing endorsement.

I drove towards the end of the Cul-de-sac, not turning on my lights until we had exited her parents street. Next stop was the Oakland airport and after that, Washington D.C., and a date with Howie Doss.

39

Howie Doss had a lot on his plate, but this was nothing new. He had long prided himself on being able to handle multiple things at once. He had to admit, juggling the possibility of being the most powerful man in the world with the chance of going to jail was definitely a first.

He'd be thinking about what he was going to tell the President one minute, and then a minute later worrying that things happening in California might land him in the Big House. It was a race between the White House and the Big House, and as he had his whole life, Howie Doss preferred white.

The information that Gloria Flores had given him was dynamite in more ways than one. It was dynamite in the sense that it was a perfect thing to hold over the president's head. Dynamite as an adjective. It was also dynamite in the sense that it was the most explosive information Howie Doss had ever held. Dynamite as a noun.

He had always prided himself on having skeletons from the closets of a lot of Washington D.C. bigwigs, but he'd never had something this big on someone so important.

Howie Doss had the president's private cell phone, but he decided if he wanted to set up a meeting, he would go through the more official route. Doss called the White House, and after he dropped his name, he was moved up the chain quickly. There were levels of secretaries in the White House, and Doss had managed to reach the top in a matter of minutes. He was amazed at how far he had come from the young man in Missouri.

Doss was connected to the White House Office of Appointments and Scheduling. From the 1800s all the way up to the 1980s, there was a position known as the Secretary to the President, but that was done away with, and now you went through the Appointments and Scheduling office.

"Hello, Mr. Doss," Jackie Handel said. Doss had talked to her a few times.

"Hello, Jackie," Doss said, and thought it must be tough to be named Jackie and work for the White House. There are constant reminders that you are never going to be the most famous Jackie at 1600 Pennsylvania Avenue. "I'd like to meet with the president as soon as possible."

"He's a busy man, Mr. Doss," Jackie said, with no hint of irony.

"I have no doubt. I'm a busy man myself. This is important, and I'd like to meet with him today or tomorrow. "

"He has 20 minutes available tomorrow at 11:00. Would that work?"

"That would be great. Listen, Jackie, tell the president that I just want this to be he and I. I'll bring no one, and I don't want any of his lackeys there either."

Doss laughed to himself after he called the president's team by that name. Lackeys were unintelligent Yes Men, and it was actually the president, and not his team, who Doss viewed as the true lackey. The man had no backbone, and was like a tree branch in the wind, blowing to wherever public sentiment pushed him.

"I'll forward that information to the president, Mr. Doss. He'll see you tomorrow."

Jackie Handel and Doss hung up at the same time. It was time to deal with the other part of the two-headed monster currently occupying Doss's brain. He called Derek Plough from a different phone.

"Hey," Plough said. He didn't sound too happy, and Doss knew something was up.

"What is it?"

"Gullicksen got a call this morning saying some longshoremen were going to follow Darby's path along the Boardwalk, picking up the path he would have taken after he met all his longshoremen buddies. I followed at a great distance."

"And?"

"And one of them just saw something a few minutes ago. I was going to call you. There was probably 20 of them, and some eagle-eyed mother fucker saw something in the water."

"Darby Bowles?"

"I'm sure it is. They just called the cops a few minutes ago, and I'll bet they are going to send some boats out here any minute. Boss, he's got to be 60 yards out there. I don't know how the guy saw him."

"You did all you could," Doss said.

This wasn't good news, but it wasn't the death of Howie Doss either. After all, no one knew the relationship between Darby Bowles and Doss with the possible exception of the kid in Oakland.

"Thanks," Plough said.

"I want you to make sure that the body is, in fact, Darby's. I have no doubt it is, but I just want to be positive. After that, I'm going to have you fly to Oakland at 6 p.m. tonight. I've decided it's necessary. But tread lightly, we don't know how this kid is involved yet."

"Anything else?"

"There's some big news I have to tell you about, but I'll wait till you get back."

"Is it life changing?"

"Our word will be the gospel of the White House."

"Jesus," Plough said.

"God actually, but close enough."

Ten minutes after Plough hung up with Howie Doss, the boats started entering the water near where the longshoreman saw something. Plough had ventured inland a little bit, not wanting to be seen hovering around the longshoremen, but when he saw the boats appear, he knew he had to get closer.

He walked back towards the boardwalk, being sure to look busy. A tourist, maybe. He looked down at the water below, not quite believing that he had been in a life and death struggle in that grotesque water.

It didn't take long for one of the boats to pull up what looked like a body. There were algae and crap hanging all over the body, and some of the long-shoremen were hoping it was something else. Plough knew better.

One of the boats zipped over to the edge of the boardwalk. Plough subtly walked closer.

"Which one of you is Gullicksen?"

Billy Gullicksen stepped forward.

"I am."

"Darby Bowles was staying with you, is that correct?"

"It is."

"We picked up a body and are taking it to the coroner. Could you meet us there and ID the body?"

Gullicksen looked like he was in shock, but he replied, "Yeah, I'll meet you there."

The longshoremen started hugging each other, and a few started crying.

"Maybe it's someone else's body," someone said, but everyone knew that wasn't the case.

All of the longshoremen made a point of going up to Billy Gullicksen. Plough figured it was time to get out of dodge. If they only knew that Darby Bowles's killer was 50 yards from them, they'd tear him from limb to limb. Derek Plough started walking away from the ocean, not turning around till he got to his rental car.

Our flight to Washington D.C. was easy. There was no long waits, delays, or anything to set us back. Evie and I's conversation wasn't as easy, as there was an obvious elephant in the room. Or on the plane, as it were.

We managed to talk about everything except our task at hand. We were surrounded by people on the plane, and it was hardly the time to be discussing taking down Howie Doss. We arrived in D.C., picked up our bags, and headed outside to catch a cab.

I told the cab driver to head to the Motel 6 on 4th Street, a forgettable hotel in a city full of memorable ones. It was necessary due to my budget restrictions, and I also thought it would be easier to keep a low profile in an out of the way, quiet hotel. And that's just what this Motel 6 was.

The cab driver pointed out some of the sites as we drove in from Dulles airport, and it only helped to emphasize the difference between Howie Doss and us. We were staying at a cheap motel while somewhere in this city, Doss was probably eating foie gras with some famous politician or lobbyist. This was truly a David vs. Goliath scenario. To make myself feel better, I reminded myself who won that battle.

Washington D.C. was a beautiful city, but we barely took in our surroundings as we made our way to the Motel 6. We had too much on our mind.

"The motel is gorgeous," Evie said sarcastically, as we pulled in.

"I figured if we are going to check out, we might as well do it in style," I said, responding with sarcasm of my own.

The cabbie heard me. "Check out? You just got here."

Evie and I laughed. He was referring to the hotel of course, and I felt no reason to let him in on what I had meant by "check out."

He removed our bags from the trunk and set them down. I paid him for the trip and thanked him.

We walked to the front desk and saw a young man who looked like he had just time warped from the 1970's. He had a tie-dyed Grateful Dead shirt on and a dazed look in his eye.

There was another reason I had selected this particular hotel. It was one of the few motels I had contacted that said I could pay with cash and no credit card. I had paid for the flight with a credit card because it was necessary, but I preferred to be invisible once we got to D.C. and planned on paying with cash, when possible. I had taken out $400 from my checking account the night before and $400 at the airport. There wasn't much left where that came from, so I had to make it last.

The employee with the long hair and out to lunch attitude notified me that I'd also have to put down a $100 cash security deposit since I didn't have a credit card. I gave him the money and filled out the form with a fake name, choosing Chief Brody in honor of Roy Scheider's character from Jaws.

"Thank you, Chief," the half-stoned employee said. "You are room 372. Here are two keys."

"Appreciate it," I said.

Evie and I took the barely functional elevator up to the third floor and found Room 372. I opened the door to a sparse, bland room. It was perfect.

We looked at the bed, and as much as I enjoyed making love to the woman across from me, I knew we had to concentrate on the business at hand. There'd be plenty of time to fool around after this was all over. Assuming we got out alive.

I sat Evie down on the bed.

"Okay, here's my full plan…" I said.

40

Howie Doss had always been the motor that made Always Right run, despite not being front and center on the political landscape. And that's the way he liked it. Political talk shows did nothing to further his cause. He preferred to think of himself as the mad genius behind the scenes, but things had changed, and Doss would no longer just be dictating policy from his websites. He would be hands on now.

It's time to fully unleash the Howie Doss playbook on the American public, Doss mused. The playbook would be as conservative as anything the U.S. government had ever put forth. And the President would have to do what Doss said if he wanted to keep his job.

Doss knew it would be best to be a little more subtle when he met with the President. The man that Doss referred to as "the empty suit" was a proud man who had overcome amazing odds to become the leader of the free world. There was no need to piss him off. After all, the President was still the leader of covert forces and could make Howie Doss's life brutal if he felt so inclined.

Of course, if that happened, Doss would release the information he had, which would be enough to get the President impeached, or more likely, to resign. That's not what Doss wanted to happen, however. He liked having the empty suit in the White House. It made his job easier.

What Doss planned was to ask the President to change some of his positions. He'd allude to the fact that he could release the tape at any time, but not overtly threaten him. If he presented it like that, Doss believed the President would have no choice but to start implementing Doss's plan.

And it's not like any of these new positions would be that big of a surprise. The country had become so divided that the general public just expected the President to take every far right position there was. He had on a great many issues, and now Doss was just going to push him a little further right.

Doss's first order of business was going to be to fuck with Blacks and Muslims. Doss didn't like Jews, Hispanics, Gays, or Asians either, but he withheld his greatest hate for the first two. Black people out of general hate, and Muslims because of their low Q rating among Republican voters. Doss thought the murders of the innocent people in 2001 was the most reprehensible act he'd ever seen. He was talking of 9-11 of course, and never saw the irony that he had innocent civilians killed via a hate crime earlier that same year.

To Doss, white people were the greatest race, so any crime committed by them paled in comparison to crimes committed against them. Doss was hoping to find the next Tuskegee experiment or the "War on Drugs" that Nixon used as a ruse to targets blacks and hippies. Doss would love to go after the hippies too. All these protests and none of them missing a day of work. Get a fucking job!

Howie Doss sat back and soaked in the anger. He didn't try to do a deep dive into how he had ended up this way. He knew a lot of the reasons, and some of his life was contradictory. He had met some African Americans and Muslims who were among the most brilliant men he had ever met. But then, you had to admit that it's the individual and not the overall race that you should judge. And that was too much work for Doss, and even more so for his voting block. Reflection and introspection were not high on the far right's priorities list.

Howie Doss wasn't afraid of the President, and he considered himself far superior intellectually. There was some nerves, however, leading into the meeting with him. After all, how many people in history have gone into the White House and told the President that they had him by the balls?

Doss liked the analogy. It was time to neuter the President. And it was time for a new, more virulent dog to take over.

"Are you fucking crazy?" and "There's no fucking way!" were the exclamations I heard from Evie as I outlined my plan. They eventually gave way to "If he agrees to meet us, maybe this could work."

"Doss doesn't have a choice," I said. "I'm going to tell him that if he doesn't meet with us, then I'm going to go to the cops, the media, and Scarlet Jackson. And not that it matters, but I'm not kidding. I want to take this guy down ourselves, but if he doesn't agree to meet us, we'll turn all the evidence over to the quote unquote experts."

"Above all else, we have to make sure we are safe. I'm not going to meet him at some out of the way place," Evie said.

"Of course not. We are going to meet him at a public park or something like that. I'd say a packed restaurant, but obviously, he's not going to talk in front of others. We will be out in the open, and there will be people around. He's not going to do anything in broad daylight."

"But what if he puts one of his goons on us after we leave the meeting?"

"That's where Scarlet Jackson comes in."

"You better finish telling me the plan," Evie said.

I did.

The coroner's office in Eureka, CA was located on I Street, and Billy Gullicksen had to use his GPS to find it. The building was as inconspicuous as any building on the street. It could have passed as just about anything. Maybe a coroner's office isn't something that you want to advertise to the public, Gullicksen thought. Probably better to be a nameless, faceless building like the one he pulled up to.

He was joined by four police officers who walked him into the coroner's office and led him down some stairs. Only fitting it would take place in a basement. He walked into the office and saw a body on what looked like an operating table. There was no operation that was going to save this guy, though. A white sheet covered his body, but his right hand was outside of the sheet, and it was quite obvious it had spent some time in the ocean.

"Mr. Gullicksen, are you ready for this?" one of the officers asked.

"Let's get it over with," Billy said.

The coroner, a tiny man with wire-rimmed glasses, pulled back the sheet to reveal the corpse. Billy knew right away it was Darby. The body was deteriorating rapidly, but the face had somehow managed to stay pretty much intact. There was what looked like bruising on the cheeks and forehead, but his eyes, nose, and mouth were clearly the same.

"Is that Darby Bowles?" the same officer asked.

Billy bowed his head. "Yeah, that's him."

Billy Gullicksen hadn't been to church since his parents dragged him there as a child, but that didn't prevent him from signing the cross as he looked at Darby.

"Rest in Peace, Darby," he said.

The coroner pulled the sheet over the body, and the officers walked Billy back to his car.

"Did Darby have any enemies?" an officer asked him.

"I don't think so. I mean, he had only been out for a damn week."

"We are just looking for potential suspects, Mr. Gullicksen."

"It was probably one of the Tweekers who hangs out down by the boardwalk these days."

The officers agreed it was a possibility.

"But no enemies that you know of?"

"No. Maybe the parents of those kids he killed. I'm sure you know about that, don't you?"

One of the officers nodded in the affirmative.

"Okay Mr. Gullicksen, you can go. We may call you into the office in the future."

Billy walked to his car and started it. He wasn't quite sure why he hadn't mentioned the young man who had called looking for Darby. He seemed like a good kid, and Billy was sure he had nothing to do with what happened. It didn't really matter now anyway. Darby was dead, and nothing was going to change that.

Billy Gullicksen went to the store and bought a handle of vodka.

Evie and I ordered a pizza to be delivered. The Motel 6 didn't have any food besides the vending machines in the lobby. We waited for the food and talked about our dreams of possibly living in D.C. this summer. We discussed our families and Evie said we owed Fiona another bowling night.

It was somber as we pondered what lay ahead of us. Evie suggested calling Darby's friend. It was about to get more somber.

"Hello," the now familiar voice said.

"Hey, this is Darby's friend," I said.

"Darby's dead."

"What? What happened?"

"They found him in the ocean. They don't know who killed him yet."

The voice sounded drunk to me. "I'm very sorry for your loss," I said.

"And don't worry, I didn't tell the police about you."

I was going to make up some bullshit story about how I had met Darby, but it seemed better to just let it go.

"I assure you I had nothing to do with it, but thanks," I said.

"I believe you. Goodbye now," the voice said and hung up.

I turned to Evie who was starting to cry.

"We are so out of our league," she said.

I couldn't disagree.

"One more day. Two tops," I said.

"In two days we might be as dead as Darby."

I looked at Evie and exhaled deeply.

"I'm going to give you your last chance to get out of this. I know I've said this many times, but I mean it. If you want out, I'll do this myself."

"Don't you remember the plan? I don't think I want to see you in a ruffled skirt," Evie said.

I managed to laugh, remembering what the plan entailed.

"People die every day," she said. "Might as well go out doing something that could change our country for the better."

I couldn't tell if her sentiment was meant to be uplifting or depressing.

We went to sleep at 11:00 pm that night. We didn't make love. Instead, I just held her the whole night. She kept pushing her back into my chest until it felt like we were one. Which was appropriate, because from here on in, we essentially were.

A little after 8 p.m. on the west coast, Derek Plough's rental car pulled up to a tiny, three bedroom house in Oakland, CA. He had flown in from Eureka only an hour previous, rented a car, and then drove to the house. He didn't even book a hotel, not sure if he'd be staying the night.

The house was nondescript, and the area wasn't very nice. The sidewalks were dirty, and the streets looked like they might be dangerous. Not to judge a book by its cover, but Plough wasn't impressed with whoever lived there. And this kid thought he had a chance of taking down Howie Doss? Plough chuckled to himself.

He looked at his phone to make sure he had the address right and drove back up the street so his car wouldn't draw suspicion. He was close enough where he could see comings and goings, but far enough away to where he wouldn't be spotted. The house was lit up, making it easier for Plough to see inside.

There was movement in the house, and Plough was able to spot two women. Very likely the mother and daughter. Sally and Fiona Waters. Doss had texted Plough all the information he was able to find out, and it appeared that the two Waters children lived with their mother.

Where the hell was the son, Howie wondered? He was the one Plough was after, not the women.

Plough sat there for 20 minutes. There was no sign of Frankie Waters. It's Friday night, Plough thought to himself. He's probably out getting drunk and chasing women.

Nothing to be gained tonight, Plough decided. He turned on his lights and was about to go get a hotel when he saw movement by the front door. He immediately turned his lights off and slunk back in his chair. He was a good 50 feet up the street, but for obvious reasons, couldn't take a chance of being seen.

The two women stepped out of the house and walked down a half block. They got into an older sedan and drove off.

Derek Plough thought hard and fast. Was it worth the risk of going in the house? He thought it was. Of course, there could be someone in the house, but it seemed unlikely. The lights had been turned off, and he hadn't seen anyone else.

The chance that the Waters kid had some information lying around was too tantalizing. He had to go for it. Derek Plough got out of his car and walked towards the front door.

Plough hit the jackpot less than 15 minutes later. Jimmying the front door was a piece of cake and took less than a minute. Plough always had a swiss army knife on his key chain, and it was enough to break into most locks. The lock he encountered wasn't much and never had a chance.

Quickly able to differentiate which was the male's room, Plough spent the first 10 minutes rummaging through that room, finding nothing. The room was sparse, and he was able to search it quickly. If the kid had anything on Doss, he had taken it with him.

The next room he checked was even smaller than the first. A few posters of handsome musicians adorned the walls, and unless the mother was into younger men, this room had to be the daughter's. Plough looked on her desk and saw a stack of what looked like mail. He rummaged through it, expecting nothing, until he got to the bottom of the stack and saw an envelope titled "Dear Fiona, please open on January 1st." It had not been opened.

Plough read the letter and realized this was the most important information he had ever discovered for Howie Doss. He started to read it again, but he had been inside for almost 20 minutes now and couldn't risk staying any longer.

Putting the envelope in his back pocket, Plough made his way out of the room and out of the house altogether. He locked the door behind him and was pretty sure they'd never know he had been there, at least until the Fiona girl realized the note was missing. And even then, what could she say. It was quite obvious that she didn't know the information in the envelope. It was unopened, and she wasn't supposed to open it until January 1st. All she'd know was that an envelope was stolen.

He walked back to his car and called Howie Doss.

"I've hit the motherlode," Plough said.

"Let's hear it," Doss said.

"I found a letter from Frankie Waters to his sister Fiona in which he outlines everything. He is coming to Washington D.C., Howie! Someone named Uncle Owen, who was once a prison cellmate of Darby Cash Bowles gave him all the information. I don't think it's their real uncle because he used quotation marks. Anyway, while they were cellmates, Bowles had told Owen all about you and Oklahoma City, and Owen was supposed to bribe you. Unfortunately for him and fortunately for you, Owen got lung cancer and died soon after getting out of jail. He couldn't just let this information die with him, so he wrote something to Frankie Waters outlining the information he knew, and how he could bribe you. Waters doesn't get into specifics with his sister, but he does have a notarized letter from Darby Bowles laying out all the reasons Darby thinks you were the man behind the murders. He also has a picture of you and I outside your house in Oklahoma City two days after the murders."

"How do you know it's two days after?" Doss asked, interrupting for the first time.

"He has a newspaper with the date on it. It's in the foreground of the picture."

"Smart fucker," Doss said.

"And he's got a young woman coming with him," Plough said.

Doss should have been upset, but he was almost intrigued. He'd have no problem killing a young woman who got in the way.

"Who is she?"

"Guessing it's his girlfriend. Her name is Evie. It appears she knows everything he does so don't take her lightly."

Oh, I'm not, Doss thought to himself.

"Anything else?" Doss said.

"I haven't even told you the best part yet!" Plough exclaimed.

Doss knew this was going to be good. "What is it?"

"The envelope was unopened. I had to break the seal of it to read the letter. On the front, it said to open it on January 1st. If Frankie and this Evie girl meet their demise, I don't think anyone else would know about this."

"Great work, Derek. Now get the next flight back to D.C. so we can do away with these fucking kids."

41

SATURDAY, DECEMBER 31ST:

What Evie and I knew for certain was that it was the last day of the year. We were going to try our best to make sure it wasn't the last day of a different sort. Our lives.

I woke up at 6 a.m., but couldn't say I was surprised. The fact that I got seven hours of sleep with everything on my mind was a blessing. Evie continued to sleep even as I removed my bearhug-like grip on her, but she woke up a few minutes later.

"What time is it?" she asked.

"Time to change the world for the better."

"Your attempts at humor may well be lost on me today."

"6:15. You can try to go back to sleep. I'm not going to call Doss's office until 8:00."

"It is a Saturday you know. Will this affect anything?"

"People will be in the office. The internet never sleeps," I said.

Evie smiled and said, "Well I do."

And went back to sleep.

Howie Doss woke up with equal parts excitement and trepidation. This was supposed to be his day. He was going to stare down the President of the United States and without saying it outright, tell him that he held his job in his hand. But there was now also the dark shadow of the kid from Oakland. At least, they now knew what his plan was. Doss had Derek Plough to thank for that.

He assumed he'd be hearing from Frankie Waters at some point today.

Doss got out of bed and walked around his opulent apartment. Most people who made it big moved to the suburbs of D.C. and bought a house. Not Doss. He didn't like to be too far from the action, so he lived in a three bedroom apartment. Of course, it was like no other apartment in D.C., costing more than those expensive suburban homes. He also owned apartments in New York, LA, and several throughout Europe.

The fact that Doss knew he'd never get married, had always led him to buy apartments. He preferred it to some huge house he'd never fill with a wife or children. I'll make an exception for the White House, Doss thought, and laughed to himself.

He spent 30 minutes in his luxurious shower and drove the five minutes to the Always Right offices on K Street. He could have afforded 100 chauffeurs, but still preferred to drive his own car.

He arrived at the offices and looked out at his employees. He liked that he could walk into an office on a Saturday, a day before a New Year, and still see it bustling. It was an office that he had built through his ingenuity, and Howie Doss was immensely proud of that. The fact that he had built it on bullying, outing people's biggest secrets, and making America a tougher place for minorities and poor people, didn't bother him at all. It actually made him prouder.

He smiled as he walked by Gloria Flores. Sure, Doss had built all this, but Gloria Flores had just given him his golden ticket. The people in the office noticed that Howie Doss was extra chipper today. With the exception of Flores, none of them knew why.

The true believers who worked for Doss would have been overjoyed if they knew what was coming. There was a segment of Always Right who leaned right, but certainly weren't true believers in the classic sense. They wouldn't have been quite as enthusiastic. Even with their conservative leanings, they were scared of Doss and would be petrified if they knew what he had in mind.

Not that Doss cared, he liked ruling with an iron fist. And his employees were not his concern right now.

As Doss walked towards his office, he started an internal monologue with himself.

Fuck the President's Chief of Staff, who had considered Doss a nuisance, not knowing it was Doss's leaks that helped the President get elected.

Fuck the Vice President who had once told him, "I'm #2 in line. Get off your high horse." Howie Doss had told the Vice President the only way he was ever going to truly be a #2 was when Doss flushed him down the toilet.

Fuck the Blacks, including the ones who had taken his father's job and dated his mother. Doss was going to have the president lessen police presence around the ghettos. Let them kill themselves.

Fuck the Hispanics who came to this country and didn't even learn how to speak the language. Doss had three words for them: *Deport. Deport. Deport.*

Fuck poor, old people who were always getting sick and bogging down the economy. Your health insurance doesn't cover you? Should have made more money in your lifetime. Universal Health Care? Not a chance. Let them rot. And Doss knew he wouldn't lose a wink of sleep over it.

Fuck the Muslims who were blowing up buildings and killing innocent people. Fuck the peace toting ones too. Fuck the whole damn religion. *I think some cluster bombs might be in order, Mr. President. May I suggest chemical.*

Fuck the poor, redneck whites in the flyover states who constantly voted against their interests based almost solely on gun ownership, faux patriotism, and a little bit of racism. We have taken you guys for a wild ride, and there's no getting off now. But thanks for putting the empty suit in office!

And finally, fuck the President/Commander-In-Chief/Empty Suit. He was the furthest thing from a true believer. His whole life he advocated for liberal policies again and again and again. *That is until I get my claws into you. Or more accurately, my puppet strings.*

Doss finished the litany of people he was going to fuck over and walked into his office. He started outlining what he was going to say to the President.

Always Right was extremely powerful, but they didn't have a very big staff and only needed three secretaries. With 37 employees, there really wasn't a need for many more. Rochelle Yardley and Anthony West would answer the main lines, and they would transfer the call to the relevant employee if they saw fit. If it were someone asking for Howie Doss, and they found it important enough, they would transfer it up to his personal secretary, Virginia Hale.

If Doss or Hale later deemed it was not worthy to have been transferred to them, then Yardley and West would have hell to pay. It wasn't always an easy job because knowing the difference between a crackpot and a guy with a real scoop was sometimes difficult.

All things being equal, they would not transfer a phone call up to Virginia Hale. They would take the name and number of the person calling, and let Doss decide himself if it was worth calling the individual back. Yardley and West preferred that to feeling the wrath of Doss for an unnecessary transfer.

Rochelle Yardley was about to be put to one of those tough decisions.

I had spent a solid hour going over what I was going to say to get Howie Doss on the phone, and then another hour going over what I was going to say to him if he agreed to meet us. I had come up with my initial plan, but it was constantly evolving.

When I had told Evie to bring a skirt with ruffles, it hadn't been because I had planned on playing tennis with her. There was a practical reason.

If we did meet with Doss, my plan was to tape a phone to Evie's upper thigh, and we would be transmitting via Facebook Live whatever Doss said to the world. It would be difficult to conceal a phone with a straight, leveled skirt. Jeans were out because I wasn't sure if the sound could be picked up through denim. I did think a ruffled skirt would make it much harder to see a phone taped to her thigh, however, and with soft fabric above it, would certainly pick up our conversation.

I was sure that Doss was going to frisk us, and he'd make us take off our shoes, and possibly even our pants or shirts. I hoped he wouldn't reach for the upper thigh of Evie, but the more I thought about it, the more I realized we couldn't take that chance. My plan evolved once again, and I knew we had to pick up some new phones at some point.

I knew that one of our big wild cards was knowing who Derek Plough was. That would be sure to get a rise out of Doss. Whether it would be enough to get him to say something incriminating was yet to be determined.

Evie had been in and out of sleep all morning. I was hoping she wasn't losing steam. She had been such a trooper through this whole thing, occasionally carrying me. But I needed her now more than ever.

I woke her up, and we went over the plan one more time. We had to be ready to go whenever the opportunity presented itself. Finally, after going over every conceivable permutation of my plan, it was time to get down to business.

"It's time. You ready to go for a walk?" I asked.

I knew that Howie Doss may well have his offices tapped and I wasn't going to let him catch us that easy. We were going to walk quite a way from the Motel 6 and call him. I'd then turn off my cell phone and not use it again. I wasn't going to take the chance that he could triangulate me if I used the same phone again. Trust me, I had thought this through.

We left the Motel 6 and started walking around Washington D.C. It certainly wasn't the part of the city that brought in so many tourists, but that was fine with me. I had a real feeling of David vs. Goliath now and I reveled in it as we passed by dilapidated buildings and defunct small businesses.

Evie looked nervous, but I couldn't tell if it was the neighborhood we were walking in or the impending call to Howie Doss.

We had been walking 10 minutes when we came upon two hotels that were right next to each other. I grabbed Evie, and we ducked into a vacant alley between the two.

"This is perfect," I said. "If they somehow can trace this call, they'd think we are staying at one of these hotels."

"Smart," Evie said. That's all I would get out of her.

"Here goes nothing!" I exclaimed.

I looked down at my phone again for the number to Always Right, typed in the numbers, and pressed the green button.

On the second ring, a female voice answered.

"Always Right. This is Rochelle, how may I direct your call?"

"I'd like to speak to Howie Doss," I said.

"And what is it regarding?"

"I have some information for him."

"You can go ahead and leave that information with me, and I'll make sure he gets it."

"No, that's not good enough. Trust me, this is information that he's going to want to hear himself."

"What is your name, sir?"

"You can tell him that Darby is calling. Make sure he hears that name."

"Please hold sir."

I looked over at Evie, covered the phone and said: "They have me on hold."

I remained on hold for several minutes. Just when I thought they had forgot about me, the woman's voice appeared back on the line.

"Transferring you to Mr. Doss," the voice said.

I was transferred, and the powerful voice I'd heard on a few YouTube interviews came to the phone.

"Howie Doss."

"Hi, Mr. Doss. I'd like to ask you a couple of questions about our mutual friend Darby Bowles."

"Can't say I've ever heard that name. By the way, what's yours?"

"I'm Joe," I said, saying the first name that popped in my head.

"That's funny, my secretary said your name was Darby also."

His voice was mesmerizing, and at the same time, patronizing. He knew my name wasn't Joe . I felt like I had already gotten off on the wrong foot. I held all the cards, but suddenly it didn't feel that way. I tried to find my footing.

"That was to get you on the phone."

"Well, it worked. What do you want?"

"I have some information that I think you may find valuable. I'd like to meet up with you and discuss it. If you don't want to, I know some people who would," I said.

"Are you here in D.C.?"

"I am."

"Listen, Joe, I'm in a meeting right now. Call me back in exactly one hour, and we'll set up a time to meet."

"One hour?"

"Yes. Oh, and Joe?"

"Yeah?"

"Tell Frankie Waters I said hello."

With that, Howie Doss hung up, and my face went ghost white.

Howie Doss wasn't happy, but he would have been a lot more shaken up if the call had come as a surprise. It hadn't been, thanks to Derek Plough, who had his back numerous times over the years. Doss was going to need his help again.

Plough had flown back to D.C. the previous night, but there would be no rest until this was over. Doss called him.

"Hello?"

"Wake up, Derek."

"I'm up."

"Then get over to my office. Right now."

Howie Doss hung up.

"Do you think he was trying to trace the phone call?" Evie asked me.

"I don't think he had enough time once he got on the line, but I do think that's why he's asking me to call back in an hour. There's no meeting that could be more important than us right now."

"I think I'm starting to realize just how big this is."

"It's gigantic, Evie. At this very moment, we are the two most important people in the future of the United States political landscape."

"You make it sound like we are taking down the President," Evie said.

Little did I know, that's basically what Howie Doss was about to become.

Never had an hour taken so long. I felt like I was watching that stopwatch from 60 minutes alert me as every single second passed by. Evie and I kept walking in the meantime. I didn't think there was any way he could have traced our first phone call, but just in case, I decided we shouldn't be in the alley between the two hotels.

"How did they find out who you were?" Evie asked.

She asked the question we were both thinking, but had been afraid to bring up.

"I've thought of a couple of possibilities. As you had mentioned, they could have tortured the information from Darby before they killed him. Or they could have tapped the phone of Darby's friend that I've been calling. Those seem the two most likely scenarios."

"This just keeps getting worse."

"I'm not saying that's what happened. Just a possibility."

"Do you think they know about me?"

I thought about it. "It depends. If they got the information from Darby, he might have told them about the two people going to Patricia Page's. If it was only from tapping the house, then they would only know about me."

"And if they have found out who you are, wouldn't you say it's likely they know who your mother and sister are?"

It was my first thought when Howie Doss had said "Frankie Waters," but it was different when I heard Evie say it. She somehow confirmed my fear.

"This is all going to end when we meet with Doss."

"That's not a denial."

"I don't want to worry them about something that may well be over later today."

"Call your Mom. For me."

I looked at Evie and knew this wasn't something I could negotiate. And for my own peace of mind, I knew I needed to make the call. I picked up my phone and called my mother's cell phone.

"Hello." It was the welcomed voice of my mother.

"Hi Mom, it's Frankie."

"Well look who it is. My son who leaves in the middle of the night."

I was just happy to hear her.

"I'm sorry, Mom. We wanted to beat the traffic and knew it would be terrible for the New Year's weekend," I said, hating myself for having to lie to her.

"So how is Tahoe?"

"It's beautiful," I said.

"Really? On the news, they said it was snowing like crazy."

I needed to get the hell off the phone.

"It is. That's what makes it so beautiful. You know how nice it is up here when everything is white."

"I do, Frankie. Taking you to Lake Tahoe as a child are some of my favorite memories. Your father loved those moments too."

I felt myself getting a little choked up at the mention of my father. I loved the man and thought about him all the time, but I couldn't at that moment. Not with all that was going on.

"Listen, Mom, I have to run. Evie and I are heading out."

"Be careful in that weather, Frankie," my mother said.

"I will. I'll see you tomorrow or Monday."

"I love you, Frankie."

"I love you too, Mom."

I put the phone down and shook my head.

"You are way too good a liar," Evie said.

"I know, I feel shitty about it."

Evie came over and rubbed my shoulders.

"Don't beat yourself up about it," she said. "You had to do it. Just glad to hear they are alright."

"Yeah, everything is fine on their side."

"And ours?"

I knew I had set myself up for that one. Having no good answer, I let the question sit there unanswered.

I looked down at my watch. Thirty minutes till I was supposed to call Howie Doss back.

<u>42</u>

The time had come for my return call to Howie Doss.

I dialed the number, once again saying I was Joe and was transferred up immediately.

"Joe, how are you doing?" The memorable, patronizing voice said, accentuating the name Joe.

"When can we meet up, Mr. Doss?"

"Please, call me Howie."

"I only call my friends by their first name," I said.

"That's the thing. I think we can be friends."

"I doubt it. Not after you find out how much I'm asking for," I said.

I had told Evie that I was going to pretend that we were blackmailing Doss. It was believable, and I thought Doss would be more likely to talk if he knew he'd be buying our silence in the end.

"Why would you possibly want any of my money? Anyway, that's something we can discuss at the meeting," Doss said.

It was obvious he wasn't going to give anything away over the phone. He was way too smart for that.

"I need a time," I said.

"I can meet very early tomorrow morning," Doss said. "As early as seven or eight a.m."

"That's not good enough. I want to meet today," I said, although I knew if I had to wait, I would.

"I'm sorry, Frankie. Oh, I'm sorry, I mean Joe," Doss said and started laughing. It wasn't the laugh of someone laughing with you, it was the laugh of someone laughing at you.

Doss continued. "Some people work for a living. We can't just all travel to Washington D.C. from Oakland, California on a wild goose chase. So if you want to meet with me, it will be tomorrow morning."

"What could you possibly have that's more important than meeting with me?" I asked.

"If you must know, I am meeting with the President of the United States today."

"Surprises me, considering you are his Puppeteer. 'I'm the fucking Puppeteer' was the exact wording I think."

I don't know what motivated me to repeat what Scarlet Jackson had played for us, but the guy was getting under my skin. I had to let him know that I wasn't just some 21-year-old in over their head. Even if that's how I currently felt.

"Maybe I have underestimated you, young Frankie," Doss said this as a compliment, not in the patronizing voice that he had adopted for most of our conversation. "I'm looking forward to meeting you."

I realized that I was staying on the phone too long.

"Where and when tomorrow?" I asked.

"8 a.m. tomorrow morning at the Always Right offices."

There was no way I was going to meet him there. He could have a goon waiting, poison the coffee, or any other of a million possibilities.

"Not a chance, Doss."

"Then where?" he asked.

"Same time, but at the Lincoln Memorial. If you are not there, then I'll give the information I've amassed to someone else."

It was an impulsive decision, but I figured he wouldn't try to kill someone at a place so public.

Howie Doss must have realized not to press his luck, because he simply replied, "I'll be there."

I hung up the phone.

"You stayed on the phone too long," Evie said.

"You're right. Let's get the hell out of here."

Evie and I started walking. I had powered my phone off, so I had Evie order an UBER. After a few minutes, our driver arrived.

"Where to?" the gruff, weathered UBER driver asked.

"1345 4th street. It's a Motel 6. But first I need to stop off at a T-Mobile store," I said.

"I know one that's close," the man replied.

Derek Plough had arrived 10 minutes before the phone call, installing chords in Doss's phone. After the phone call had ended, Doss asked if he was able to get a reading.

"It takes a few minutes," Plough said.

It was rare when Plough was the expert on something, but when it came to tapping phones and such things, Doss deferred to Plough. The meat-headed football player had become a bit of an expert on surveillance.

A few minutes later, a reading came in.

"It looks like the call was made from the Northeastern part of D.C. Looks like Woodridge. No business comes up as the point of origin so he may have been walking on the street."

"Head over that way. It's a long shot, but maybe there's a chance he's still walking around that area."

"I'll go now."

"And Derek, If you don't find anything, why don't you find out where Scarlet Jackson is."

"Why her?"

"You know that line he said about the Puppeteer? The only time I ever used that phrase was to Scarlet Jackson. Maybe they are in contact with each other."

"I'll head in the direction of her office after I scope out Woodridge."

"Good work, Derek. Now it's time we part ways. I have to go meet the President," Doss said.

Plough looked on quizzically, and Doss remembered that he still hadn't told him. He spent the next few minutes updating Plough on all that had happened.

I had decided the odds were way too high that Doss would find the phone we'd have on Evie's thigh. His livelihood was at stake after all, so I had to assume he would do everything in his power to make sure he wasn't being recorded. The plan I had come up with was starting to sound better and better.

It would involve several prepaid cellphones, so I stood in line holding five of them in the T-Mobile store. I looked ridiculous, but I didn't care. All of my focus was on keeping Evie safe and exposing Howie Doss for the murderer he was. Those were the only two things that mattered.

I looked over at Evie, and she looked nervous. She hadn't been herself the last few days, for obvious reasons.

"You want to go to the cops, don't you?" I whispered.

"No. I said I'd see it out and I will. But there is someone I would like to meet."

"Scarlet Jackson?"

"Yes," Evie said.

"Let's get back to the hotel, and then you can call her."

"Alright."

I arrived at the front of the line and bought the five phones. The teller gave me a peculiar glare, but as I said, nothing else mattered at this point.

What Howie Doss appreciated most about being a visitor to the White House was that they always sent a car for you. While Doss had prided himself on being one of the last of the D.C. political big shots to still drive himself, he could never say no to the President. At least not when it came to free transportation.

Doss was picked up outside of his offices, and he took his seat in the back of the black, tinted town car. There would be no small talk on this ride, so Doss concentrated on his impending meeting with the President.

The drive was barely over a mile, but with traffic, it took 15 minutes. They took K street to 20th, got on to L Street for a few hundred feet, and then took a right on 19th street. The left on E street and the buildings that appear made Doss take notice. He started looking around like a tourist who had never been to D.C.

As powerful as he had become, he never grew tired of approaching the White House. Whatever could be said about Doss, he was a man of history and knew a great deal about America's most famous house. Doss laughed to himself, imagining this as his move-in day into the White House.

Doss went through the usual protocol before being ushered into the West Wing. He was frisked, escorted between two separate groups of Secret Service agents, and finally was able to enter the White House. They all knew who Doss was, and he remembered it taking longer when he visited for the first time.

It had become almost routine for Doss, being the eighth time he had visited the President since he took office. Of course, none of the other meetings were going to go down like today's.

Doss was led through the now familiar path to the Oval Office. He still had three secret service agents with him as he approached the door of the most famous office in the world.

"The President will see you now," one of them said.

The Oval Office doors opened and out walked the President of the United States of America. He had on a red power tie that Doss thought hung too low. He walked with authority, careful to never look like he was rushed.

They shook hands and then the President put his hand on Doss's shoulder and escorted him into the Oval Office. The door closed behind them. They were alone.

"Nice to see you, Howie," the President said.

"Hello, Mr. President."

Doss knew the President well enough to call him by his first name. But because this was going to get ugly fast, he decided to show civility before the shit hit the fan.

"This better be important, Howie. That loon in North Korea is causing me more headaches than the media is."

"Why don't you take a seat, Mr. President?"

"I tell people when to sit, Howie," the President said sternly.

"Not anymore," Doss said.

So much for being diplomatic. Howie Doss was going to enjoy this. He had always been a man to whom power was like a drug, and this was the strongest one he'd ever been on.

"I like you, Howie. I don't want to have to throw you out, but if you talk to me like that again, I will," the President said, standing more upright to emphasize his height advantage.

People had used this ploy on Doss his whole life. Trying to stake their claim by showing that they were taller. It never worked.

You just have further to fall when I chop you down, Doss thought, and decided it was time to start chopping. There was no need for small talk.

"Did I ever tell you that my employee Gloria Flores has a daughter named Michelle?"

The President took a step back, looking for a moment like he had been shot. His heel clipped his chair, and he almost went down.

"And she likes to record conversations from time to time."

Doss took out his phone and started playing a few seconds of the audio that Gloria Flores had given him. The President started rubbing his forehead.

"Stop it! Turn it off!"

The President had to put his hand on the desk to keep himself upright.

"You're looking a little peaked, Mr. President," Doss said.

"Maybe I will take that seat."

The President of the United States, or 'the empty suit' as Doss commonly referred to him as, took a seat in his Oval Office chair. Love him or hate him, and he had plenty on both sides, most people would agree that the President had been a proud man for his entire adult life. He didn't look like one now.

He was slouching in the chair, a man who appeared defeated. He was rubbing his forehead and staring at the ground. It was almost like he couldn't muster the strength to look up at Doss.

"Can I get you a water or something, Mr. President?"

The Commander-in-Chief managed to raise his eyes to Howie Doss. He had never liked the guy.

They both had been great at using each other, and the President had been fine with that. He knew that Doss and his websites had helped him get elected, and for that he was grateful. He also knew that he never wanted to be on Doss's bad side. Unfortunately, that's where he now found himself.

"A glass of water, Mr. President?" Doss repeated.

"Stop being condescending. I'm still the most powerful man in the world."

"That's currently up for debate."

"What do you want?"

"I want your job."

"It's not for sale."

"Well, that's where we differ. I think it is. Don't worry, you'll still be the man with your face in the limelight, just how you like it. But behind the scenes, I'll be the one pulling the strings."

Howie Doss loved dropping the Puppeteer reference. Not that the empty suit would ever understand what he was referring to.

"Will never happen," the Commander-in-Chief said.

Howie Doss ignored what the empty suit said.

"Mr. President, wouldn't you say we agree on about 85% of issues?"

"Sounds about right," he said, still rubbing his forehead with his fingers.

"Then all you have to do is change 15%," Doss said.

He held all the cards and enjoyed looking down at the beaten man. It gave Doss great pleasure eyeing the empty suit in this light. A true believer holding the power over a flip-flopping joke of a man. It was perfect.

"Screw you," the President said, but it was half-hearted at best. Howie Doss knew he had him.

"We're not going to do this all at once. That would be too obvious. However, slowly but surely, the things we disagree on will tilt in my direction."

"And for that, you will not go to the press?"

"Yes, although that would be the least of your worries, sir. Does the word treason mean anything to you?"

"You wouldn't do that. You need me."

"That's why I'm trying to work with you. I'm giving you an out, Mr. President."

The President nodded.

"One thing I didn't mention," Doss said. "If I should somehow befall an injury, the information I have would be sent directly to the proper authorities."

The President nodded at Doss. It was as if the ability to form sentences had been zapped from him.

Doss continued. "If nothing happens to me, then no one will ever be made aware of this audio. That includes your Chief of Staff and your VP. No one. In fact, I prefer to be the only one that knows."

"What about Gloria Flores?" the President said, barely above a whisper.

"Have you met the woman? She's further right than me. She's not going to say anything. She brought it to me."

"And her daughter?"

"You have no worries about her. She's a very sexy girl Mr. President, but I'm really shocked you could be so dumb to talk about that information. It's unfathomable to me."

The President didn't respond, basically confirming Doss's opinion of how mindless and idiotic he had been.

"I mean, how could you be so careless? I know you aren't the sharpest tool in the shed, but this is pathetic, even for you."

Howie Doss would never have talked to the President of the United States like this. Until now. He knew he could get away with anything.

"I need to think about this," the President said, but it was a bluff, and they both knew it.

"No offense Mr. President, but there's nothing to think about. You play ball with me, or your life is in ruins, and your time as President is over."

The President put his head in his hands.

"So what's next?"

"We'll meet sometime next week. I'll have a list of the first few policy changes I think you should propose."

Doss couldn't just leave it at that.

"You've always been a weak-minded jellyfish, sir. You have no thoughts of your own and people have been making the decisions for you since the beginning of your candidacy. You get all the blame and all the glory from the country, but they don't realize you are just a pawn. Or a puppet, as it is. And the only thing that's changed is that you have a new Puppeteer.......Me!"

"You're a slimy asshole, Doss!"

"What happened to Howie?" Doss asked.

The President ignored taking the bait. The obvious answer was that they were no longer friends.

"I'm going to leave now," Doss said.

"You know how to show yourself out."

Howie Doss got to the door and said, "You're looking really handsome, Mr. President."

The President looked up and saw that Howie Doss was talking to his reflection in the mirror.

43

We arrived back at the hotel, and I could tell that Evie was antsy to call Scarlet Jackson.

"Go ahead and call her," I said.

She reached for her own cell phone, but I grabbed it and gave her one of the cheap phones I had bought.

"Let's use these from here on in," I said.

Evie nodded. She wrote down Scarlet's number from her phone and dialed the number with one of the phones from T-Mobile.

Someone picked up almost immediately. Scarlet Jackson must have been taking our little story very seriously.

I only heard Evie's end. "Hi, Scarlet....Yeah, we're in D.C.....We know what we are doing.....Thanks, but no thanks.....but yes, we would like to meet with you today.....8 p.m. is the earliest you can meet?......no, that's fine.....you tell me where.....Florida Avenue Grill?...We'll be there."

"Eight p.m. at the Florida Avenue Grill?" I asked.

"No fooling you," Evie said.

"Eight p.m. with Scarlet, eight a.m. with Doss."

"Indeed."

"I've been extremely cautious in planning this out, and I think it's better if we stay in the hotel until we meet her. Especially since Doss knows who I am. We can meet Scarlet at eight, come back here and sleep, meet Doss in the morning, and then this will all be over."

"Promise me one thing, Frankie."

"Anything."

"After tomorrow morning, we wash our hands of this. Even if Doss doesn't admit anything, or the phones don't record, or he doesn't show at all. Etc. Etc. No matter what happens, promise me this is it."

"I promise, Evie. I didn't go through all of these precautions because I'm taking this lightly. I just don't think we have enough on Doss to prove that he ordered those murders in Oklahoma City, so I think we need to take this extra step of trying to get him to admit something. Obviously, it's going to take considerable cunning and most importantly, charm," I said.

I got Evie to flash a brief smile. I considered it a win with all the tension we were under.

"And we are going to be safe?" she asked.

"The last call I made from my cell phone was two or three miles from here. I turned that phone off. We are now at a fleabag motel under an assumed name, and I have no plans on turning that phone back on. We have new phones we can use if we have to. As for Doss, he is not going to shoot us in front of the

Lincoln Memorial. And right after the meeting is over, we can drive to the entrance of the Washington Post and tell our story if you'd like."

"That actually sounds nice."

"It does, but I'd prefer having Doss admit to the murders live to the world."

"I understand your reasoning, and I've had the adventure of a lifetime, but I'm ready for it to end."

"I am too."

We embraced.

Howie Doss walked away from the meeting thinking he could add veterinarian to his resume. After all, he had just neutered the President. The empty suit was now, what they would call in the horse racing business, a gelding. Doss rode back in the same car that had brought him, smiling the whole time. Everything was coming together.

He returned to Always Right and went up to his office.

With one of his secured cell phones, Doss texted Derek Plough for an update. Plough said he hadn't seen the kid in the vicinity of where the call was made. He was headed to check on Scarlet Jackson. He assured Doss that if he used the same cell phone again, he would be able to track him down. And from there, Plough would do away with him, just like he had Darby Bowles. Doss smile only brightened.

Doss went over everything in his head again, trying to think if he was missing anything. He was so close, for all intents and purposes, to becoming the de-facto leader of the country and he couldn't risk that by overlooking anything.

He decided that there was one last thing he could do. It was an insurance policy more than anything else. Most likely it wouldn't be necessary, but Doss couldn't leave anything to chance.

Doss had only trusted a few people in his whole life. Derek Plough was one of them. As was Gloria Flores. And both of their trust had come over time.

He had trusted Hunter Lockley from the first moment he had met him, being introduced by a conservative operative who shared Doss's political leanings. They immediately got along, aware they were aligned politically, and more importantly, would do anything to get what they wanted.

Lockley had worked for the CIA in South America for years and judging by the rumors, his first name was apropos. Although Hunter Lockley had not been hunting animals.

He was now working more as a covert political operative, but that doesn't mean he didn't occasionally miss the old days. Old habits die hard.

Howie Doss knew he was still based out of San Francisco, planted there to find dirt on Dems in the most liberal of America's big cities. He had given

Doss more than a few inside stories over the years, although it would be his former job in South America that made Doss call him on this day.

Doss dialed his number from one of his secured phones and told him he had a job for him. He was to go across the bay and stake out a house in Oakland.

Hunter Lockley knew he was going to take the job well before Doss finished his pitch.

Over the next several hours, I updated Evie on our plan, and what I had in mind for the five phones I had bought. I proceeded to set up five new Facebook accounts, knowing I could only stream Facebook Live from one account at a time. I made each Facebook account open to the public so there would be no problem for people trying to listen in.

Evie and I didn't talk much as I set up the phones. Time seemed to be moving at a snail's pace. There would be no light-hearted banter. We were both extremely nervous. Two twenty-one-year-old kids on the trail of a powerful murderer. Two twenty-one-year-old kids in way, way over their heads.

"It's seven o'clock. Should we get ready?" Evie asked me.

"Yeah. I'll take a two-minute shower."

I went to the door of the Motel to make sure it was locked. Evie gave me a knowing look.

"Remember not to turn our personal phones on for any reason. And I mean yours as well. Use the phones I bought if you have to. I'm 90% sure they don't even know who you are, but no need to take that chance."

"I'm not going to turn on the phones, Frankie," Evie said.

"Sorry if I keep repeating myself. Just trying to make sure we don't deviate from our plan."

"I get it," she said.

I jumped in the shower, using a bar of soap that was about the size of the parting mint they give you at a restaurant. Evie was next, and if she didn't like the bathroom arrangements, she didn't complain about them.

When she finished, I called downstairs and had the front desk call us a cab. He said it would be downstairs in 10 minutes.

The Florida Avenue Grill claimed to be the oldest soul food restaurant in the world. While that may be up for debate from some people in the Deep South, what can't be argued is that it was a Washington D.C. landmark. It's been open since 1944 and has been serving oversized portions of southern comfort food ever since.

We waited outside for Scarlett Jackson who arrived a few minutes after us. She walked us in like she owned the place.

The red stools were made of plastic that looked like they had been cracking since 1944. The laminated menus weren't much cleaner, but that seemed to be part of the charm. Presidents, Senators, and Congressmen had been coming there forever, so they had to be doing something right.

And while Scarlett Jackson may not have owned the place, she was obviously a regular. At least three people said hello within the first few seconds of us walking in. I saw a plate that was covered with some delicious looking fatty food.

"They don't hold back here do they?" I asked.

"No one has ever left the Florida Avenue Grill hungry," she explained.

It was really busy, and I wondered why the hell Scarlet Jackson would want to discuss important issues here. I got my answer a few seconds later.

Scarlett led us to the checkout counter.

"Pickup order for Scarlett Jackson," she said.

"Of course, Mrs. Jackson," a young woman said.

She went in the back and picked up the order.

"That will be $42.93."

Scarlett paid cash and left a few dollars in the tip jar.

"Let's go," she said.

Evie and I followed her out of the Florida Avenue Grill, not sure exactly what was going on. A tinted, black SUV came to the front of the Grill, and a driver came around and opened the back seat for the three of us. We all got in. The car pulled around the corner and parked.

"You can't come all the way to Washington D.C. without trying the Florida Avenue Grill. That's my treat. You guys can eat at your hotel. I got you a little of everything."

"Thanks a lot, Scarlett," I said, remembering she liked to be called by her first name. "I wasn't sure that was the best place to talk."

"No, your secrets wouldn't last long in a place like that. A lot of my fellow congressmen and women go there, but it's never to talk business. It's to have some great soul food and fill up our tummies a little bit."

"So what's in the bag?" Evie asked.

"Ribs, Fried Chicken, Cornbread, Greens. Trust me, you'll love it."

"Sounds great."

"So, where are you guys staying? I'll take you there after we talk."

"The Motel 6 on 4th street."

"Ouch. I could have gotten you better arrangements if you wanted it."

"Thanks, but we are trying to keep a low profile," I said.

"By coming to Washington D.C.?" she said.

Her words just hung there, and I had no good response.

"Okay, tell me your plan and leave out nothing," she said.

"I'll tell you, but you have to guarantee me you will let us go through with it,"

"Why should I do that?"

"Because if you don't, you'll never know the information I have on Howie Doss," I said.

It was an obvious bluff, but Scarlett decided not to call me on it.

"As long as I like what I hear, I'll let you go through with it," she said.

"That's fair," I told her and proceeded to tell her what I had in mind.

She hated every single part of it.

After getting about five disapproving looks from Scarlett Jackson while telling her my plan, I pulled the rip chord at the last second.

"So when are you planning on implementing this terrible idea?" she asked.

I paused, thought about it, and decided I was going to lie to a United States congresswoman.

"The day after tomorrow. In Doss's offices."

I stared at Evie, hoping she wouldn't spill the beans. I had lied about the time, the place, and I had left out the part about using the other phones. She looked at me stoically, and I knew I had nothing to fear.

"Are you crazy? I would need to plant some of my people around the office buildings. We'd have to scope the place out, and have you wear a wire or something."

"He's going to search us. A wire wouldn't work."

"It's just too risky, and I can't let you do it. So here's what's going to happen," Scarlett said. "I'll run your plan by some people I know and see how we can make you safer. How about meeting tomorrow around noon?"

It was time for one last lie.

"Noon sounds fine," I said, knowing we were meeting Doss at 8 a.m. and there would be no need to meet Jackson.

"I'm glad you two have come to your senses," Scarlett said. "I'll drop you off at your hotel now, and we'll come by and pick you up tomorrow at noon."

Scarlett Jackson knocked on the partition window of the SUV and told the driver to head to the Motel 6 on 4th street.

The SUV pulled away from the curb. The driver didn't notice that another dark SUV pulled away from the curb a few seconds later, following from a safe distance. Derek Plough had found his targets.

"We can't wait to have Scarlet make things safe," I told Evie when we made it back to the hotel. "Doss would figure something was wrong if we suddenly called back and said we wanted to delay our meeting."

"I agree," Evie said. "Doss is no idiot."

We heard some fireworks go off in the background. Followed by some more. It was the first time that we had consciously realized that it was New Year's Eve.

"This has to be the strangest New Year's Eve in history," Evie said.

I grabbed one of the bags from the Florida Avenue Grill.

"Soul food in a Motel 6. Yeah, I'd say so."

I put some ribs, chicken, and some greens on Evie's plate and handed her a plastic fork.

Neither one of us had much of an appetite, which was unfortunate because it was some delicious food.

"I've found your targets," Plough said.

"Targets?" Doss asked.

"Remember the girl? Evie. And let me tell you, she's a peach."

"Of course," Doss said.

He cursed himself, already forgetting about the girl. He had way too much on his mind.

"I followed your advice to check out Scarlet Jackson. I know who her private driver is, so I staked out his house."

Doss was going to interrupt and ask how he knew Jackson's private driver, but it shouldn't have come as a surprise. Plough was good at what he did.

"Sure enough," Plough continued, "He went and picked up Jackson about an hour ago. I followed from a safe distance. He drove her to the Florida Avenue Grill, and they met up with Frankie and Evie. They grabbed some food to go and sat in Jackson's car for about 10 minutes before driving them back to a Motel 6. I'm sitting out front of it right now."

Howie Doss felt his world crumbling around him. They had just met with Scarlet Jackson and surely had given her any information that they had. This whole empire he had built was going to collapse. Fuck! Fuck! Fuck!

"I haven't told you the best part," Plough said.

"Best part? There's nothing fucking good about this! Someone has information on me and is meeting with a United States congresswoman? What could be fucking good about that?" Doss yelled.

Plough could feel the rage coming from Doss's end, but it was time to turn that rage into appreciation.

"I may ask for a raise when this is all said and done," Plough said.

"You better make me happy. And quick."

"As I waited for Jackson's driver, I figured putting a bug in his car couldn't hurt. He was in his house, and it was easy to jimmy the car and put a microphone in it."

"I'm listening," Doss said.

"I heard their whole conversation. You have nothing to worry about. The kid lied to Jackson, saying you two were going to meet at your office in two days. Most importantly, he didn't tell her what he had on you."

Howie Doss smiled. Just like the politicians he had brought to their knees, this kid had wanted too much power. He wanted to take Howie Doss down all by himself, and it would cost him. With his life. And the life of the young girl who was with him.

"Did they discuss their plan?"

"They did. I'll make sure they never meet you in the morning, but would you like to know?"

"Humor me," Doss said, in the most unhumorous way possible.

"The girl was going to have a phone on her upper thigh, under her skirt. They were going to live stream it to the internet and get you to admit incriminating things."

Howie Doss was floored. These were smart fucking kids. It was almost a shame that Doss wouldn't get to meet them face to face. Almost.

"And they told Jackson nothing about what they had on me?" Doss asked.

"Nothing. Trust me, she tried to get it out of him, but he wouldn't budge."

"You've done amazing work, Derek. When will you be completing the final piece? The extermination."

These were secured phones and Howie Doss had no problem using this type of language.

"Not until early tomorrow morning. I was able to see what room they walked to and I'm staking it out the front of the Motel now. It's New Year's Eve, and there's just too many people walking around the hotel. Probably be that way till well after midnight. I'll feel safer doing it around five tomorrow morning. All the New Years' Eve drunks will be passed out by then."

"Tell you what," Doss said. "Why don't you meet me at the steps of the Lincoln Memorial tomorrow morning at eight. Since the other two will not be making it, you can sub in for them. And tell me about their demise. The demise at sunrise."

Doss laughed at his own joke. Plough did not.

"I'll be there," he said instead.

44

SUNDAY, JANUARY 1st:

In the most subdued countdown in New Year's Eve history, Evie and I looked on as our little clock radio struck midnight and we raised our water-filled plastic cups to each other. We had been struggling to fall asleep, and against our wishes, we were still up as midnight struck.

"We really need to get some sleep now," I said.

Evie turned the lights off and climbed into bed, and we tried to get the sleep that had been so evasive. It didn't come easily, and I spent the next few hours tossing and turning. Evie looked to be doing better than myself as I heard her snoring away the hours from one to five a.m.

Sometimes when I couldn't sleep, I'd get up and walk around for a little bit. I'd had the habit since childhood, and sometimes it would help me fall asleep.

I removed my arm from Evie's waist and got out of bed, making sure not to wake her. I put on some sweatpants and walked out the door, making sure the door was locked behind me. I made my way down to the hotel lobby and decided to get some pretzels. I had no idea why, but it helped pass the time.

Looking out in the parking lot, I saw a black SUV. It stood out in the Motel 6 parking lot. Old Honda Civic's, Toyota Camry's, and Ford Fiesta's were more the car of choice for people staying at this particular Motel 6. I made a mental note of it and started walking back towards the room, devouring the pretzels as I did.

I got to the outside of our room and looked down at the SUV one more time. I opened the door, and Evie was awake and sitting up in bed.

"Are you trying to give me a heart attack?" she yelled.

"I couldn't sleep," I told her.

"Don't leave me again."

"I'm sorry. I won't. Come here for a sec," I said.

Evie walked out of the room, and I pointed down to the SUV below.

"Do you remember seeing that SUV earlier today?"

"No, but I wasn't exactly keeping tabs on the parking lot."

"It stands out like a sore thumb, doesn't it?"

"Is there a rule that says you can't have a nice SUV and stay at a seedy Motel 6?" she asked.

"Let's find out," I said.

I grabbed her hand and started moving her rapidly in the direction of the stairs. We were in the line of sight of the SUV, and if there was someone in it, he surely would see us.

As we approached the stairs, the SUV turned on its lights and started backing out of the parking lot.

"Get your stuff together," I said. "We're getting the hell out of here."

Derek Plough had to stay close to the Motel to make sure that they didn't leave under his nose. He didn't like parking the SUV in the dilapidated parking lot, but he didn't have much of a choice. He couldn't see their hotel room from the street, so he had to.

It was shortly after five a.m. when Plough saw Frankie Waters exit his hotel room and walk down to the lobby. He had planned on executing his plan within the next half hour and wasn't happy about seeing Waters walking around. Plough saw him looking at his car, but there wasn't much he could do. To just get up and drive away would only further the kid's suspicions, so Plough stayed put.

Then Frankie started pointing the SUV out to Evie and began running towards it. At that point, Plough had no choice. He had to get out of there. One time it could have just been curiosity, but running towards him was definitely more suspicion than curiosity.

They could call the cops or take down his license plate, and Plough couldn't have that happen. He turned on his lights and backed out of the Motel 6 parking lot.

"How the hell could this have happened to your perfect plan?' Evie asked, as we quickly put her stuff together.

"I don't know. I turned my phone off after the first call. There is no way they pinged us here. Fuck!" I yelled.

"Rack your brain, Frankie. There has to be something you hadn't planned on."

I thought and thought, and finally, it came to me. I had gone off script one time.

"The Puppeteer," I finally said.

"What?"

"When I said The Puppeteer he must have remembered who he said it to. And then he might have put a tail on Scarlett Jackson."

"You had to try to one up him with your knowledge, didn't you?" Evie said rhetorically.

She was right of course. I never should have repeated the phrase that Jackson had told me.

"I fucked up," was all I could muster.

"We'll worry about that later. For now, we need to get the hell out of here."

I finished packing my bag, making sure I still had all the cell phones. I did.

"You ready?" I asked.

"Yeah."

I didn't want to run out of our room at that moment, with the man in the SUV likely still out there somewhere.

"I have a plan," I said.

Evie's face said everything her voice wouldn't say.

I turned on one of the phones. The seconds felt like minutes, but my plan needed a cell phone and the hotel phone.

"Now what?" she asked, as the phone finally powered on.

"Call the front desk and say you left a bomb at the hotel. Tell him if he wants to save lives, he better evacuate everyone right this second."

"You're crazy," she said. I couldn't tell if it was a compliment or a put-down.

"Whoever this guy is, he's not going to start shooting with 100 people walking around the lobby."

Evie looked for the number and started calling the front desk, but I grabbed the phone. I realized it might sound more realistic coming from a man. A voice from the front desk answered.

"Hello, Motel 6."

"I have left a bomb at your hotel. This is not a joke. If you want to save lives, you better start evacuating. And you better do it now!" I said and hung up.

I then had Evie call 9-1-1 from the hotel room, and I told her what to say.

"9-1-1, what's your emergency?"

"I'm staying at the Motel 6 on 4th street, and we've just been alerted there's been a bomb threat. Please send police now. I'm so scared," Evie said.

She had done great.

"We might be joining Howie Doss in jail," Evie said. I had no answer.

I decided to use the hotel phone for the 9-1-1 call, so it sounded like a concerned hotel guest. We didn't need police officers pinging our phone and coming after us. Not when we were hours from meeting Doss.

"I'm assuming the SUV won't hang around once the police start showing up. And then we can get an UBER and get the hell out of here," I said.

"This is freaking nuts," Evie said. "But your plan isn't half bad."

Less than 30 seconds later, a piercing siren started emanating from downstairs. It was loud and unmistakable. I don't care how deep in sleep you were from New Year's Eve drinks, that noise was going to wake you up.

Within seconds, people started walking from their rooms towards the lobby. There were some pissed off people, and I felt a bit guilty, but my only concern was to keep Evie and myself alive. The majority of the people walking by were midway between still being drunk and waking with a hungover. Not a fun state to be in.

We heard the first police siren less than a minute later, and within three minutes there were several cops downstairs. Fire trucks followed a minute later. A bomb threat was no joke, and I was sure I'd eventually have to answer for it. The place was a total madhouse, with people in their pajamas smelling of booze surrounded by Washington D.C.'s finest. It would have been comical if there wasn't so much at stake.

Evie and I walked downstairs with our bags, keeping our eyes on the surrounding areas for any sign of the SUV. The half-stoned guy who had checked us in was back at work and answering questions from police officers. He looked like he'd literally rather be any other place in the world.

A steady stream of cabs and UBERs started showing up as people realized they would probably not be allowed back to their room's anytime soon. I looked around and still saw no sign of the SUV I had seen earlier. Was there any way I had caused this huge ruckus for no reason? No, I was pretty sure that the SUV was there to deal with Evie and I. After all, it had taken off at the exact moment Evie and I headed in its direction.

I told Evie I was going to call an UBER, and the timing couldn't have been better. As I ordered it, we heard one of the officers say to the half stoned clerk, "Who is in Room number 372? They called 9-1-1, and we'd like to talk to them."

I guess my plan hadn't been foolproof after all.

The clerk went through the paperwork for each room. Apparently, that was easier for him than getting on the computer, even though the front desk was hardly a masterpiece in cleanliness. Finally, the clerk found what he was looking for.

"Room 372 is inhabited by someone named Chief Brody," he said.

An officer smirked. "Chief Brody?"

"That's what it says here," the clerk said, showing the paperwork.

"Chief Brody is a character from the movie Jaws."

"I just thought maybe he was Native American."

This was a serious situation, but a few of the officers couldn't hold back and started laughing.

"Come with us sir, and see if you can point out this Indian fellow," one of the officers said.

I grabbed Evie's hand, making sure to walk in the opposite direction of where the officers were leading the clerk. We walked 50 feet up from the Motel. There was a good 15 cop cars surrounding the hotel by now.

Our UBER arrived two minutes later, and as I opened the door to let Evie in, I did one last look around, not seeing the SUV.

I got in the car and looked down at my phone, which I had powered back on to order the UBER. I had planned on turning it off immediately, but I had a message from Fiona. It managed to scare the shit out of me.

"Hey Frankie, the letter you told me not to open till the 1st is gone. It wasn't in my room a few hours ago. Are you playing some joke on me? It's not funny. Text me back please."

"Fuck!" I yelled, scaring both Evie and the UBER driver.

I was so busy reading the text that I didn't notice that the SUV had started following behind us.

The SUV hadn't gone far when it pulled out of the Motel 6. Plough parked about 100 yards outside the entrance to the motel, but he parked behind another big SUV, making it tough to see. Plough heard the fire alarm going off and saw the arrival of the police minutes later.

Great idea by the kid, Plough thought, even if it was only going to delay the inevitable.

After around10 minutes, he saw his two targets walk out the front of the motel. He grabbed her hand and escorted her along, and it was obvious they were in a rush. The kid's eyes darted around, but Plough knew he hadn't seen him. They got in an UBER, and after about 15 seconds, Plough pulled the SUV out and started following them.

I dialed Fiona's number. I knew it was approaching 2:30 a.m. on the west coast, but since it had been New Year's Eve, maybe she was still up.

She answered on the second ring.

"Frankie, what is going on?" she said.

"Where are you?" I asked.

"I was at a friend's NYE party."

"How did you get there?" I asked, knowing Fiona didn't have a car.

"Tricia."

"Listen to me carefully, Fiona. This is very important! Take an UBER home right now! When you get there, I want you to turn on every light in the house. I want Mom's house lit up like a Christmas tree. After you have done that, I want to you to call the police. Tell them that there has been an intruder in the house and that you have reason to believe he's close by."

"Are we in danger, Frankie?" Fiona asked.

"Maybe. Go home now!"

"Okay, I will," Fiona said, and I could tell she was starting to cry.

She would not make it to the front door.

After I was done calling Fiona, my eyes went to look at Evie, but they found their way to the rear view mirror. I saw a SUV about 50 yards back. I couldn't be sure, but it looked a lot like the one that was parked at the Motel 6.

"Do you see that SUV back there?" I asked our driver.

He looked in his rear view mirror. "Yeah, I see it."

"That person means to do us harm. I'm not kidding. If he starts accelerating towards us, do anything you can to get away."

The driver, a middle-eastern man in his mid-50s, looked back in the rear view mirror, but this time he was looking at me.

"You're serious?" He said, with a thick accent.

"I absolutely am," I said.

"Why don't you call the cops?"

"I can't be in a police station this morning. I have more important things to take care of."

It was a pathetic answer, but the man didn't call me on it.

I thought about the situation and realized we had no chance against an SUV in which the driver was likely carrying a weapon. It was time to make up a plan on the fly, something that had seemed to become my modus operandi lately.

"Take us to the closest big train station. Right now!" I yelled.

"That would be Union Station, about four minutes away."

"Head there."

As our driver accelerated, I saw the SUV do the same.

Hunter Lockley, the ex-CIA man, turned political operative, looked down at his watch. It was 2:29 in the morning. His instructions from Howie Doss had been to watch the house, and that's exactly what he had been doing for the last several hours. He had encountered many drunks over that span and seen his fair share of fireworks going off in the sky.

Not that Lockley minded sitting in his car on a stakeout during New Year's Eve. Howie Doss hadn't asked him for a favor like this in years, so he knew it must be important.

He was situated less than a block from the Waters house. Some people of his ilk would say that he was situated too close, but when Doss told him that it was a woman and her daughter, Lockley didn't think it was too likely he was going to be ID'd. So he stayed closer than usual.

Doss had sent pictures he had found online of the two women. Sally Waters looked to be in her mid to late 40s, while her daughter Fiona, was probably in her late teens.

Lockley looked down at his phone one more time, and as he did, he saw a car pulling in front of the Waters' home. It had the UBER logo on it, and he saw a young woman step out. He recognized her immediately as Fiona Waters. She looked disheveled and appeared to have been crying.

It was a risk, but Hunter Lockley knew he had to get closer. He got out of his car and started walking towards Fiona Waters. The UBER drove away, and as the young woman approached the front door, she dropped her bag, and everything spilled onto the ground.

She was now sobbing loudly. Hunter Lockley was in the shadows 50 feet away, quietly moving closer.

Fiona Waters started picking up everything she had dropped, but then she held her purse at the wrong angle, and it all dropped out again. She started crying louder.

A light came on from inside the house. Hunter Lockley inched closer.

Sally Waters walked out of the house.

"What the hell is going on Fiona? Are you drunk?"

"You know I don't drink!" Fiona said and then started to gather herself. "Frankie called me. He said we need to turn on all the lights in the house and call the cops."

Hunter Lockley inched closer still. He was now only 15 feet from the women. He stood in the shadows, and the women were so focused on each other they didn't notice him.

"What the hell are you talking about? Why would we need to call the cops?"

"Somebody was in our house yesterday and stole something. I think Frankie is in some serious trouble."

"Get in the house, and we'll talk about this," Sally Waters said.

"You don't understand, we need to call the cops!" Fiona yelled.

Sally Waters walked from the front door to her daughter and helped her get everything in the purse.

"Okay," she said, "We'll call the cops."

They finished packing up Fiona's purse, and Sally Waters put her hand around her daughter and led her towards the door.

Hunter Lockley knew he couldn't let them get inside and call the police. Doss had called this a stakeout, but things had just changed.

The two women approached the door. Hunter Lockley was on them before they knew it, shoving them inside the door and quickly shutting the door behind him.

45

As the car in front of him accelerated, Derek Plough gave his gas pedal a slight nudge in order to keep up. The car he was following was some sort of mid-2000s sedan, and he knew he was in no danger of losing touch. After a few minutes, Plough had an idea where the sedan was headed. Union Station.

The sedan kept on the path that Plough expected, pulled up in front of Union Station, and his two targets ran towards the entrance. The sedan sped away.

Plough parked in a handicapped spot close to the front and grabbed his gun as he stepped out of the SUV. He looked towards the entrance and saw that the two of them were watching him. He didn't see anyone else around and figured he could go for a kill shot right then. It was risky, but the biggest risk of all was letting them get away and go to the cops. Doss and Plough would be spending their lives in jail if that happened.

He decided it was worth the risk. He raised his gun, aimed and fired.

I told our driver that I wanted him to pull up to the very front of Union Station and let us out.

"Grab that ruffled skirt," I said to Evie. "Stuff it in your jeans."

It was too important for the plan to leave without it. I grabbed the cellphones and scattered them throughout my jeans. We exited the car, sans bags.

Union Station had three beautiful columns at its entrance and a gorgeous dome-like interior that would be breathtaking any other time.

As Evie and I approached the columns, we turned around and looked back. The man had parked right out front and was heading in our direction. We saw him holding something in his jacket pocket. This was no longer just an overactive imagination. We had to assume it was a gun. This man was definitely there to kill us.

The man was big and tall, and I had to assume it was Derek Plough. He had been with Howie Doss from the beginning, and it would make sense to send him to do the dirty work for anything involving the Oklahoma City murders.

As he looked over and saw us staring at him, he readied his gun. I grabbed Evie's arm and swung her inside the station, hearing two bullets career off the front surface of Union Station.

We were arm in arm as we ran into the station, bypassing the place where you bought tickets and jumping over the turnstiles. The station was still open, and you could hear drunk voices permeating the station, despite it being just after 5:30 in the morning.

Evie and I ran as fast as we could, not sure exactly where we were going. I just knew that we needed to create some distance between ourselves and Derek Plough. If he was only seconds behind us, we'd have no time to do anything. He had a gun, and we had some cell phones and a ruffled skirt. Hardly a fair fight.

We continued running through Union Station like two bats out of hell. There was no police presence. We hadn't seen him in over a minute, and yet, I knew we hadn't lost him. There's no way it was going to be that easy.

I heard an announcement that it was the last call for a train on Ramp #7.

"He's hearing this too, but we have to risk it," I said.

I looked at the nearest map and grabbed Evie's arm, heading in the direction of Ramp #7.

Plough heard the call for the oncoming train and knew he had to get there. They had managed to get away from him, and he couldn't let them board that train. If they did, they'd go to the police, and it would be the end of Howie Doss, and by extension, Plough himself.

He ran towards Ramp #7 praying he wouldn't be late. It took him just over a minute to get there. Once there, he took the stairs three at a time, reaching the ramp just as people were starting to board the train. He looked down at the first train while walking along the edge of the platform. He put the gun to his side and started walking the 30 feet between him and the front of the train.

We arrived to Ramp #7 in less than 30 seconds. Soon after we got to the bottom of the stairs, I heard a ruckus coming from above. I looked up, and the man who had just shot at us was pushing people aside and rushing down the steps. I was sure that he hadn't seen me, however.

I told Evie to go hide behind the stairs. If something did happen to me, I wanted to make sure she would get away unscathed.

"I love you," she said.

"Go now!" I yelled. We didn't have time for that.

Evie ran to where she couldn't be seen. I looked up, and the man was getting closer.

There was about 30 feet from the base of the stairs to the front of the train, and then another 25 feet from the front of the train to the doors of the first train car. The man would be hugging the space parallel to the train tracks as this would give him his quickest path to the front of the train. I was sure he would head there, looking to see if we had entered the train.

My goal was to push him onto the tracks. It wasn't going to be easy, considering he had a gun. I'd have to surprise him or push him from behind. The train wasn't moving, and he probably wouldn't be killed, but it was a good 10-foot drop, and there was hard steel that would greet him when he landed. He wouldn't be getting up to come after us, that was for sure.

I knew that I had to push him within the first 30 feet because once he made it to the start of the train, it would be shielding him from any fall. I quickly hid behind a huge pillar as I saw him arrive at the base of the stairs.

As he arrived on the platform, I saw him pull out his gun and put it to his side. I was not in his line of sight, as he was looking directly at the front of the first car, while I was hiding behind the pillar, which was roughly 10 feet before the front of the train.

It was now or never. I had to time it perfectly. Right when he appeared on the other side of the pillar, I would need some momentum built up to push him to the tracks. If I was a second too early or late he would have a chance to use his gun to start firing at me. I'd certainly be killed, only being a few feet from him.

The man was approaching the pillar. When his body appeared at the other end of the pillar, I would take two big steps and hopefully have the power to shove him onto the tracks.

He had gone to the train side like I knew he would. I could hear him coming. It was only a second or two until he passed the pillar I was hiding behind. It was a life or death moment. My life flashed before my eyes.

The man took his first step past the start of the pillar. Our bodies were now parallel, on opposite sides of the pillar, just a few short feet from each other. A second step revealed his shoe as he started to make it past the other side, and I knew the next step would be the one where I'd have to connect with him. I backed up a few feet, hoping that would give me the extra momentum I needed.

His other foot crossed the end of the pillar. It was go time!

I accelerated, and as his body fully passed the pillar, I was on him before he knew it.

He literally had no time to react. When his body came into view, my chest made contact with his left flank, and I extended my arms, pushing him as hard and far as I possibly could. There was only two to three feet until the 10-foot drop to the train tracks below, and I had to make sure I pushed him over the edge.

With my momentum and strength, he never had a chance, and went over the edge. He started falling in what felt like slow motion as I saw him go over the small ledge with his arms flailing.

As he was falling backward and downwards, he grabbed his gun and tried to get off two shots in my direction, but the shots did nothing but hit the ceiling of the platform.

He landed with a great thud and his gun hit the train tracks, ricocheting 15 feet away from him. I walked over and looked down on him. There was no more doubt that it was Derek Plough. I had seen a few pictures online, and that was enough.

Plough was looking up at me, but I knew he wasn't going to be moving anytime soon. There was a piece of metal protruding through his left leg, but more importantly, he couldn't seem to raise his back. I didn't know if his back was broken, but it certainly was going to keep him there for the foreseeable future.

There had been several people who had seen me push him onto the tracks, but then they heard or saw the man fire his gun, so they weren't sure if I was a hero or a sadistic asshole. They looked down at him and saw the weapon, so they seemed to give me the benefit of the doubt.

With the exception of the people looking down at the tracks, everyone else had scattered at the sound of the gunshots. The train obviously wasn't going anywhere with a man lying at the base of it, so everyone in the first car ran out onto the platform.

Evie came around from the other side of the stairs. We quickly embraced and I grabbed her hand, guiding her towards a different set of stairs since everyone was headed towards the one Plough had come down.

I looked down at the man on the train tracks as we passed him on the way to the stairs. He stared up at me. If looks could kill, I'd be six feet under.

"Let's get out of here," Evie said.

Cops were going to be there any second, so I heeded her advice. We walked pass Plough and headed towards another exit.

I was reminded of a scene from *House of Cards* where Kevin Spacey's character, Frank Underwood, shoved a member of the media onto the tracks, killing her. It was a case of corrupt power using anything in their repertoire to silence someone seeking the truth. The irony was not lost on me.

Only this time, the roles were reversed, and I was playing the role of the truth seeker, and the man down on the tracks was the corrupt member of Washington D.C.

As we walked up the steps toward the exit to Union Station, we were passed by several police officers. Word of the man on the tracks and the gunshots fired had traveled fast. It was the second time in less than an hour that we had created a bit of hysteria in Washington D.C. First the bomb threat and now this.

I knew I had better get Howie Doss to admit to the murders that he had commissioned years ago. If not, I might just be public enemy #1 when Washington D.C. woke up in a few hours.

Howie Doss had hoped to stay up and find out about the demise of his two adversaries, but had passed out around 2:00 a.m. He was woken up by his alarm clock at 6:00 a.m. and looked down at his phone, expecting to see good news. He had been bombarded with several texts.

Plough had texted at 4:45 a.m. saying he was outside Frankie Waters's hotel and he would be going up to finish his mission within the hour. There was still too many drunk people coming back to the hotel to risk going in.

He texted back at 5:14 a.m. saying he was sure that Waters had reported a fire or bomb scare or something because a really loud alert was followed by the place crawling with police and fire trucks. Doss couldn't help but smile. This 21-year-old had a bunch of tricks up his sleeve.

At 5:26, Plough texted he once again had a track on Waters and the girl, having followed behind an UBER they had picked up. At 5:31, Doss received his final text from Plough, saying he thought they were headed to Union Station and that he would text Doss when it was over.

Doss had received only one text from Hunter Lockley, which came in at 5:47.

It read, "Waters girl came home and told her mother they needed to call the police. I'm assuming you couldn't let that happen, so I took matters into my own hands. Currently have them duct taped inside their house."

Doss texted Lockley back, telling him to take a picture of the two women. He received a text back and laughed as he looked at the petrified faces of the two women.

He knew he had Frankie Waters by the balls, although it wouldn't really matter once Plough confirmed he was dead. Twenty minutes passed, however, with no text back from Plough, and Howie Doss began to get a sinking feeling.

He went to his closet and grabbed a Smith & Wesson M & P shield, his favorite of the three handguns he owned.

Evie and I walked out of Union Station just as more police were pulling up. We walked away from the commotion and didn't say a word till we had walked a quarter of a mile away.

"We have caused quite a mess, haven't we?" I asked Evie.

"Nothing that can't be explained away if we get what we want today."

"We've got a little over two hours until we meet Doss, but we should get there early."

"If we get there by seven we're fine, right?" she asked.

"Yes," I said.

"Good then let's walk there. It's probably 45 minutes from here, but to be honest, I'm tired of trains, UBERs, and the like."

"You can say that again. Plus, I have some things I have to do as we walk. But first things first, I need to call my sister."

I called Fiona, but she didn't pick up.

"No answer," I said to Evie.

"I'm sure she's busy with your Mom and the police."

"I hope you're right," I said.

But I wasn't sure she was.

Evie grabbed my hand, and we started walking in the general direction of the Lincoln Memorial. She had lived in D.C. for a summer, so I followed her lead. My guess was that very few people ever walked from Union Station to the Lincoln Memorial. We didn't mention that someone had tried to kill us.

Evie led us away from Union Station and towards the Smithsonian National Postal Museum. She explained that this wasn't the quickest way, but we had time to kill. I wish she had chosen a different phrase. We passed the Verizon Center, and then we came upon the International Spy Museum.

"Maybe we'll have our own wing there someday," she said.

I didn't respond.

We headed down 14th street and ran into the real Smithsonian. She pointed in the direction of the National Mall and the Smithsonian Castle, but it was approaching 7:00 at this point, and I said we should get to the Lincoln Memorial.

She adjusted my body and pointed it towards the Washington Monument. I knew we were getting close.

I saw a bench and told her I needed some time to set up the phones.

Howie Doss took a shower, hoping he would see a text from Derek Plough when he got out. He did not. The sinking feeling became worse.

To make him feel better, he once again looked at he picture Hunter Lockley had sent. If Frankie Waters had somehow survived the night and made it to the Lincoln Memorial, Doss couldn't wait to show him this picture.

He got dressed in one of his best looking suits, matching dark blue pinstripes with a light blue tie. Regardless of who showed up, this was a monumental moment in Howie Doss's life. He wanted to look the part. He checked his phone again. Still no text back from Plough.

Doss sat around for a while longer, going through the potential obstacles he would face if, in fact, the two kids showed up. Knowing that Evie would be wearing a phone on her upper thigh was a huge advantage that Doss had. He could decide when and what information he would give out.

More importantly, he could show him the picture of his sister and his mother. That would surely stop any crazy ideas he might have, like going to the cops or the media. Howie Doss started breathing easier.

At 7:15, Doss left his house and drove himself towards the Lincoln Memorial. He was less than 10 minutes away but figured the earlier he got there, the better. He wanted to be the first one there. Less surprises that way.

"Please let it be Plough who shows up," Doss said to himself as he neared his destination.

He felt his side. The Smith & Wesson M & P Shield was still there.

The phones took me longer to set up than I had imagined. By time I finished, the sun was starting to peak itself over the horizon as Evie and I stood and started taking our final walk towards the Lincoln Memorial. I had set the phones to their respective Facebook accounts and just had to turn on Facebook Live when I planted the phones.

In the meantime, Evie had changed into her ruffled skirt that made it look like she was going to play tennis. My doubts that her phone would last were only amplified.

The sun rising was a reminder that Evie had slept only about four hours and I had maybe snuck in an hour. On top of that, we had experienced the most intense night of our lives.

We may have been running on fumes, but there was no chance we would run out of gas. We saw the finish line, and we had no choice but to get there.

I looked into her eyes.

"Are you ready for this?" I asked.

Evie grabbed me and kissed me on the lips. We were nervous as hell, and it wasn't a romantic kiss, but it still felt right.

"Make sure to be cautious," she said. "He could have a gun or some goons around. I know he's not going to kill people outside of a famous monument, but let's be prepared for anything."

It was sound advice.

We set out in the direction of the Lincoln Memorial. The time had come. Our date with Howie Doss was at hand.

46

The Lincoln Memorial has been one of the most popular tourist destinations in Washington D.C. since its dedication back in 1922. The memorial took eight years to build and had a different architect, carver, painter, and designer of the statue.

The marble making up the exterior is named Yule Marble and is found exclusively in the Yule Valley in Colorado. The marble itself is quarried inside a mountain that is 9,300 feet above sea level, differentiating itself from most marbles which are quarried in an open pit and at much lower elevations. The marble is 99.5% pure calcite and gives the grain a smooth look and a bright, radiant surface.

The Memorial sits directly across from the Washington Monument, and they both served as the backdrop for the "I have a Dream" speech by Martin Luther King Jr. in 1963. There have been numerous other well-known speeches conducted there, along with scores of movie scenes, including *Mr. Smith goes to Washington.*

The Park Service did not want the movie's director, Frank Capra, to film at the Lincoln Memorial, so Capra sent a big crew elsewhere in the area to distract the Park Service, then had stars Jimmy Stewart and Jean Arthur film the scene with a very small crew. It worked, and the scene shot with the tiny crew made it into the movie.

It's a must see for anyone who ever visited Washington D.C. and is one of the city's most famous structures.

Of course, no one had ever come to the Lincoln Memorial with as much at stake as Evie and I.

The memorial was open 24 hours a day, but as we looked around, we realized that early on the first day of a new year wasn't one of the more popular times. There were a few people walking around the statue, but very few people were walking around the grounds below.

This worked right into my plan. I couldn't just walk up to the statue of Lincoln, in plain sight of Doss, and set the phones down. Obviously. Knowing Doss wouldn't want to talk around other people, I was hoping we could lead him towards where I set the phones.

We passed the Washington Monument and looked at the Lincoln Memorial, taking it all in. It was truly beautiful. I heard that sunset is the most visited time to the Memorial, but I couldn't imagine it being any prettier than it was at that moment.

I explained to Evie why I wanted to leave the phones down at the base of the memorial. She looked a little tepid but agreed with me. I logged in to the accounts I had created the night before and set the four of them on Facebook Live. I set the fifth phone to my personal Facebook account and posted the following:

"The conversation I will be having this morning is with none other than Howie Doss, the founder of the Always Right website. If you can't hear the audio from this account, please try the other Facebook accounts that I have linked to below. Check out the Evie Somerset account first because the conversation should start there. Please share with all your friends!"

My hope was that none of the other phones connected to Facebook Live would be necessary, but I was going with the assumption that Doss was going to frisk us. I wasn't sure how long the phone we planted on Evie would last.

I didn't mention the location in the Facebook post. I didn't want the police or the media to get wind of where this was taking place and show up, preventing my conversation with Doss.

At the base of the Lincoln Memorial, on the left hand side, below the stairs you walk up, I planted five phones. I hid them in shrubs, so they weren't visible.

There were more people on the right, and I was again using the logic that Howie Doss wouldn't want to talk around others, so I planted them all on the left. I had a final phone and I placed it where some grass and a small set of stairs met. It would be the perfect spot if we could subtly lead him in that direction.

Finally, I had Evie connect her phone to Facebook Live. And just like that, we were live and broadcasting to the world.

She put the phone on her thigh and was able to secure it by sliding the side of her panties around it, protecting it against her thigh. It was hardly optimal, and tape would have been easier, but we didn't have that luxury.

We walked from the left back to the middle and started taking the steps up to the Lincoln Memorial. Halfway up we saw the silhouette of Howie Doss. He was blocking our view of Abraham Lincoln. I guess he liked to be early as well. It looked like the 8:00 meeting had become a 7:30 meeting.

I was pleasantly surprised. Facebook Live could run for two hours, but the sooner we got near the phones, the better.

Evie looked at me, and we had to hope he hadn't seen us drop the phones. He had just come into view, so I assumed he had just arrived. I thought we were safe. In that regard, at least.

I didn't know if it was intentional on his part, but I took great offense to Doss standing in front of the statue of Lincoln. It was hard to explain, but I had a very visceral reaction to this, and my hate for Doss only increased. As we made our way up the stairs, our angle changed and we now saw the Lincoln statue towering over the diminutive Doss. As it should be.

We finished walking the steps. Although Doss must have realized it was us as we made our way up, he still couldn't hold back his shock.

Seeing him in person, I finally understood why people joked that he was the albino devil. The gray hair from his younger years had given way to an almost purely white tint. More importantly, his skin had the slight reddish hue that so many people alluded to.

His overwhelming intensity was only magnified by how he stood. He wasn't a very tall man, but his rigid posture made him appear immovable. He was obviously comfortable in his own skin. His devilish, reddish skin.

I knew I was overmatched. I was a smart, young man, but the guy in front of me had taken down political adversaries for years, all while building an empire. What had I ever done? I told myself all I had to do was get the best of him here and now. Nothing else mattered.

I had to be confident, or at least portray that to him. If he viewed me as amateurish, it would just give him another advantage.

He walked over towards us. We faced each other. Everything Evie and I had done had led to this point. I put on my game face and breathed in deeply.

Sometimes life comes down to a few pivotal moments. This was undoubtedly one of mine.

"You look surprised? Were you not expecting us?" I asked.

Doss paused, taking us in.

"Of course I'm surprised. You never mentioned you were bringing a girl," he said.

There was a lot of meaning to his response. While I was alluding to his surprise being that we weren't dead, he made it sound like his surprise came from the fact that there were two of us. Calling Evie a girl was intentional as well. He was trying to diminish Evie, making her feel inferior.

"This *girl* is the reason we are here right now," I said, sarcastically accentuating the word girl.

I looked over at Evie, who ushered a brief smile towards me, but I could tell this was all too much for her.

"Ah yes, the reason you are here," Doss said.

His voice was even more mesmerizing in person. It was truly amazing.

We stood there looking at each other, neither one knowing what to say next. Doss looked around, and there was now six or seven people near us, hovering near the statue of Lincoln.

"I think it's better if we talk alone. Wouldn't you agree, Frankie?" Doss said, his condescension obvious in using my first name.

I knew I couldn't let him get me rattled.

"Whatever you say, Howard."

He stared intently at me, furious I had used his given name. He then smiled, pretending it hadn't bothered him. I knew differently.

We started walking down the steps of the Lincoln Memorial. At first, he had motioned for me to take the lead, but I declined and let him go first. I didn't think he was going to try and kill me by pushing me down the steps of the Lincoln Memorial, but I thought it was good protocol not to turn my back on Howie Doss.

We continued walking down the steps, none of us saying a word. I didn't know how long he was going to keep walking once we reached the bottom, but I couldn't have him walk past the phones I had planted.

I decided to say something shocking when we were in the vicinity of the phones. Hopefully, that would get him to stop in his tracks and then we could start talking where I knew the conversation would be picked up.

We had the phone on Evie's thigh, but I was less and less confident it wouldn't be confiscated.

The three of us continued walking down the stairs in silence. We reached the bottom and Doss took a quick right, heading towards where I had planted the phones. There was grass and small shrubs that stood in stark contrast to the concrete stairs. Most importantly, there were no people on that side of the stairs. My plan appeared to be working.

I could see Evie looking at me out of the corner of my eye, but I couldn't risk looking back. Doss might notice something was up.

He started to slow down, and I was hopeful he would stop. It wasn't to be. He kept walking. We were passing the point of where the phones were, so I had to try something.

"Don't you want to know what happened to your friend?" I said. "Derek Plough is his name, I believe."

I had wanted to save Derek Plough for later, but none of this would matter if we didn't get him to talk in the vicinity of the phones. I had to go for it.

Doss stopped in his tracks. He looked around. He saw the small set of stairs where I had planted one of the phones. They were only 20 feet away.

"We'll go talk there," he said.

Evie and I didn't say a word, following Doss.

We arrived at the stairs, but Doss remained standing. Evie and I did the same.

"That Plough was always so rogue, going out and doing things on his own. What did he do now?"

It was pretty obvious why Doss chose to call Plough rogue. He'd be able to say he had done everything on his own.

"As of an hour ago, he was on the train tracks of Union Station. And I have to say, he didn't look too good. He's probably in jail talking to D.C.'s finest at this point," I said.

It felt good to needle Howie Doss.

He had a full-fledged poker face going, but I stared into his eyes and knew he would love to kill me if he could.

"Quite sure it has nothing to do with me, but thanks for the information," Doss said.

"I wonder if the police are talking to him about Darby Cash Bowles," I said.

I wanted to get Darby's name on the record, but it wasn't to be.

As I started saying the name of Darby Cash Bowles, Howie Doss leaned in the direction of Evie and started coughing loudly. Somehow, I didn't think it was a coincidence.

"I have never heard of Darren Bowen," Doss said.

There was no doubt why Doss had changed the name. He was trying to prevent the name Darby Cash Bowles from being heard.

He either knew or suspected that we were recording him. Not that I was surprised. I had expected exactly that.

"Actually his name was….." it was the first words that Evie had uttered, but she wouldn't finish them.

Doss put his hand over her mouth before she could finish. He then put a finger up to his mouth, telling us not to say anything.

"It's pretty early in the morning for a skirt. Wouldn't you say, Evie?"

We all knew what was coming next. Although I'd want to kill Doss for touching Evie's thigh, there was really no way around it. My hope was that he'd then be willing to talk, thinking he had found the only recording device.

He put his hand on Evie's shoulder, holding her against one of the stair railings, and reached under Evie's skirt. Despite knowing it was bound to happen, I had to restrain myself from leaping towards him and ripping his eyes out.

Doss had a sly smile on his face as he did it, staring at me the whole time. I looked at Evie, who must have been disgusted, although I saw the semblance of a knowing smirk, as if she knew this was necessary.

It only lasted a few seconds as Doss removed the phone from Evie's thigh. He hadn't done anything gratuitous, thank God. If I had sensed that, I wouldn't have been able to restrain myself.

Doss spoke into the phone and said, "It was very nice meeting you guys, and I hope you have a safe trip back to California. Thanks for your interest in Always Right."

He powered the phone off and slammed it on the ground, breaking it into several pieces. He proceeded to stomp it into several more pieces, enjoying it way too much.

"Fuck, that felt good," he said.

He came over to me and motioned for me to empty my pockets. All I had was my original cell phone, wallet, and a tiny purse of Evie's. I took them out and showed Doss that my phone wasn't turned on.

I tried to look defeated. I hoped there wasn't a twinkle in my eye that gave away my true sentiments.

"How about your phone?" I asked.

"Not that it's any of your business, but it's powered down too," Doss said.

It was a risk I was taking, but I didn't want him getting phone calls from friends if our conversation went viral. Knowing it was powered down was a huge win for us.

"So you have heard of Mr. Bowles?" I asked, changing the subject.

"Your uncle's notes tell you that? Better not believe everything you read," Doss said.

I pretended to look shocked. I knew he had someone intercept my letter to Fiona, but I had to act like it was news to me. Evie noticed I was trying to look surprised, so she jumped in. We were playing off each other now.

"Don't believe everything you read? That's cute coming from a guy whose website spews out bullshit on a daily basis," Evie said.

The fact that Doss had grabbed her seemed to wake Evie up. She no longer looked scared. Only determined.

"Always Right, my ass," I added.

"You two are so cute together. This must just be one hell of a school field trip."

The condescension in his voice was only surpassed by the irritation in it. No, not irritation. More like hatred.

"We've learned quite a bit on this field trip," I said.

"I guess I can understand how two youngsters like yourselves could fall for an epic tale of intrigue like the one your Uncle Owen spun for you."

I tried once again to feign shock at the second mention of Uncle Owen.

Sensing he had taken the upper hand, Howie Doss said, "Are you alright, Frankie? You look like you've seen a ghost. Maybe the ghost of your Uncle Owen?"

"No, just looking forward to the death of Always Right. That's the only ghost I see."

Howie Doss laughed.

"You two are impressive. Another time, another place, things could have been different," he said.

We just stood quietly. The more he talked, the better.

"Did you really think you were going to take down Howie Doss that easily?" he asked.

"There's still the matter of all the information that we have," I said.

"Hearsay and circumstantial evidence, Frankie. Guess you're not Pre-Law out there at San Francisco State."

I could tell that he enjoyed showing how much he knew about us, so I thought it might be a good way to let him hang himself.

"You really know a lot, don't you?" I asked.

I knew he wanted to show how smart he was so I threw out some rope to the narcissist in front of me.

"Did you not think I would do my homework, Frankie? When I heard that some little fuck was calling a friend of Darby Bowles's, was I just going to sit idly by? The best part is that while you were looking for him, Darby was floating in the Pacific Ocean. And he wasn't doing the backstroke."

"And you had him killed?"

"Of course I fucking did! I wasn't about to admit that to Evie's wonderful thighs, though."

My skin crawled. I looked at Evie, and there was no doubt that the tough-minded woman had returned. She didn't even flinch at Doss's comment.

Doss realized what he had just admitted. He looked us over again.

"Pull your shirt up, Frankie."

I gladly did as he asked. He wasn't going to find anything on either of us. He frisked Evie again, without giving me the sly smile this time. He was all business now.

"How many times are we going to do this?" Evie asked. "Let's get back to Bowles."

"Why do you guys want to know everything? You are here to blackmail me, so I don't see why you need to know all the details."

"We've spent the last three weeks trying to figure out how everything was connected."

"It's pretty simple, actually. We knew a guy in jail and put out word that we needed a driver. He sent Bowles to us. I had never heard of the guy."

"And when he joined the crew, you decided to graduate to murder?" I asked.

"It's caused me great inconvenience lately."

"Inconvenience?" Evie said incredulously. "You had two people murdered."

"Two?" Doss looked at us knowingly. Evie was referring to the innocent civilians, but Doss was thinking about the co-conspirators he had murdered as well.

Doss continued.

"You must be referring to the black woman and the Hispanic man. But I guess technically, you're right, they are people."

I was repulsed by the man across from me and wanted to jump over and strangle him to death.

But why would you strangle someone who was hanging himself?

"I have a question for you," Doss said. "How did Bowles find out who I was?"

There was no need to lie.

"He heard your voice when he was in jail. Some Fox Business News interview."

"This voice of mine has been a blessing and a curse."

"And soon after Darby Bowles heard your voice, Uncle Owen became his cell mate," I said.

I figured the more information that I threw at Doss, the more likely he would be to give us some of his own.

Something didn't feel right, though. He was too confident. We held all the cards, or at least I thought we did. Was I missing something?

"And I heard he met his maker soon thereafter. Lung cancer. What a way to go," Doss was pretending to sound empathetic, but his patronization was obvious. "He did outlive your father though, didn't he, Frankie?"

I was furious, but not surprised. Doss was known for using absolutely anything at his disposal to crush his opponents. This situation was no different.

But I had to stay calm. I decided to ignore the comment about my father and concentrate on Uncle Owen.

"You can ridicule the dead all you want, but Owen's writings are what got us here. If you don't watch it, he might get the last laugh."

"I doubt it," Doss said.

It was time to up the ante, and play one of the aces up my sleeve.

"How far before the murders had you planned on Derek Plough cleaning up your mess and killing your co-conspirators?"

Howie Doss tried to smile, but the fury behind his eyes made that impossible. He had proven that he knew a lot about me, but two could play at that game.

"We can get to that, but first let's talk about how much money you want. That is why you are here after all."

"We want millions," I bluffed.

Doss tried to feign surprise, but he laughed instead.

He was borderline giddy. Something was definitely wrong.

47

Austin Ingles was a precocious 16-year-old living in Antwerp, Belgium who had excelled at computers from an early age. Well, not computers per se, but video games. He had set up a YouTube channel by the time he was nine years old and gained followers by the hundreds of thousands over the intervening years. He showed how to improve your video game skills and young boys and girls flocked to his YouTube page in record numbers. He also built a huge following on Twitter, and although he rarely looked at his followers, one day a young woman named Paige Muller tweeted back at him, and they struck up something of an online friendship. Paige Muller was friends with Evie Somerset at Brown University.

Sherry Poe was a 51-year-old housewife from Rochester, New York. She had been conservative her whole life, still believed in the sanctity of marriage, and was extremely pro-life. She was also a writer and didn't like the muzzle that was being put on the media by the current White House administration. As conservative as she was, when it came to freedom of the press, she was very liberal. Her most recent target was Howie Doss, who she felt went after every liberal he disagreed with, going after their personal life, family, even kids. It was beyond the pale in her view. Her conservative friends barely recognized some of her recent rants on social media. What had happened to their conservative friend? Poe's son had gone west to college, landing at San Francisco State, where he became friends with a young man named Frankie Waters.

Maxfield Unger was a 23-year-old recent college graduate living in Dallas, TX and trying to make it in the ultra-tough world of political blogging. He had slowly but surely gained 20,000 Twitter followers, and he felt like he might have finally turned a corner. His posts were being liked and retweeted by more and more people, and despite what his parents thought, he knew he was going to make a success of himself in the political sphere. Months previously, he had gotten in an intense, but civil, political debate on Twitter with a woman named Sherry Poe. They followed each other back on Twitter.

What these three people had in common, besides being very active on social media, was that they were some of the first people to see the posts about what was going on at the Lincoln Memorial.

Paige Muller saw Evie Somerset's Facebook Live post and then watched as Evie's feed went dead. She had linked to someone named Frankie Waters, and Muller went and listened to his Facebook Live. There were four other links on his page, and she finally found the one that was picking up the conversation. She knew something big was going on, and posted a link to Facebook via her Twitter account.

She tweeted at Austin Ingles asking him to retweet the link to the conversation, knowing he had a huge following. Ingles' specialty wasn't politics, after all, he was only 16 years old, but he did enjoy his banter with Paige Muller, so he retweeted it for her.

Sherry Poe saw her son share a Facebook post from a young man named Frankie Waters. It claimed to be a conversation with Howie Doss, the man she had come to despise. She shared her son's post and like Paige Muller, sent a Tweet out with the same information. She started texting her friends as well. If this was actually true, she'd love to see the downfall of Howie Doss.

Maxfield Unger saw Sherry Poe's Tweet and clicked on the link. Being a political buff, he recognized Howie Doss' voice right away. He retweeted it and being that most of his followers loved politics, the post went rival within seconds.

Unger started texting friends, telling them they were missing out on a part of American History. The video wasn't much to look at, as the majority of the screen was concrete and grass, but the audio was surprisingly good, and Doss's voice was unmistakable.

Within a minute of Austin Ingles posting it on Twitter, the link had been retweeted 10,000 times. After two minutes, the number was 30,000. At four minutes, when the conversation started getting juicy, the number was over 100,000.

The Facebook numbers were even higher, to say nothing of live streaming YouTube videos that people had set up.

After less than a minute of amateur detective work, Paul Bentley, a 19-year-old from Annapolis, Maryland was able to figure out from the grass, concrete, and the slight view behind it, that this was taking place at the base of the Lincoln Memorial. Bentley posted a live stream to Twitter with the title, "Honest Abe vs. Dishonest Howie." The video was shared 50,000 times within the first minute.

The conversation between Howie Doss and two young adults was going viral in the early morning hours of the New Year.

48

When I mentioned that we wanted millions, I didn't like the reaction that I got from Howie Doss. It was not only that he had laughed, but he had the smug look of someone who held the upper hand. But that wasn't possible. Was it?

"And how do you want this money?" he asked. "I'm sure a million dollar personal check wouldn't arouse any suspicions."

He smiled again. His ease and composure was making my nervous.

"First things first, Doss," I said. "I want to hear about Oklahoma City."

"You're going to get your money. Enough of these questions."

"Call it creative curiosity. We've spent a lot of time investigating this."

Doss looked at us. Despite having found Evie's phone, and searched us twice, there's no doubt he was still suspicious.

"If you don't want to tell us, we can always say fuck the money, and just go to the media."

Howie Doss was stuck in a corner without much leverage, or so I thought.

"Lift your shirt up to your ribcage. Both of you."

He patted us down a third time. When he was satisfied we didn't have any other recording device on us, he turned to me.

"You want to hear about Oklahoma City?" he said

Doss said this like a man wanting to brag about his accomplishment. But why would he tell us? He would be giving us more ammunition. The feeling that I was missing something deepened.

Still, I said, "Yes."

"And then we can talk about how much money you want?"

We had no plans of taking a cent from Howie Doss, but if he saw an end to this via a payoff, all the better. I just wanted him to keep talking.

"We'll get to the money after we know the whole story."

Howie Doss took a deep breath and smiled.

"I had planned on killing my co-conspirators early on. The four guys I had working for me had done, and knew, too much. Several robberies, the swastikas on the churches, etc. If I was going to make it big, which was only a matter of time, I couldn't have them attached to me any longer. I had to convince Derek Plough, however, and that was going to be the tough part. He was friendly with one of them. I can't remember his name, but I knew it might be tough to sell Plough on it."

Evie and I did a double take when Doss said he couldn't remember the guy's name. Couldn't even remember the names of the men he had murdered. Scum. Deviant. Cretin. There wasn't a name that covered how despicable Doss was.

"Eventually, Plough came around like I knew he would," Doss continued. "And my plan was a brilliant one. Kill a couple of dirty minorities and then have my only ties to the crimes done away with by Plough. Of course, he was supposed to ambush them when they parked at the Jew Church, but that all changed when that one officer tried to play hero. Luckily for me, Plough was still close enough to get there and kill all of them. Except Darby Bowles, of course."

"And then Bowles went off the radar?"

"Trust me, we tried for a while. I had Plough pay an old friend of Bowles a visit, but that just made the death toll higher."

Evie looked over at me. This was news to us.

"What was his name?"

"Jake something. Old drug dealer that Bowles was friends with."

"You say this all so matter of factly," Evie said. "You don't even care that you caused these people's deaths?"

"Sometimes you have to get your hands a little dirty on your way to the top."

"And that's where you ended up?"

"You're damn right! Look at me now. I own and run the most influential conservative website in the nation. Fox News is yesterday's news, Breitbart is stuck in the mud. Always Right is the present and the future."

Doss beamed like he was talking about a new born baby.

"So you think all of this is going to go away? Are you crazy?" Evie asked.

"Of course it is," Doss said. "You guys are the only link to everything that has happened. Darby Bowles is dead. So is your Uncle Owen. And your little note to your sister never got to her."

I already knew this, but I was starting to get nervous. He was building up to something else.

"That may all be true, but what's to prevent us from going to the media?" Evie said.

"Well, that's why we're here, right? And let's just say, if you can't be bought off, I have a little contingency plan."

My heart sunk. I knew what was coming before he said another word.

"I'd like to show you a picture, Frankie. I've nicknamed it *Still Waters* in honor of your family name."

Howie Doss removed two phones from his pocket. One was powered off, and he put that one back in his pocket. He raised the other phone to me.

It was a picture of Fiona and my mother, with duct tape around their mouths. They were clearly alive, and after he had said Still Waters, I had suspected the worst for a split second.

The nozzle of a gun was clearly visible in the foreground of the picture. Evie let out a little shriek when she saw it. I was in too much shock to open my mouth.

I knew I had put Evie in harm's way, but my sister and mother were different. Evie had been a willing participant, while my family had been anything but. I saw the scared look on Fiona's face, and it was almost too much to take. I had never felt such rage and sadness in my whole life. Nothing even approached it.

Fiona must have been intercepted when I told her to go home. I should have had her call the cops before she went home. This was my fault!

Since Plough was in D.C., Doss must have called another goon to abduct her when she got home. I wanted to crawl into a hole and die, but I knew I couldn't. It wasn't over, and my family still needed me.

Once again, I considered jumping at Doss and beating him to death, but that wouldn't solve the problem at hand. What I needed was for Doss to say out loud that he was holding Fiona and my mother hostage. He had showed me a picture, but that couldn't be seen on Facebook Live.

If the phone was doing its job and broadcasting our conversation, I just hoped that someone would alert the police that my family was being held hostage. It was my only chance.

I shuttered at the idea of anything happening to them. I knew I had to get Doss to say something and just pray that he didn't catch on.

"So if we agree to take a payoff, you will let my family go?"

"Payoff? Not sure you are in a position to ask for money now, Frankie. But I don't want to have to kill a nice, white family like yours."

I grew more revulsed by the guy across from me with each passing second, but I had to keep my head on straight. I had to let the people listening know that they were being held at my mother's house.

"I don't care about the cash. Will you have your guy leave my mother's house if we agree to a deal?"

"That remains to be seen."

I looked over at Evie and saw that she was near tears. She was probably blaming herself for the situation my sister and mother were currently in. Evie had been as persistent as I in following Uncle Owen's book in whatever direction it led us. We had realized weeks ago that we were in over our head, but we continued on this path anyway. And that path had led to my family being held at gunpoint.

When I glanced at Evie, I noticed people starting to mingle well beyond the Washington Monument. Doss's back was to this, and he couldn't see it. It was a surprise, considering there were so few people around the Lincoln Memorial. Is it possible that our conversation was going viral and they had figured out where we were? And if that was the case, why weren't they coming closer? Had the police set up a perimeter?

I had more questions than answers. But of the utmost importance was getting Doss to release my family. I would agree to anything at this point if I could guarantee their safety.

"Anything you want, Doss. I will agree to whatever you have in mind, if you'll just release my family right now."

"One of my tactics when dealing with people is to always have the final trump card. Whether it be having dirt on them or threatening their family, if you have the trump card you tend to get your way."

I didn't know what to do, so I decided to stall. Give the authorities as much time as I possibly could. I blindly prayed that the phone sitting at the base of the stairs was picking up our conversation. The lives of my family sat in the balance.

"I don't want a dime, Doss. If you release my mother and sister, I'll walk away from here and never say a word."

"That sounds nice, Frankie. But somehow, I'm not sure I can trust you. After all, you and Evie tried to record our conversation. Remember that? Thanks for the offer, but I'm going to keep your family hostage a little while longer."

Doss let loose with a horrific laugh.

That's when I knew he had no plans of ever releasing my family. He couldn't risk it. He was going to kill my family and then try to kill Evie and I. It was Doss's only shot at escaping unscathed. I knew he wouldn't kill us in the middle of the Lincoln Memorial, but once we left, we were in imminent danger.

"I will do anything I can. Want me to say I was full of shit? I'll sign a non-disclosure agreement. Whatever it is you want."

"Forms and Papers? No, I don't think I want you informing another living soul of what you know. I'm trying to eliminate connections to Oklahoma City. Not create more."

The way he said eliminate chilled me to the bone.

I looked out past Evie and saw that the crowd past the Washington Monument was growing. Doss was facing us, but if he turned around and saw the growing crowd, I had no doubt he would figure out what was going on. I couldn't let that happen.

Max Morris received his first call regarding the Waters house at 4:44 a.m. local time. Morris was a 22-year veteran of the Oakland Police Department. He was a competent, if uninspired, officer who continually received mediocre reviews from his commanding officers. He had never risen very high, and he was fine with that.

He preferred the early mornings where he could sit at his desk, and nothing seemed to happen. He arrived at four a.m. each day and the drunks, gangs, and all of the other troublemakers were usually asleep by then. That was just fine by Morris.

While his shift was generally the quietest one of the day, that would not be the case on the early morning of January 1st.

The conversation going viral at the steps of the Lincoln Memorial was slower to gain momentum on the West Coast. After all, it was only a little after 4:30 a.m. in Oakland when the conversation had started. That all changed when people heard Howie Doss admit that Sally and Fiona Waters were being held hostage in their own home.

People who lived on the same block as the Waters's started getting phone calls from concerned friends. The Arnold's, the Zell's, and the Young's, all who lived close to the Waters, got calls alerting them that their neighbors were likely being held hostage at that very moment.

In fact, the only house in the area that wasn't receiving any calls was the Waters house itself. Hunter Lockley had taken the house phone off the hook and had powered down the two women's phones.

For every call to the Waters' neighbors, there was twice as many going to the Oakland Police Department. Max Morris started receiving calls telling him there was a hostage situation in his jurisdiction.

The first caller told Morris he could listen to it all on the internet. He wasn't exactly a computer savant and figured there had to be a better way.

When the second and third callers said the same thing only seconds later, Morris called over one of his younger officers and told him to find the live stream that the callers were referring too.

Morris immediately called his superiors who had all been woken up with calls of their own. Apparently, something huge was going on in Washington D.C., and Oakland was now part of it.

One of his superiors, on word from the Chief, told Morris to send six of his men to the Waters home. From what he had been told, time was of the essence. He dispatched two officers from police headquarters and two cars that were in the vicinity.

They were to surround the house and gauge the situation but were not under orders to storm the house. They were taking a wait and see approach. At least for the moment.

Morris was told that he was in charge until one of his superiors got there, which could be several minutes. If he felt it was necessary, he had the authority to order the officers to storm the house.

It was more responsibility than Morris was usually given and he didn't like it.

There was a very real chance that Doss and I would both end up losers, with Doss in jail for life, and for me, a future worse than jail; knowing I had caused the deaths of my sister and mother. It made me shiver.

"Then what can I do to get you to release my family?" I said.

I knew I was repeating myself, but I didn't have many options.

"At this point, I'm not sure there's anything you can do, Frankie. Looks like you got involved with the wrong guy."

"There has to be something," I said.

Doss thought things over. I knew what was coming next. It was his only out.

"If you and Evie leave with me, I'd consider calling my guy and telling him to release your family," he said.

His evil intentions were so obvious that there was no need to respond. He couldn't kill us at the steps of the Lincoln Memorial, but if he could get us alone in private, he'd jump at the chance.

He knew if we didn't leave with him, we'd go straight to the police and the life he had built for himself was over. He had no choice but to try and get us to leave with him.

And as much as I knew we couldn't leave with him, I also knew I couldn't separate from Doss right now. He'd surely call his guy and tell him to kill my family.

We were both between a rock and a hard place.

"I'll go with you if you allow Evie to stay," I said.

It was a non-starter, and I knew it.

"Not a chance. You two are a package deal."

I didn't know what to do. I could attack him, but that would do nothing to help my family. It would have to be Doss who called it off.

"Stop stalling, Frankie. We can't just sit here in a Mexican Standoff."

Stalling was exactly what I was trying to do.

"I'm thinking," I said.

"Let me lay this out for you. I'm leaving here in one minute. If you and Evie don't come with me, I'm going to call my guy on the way out and tell him to kill your sister and your mother. Do you understand?"

I had no good options.

"I said I'm thinking," I yelled.

"Too late for that. You have 30 seconds."

Nothing felt right. I didn't know what to do.

"Okay, we'll go with you," I finally said.

"Well let's get moving then. If you really want to save your family that is," Doss said.

When he turned around, Howie Doss would see the gathering crowd, and then who fucking knew what was going to happen.

Everything was about to come to a head.

Max Morris remained at headquarters and was in touch with the six officers as they surrounded the house. A kidnapping situation was one of the toughest in law enforcement. Sometimes, like when you were sending in a negotiator, it's preferable to let the kidnapper know you were there. But this wasn't that type of situation.

In this case, the element of surprise was much more valuable than setting up a dialogue with the perpetrator.

Morris ordered more officers to the scene and had them set up a perimeter around a two block radius. He had six officers staking out the house, and that was plenty. Any more and the risk of them being seen would be too great. He would have sent less, but his superiors had told him to send six, and Morris followed orders.

Junior Ballard, a tough SOB and a great cop, radioed back to Morris a minute later, saying there was a light on in one of the bedrooms. The two women were likely being held there. This was a good sign. If the lights were on in the kitchen or family room or something facing the street, it would make the officers job much more difficult. They would be sitting ducks in that scenario, but if the hostage taker was indeed holding them in a bedroom, they might be able to enter the house without being seen.

Morris listened to the live stream and heard the voice of Howie Doss telling Frankie Waters that they should get moving. He couldn't believe none of his superiors had arrived yet, but when he looked down at his watch, he realized only a few minutes had passed.

This was all playing out too quickly for Morris.

49

The live streaming video from below the Lincoln Memorial was now a world-wide phenomenon. In Europe, it was the middle of the day, and people were riveted to their computers. They may not all have heard of the name Howie Doss, but they had all certainly heard of Always Right. He was met with contempt in most of Europe for his constant use of the phrase "the pussification of Europe."

Australia, no fan of Always Right, was positively infatuated with the live stream as well. It was approaching 10 p.m. in Sydney, and several local TV stations had changed their regularly scheduled broadcasts to update their viewers on the latest. The most recent report said perimeters were being set up around the Lincoln Memorial, but there had been no word about when the FBI, CIA, or D.C. police would be going in.

Searches of "Oklahoma City murders," "Howie Doss," and "Darby Cash Bowles" dominated the search engines of Google.

Employees of Always Right were trying to text and call Howie Doss to warn him, but the calls went unanswered as Doss had his primary phone powered down. A few of them realized the possible repercussions and thought better of calling him.

Gloria Flores didn't err on the side of caution as she frantically called Doss 10 times. The information she had given Doss, the biggest dirt anyone ever had on a sitting President, was going up in smoke. Flores's lone positive was that at least Doss hadn't mentioned the information she had given him.

Flores was certain he knew better than that.

I looked past the Washington Monument, and the crowds were getting bigger. They were far enough away that we couldn't hear them, but when Doss turned around, there's no doubt he would see them. I had to get his phone from him before he realized what was going on. Once he knew his world was imploding, I had no doubt that he would have his goon kill my family. Even if it was just out of spite.

"I have one more request," I said.

"You don't have a whole lot of bargaining power," Doss said, "but let's hear it."

"I want you to give me your phone until we get out of here. Just so I know you won't text your guy and tell him to go after my family."

"You know there's no chance of that happening, but it will remain powered off until we leave the premises."

"But you have two phones," I said.

"You don't miss a beat, do you, Frankie?"

"I saw two phones. Hardly groundbreaking stuff," I said.

Doss ignored my sarcasm.

"I will not touch my phones until we are gone," he said.

That was all I was going to get, but I had realized something of vital important. The phone that was turned on, the one that had the picture of my family, had to be the phone in which he was coordinating with his goon.

It also explained why he wasn't getting messages alerting him to what was going on. His main phone was powered down.

My goal was to get the phone that had the picture. I could message back whoever sent the photo and tell him not to touch his hostages.

It was as good a plan as any. I decided when we left the stairs, I was going to attack Doss. Evie and I were in imminent danger if we left and I had found a plan to possibly save my family.

The time had come to attack Doss.

Unfortunately, I never got the chance.

Doss heard something, swiveled around, and he immediately saw the crowd beyond the Washington Monument. I was just getting ready to rush him when I looked down at his side. He had grabbed a gun from his pocket and was pointing it at Evie and me.

"What's with the crowd?" he asked.

"People here to see the monuments I'm sure," I said.

"Oh yeah? That 8:00 a.m. rush on New Year's Day? I don't think so."

He could tell that I was eyeing the gun.

"If you even make one move towards me, I will shoot Evie. Do you understand, Frankie?"

"Yes."

Howie Doss grabbed the powered down phone from his pocket with his right hand. His left hand continued pointing the gun at us.

He pressed the power button, and I knew within seconds that he would be inundated with texts telling him what had been going on. At that point, he would be like a wounded animal, and there would be nothing to prevent him from killing Evie and I, as well as ordering the death of my family.

I had to do something, but I didn't know what. He was still a good 10 feet from me, and if I lunged for him, he'd have plenty of time to shoot me. Or worse, shoot Evie, who was standing closer to him. I had my girlfriend and my family in harm's way, and I was utterly defenseless.

I decided that I had no choice. When he began to look at his phone, I had to lunge at him. Even if he shot me, maybe I could smother him long enough to have Evie get away and notify the cops about my family.

At this point, I was very willing to sacrifice myself. I had gotten all of us into this mess, and it was my obligation to get everyone else out of it. If I died as a result, so be it, but I couldn't live with myself if anyone besides myself was hurt.

Scarlett Jackson was one of the first people on Capitol Hill to become aware of the live streaming video. She had never been a sound sleeper, and when she heard the beep of a third text message shortly after 7:30 a.m., she realized something was up. Jackson got out of bed and checked her phone, alerting her to the live stream. She turned on her laptop, found the link, and listened intently.

At first, she cursed Frankie and Evie for lying to her, but then realized they were doing a great service to the country. They were trying to get Howie Doss to admit all of their suspicions to a national audience. Jackson couldn't help but smile as she heard Howie Doss admitting to his part in the murders in Oklahoma City years ago.

It was all very bizarre. One of the most influential men in the United States was live to the world, admitting to murders he helped commission. She couldn't believe her ears. When Doss admitted that he had Waters' family hostage, Jackson realized she was fully immersed in this. The two crime scenes were her adopted home of Washington D.C. and her birthplace of Oakland, CA.

She couldn't wait for her driver, so she linked her phone to her car and started driving towards the Lincoln Memorial, playing the live feed as she drove.

Hunter Lockley was a big, strong man and when he pushed the two women into the house, they both collided with the wall opposite the front door. They crumpled to the ground.

"Don't move and don't scream," he said. "Where do you have duct tape?"

"In the kitchen," Sally Waters said, trying to stay stoic for her daughter.

Lockley picked up Fiona off the ground.

"I'm taking her in the kitchen. If you attempt to leave, I think you know what will happen to your daughter."

"I'm not going anywhere," Sally Waters said.

Lockley left with Fiona and returned a minute later with duct tape in his hand. Sally Waters looked at her daughter and saw the tears flowing. She wished she could kill the man in front of her.

They were led into Sally Waters's room, the biggest one and easiest to watch them in. The bedroom was also facing away from the street which Lockley preferred. He could have kept them in the family room, but they could be seen or make some suspicious motions to passersby. The bedroom was infinitely better.

He removed their phones from their pockets and powered them down. He put the two of them on the bed and proceeded to duct tape their mouths and their hands behind their backs.

"If you don't get out of line, and do exactly as I say, you will get out of this alive."

It was the last words Lockley would say to them. He walked to the kitchen and unplugged the landline.

Sally Waters felt completely helpless, partly because she had no idea why they were being held hostage. She'd heard Fiona say that Frankie was in D.C., but surely that couldn't have anything to do with it. Could it?

She slowly tried to move her hands behind her back to create a little friction on the duct tape, but she could tell early on it would be to no avail. The kidnapper had made it extremely tight. Unlike movies and TV shows she had seen, the duct tape was not going to loosen and give her a chance to escape.

An hour passed and then another one. The man remained in the room, occasionally checking his phone, but never saying a word.

`Sally and Fiona Waters were at the mercy of the man in front of them. And he didn't look like a man who believed in being merciful.

Howie Doss's phone continued to power on. I don't know if it was the situation or the likelihood that he was opening his phone to 50 messages, but whatever it was, it was taking forever and each second felt like an eternity. I was just looking for him to get distracted or point his gun somewhere else, but the possibility never arose.

I heard the sound of the iPhone coming to life, and I knew we were fucked. The sound went off alerting him that he had a text message, and then again. And again. And again. The same went for his voicemails. Again, and again, and again. There must have been 20 sounds and alerts that went off.

He looked over at me, and for the first time, I saw dread in the eyes of Howie Doss. I had seen uncertainty and fear, but I had yet to see dread. But that was undoubtedly what was staring back at me. He looked at me and took a deep breath. I think he knew what was awaiting him.

Doss started to read the text messages aloud, more to himself than to us.

"You are being recorded Howie, stop talking...Stop fucking talking, you idiot.....Pretend this is all a joke, it's your only chance...It's over, Howie. You're done...Today is a great fucking day, you asshole."

I continued to watch him, waiting for the right time to pounce. He put his phone away. He walked towards Evie and put his free hand up her skirt. Not finding what he was looking for, he looked at me for an answer.

"You knew I was going to find the one on her thigh, didn't you?" he asked.

There was no use denying it now. "I thought it was a possibility," I said.

"And somewhere around here is another recording device and I'm live to the world?"

"Yes," I said.

Doss bowed his head. The magnitude of what was happening was fully hitting him.

"You've done much more than you will ever realize. I was going to run this fucking country," Doss said somberly.

We had no idea what he meant. He seemed to go deep in thought and loosened his grip on the gun for just a second.

Evie noticed this and being closer to him than I was, went for his gun. She tried to knock it out of his hand by bringing her forearm down on it. She was partly successful, knocking it loose from his grip, but the gun was still dangling by the tips of his fingers.

I took two steps and leaped at Doss. He was able to bring the gun back to his fingers just before I collided with him. He fired the gun, and I felt the bullet entering my body as I knocked Howie Doss to the ground.

The FBI, CIA, and Washington D.C. police were all alerted to the developing situation within seconds of the first words between Howie Doss and two yet unnamed individuals.

After the post by Paul Bentley confirming this was taking place at the base of the Lincoln Memorial, agents and police officers from all three agencies were sent there. They set up a perimeter outside of the Washington Monument, deciding not to get too close until they knew exactly what was happening.

It was mayhem, and no one knew exactly who was in charge.

The D.C. police, FBI, and CIA all had many interactions with Doss over the years, mostly dealing with threats on his life. Even the most conservative of the officers and agents thought he was a conceded prick, and many took great satisfaction in hearing him admit to the Oklahoma City murders.

There was debate early about whether they should head towards the Lincoln Memorial immediately, but they decided to set up the perimeter instead. Less than a minute after the police arrived, the first members of the public started showing up. The officers kept the public behind the perimeter, hoping not to alert the active parties to the police presence.

As each minute crept by, the public's interest grew greater, and hundreds were now looking out towards the Lincoln Memorial, hoping to catch a glimpse of American history. Everyone was listening to the conversation on their phones . Oohs and aahs could be heard as Howie Doss started admitting some pretty amazing stuff.

The CIA slowly tried to take over the jurisdiction and were about to give the okay to send in officers when everyone heard a gunshot. Scores of FBI &

CIA agents, along with some of D.C.'s finest started running in the direction of the Lincoln Memorial.

The police tried to prevent members of the public from joining, but there were too many of them, and they couldn't hold them all back. It was complete madness as everyone headed towards the sound of the gunfire.

As the gunshot went through me, I collided with Howie Doss. I could tell it hadn't hit any vital organs. Not that it mattered. If I had been shot through the heart, I was still going to find a way to hold Doss down and let Evie get to safety.

I had two immediate priorities and being shot wasn't one of them. I needed to get Doss's gun to prevent him from shooting Evie, and I needed to get his phone to stop him from texting the man holding my family.

When I collided with Doss, he went straight to the ground, back first, landing on the grass that neighbored the stairs. I was bigger than him, and I had all the momentum created when I had leaped through the air. The only advantage he had was that I had been shot, and that really wasn't much of an advantage as I was running on extra adrenaline at this point.

I ended up on top, and he tried to swing me off of him. The gun remained in his left hand, and I grabbed it with my right hand, holding it down, trying to burrow it into the grass.

With my left hand, I started pummeling the right side of his face. I tried to hit him in the nose to try and break it, but he kept dodging his face to avoid being hit straight on.

"The police are coming," Evie screamed. "Just hold him down a while longer."

I turned around and saw a mob of people running from the direction of the Washington Monument. It was a big mistake on my part.

Howie Doss moved his head back and then accelerated it with extreme velocity, head butting me squarely in the center of my nose, making it explode with blood. He had broken it. He used his right hand to hit me, and I fell to the side of him, no longer having my dominant position on top.

My right hand had remained on the gun, however. I couldn't let that go no matter what happened.

"Run towards the police!" I yelled to Evie. She wanted to help, but I couldn't risk her getting close to the gun.

"Now!" I yelled. "And tell them to storm my mother's house."

Evie started running towards the police.

As I concentrated on holding down his wrist and not letting him get a firm grip on the gun, Howie Doss showed how completely and utterly evil he was.

With his free hand, he grabbed one of his phones. Before I had a chance to stop it, he said "Text Hunter Lockley. Kill the family. Send."

We were now a good 30 feet from where I had hidden the closest phone, and I doubted Facebook Live could pick up what Doss said at this distance. I had to get to the phone immediately, but I couldn't just let go of my grip on the gun. Every second mattered at this point, with my family possibly waiting to be slaughtered.

I bent his wrist back as far as I could and saw him writhing in pain. I kept pushing and heard it snap, and Doss screamed out in pain. The gun fell to the ground, but before I could pick it up, Doss used his foot to kick the gun a good 20 feet away.

His next move was brilliant as well.

Doss threw the phone in the direction we had come from, landing near the stairs.

I had to make a decision. The gun or the phone. I punched Doss twice in the face as hard as I possibly could, and he remained on the ground.

Most people would probably say I should have run for the gun, and then gone back for the phone. Not a fucking chance. I was imagining Doss's goon getting close to killing my family. At that very moment, the phone meant more to me than the gun.

I ran in the direction of the phone, picked it up and yelled "Text Hunter Lockley. Keep the family alive. Send." I looked down, and nothing seemed to be happening.

I tried again. "Text Hunter Lockley. Do not touch them. Send."

Looking down at the screen, I saw it was black. I was so fired up that I failed to notice it the first time. The phone must have broke when it hit the stairs.

I was more petrified in that split second than I had ever been in my life. I ran over to the phone that was still lodged between the grass and the stairs. I screamed into it.

"Doss told his guy to kill my family. If you are listening to this, please storm my mother's house. Now! Please!" I yelled directly into the phone.

In my fervor to alert the authorities, I had given Doss a chance to get the gun. He had managed to get off the ground, and as I looked up, he was only a few feet from grabbing it. His face was a bloody mess.

Luckily, I was now almost 30 yards from him because the phone and gun had gone in different directions. Doss couldn't get a good shot at me if I hid down below the stairs.

Of course, he could run over and shoot me, but I suddenly had an advantage.

Scores of police officers were running in my direction. They were only a few hundred feet from us now. Evie was amongst them. There were so many, and they all had their weapons drawn.

I peeked out above the stairs and looked at Howie Doss. We made eye contact for a final time, and instead of running towards me and the oncoming police, he turned around and started running back in the direction of the Lincoln Memorial.

For the first time, I had the time to notice the hole on the left side of my body and the blood oozing from it.

Max Morris was still sitting at police headquarters, waiting for his superiors. None had arrived yet. He had been listening intently to the live streaming, but he hadn't heard any voices in over a minute. He had the six officers right outside of the house, and he was just waiting for the right time to send them in.

It wasn't an easy call one way or the other. If he sent them in too early, and the gunman decided to kill the family because of it, Morris would be the fall guy. If he waited too long, and the gunman killed the family while he waited, he would be equally at fault.

Something told him he shouldn't wait too long.

Junior Ballard called Morris.

"Do you want us to go in?" he asked.

A split second after Ballard asked this, a voice could be heard on the live stream.

"Doss told his guy to kill my family. If you are listening to this, please storm my mother's house. Now! Please!"

Without a second's pause, Morris said to Ballard, "Go in! Now!"

Junior Ballard led the men into the house. The door proved easy to open, as they were able to use a lever, which helped keep the noise to a minimum.

The officers heard muzzled noises coming from the room with the light on. It sounded like people were trying to scream, but couldn't. Ballard knew time was of the essence. From what was said on the live stream, the man was given permission to go through with the murders.

Ballard motioned to one of the officers to come with him. He motioned to the other four to stay at the front door. He couldn't risk them being heard. He moved down the hallway as quickly, yet quietly, as he could, another officer at his side.

He approached the room with the light on, hearing the muffled voices getting louder. Something was about to happen.

Ballard assumed the kidnapper's back would be to the door, likely putting his victims on a bed or up against a wall. Of course, there was the chance he had them sitting against the wall nearest the door, and if that were the case, Junior Ballard would be a sitting duck when he entered the room.

He had no choice though. This was what he had signed up for, and he knew if he waited any longer, these people were dead.

They were now directly outside the door, and the muffled screams became louder still. He gave the lone officer with him the okay to kick the door open, and Ballard readied his weapon to fire.

His fellow officer kicked the door as hard as he could, knocking it off its hinges and in the split second he had, Ballard saw two people duct taped and sitting on the bed. The gunman, who had his back to the door just as Ballard had assumed, was aiming his gun at the hostages. When he heard the door kicked open, the gunman tried to swivel around and face the officers.

Just as his body turned around to face the officers, Junior Ballard shot Hunter Lockley. Ballard decided to use a head shot, knowing that the hostages would be in harm's way if he shot for the body and missed. It was quick thinking on Ballard's part and the absolute right decision.

Hunter Lockley fell to the ground at the base of the bed, dead before he landed.

Junior Ballard quickly untied the hostages and escorted them downstairs. He told the officers to look after them, especially the young woman.

Ballard returned to the bedroom, calling Max Morris to tell him the mission had been a success. He surveyed the crime scene, looking down at the hollowed out forehead of Hunter Lockley.

Howie Doss couldn't believe it had come to this. Two days earlier, he had been given information that was going to make him the most important man in the United States, and by extension, the world. He had met with the President less than 24 hours ago and had the empty suit acquiescing to everything he had asked for.

He had loved seeing the President flailing in the wind. The empty suit had ridden the coattails of people like Doss to get elected. He was nothing like the ultra-right true believer that Doss saw himself as.

Doss had planned on imparting his political agenda and returning this country to where it should have stayed.

He had risen from a child who was almost aborted to unbelievable heights. And he was going to unleash his wrath on those he despised.

But not anymore.

Instead, he was making eye contact with a 21-year-old kid who had somehow, against all odds, gotten the better of him. He looked in the kid's direction one last time, but as he saw the approaching mob of law enforcement headed his way, he knew he'd never get to him.

Doss turned around and started running towards the steps of the Lincoln Memorial.

If this was the end of his life, and Howie Doss had no intention of turning himself in, then he was going to give them all a show.

I saw Doss running up the steps of the Lincoln Memorial and a huge police presence head in his direction. Saying it was surreal didn't do it justice.

Evie ran towards me, took my shirt off, and used it to help cover the hole in my side. It was a fantastic gesture, but medical help arrived simultaneously and took over.

I appreciated the attention from them, but I still only had one thing on my mind.

"I need to know what happened to my family!" I yelled.

An undercover member of law enforcement, I assumed he was FBI or CIA, walked towards me and raised the phone to his ear.

"Put me through to the Oakland PD," he said.

As I waited, the EMTs continued to work on me. They put gauze in my bullet holes and loaded me on to a gurney.

I didn't care about myself.

"I need to know what happened to my family!" I screamed for the second time.

I saw the official talking on his phone. I tried to read his body language, but he wasn't giving away a thing. If anything happened to my family, I would not be able to go on living. I looked at Evie.

"Please say they are okay," I said.

Tears were streaming from Evie's eyes. We were now forever a part of American history, but none of that would matter if my family had been killed. Evie knew this as well as I.

I couldn't handle it anymore.

"Will someone please tell me something!" I screamed.

I saw the undercover man walking towards me. My heart was about to jump out of my chest.

He leaned down to the gurney and whispered to me. Evie listened in.

"Your family is fine. They raided your house and killed the intruder. They are being taken to the Oakland Police Department as we speak."

Evie leaned over the gurney, hugging me, as we both started crying tears of joy. We embraced for a few seconds until she rubbed close to my bullet wound and I cried again, this time in pain.

I looked up and saw an ambulance approaching. They wanted to load me from the gurney into the ambulance, but I had other plans.

"Put me on my feet," I said.

"Sir, we can't," an EMT started to say.

"I need to see how this ends," I said.

I think everyone understood.

Two EMTs got me on my feet, making sure the gauze was still blocking my wound from leaking blood. I held on to Evie, and we looked towards the Lincoln Memorial.

Howie Doss had reached the top of the steps and was now tiptoeing backward, keeping an eye on the throng of law enforcement that were making their way in his direction. His hand was by his side, but he hadn't brandished the weapon, or he would have been shot already.

People had either heard what was going on or had been evacuated because Howie Doss was the only person at the top of Lincoln Memorial.

He continued backpedaling towards the statue of Lincoln. There was now at least 40 law enforcement agents walking up the steps of the Lincoln Memorial. It was like nothing anyone had ever seen.

You could hear voices yelling at him to put down the weapon. Doss back tracked a few more steps until he was at the base of the statue of Abraham Lincoln.

The last of the officers made their way to the top of the steps. There were dozens of guns pointed at Howie Doss.

I looked over at Evie. After all we had been through over the last several weeks, it looked to be coming to an end. And in such a grandiose fashion we never could have imagined. Two twenty-one-year-olds had changed the course of American politics forever. We shared a moment that no one in the world could have understood.

There were more shouts for Doss to drop his weapon. It was too late for that. Everyone could tell this wasn't going to end peacefully.

We heard Howie Doss scream "Always Right" and then his hand reached down towards his pocket. It would never get there. The sound of hundreds of gunshots rang out and echoed throughout the Lincoln Memorial.

Howie Doss fell backward, staining the base of the Lincoln Memorial with his blood. The shots that missed him ricocheted off the base of the statue. Even in death, Howie Doss had managed to harm a symbol of American tolerance.

That would only be temporary, however, and they would fix the Lincoln Memorial back to the way it had always been. There would be no repairing Howie Doss, however. He was gone forever.

I was starting to get light-headed and thought that maybe shrewdness should replace valor for the moment. I called an EMT over, and she quickly put me back on the gurney and prepared to load me into the waiting ambulance.

Evie sat next to me kissing my forehead and telling me I was going to be just fine.

We looked up towards the Lincoln Memorial. The contrast between the dead man and the statue towering over him was impossible to avoid.

On the ground was a mean-spirited, cowardly, murderous excuse for a man who had demolished any opponents in his path, using the most personal information and lies to crush politicians he didn't like. He had contributed to the polarization of Washington, which led to the horrible climate our political parties now found themselves in.

Above him, both literally and figuratively, was the statue of a man who was a true American hero. He had stood up for what he thought was right and the country was better for it. He was far from a perfect man, but he had good in his heart, and the same could not be said of Howie Doss.

None of this was discussed, but as Evie and I looked at the Lincoln Memorial for a final time, I knew she was thinking similarly.

I looked over at her, and we both decided we'd had enough of Howie Doss. We shifted our eyes away from the statue and looked out at the sunrise of the coming day.

The EMTs gave us a few extra seconds, but the time had come. They loaded me into the ambulance, and we set out for the hospital.

50

The immediate concern of the EMTs was to prevent me from bleeding out. I had lost a lot of blood before they arrived, but they had done everything possible once they got to me. Two EMTs joined Evie and I in the back of the ambulance, and they seemed confident I would make it.

We arrived at George Washington University Hospital. Word had leaked that one of the people responsible for the demise of Howie Doss was arriving and there were at least 30 members of the media waiting for us.

As I was taken out of the ambulance, I was greeted by incessant flashbulbs as the media took pictures of Evie and me until hospital personnel alerted them to stop. I heard people yelling questions in my direction. "Who is Darby Bowles?" "Have you talked to your family?" "How does it feel to be responsible for the death of Howie Doss?" I was in and out of consciousness and just held on to Evie's hand as I was bombarded with all these questions.

In a moment of lucidity, I heard the paramedics say that they had a gunshot victim and they were taking me to the ICU. I couldn't wrap my mind around the fact that I was a gunshot victim. It was all so unbelievable.

My mind once again started focusing on Fiona and my mother. I knew I owed them a lifetime of apologies. I hoped they hadn't endured too much.

Once we entered the hospital, the questions and flashbulbs stopped. I'd credit the media for knowing where to draw the line, but it was more likely they weren't allowed in the hospital.

At some point, I lost consciousness, and don't remember being taken to the ICU. I woke up several hours later with a throbbing pain in my side, but as I looked at the smiling girl across from me, I knew I was going to be just fine. I guessed it was early afternoon, but couldn't be sure.

Evie alerted the doctors that I had woken up and came in to give me my prognosis.

They said I had suffered a gunshot wound and when I said "No shit," they realized I had escaped with my sense of humor intact. I was told that plenty of rest and relaxation was on the docket and that if I followed their orders, I would be as good as new in a few short weeks. The bullet, like I had assumed, had hit no major organs.

I asked the doctors for some alone time with Evie. They granted it.

As they left, I saw the TV on above my bed.

"Anything interesting on the news?" I asked.

Evie started laughing uncontrollably, and I joined her before realizing that it exacerbated my pain.

"Did you ever, in a million years, think it would come to this?" Evie asked.

"Not even close. Do you know why I originally brought you on to help me?"

"To be close to me?" she smiled.

"Yeah, pretty much. Although you did say you were looking for an adventure."

"Yeah, that. It feels like 20 years ago. After all the craziness we've been through, I don't think I'll ever worry about a lack of adventure again. Thanks for that."

"I do what I can," I said.

We both heard some rustling and several members of law enforcement were talking to the doctors outside my room. One of them walked in.

"Mr. Waters, do you think you are ready to answer some questions?"

"There's one thing I have to do. Can you give me five minutes?"

"Yes. We'll be back in five."

The man left, and I turned back to Evie.

"Can I borrow your cell phone?"

"I don't think we are getting those back anytime soon. They are part of the investigation now."

"Should have guessed that," I said.

"But there is a phone right back here," she said, pointing behind me. "I'm assuming you want to call your family."

"Yup."

"I talked to Sally and Fiona when you were asleep. They know you are going to be alright."

"How are they holding up?"

"They are tough. They are going to be just fine."

"I still want to talk to them," I said.

"Of course."

Evie grabbed the phone, asked for our home line, and dialed the number. She gave me the phone as it rang. I didn't have to wait long as my mother answered on the first ring.

"Hello?"

"Mom, it's me," I said.

The waterworks started on both sides of the phone. It was a good 45 seconds before either one of us could talk.

"I'm so sorry, Mom. I never knew it was going to involve you and Fiona."

"Don't apologize, Frankie. We are just happy everyone is alive."

"I'm going to have a little scar," I said.

"Well, you'll have quite the story to go with it," she said.

I laughed briefly but stopped as I started feeling the pain in my flank again. I had to remember to stop laughing.

"When can I see you guys?"

"Soon. We are flying out to Washington D.C. tonight."

"You don't have to do that."

"I hope you're kidding, Frankie. Do you know how big a story this is? My son is a national hero right now. You are the lead story on every news channel in the world. I imagine it will be that way for weeks. And we are going to be there for your recovery. And one last thing. Your father would be so proud of you. I'm sure he's sitting somewhere smiling down on you."

"Thanks, Mom. That means so much. I hope Fiona didn't have to go through too much," I said.

"We can deal with all of that stuff later, Frankie. For now, I just want you to get better. And don't do any interviews or anything like that. I'm sure you are in high demand right now."

"I've got some FBI or CIA outside my hospital room right now. Don't think I can avoid that interview."

"No, of course not. I was referring to the media."

"Yeah, I'm a little tired of the media right now," I said.

The fact that I was referring to Howie Doss and Always Right was implicit.

"Get some sleep, Frankie."

"I love you, Mom. Tell Fiona I'm sorry."

"I love you too. We'll see you soon."

"Bye, Mom."

"Bye, Frankie."

Evie grabbed the phone from me and hung it up.

"Do I want to know what they went through?" I asked Evie.

"Probably not," she said. "But they are tough. They'll get through this."

"Just like we will."

Evie grabbed my hand and kissed me on the forehead.

"Guess it's time to get this over with," I said, motioning to the people waiting outside my room.

"I'll go get them."

51

The first of my many interviews with different law enforcement agencies lasted just over an hour. There were three of them in the room, one each from the FBI, CIA, and the D.C. police. They told me that this was a joint task force and they were all equal partners. I doubted that, but didn't bother saying so. Someone always has the final say.

They started by asking a few questions, and I told them it might be easier if I just started from the beginning and told them everything. If they had any questions after that, I would answer them. That seemed fine by them.

I told them the story from the beginning, starting all the way back when Uncle Owen had given me "The Greatest Novel Ever" when I was 16 years old. I looked around my own hospital room. What had started in a hospital room had come full circle.

I described the writings of Owen and how we investigated the murders that took place in Oklahoma City on February 26th, 2001. I talked about Darby Cash Bowles, Patricia Page, Derek Plough and everyone else involved, and how it was my idea to come to Washington D.C. and broadcast our conversation with Howie Doss.

It wasn't a perfect recap, but for someone who had just been shot and was on a lot of painkillers, I thought I did just fine.

"And why didn't you just go to the authorities early on?" the FBI agent asked. Or was he CIA?

"We really didn't think we had enough concrete information. Like I said, a lot of it was circumstantial, and this guy was a media mogul. I thought if we went to the cops or the media, he would just get everything squashed. If we could get him to talk live to the world? Now that was different."

"And it was your idea to hide phones around the Lincoln Memorial?" The man asked. He looked on in awe as he said it.

"Yes."

"Fucking smart," said a different agent, showing he was impressed as well.

"And that was in case Doss found the phone on Evie's thigh?"

"I figured he was going to frisk us. Plus, I thought if he found that phone, he'd think he was in the clear and be more likely to talk."

"You're a smart young man, Frankie," said the third.

It was unanimous. They all thought I was intelligent.

It was my turn to ask a question. "What's Derek Plough's prognosis?"

They all looked at each other and decided to answer.

"He broke his lower back when you pushed him on to the train tracks. He's cooperating, and I'm sure we'll learn a great deal from him, but I'm not sure he'll ever walk again. He knows a great deal about all of the terrible shit that Howie Doss did, so I'm actually glad he's alive."

I was ambivalent.

"Did Plough kill Darby Cash Bowles?" I asked.

"Yeah. And then he came back to D.C. Howie Doss hired someone else to subdue your mother and sister."

I knew there were going to be a lot of interviews, but I was getting exhausted and needed to end this one.

"I'm really tired, guys. Can we continue this after I sleep for a few hours?"

"You've been very helpful, Frankie. Get some rest, and we'll talk later."

They walked towards the door.

"One more thing," I said. "Let me know if you find out who called in that bomb threat at the Motel 6. I think they saved our lives."

For possibly the first time ever, members of the FBI, CIA, and local police all laughed at once.

"I think we are going to give a pass to whoever made that call," one of them said.

"Good," I said. "They deserve it."

After the death of Howie Doss, Gloria Flores went to Always Right to pick up her things, but the Feds had already blockaded the building, and she couldn't get in.

She decided that it would be best if she got out of town. After all, with Howie Doss dead, Gloria and her daughter were the only people who had the information Doss was using to bribe the President.

Flores called a hotel in Baltimore and gave them a fake name. She said she needed a room and would pay cash up front. Gloria Flores figured a week away from D.C. was probably a good idea. She could gauge the temperature of the city in seven days, and see if she wanted to come back.

The immediate aftermath of Howie Doss's death focused on five separate crime scenes. The FBI and CIA were sent in record numbers to Oklahoma City to investigate the murders in February of 2001. There were also 20 agents sent to Oakland, CA and over 30 agents sent to Eureka, CA. The final two crime scenes were Union Station and the Lincoln Memorial. The Motel 6 was not considered a crime scene.

It was confirmed that Derek Plough would spend the rest of his life in a wheelchair. And surely a prison cell. He continued to tell his story, and the Feds were able to build a timeline for the last few days of Howie Doss. It lined up exactly as I had told them.

Apparently, Howie Doss had a meeting with the President the day before he died, but the President claims nothing special was discussed.

My mother and sister arrived in Washington D.C. at 11 p.m. on January 1st, less than 20 hours after being held hostage. They walked into my hospital room, and we all embraced. There were many tears shed, and when I tried to ask about what they had gone through, they said we could talk about that over the coming days and months.

We talked for over an hour until a doctor came in and told them that they should let me get my sleep for the night.

"We have a hotel a few miles away, Frankie. We'll be back early in the morning," my mother said.

"I love you both so much!" I looked at Fiona when I said it.

I could tell that she was a little fragile at the moment, and I couldn't say I blamed her. While I didn't know everything that had happened, I did now that a man was shot and killed in front of her. That would traumatize anyone, especially an 18-year-old girl. Okay, woman. Still had to get used to thinking of my sister as a woman.

My mother had been the rock of our family ever since my father died, and she continued to be the same through this incident. She was a strong woman, and I didn't worry about her.

"How about you, Evie, and I go bowling again sometime soon?" I asked, looking at Fiona again.

"Only if you finally admit that Evie is your girlfriend," she said.

Evie leaned in, and we kissed.

"Where have you been? That's been official for like a week now, " Evie said.

That seemed to make Fiona happy.

"Get better, Frankie. I love you so much. And I'll get better too, so you don't have to worry about me," Fiona said.

"I'm sorry for whatever you had to go through," I said.

"You're going to owe me, that's for sure," she said and smiled. She was a tough kid, and I believed her when she said she'd get over it.

"Fiona, let your brother sleep," my mother said. She winked at me and took Fiona out of the hospital room.

Evie and I remained, and she took the remote control and turned on the T.V. We watched CNN, FOX, MSNBC, and many other stations as they plastered our faces all over the television. Supposedly there were so many videos of Howie Doss being shot to death that YouTube was having a tough time restricting them. That part didn't interest me.

We were being hailed as heroes, although some of the stories didn't have all the information correct. One story reported that Evie and I were brother and sister.

"Let's give them a big kiss for the cameras tomorrow. That will get them talking," she said.

"Stop trying to get me to laugh," I said, grabbing my side again.

"Have you thought about your future at all?"

I looked up at the T.V. and saw another photo of me. "Think I'm just going to soak up being a national celebrity. Maybe get a few free meals out of this."

It was Evie's turn to laugh.

"I talked to Scarlett Jackson today," she said.

"And?"

"And she forgives us for lying to her. She realizes that if we had rescheduled with Doss, he would have known something was up."

"That's what I was saying all along."

"And you were right. People think we are nuts, and maybe we are, but it worked out pretty much like we had hoped."

"When I dreamt it up, I hadn't planned on getting shot."

Evie smiled. "Well yeah, except for that."

"It's not so bad, I guess. I'll just have you at my beck and call for the next few weeks."

"There's no place I'd rather be," Evie said.

"Have you talked to your parents?" I asked.

"Yeah. They are flying in tomorrow morning."

"They are going to want to shoot me a second time."

Evie smiled again. "Yeah, you're probably right."

I changed the subject. I could deal with the Somerset's tomorrow.

"Did Scarlett mention if our job offer was still on the table?"

"She didn't bring it up. But I don't think we will have any trouble getting a job in this town. Every single Democrat loves us, and quite a few Republicans do too. Howie Doss was a murdering thug. People, Reputations, Public Civility. He murdered a lot of things. No one wants to claim him."

I didn't want to talk about Howie Doss anymore. There would be plenty of time to talk about all we had accomplished.

For now, I just wanted to spend time with the beautiful girl across from me.

"Come lay down," I said.

"Are you crazy?"

I slid over to the far right of the hospital bed so my wound wouldn't be near Evie. She looked on reluctantly and slowly climbed into bed, being careful not to rub too hard up against me. It was uncomfortable, and yet I was as content as I had ever been.

I kissed her, and she kissed me back.

"It's crazy, but we are the darlings of the whole country right now."

"Our lives will forever be different, won't they?" Evie asked.

"Probably. But forever can start tomorrow. Right now it's just you and I."

Evie smiled and slowly laid her head on my chest.

"We changed the world, didn't we, Frankie?"

"We sure did."

"And we rid the world of a horrible man, didn't we?"

"We sure did," I repeated.

"Maybe we have found our life calling."

"Waters & Somerset."

"I like the sound of Somerset & Waters better," Evie said.

"You can have top billing any day," I said.

She leaned in and kissed me. We were 21 years old, the most famous people in the country, and the world was our oyster. But at that moment, there was no place we'd rather be than in that cramped hospital bed, lying in each other's arms.

THE END

Made in the USA
Columbia, SC
11 October 2017